Suspects

OTHER NOVELS BY THOMAS BERGER

Robert Crews (1994)

Meeting Evil (1992)

Orrie's Story (1990)

Changing the Past (1989)

The Houseguest (1988)

Being Invisible (1987)

Nowhere (1985)

The Feud (1983)

Reinhart's Women (1981)

Neighbors (1980)

Arthur Rex (1978)

Who Is Teddy Villanova? (1977)

Sneaky People (1975)

Regiment of Women (1973)

Vital Parts (1970)

Killing Time (1967)

Little Big Man (1964)

Reinhart in Love (1962)

Crazy in Berlin (1958)

Thomas Berger

Suspects

A Novel

WILLIAM MORROW AND COMPANY, INC.

NEW YORK

Library of Congress Cataloging-in-Publication Data

Berger, Thomas, 1924-
   Suspects : a novel / by Thomas Berger.
      p.   cm.
   ISBN 0-688-11925-5
   I. Title.
PS3552.E719S87   1996
813'.54—dc20   95-42513
                                                              CIP

Printed in the United States of America

 ˙ 3   4   5   6   7   8   9   10

BOOK DESIGN BY BRIAN MULLIGAN

To Brooks Landon

Suspects

"No answer, missus," said the young policeman, stating the obvious, but he knocked on the door still another time before turning to Mary Jane Jones, whose call was the reason why he and his partner had come to 1143 Laurel. Mrs. Jones, a tall, big-boned but not heavy woman in her mid-sixties, though with the voice of a plaintive little girl, lived next door at 1145, in a larger and older house. She and Jack Marevitch, the other cop, stood together at the bottom of the two-step entrance. There was no porch here.

Art McCall, the policeman who had done the knocking, came down to join the others. "I'd wait awhile if I was you," he told Mary Jane. "Sometimes people change their routines, you know, without warning. Sometimes something comes up."

"I tell you she's in there," Mary Jane insisted, in her high-pitched whine. "She hasn't gone *anyplace*."

Marevitch now was heard from. "Ma'am, you might be right. But maybe she's busy, see. You know, in the bathroom."

"For an *hour*?" Mary Jane turned to share her incredulity with McCall, but he remained professionally noncommittal.

Marevitch was a strong-featured, thick-trunked man in his late forties. "How old's the individual? My seventeen-year-old, she'll stay in there all evening. Our mistake was giving her that portable phone." He smiled at Mary Jane.

"I know Donna," Mary Jane said, "and she—"

"What's the name again?" McCall asked.

"Donna. Mrs. Larry Howland."

"The Howland residence," McCall said, the shiny black bill of his navy-blue cap pecking the air as he nodded.

"Can't you go in and look? I tell you, I've been calling over there an hour."

"You been phoning to this residence?" asked Marevitch. "This phone's been ringing?"

"Oh, it's not out of order. I can tell you that," said Mary Jane.

"Well, we can't just break in, missus," said Officer McCall. There was a radio unit clipped to his left epaulet, and it made a quacking sound now. He replied to it, lips close to its grillwork, in an almost metallic voice of his own, then straightened his head to say, "We got another thing we gotta go and do now, Mrs. Jones. If you're still worried, give us another call later on. But I bet everything will be okay and your friend is just fine. You'll see."

He tipped his cap, and he and Marevitch walked to the curb and their patrol car, a shiny white vehicle with so many markings in royal blue and gold as to seem gaudy: official seal; the name of the city; the slogan "To protect and to serve" and another with an antidrug message; and "Dial 911."

McCall took the wheel. On the passenger's side, Marevitch lowered the window and smiled out at the woman, which made his nose more evident than ever. "Probably everything is completely normal. But you always know where to get ahold of us."

They drove briskly away. They had not even bothered to go around back. It was true that nothing could be learned looking in the windows and through the glass panes in the doors, which Mary Jane had proved before calling the cops, and she was aware that they could lawfully enter private premises only if invited or with a search warrant, but there was no one else to blame, unless of course Donna *was* soaking in the bath, listening to music loud enough to obscure the sound of the phone and the knocks on the door as well, and furthermore this had been true for a good hour, though Mary Jane knew that Donna invariably took showers after her daily exercise, not tub baths, and furthermore, with an ear against each of the doors in turn, she had not heard any radio or stereo noise.

She had not considered it her place to turn a doorknob. When Mary Jane was a girl, in this same town, though two miles away, over on Dimsdale, her mother had felt free to trot into the houses of the neighbors on either side without knocking, to borrow instant coffee or a cup of milk, or simply to talk, and they returned the favor whenever they felt like it. But people kept their doors locked nowadays unless they had children who came and went. Mary Jane's sons were long grown up and lived elsewhere. Donna's little daughter at three was still too young to go outside on her own in an unfenced yard.

Mary Jane decided to take the advice of the officers and go home, having anyway forgotten just why it was she had called Donna in the first place. She had come over to knock when the telephone had not been answered: that was clear. The policemen had not suggested she was wrong in so doing. It was important to Mary Jane that she keep things straight, for nowadays, having nobody to answer to, she was wont suddenly to lose track of what she was doing. Sometimes she went for several hours on the assumption that her husband would be back from work at the usual time, wanting his dinner, and would plan an elaborate menu.

Mary Jane suddenly remembered why she had phoned Donna. The young woman had invited her to supper, as she had so frequently done since Karl Jones's death, one or more evenings per week. Larry Howland was out of town at the moment, in fact all the way out on the Coast, attending a sales-training seminar given by his air-conditioning company. Donna had called Mary Jane that morning: how about coming over for the evening meal, women only? Just us three ladies, meaning she was counting little Amanda, and that was quite okay with Mary Jane, who had had only boys herself, two of them, and while she could not say she was disappointed, it would have been nice to have one other female in the house of men, which could sometimes be coarse, with all those sweaty clothes from sports and the mutual punching, though usually good-natured. They were fine sons.

So Donna had invited her to supper, but on this occasion Mary Jane had not accepted immediately. She had made one small beginning effort to reclaim her lost pride. She loved being entertained at the Howlands', and she had no place else to go, but she simply had to make a start at recovering her strength of character. So she pretended to have other arrangements that had to be altered, and Donna, who was the soul of delicacy, said the right thing: that the invitation would remain valid right up to suppertime. That had been just an hour earlier, but Mary Jane saw no reason to keep her in suspense. Donna might need to buy extra food if a guest with *her* appetite was coming.

That Donna would have gone out before getting Mary Jane's answer was unreasonable. Thus, when the phone was not answered, Mary Jane had walked on over. That she should go home now without solving the mystery might be acceptable to the police, but it would be a violation of her personal moral code.

She strode purposefully around to the back of the house, where, unlike the front, there was a porch, though only a little one, five or six feet deep, two steps up from the yard. She mounted the porch, opened the screen, and knocked forcefully on the wooden door. There was no bell in back. Without waiting for a response this time, she turned the knob. The door opened readily, on silent hinges.

She bent forward and poked her head into the opening so offered, speaking Donna's name at normal volume. When no answer came, she tried a somewhat louder version. Finally she stepped across the threshold onto vinyl tiles that she nowadays never trod without recognizing how much cleaner they were than her own had been since her husband's death. As always, the entire kitchen was spotless, a miracle with a small child in residence. It was also, at this moment, deserted.

She continued to shout. "Hello, Donna? . . . Hi, Donna. It's Mary Jane. . . . Your phone didn't answer. . . . Donna, if you're here, I beg your pardon. But I just can't keep waiting out there."

The kitchen had two exits: one gave onto the dining room, which at a certain arbitrary point, defined only by the change in furniture, became a living room with a large picture window that provided a view of the street. Neither Mary Jane nor the policemen had been able to see clearly through this from the yard, that is, through the reflections of the bright afternoon into a darkened interior, and at a distance that was due to the thick rose bushes beneath the window, which were not yet in flower but were heavily budded.

In the kind of gingerly search Mary Jane was making, you could look out of the kitchen and see the entire dining-living room at one glance, not missing an occupant unless she was willfully hiding behind a sofa or drapery. Mary Jane therefore did not explore that area on foot but instead went into the hallway through the right-hand door. Here the three bedrooms were placed in line against the west wall, but separated each from each by sanitary facilities: a full bathroom between the back corner bedroom and the middle one; then came the lavatory, washbasin and toilet, that was near enough to the living room to be used by visitors; and finally the bedroom at the front corner of the house.

The back bedroom was the master, the middle served as nursery, and the one that faced the street was for guests if any, though there had never been any to Mary Jane's knowledge other than Larry's kid half brother Lloyd, who dropped by sporadically, between changes of address.

She headed for the middle bedroom, for the simple reason that its door was open, as that to the master bedroom was not. She was still more puzzled than fearful. Her apprehensions began only when she looked in through the open doorway and saw little Amanda, sleeping placidly on one cheek, silky fair hair strewn across the other side of the pillow, pink blanket pulled up to her pink ear. A serene image if there ever was one, except that the time must now be almost four-thirty, far too late for her normal nap.

She continued on to the top of the hall, past the lavatory, the door to which was normally kept slightly ajar, except when it was in use. It now stood in the wide-open position, as did those to the bathroom and the front bedroom beyond. There was no one in the lavatory or the bathroom, and the guest bedroom had no occupant.

Mary Jane walked slowly down the hallway to the closed door of the master bedroom, producing heavier steps than usual so as to alert Donna if the latter was napping within. But no response was forthcoming. When she eventually reached the door and put limp fingers, not yet clenched, on the knob, she received a violent shock as if the thing were electrified. It took her a moment to understand that the sensation was due only to the ringing of a telephone, and not a single instrument but several, many, too many and too loud for one small house. Apparently there was one in every room, and she was equidistant from them all. The din was unbearable. She covered her ears, but the noise seemed as loud as ever. The only way to stop it was to answer one of the phones. Obviously there was one in the room behind the closed door, though because of the barrier its ring was not so loud as that on the kitchen wall through the open door across the hall. Though this event offered an additional incentive to invade the master bedroom, Mary Jane was now grateful for an excuse not to intrude there.

She strode into the kitchen and seized the white telephone from its holder on the wall to the left of the sink.

"This is Mary Jane Jones."

After a short pause, a man's voice said, "Mary Jane, I'd know you anywhere. It's Larry."

"Larry, I want you to know what I'm doing over here. I—"

He interrupted jocularly. "I'm pretty sure you aren't stealing the valuables. You're welcome to all you can find. Listen, we're due back from lunch in a minute, out here, but I thought I'd say a word to my sweetie because I'll be tied up later in the day and evening, at least till after her bedtime. So."

"Nobody answered the phone, so I did," said Mary Jane. "I don't know what's going on. Amanda's in bed. Donna's I don't know where. You left the car at the airport, didn't you?"

"I can clear that up for you," Larry said in his jovial voice. "She's taking a shower. She wears that cap that bunches her hair over her ears. What with that and the water, she can't hear you if you shoot a gun off. Take my word for it."

"The water's not running, though," Mary Jane said. "And the bathroom door is wide open. The back bedroom's the only one closed."

"Huh," said Larry. "Well, she's got to be around somewhere. Running the washer?"

"Wait a minute, Larry." Mary Jane looked for a place to rest the phone but, finding none, let it dangle. She had forgotten about the cellar. She opened the appropriate door, next to the stove, and peered down the stairs. The Howland basement was a cheerier one than her own, with lots of light on the floor from its high windows. She would not have hesitated to go down and look around, but she heard no sound of washing machine or dryer, and her calls of Donna's name brought no response. And Larry was waiting on a long-distance line.

She reported back to him. "Nothing's on down there."

"Well, gee, Mary Jane, my time's all gone now, I see. I got to rush. I *will* try and find a minute later, tell her, but if not, then sometime tomorrow. We got these real late sessions—I mean, counting the change of time zones. You take care!"

He hung up before he could be made to appreciate that the real problem was not his tight schedule but his wife's whereabouts. But being annoyed made Mary Jane feel less fearful. With her newfound confidence she now crossed the hall, knocked sharply on the closed door, and called out Donna's name. She suddenly remembered an odd failure on Larry's part: when she had told him the door to the back bedroom was closed, he had not suggested she go and open it. Did that mean she wasn't supposed to? On the other hand, he hadn't said she should not, either.

She knocked again while turning the knob, and called Donna's name one more time, as loudly as ever, and then, inside the room, continued awhile to repeat it softly in a series that soon became a single prolonged whimper. But at no point did she scream, though she had never before seen blood in this abundance.

The white bedspread was a swamp of it, so supersaturated that it had overflowed, cascading onto the bedside rug below. The redness was what Mary Jane first fixed on, as being more incongruous than the nude white body lying prone on it, in it, for the body was Donna's, whereas the blood seemed altogether out of place, having no visible place of origin, Donna's back being unmarked from shoulder to heels.

Mary Jane tried to believe her friend was still alive, despite the hemorrhage, and while being incapable of coherent speech, pretended to talk to her. When she received no answer to the questions she had not been able to ask, she leaned over the bed, to the left of the protruding feet and ankles, trying to avoid the once fluffy rug that squished with blood. Donna lay at a right angle to the axis of the large bed, queen- or king-size or whatever they called them; Mary Jane had slept her entire marriage in a just plain double. She touched Donna's shoulder cap now and was relieved to find it warm-ish, certainly not really cold.

Once again she tried to speak, addressing the bloody tangle of hair above the serene smooth white groove of spine. She wanted to say she'd try CPR before calling anybody: you could never tell. But it was useless. She could not produce a sound. Not even her strenuous gasps for air seemed audible.

She tried one-handedly to roll Donna over to the supine. But the body had too much inertia to be moved, and it was glued down by the dense blood. Then at last, with a heroic effort, using both hands and putting her weight into it, she succeeded.

Donna, face up, was inaccessible to the kiss of life. Her upper teeth were embedded to the gum in her lower lip. Below her chin she was all raw flesh, with a continuous open wound from groin to breastbone.

Mary Jane remained soundless. Her emotions had been instantaneously annealed by the horror before her. In the next moment she was down the hall and at Amanda's bed. The child at least must be saved. But when she pulled the pink blanket aside, she saw that Amanda's delicate throat had been slit from just below one pale little earlobe to the other.

The morning began with Lloyd Howland's butter-fingered loss of an electric razor to a washbasin full of water. The fuse blew, and the shaver was probably permanently ruined. He could not go to his job without shaving. He was on thin ice at work for many reasons, and had already been chided for a recent appearance with a stubbled chin, which he had failed to get the boss to accept as being in the current fashion of many popular young film stars. "This is not a movie, Howland. This is a supermarket. Also wear a clean shirt tomorrow. Stay in back today. Keep off the floor." So he unloaded produce from the big tractor-trailers that pulled around to the rear of the shopping center. He hated truck drivers on the highway and liked them even less close up. For one thing, they were habitually overweight, and Lloyd, himself constitutionally slender irrespective of diet, had an instinctive contempt for anyone he saw as obese. So he was wont to wisecrack in the hearing, sometimes even into the face, of some tub of lard who had climbed down from the high cab to waddle back and unlock the truck doors, and not all who were so derided had a sense of humor about it.

"You're going to get your tail kicked one of these days," the produce-department manager told him with obvious pleasure. "You got it coming."

"Any time they want to try," Lloyd said, "I'm available." He thrust his jaw at the man. "Or anybody else."

"That's really going to throw a scare into 'em," sardonically murmured this narrow-shouldered, balding person. "Now get back to work."

Lloyd would have liked to smash him in his smirking face. But he had already lost one job since the year began, and his duties here were easy enough to shirk. Not to mention that if he took on everybody whom he found objectionable, he would have to fight most of the world. So he had grimaced hatefully but pretended to do as ordered.

He had the definite feeling he could not get away with showing up unshaven so soon after the episode of last week, even though he now had a genuinely reasonable excuse. When they were against you from the start, they would never grant you a single point.

So he went to the pay phone down the block and got through to his boss. "Jack, Howland. I'm calling in sick today."

"No, you're not," Jack responded crisply. "You're calling in to quit."

"No, I'm really sick. I mean it."

"Have it your way. I was just letting you save face. So you're fired."

"*Fired?* What the hell for?"

"You figure it out, Howland. You haven't put in a decent day's work here since you were hired, and you called in sick how many times in three weeks? If you're in that bad a condition, you ought to retire. I'm making it convenient for you."

Lloyd slammed the phone into its chromium hanger. Well, he had tried, and see where it had got him. He was on the downward route again, three weeks after beginning the latest effort to climb out of the hole. Nobody even knew he was back in town. His plan had been to collect a paycheck or two, stay off anything stronger than ice cream, buy some presentable clothes, and show up one Sunday soon over at 1143 Laurel with an armful of presents for everybody: flowers for Donna, a classy bottle of wine for his brother, and of course all kinds of toys for Mandy, dolls and whatever else little girls liked: he'd ask a female clerk in the toy store, but only after explaining that he legitimately had a niece, so he wouldn't be accused of being a potential child molester. He had always to stay on guard, being the kind of guy many people instinctively thought the worst of.

And time did not diminish the effect of any injustice he had ever suffered. A dirty deal tended to get worse in memory. Jack Duncan, the produce-department manager, would not be forgotten, though Lloyd was aware, if precedent meant anything, that he was unlikely to have the opportunity to take revenge on the man, Duncan being the sort to call the law on the slightest pretext, and if ordinary people were inclined to detest Lloyd on sight, make that to the tenth power for cops.

He was in a foul mood as he arrived at the supermarket in late morning to collect what money was due him, but he was also under control until he went to the accounting department in the mezzanine office and found that not only was a check not waiting for him there, but Jack Duncan had thus far failed to notify Personnel of the dismissal.

Lloyd went down and found the man, with his bow tie and name-plate, out on the floor near the lavish array of tomatoes—regular, plum, aquacultured, cherry, yellow, organically grown, imported Israeli, sun-dried—that was his self-described "baby."

"They don't have my money ready. That mean I'm not fired?"

"You're dreaming," Duncan said. "They'll send you a check when they get around to it." He was drab against the background of brilliant red fruit.

"If you fire a person, you should pay him right away," Lloyd said sullenly. He brought his hand out of his pants pocket.

"You must be an authority on the subject," Duncan said wryly, but then looked at what Lloyd had brought from the pocket and blanched. He took a step backward, pressing himself against the display of tomatoes, and stared wildly around the store. As it happened, no customers or staff were nearby at the moment. "Oh no, please—!"

"What's your problem?" Lloyd asked, feeling good for a change as he extended the closed utility knife. "I preferred this to the box cutters you got back there: opens cartons better. I took it from Hardware. It wasn't pilfering: I only used it in the store. Here, I'm giving it back."

"Get out," said Duncan, recovering his courage.

"Here, take it," Lloyd said. "Look, the blade isn't even out. How could I have carried it in my pocket otherwise? It's the store's property. Take it."

"I'm calling Security," said Duncan.

"All right," Lloyd said. "I tried." He returned the closed knife to his pocket. "You dirty little yellow bastard." He turned quickly and left the store. At that moment he did not care about his money, but neither did he feel the demands of his pride had been satisfactorily answered by simple name-calling. He needed the ear of a woman who had some affection for him, a characterization that could not be applied to any with whom he had ever been intimate. This was an unpropitious time to make his peace with Donna. He had to do some drinking first to work up his nerve, but not get so drunk that his sister-in-law would not let him in the house.

2

Yellow tape had been stretched around the entire property at 1143 Laurel, and the van of the crime-scene team was at the curb in front, along with many police cars, marked and unmarked. Vehicles sent by the local TV channels and the daily paper were kept at the end of the block. Uniformed officers were on hand to restrain the newspeople and the gathering crowd that had begun as the immediate neighbors but had gradually attracted those from nearby streets and others in transit.

Dr. Pollack, an assistant medical examiner, had made a preliminary examination of the bodies, and they were taken to the morgue, to be thoroughly autopsied in the lab upstairs. Pollack's estimate of the time of death was any time from six to two hours before he arrived on the scene of the crime. He would not know for sure until the body was on his steel table—and perhaps not even then, for forensic medicine was not mathematics, as he was wont to remind complainers. With her smaller body, the little girl's death was even harder to time: so little flesh cooled quickly. The cuts had been made by a very thin and very keen blade, perhaps a straight razor or the like, or so it seemed.

Photographs had been taken before the bodies were touched by anyone in an official capacity. The detectives for whom the case was the primary assignment had looked at the bodies and walked through the house, again without touching any surface, and promptly left the premises to the Identification team, who would gather evidence and fingerprint the place.

One of the members of the Ident team was a blond and very fit-looking officer named Daisy O'Connor, whose policeman father, a year before his retirement a decade and a half before, had been given as partner a rookie by the name of Nick Moody. Moody was now, with his partner, Dennis LeBeau, the detective assigned to the Howland murders.

Moody, a detective first grade, was the senior man, but after putting a few questions to Mary Jane Jones on the subject of her discovery of the bodies, he turned the job over to LeBeau and joined the other detectives in interviewing the rest of the neighbors. It was Moody's theory, and not LeBeau's, that because of Dennis' headful of curls and big brown eyes he was more successful with the female subjects. But it was Moody, not LeBeau, who was always on the prowl. LeBeau was very married, whereas Moody was twice divorced. The breakup of his second marriage, the year before, had impoverished him financially and emotionally.

Without the sum the store owed him, Lloyd's funds were insufficient for the drinking he wanted to do. Not for the first time in his life, he thought about getting money in a criminal way. The problem was *how*. He had done some shoplifting as a kid and been picked up for it a few times, but was always put on probation or simply warned. All that he had been caught at as an adult was employee pilfering, for which the punishment was, at worst, being fired. Therefore he had no police record. He took that fact into consideration whenever he thought about raising funds by illegal means. He hated cops and did not wish to give them an advantage over him. Also, he feared losing control of himself under certain conditions. It had never yet happened, but he believed he had the capacity for it. Could he trust

himself to keep within bounds if he tried to mug someone who resisted violently? There were fools who fought back with bare hands
against an armed adversary. He should probably avoid crimes against
the person. He could not stand being shamed. He did not consider
what happened with the produce manager as being personally degrading, but it would have been had he not backed the man against
the tomatoes.

Thinking of the supermarket gave him an idea for a quick source
of funds. He had observed how careless women food shoppers were,
especially those with small children. They often carried shoulder-
strap purses, which with their movements, sometimes abrupt ones
necessitated by what the kid was getting into, swung to a blind spot
back of one hip. Often these big bags even yawned open to offer
easy access. Sometimes they put their purses in the carts and left
them to inspect the shelves.

It would be only justice to work the store from which he had just
been fired, but he might be too conspicuous there to the other employees, some of whom, after three weeks, he knew slightly.

There was a big PriceRite on the same road as its nearest com-
petitor, but a mile and a half distant, which meant a walk for Lloyd,
who had no car. Three months earlier, he had come to town by bus
for his father's funeral.

"Well, okay, my car was repoed," he had told Donna over the
slice of her warm Dutch apple pie not long from the oven.

"Why couldn't you just say that in the first place?" She cut a
backup wedge so that it would be ready whenever he finished the
first. Donna was like that.

He swallowed, then took a sip of the only fresh-brewed coffee he
ever tasted. First time he watched her make it he hadn't known what
she was doing: where was the jar of powder? "I was embarrassed,"
he said. "I couldn't keep up the payments. Old story. I get tired of
telling it."

She showed him the most beautiful smile in the world. He knew he shouldn't make too much of it, but it was always as if for him alone. "*Old?* You're not even twenty-two."

"Come on, *Donna*," he whined for effect. "I'm almost twenty-three, and you know it."

"Do you count leap years? I don't when it comes to *me!*" She stuck the wedge-shaped silver gadget—leave it to her to have just the right tool for every job—under the already cut slice of pie. "I'm determined to fatten you up, so you don't make your brother feel heavier than he already does."

"Did Larry put on more since last time?" This was Lloyd's first visit since early fall. He tried to limit himself and would not have made it for several months now, had it not been for their father's death.

Donna immediately acquired a slight stiffness. She was supersensitive regarding any hint of negative reflection on her husband—even when it was she who had brought the subject up. "He's still in great shape," she said. "But you know how people are. They always think they could stand to lose a pound or two. You can't be too thin or too young or too . . ."

"It's 'rich,' isn't it?" he offered after waiting politely. It was the only one of the three that mattered to Lloyd, who was slender without trying and this early in life cared little about age, but, significantly, it was the one Donna had difficulty remembering. With another kind of woman, he might have observed now that *she* certainly had no problem with her own figure, but of course he would have been mortified to have Donna know he had so much as thought anything of the sort, he who averted his eyes when passing the open doorway of the master bedroom on a trip through the hall. "It's *rich*," he repeated. "What I still hope to be if I can find the right thing."

" 'Still'? At your age you shouldn't use that word. You've got lots of time for anything you want to do, but if you don't mind some advice from an old woman, you could use some focus. What are you doing at the moment?"

"Now who's misusing words?" he asked. She was twenty-five. He then lost his smile and looked away. "I've been trying various lines of work. . . . Look," he said hastily, "I'm trying to learn how businesses are run, you know, profit margins and taxes and all, how to get the best out of people who work for you, and . . ." He smirked at the expression she was showing him. "I shouldn't have told you the truth. I should have lied."

"It wouldn't have worked," Donna said, putting her hand lightly on the back of his, setting his afire. "I know you so well. I know you like I feel I would have known my own little brother by now, if he had lived."

He disliked the comparison but could not hint that he did, for it was dear to her, and he cherished any kind of intimacy he could get. "You *do* know me like nobody else."

"Now, don't say that. It's Larry who knows you best. You're brothers."

Lloyd finished the coffee that with the half-dissolved sugar made a pool in the bottom of the cup. "As you know, we never lived in the same house. My father ran off with my mother, leaving Larry's mom and Larry behind, but he didn't stay long with us. Larry may have forgiven him, especially when he got old and sick, but I never did. I'm here for the funeral because of Larry, not *him*." This too was a lie, but he could hardly confess he was using his father's death as an excuse to see *her*.

"Why," Donna said, gasping, "that's an awful thing to say about your father when he's dead."

"Dying doesn't make him a better man."

She shook her head. "I'm not saying you don't have a grievance, but his last few years must have been pretty rotten, all alone in that Medicaid place. Larry had lost track of him. He never bothered us before. I guess it was by some kind of accident he found out where Larry was, from somebody at the nursing home."

"So Larry is burying him. That must cost a pretty penny. But that's good old Larry for you."

Donna's eyes flashed. "What's that supposed to mean?"

Lloyd was suddenly so inflated with conflicting emotions that he could hardly stay in the chair. "Who is he to be so forgiving?"

It took Donna a long moment to interpret this outburst, and she was never more lovely, with the profusion of amber curls, the incredible gradations of rose from cheek to lips, and, always, the jewel-like eyes that could grow huge with tenderness, or contract in disapproval as they were doing now. "Let me get this straight," she asked. "You are condemning him for his virtues?"

"I'm condemning myself," Lloyd insisted. He had screwed this up, as usual. What he wanted least was to center the focus on his brother, who had too much already. "Forget it. I apologize. I didn't mean it like it sounded."

"All right, I will," Donna said quickly, smiling gloriously. "You know I love you both."

What he knew was that her love for him was as a brother. He was not demented. But he was aroused all the same. Not erotically: to desire someone you so adored was impossible. To have any hope of gratification was not to adore, which could admit no compromise and remain what it was supposed to be. And there was no serious desire that could rule out all hope of gratification. He was therefore safe, unless all existing categories were false. "Well, I love you . . . you both. I mean, all three."

He immediately regretted the reference to Amanda, which caused Donna to rise from the table. "The nap should be over by now. I don't know if something's wrong with her, sleeping so much. Until now the problem always was she didn't want to ever go to sleep at all. Is that just growing up?"

But she stayed awhile longer, smiling down at Lloyd. She wore a shapeless pale-blue sweatshirt. He had never seen his sister-in-law in as little as a modest bathing suit, and did not want to: call him a prude.

"Speaking of sleep," she went on, her hands on the knobs that topped the corners of the chairback, "how's your insomnia? Did you try my treatment?"

"I did," said he, lying, "and it worked. I should have told you that before now." Donna's method, used by herself since childhood, was to trick sleep into coming by pretending to be someone else: that is, by acting a part in an impromptu play. You could be your favorite person, not the one you actually were, and could do anything you wanted, without hurting or taking anything away from anyone else. Usually you went to sleep before very long, because it was relaxing not to be yourself, but if you stayed awake at least you were having fun doing so.

Only Donna would have come up with such a technique, and probably only she could use it successfully. Lloyd certainly could not. He had no idea of how to be somebody else. It was hard enough to be himself: that in fact was his problem.

"I was wondering," he asked now, "if Larry uses your method. I don't remember if he said, whenever it was you were telling about it." In truth he never forgot where and when Donna told him anything. In the case of her insomnia cure it was as he dried the dishes she washed after dinner one night the previous fall. The dishwasher, eccentric all week, suddenly refused to operate except on the rinse cycle, and the job had to be undertaken by hand. Lloyd eagerly volunteered. It was a way of being Donna's partner in an innocuous but nevertheless intimate association, of which the warm, steamy water in one compartment of the sink, winking with iridescent bubbles, was an element, as was the hot clear rinse she gave each plate with the flex-hosed spray before inserting it into the draining rack, from which Lloyd plucked it up and vigorously abraded off the remaining droplets with the thirsty-fibered towel. Larry was not in the room. He was putting Amanda to bed.

Donna now tossed her head merrily. "*Larry?* He's never taken more than two minutes to go to sleep in his life. He's out soon as his head hits the pillow."

What Lloyd heard was no doubt mostly wish fulfillment and therefore suspect: if this was true, how often did his brother then—? But he rejected the ugly question, which was no business of his. And, happily, Donna could be counted on not to have gotten so up-to-date as to reflect publicly on her marriage bed, unlike some of the sluttish types with whom he had worked. At times this was obviously intended as sexual invitation to the male listeners, but even more often, to Lloyd's mind, it was unconditioned exhibitionism and repelled him.

"He's a lucky man," he said now.

Donna's eyes quickened but did not spark. "What might seem luck is mostly hard work. He's running himself ragged these days. You know, he's up for assistant sales manager. The present man is going to retire in the spring. Larry's certainly qualified, with one of the best sales records in the whole Northeast, but there's stiff competition. The boss's second cousin is in the running."

"Then Larry can kiss the job good-bye," Lloyd said, his lip curling. "There's always some dirty inside stuff, wherever you go. Unless you're in on it, you haven't got a prayer."

Donna had been about to leave and wake her child, but was detained by his bitterness. "Now, that's not always true, else how could anybody get a start? Your brother didn't have any connections when he joined Glenn-Air. He soon made them, though, by hard work, and he's done mighty well."

Donna wouldn't be Donna without the naïveté. That was much of what Lloyd loved about her. She was older than he in the chronological sense, but as innocent as Amanda, and it was by nature, for she had worked a few years in the world before meeting Larry: she could have seen what went on there, but was blind to it. Lloyd knew little about Glenn-Air, but he was certain that if his brother had prospered in the association, it was by the same means used by everybody else who succeeded anywhere and had nothing to do with real talent or true quality.

He sneered. "I've heard that too often."

It didn't seem all that offensive to him, but Donna was suddenly incensed. Her body grew rigid, and her soft face had become hard. "And you'll hear it a lot more if you come here! Don't use that tone with me!"

"All right," he said, pushing back his chair and rising in one stark movement. She was not the only one who could be hurt. "You don't have to listen to it any more." He wanted to get away from her as soon as he could and therefore headed for the back door. Even so, he thought she might call him back before he took the four steps to get there, but she did not. She had coldly left the kitchen by the time he turned, before stepping onto the back porch, to thank her at least for the coffee and pie. His resentment was not so great as to eradicate his manners. But she was not there to hear him. He left town without attending the funeral.

3

Detective LeBeau was trying to locate Lawrence Howland, husband of the deceased female, father of the murdered child, but as of six hours after the homicides had been reported, he had had no success. The Jones woman had stated that Howland was out of town on some business matter, but she could not name the firm for which he worked, nor had such information yet been discovered in the search of the house. She did, however, say he had "something to do with air conditioners," and one of the neighbors across the street, an accountant named Lundquist, confirmed this, but in the same general way without a brand name.

While Moody was phoning the local airline offices, LeBeau went to the yellow pages and began to call firms listed there under "Air Conditioning." By the time he was able to get started on the quest it was well into evening. He received no answers at any of the local offices. He then tried the 800 number of the best-known maker of window units and got a woman who worked for the national twenty-four-hour service that provided suggestions for self-help in the case of emergency breakdowns at night or on holidays. She was not equipped to find every employee of the firm, and anyway there was no reason to suppose that Howland worked for that particular company, but like many civilians nowadays, the woman was eager to help the police even when, as in this case, they were halfway across the country from where she said she lived. She gave LeBeau a phone at which the chief engineer could be reached, and this man was able to supply a number for the central personnel office, which, conveniently for LeBeau's purposes, was on the West Coast, where the time was only four forty-five.

The result of all this effort was only that he finally learned Howland was not employed by the firm in question—at least not under the name given: you had to allow for all possibilities, though most crimes, murders especially, had no mystery about them. They were almost always committed by the most obvious suspect. Both LeBeau and Moody assumed, routinely, that Donna Howland had been murdered by her husband. True, the killing of the little girl was a complication, but not to have suspected Howland would at this point have been unprofessional. And that the man could not promptly be found was hardly at odds with the routine assumption.

"Isn't it funny," LeBeau asked Moody across their facing desks, "nobody knows the name of his company? The neighbors usually do on a street like that."

Moody was about to respond when his phone rang. He hardly spoke again after identifying himself, but he took some quick notes on a pad of yellow paper. "Thanks, Doc," he said finally. "Sure. Okay." He hung up and spoke across to LeBeau. "Pollack's going to do the autopsy tomorrow morning. I guess it's my turn to observe?" Neither enjoyed watching a postmortem, but someone had to, to protect the chain of evidence for legal purposes. Else a defense lawyer was not above suggesting that the medical examiner opened up the wrong body, thus discrediting the whole case against his client. "Meanwhile, it looks like, in addition to the cutting, she's got a bad head wound from violent contact with something more or less blunt. No visible semen anywhere on the body." He went over his jottings. "The little girl probably died of the clean slash at the throat. No other signs of damage on her." He looked across at his partner. "Let's hope it was while she was still asleep."

LeBeau's youngest daughter was only a year and two months older than the dead child. He said, "I'm going to drop around home, maybe get a hot meal. There'll be more than enough for you, Nick. I'll give Crys a call."

Moody was given to saying, and sometimes even believing, that if he could find a wife like Crystal LeBeau, he would settle down forever, but when in the depths of drunkenness he could identify and accept the truth, he knew he would never recognize such a woman if he did meet her. "Thanks, but you go on. Maybe I'll get a bright idea meanwhile."

"How about I bring you back a sandwich? If she doesn't have some nice meat, I'll get her to make one of those bacon-and-eggers you like, on white bread with lots of ketchup."

"Swell," said Moody, for whom the described sandwich was a favorite only because it was one of the few dishes he could cook for himself. If a woman was feeding him, he preferred almost anything else. He knew LeBeau's real reason for stopping off home was to tuck in his little daughter even though she was probably already asleep. When Moody had first seen the Howland child, he would have liked to keep Dennis out of the room, but there was no way that could be done, and his partner would anyway have resented the effort as an implication that his competence was at the mercy of a selfish emotion. LeBeau had three kids and would likely father more. Moody's lone offspring, by his first wife, was a twenty-four-year-old graduate student, living with his mother in Oregon. He was a left-winger and despised the police, though he was civil enough when his father phoned him every Xmas.

Hardly had LeBeau gone out the door when Dennis' phone rang. If the call was important, Moody could catch him by raising the back window and yelling down to the parking lot. Homicide occupied the second floor of the Tenth Precinct stationhouse: one big shabby space full of paper-cluttered desks, with a couple of private offices for the brass up around the perimeter, a squalid locker room with adjoining shower, and two interrogation rooms in the rear.

Moody stood up, leaned over, and seized the phone from his partner's desk. He did not identify himself.

The voice was female. "Denny? I found the address book."

"Daisy, it's Nick."

"Oh, well, okay," she said with somewhat less enthusiasm. "I found their address book. Know where it was? The little girl's room, on a shelf with kids' storybooks."

"You're real good, Daze."

"I wish I could claim it was more than luck. I wasn't looking for evidence at that point. I was just seeing if any of the books were ones I had as a girl."

"I won't tell anybody," Moody said, in the tone he sometimes used to cultivate the confidence of arrested felons. "Besides, you would have found it sooner or later anyhow. You're doing great." She was not long out of the Academy.

"It looks like the husband's employer might be something called Glenn-Air. Here's the number."

Moody took it down. "There won't be anybody there tonight. What about relatives?"

"The book is full of names."

"I'll run over to get it."

"I'll drop it off," O'Connor said. "We're finished here. Small's taking a few last prints, down cellar."

"I'll be here," said Moody.

But it was her partner, Harry Small, who delivered the address book about a half hour later. It was tagged as evidence, and Moody had to sign a receipt for it.

Small looked more like a professor than a cop. He was an authority on fingerprinting, who kept up with all the latest technology in that area. The department even once found the money to send him to a national convention of fellow specialists in the craft.

"Daisy go on ahead?" Moody asked.

"She wanted to get started with the prints," Small said. He had a perpetual squint under bushy dark eyebrows.

"She's doing good?"

Small nodded noncommittally. "There's a lot to learn about prints."

"But she's doing okay? She's pretty young."

"Sure," Small said and left.

He was probably worried she might be promoted over him, what with the department's new policy, instigated by a pushy female city councillor, of giving preference to women wherever feasible. Moody was opposed to the policy on general principles, but when it came to particulars of which he was aware, as in this case, he saw some justification for it. Daisy after all was extremely bright and very pretty, whereas Small was without personality and seemed to have no existence beyond fingerprints. And Moody had known Daisy since she was born.

Small on the way out passed LeBeau coming in. LeBeau was carrying a plastic bag.

He said to Moody, "Don't tell me he's classified and identified all those prints already. That's guy's a wonder."

"He just dropped off the address book that *Daisy* found," Moody said. "She's the one working on the prints."

LeBeau handed over the plastic bag. It was pleasantly warm to the touch, and when Moody opened the flap his nostrils were greeted with a delicious aroma. The sandwich thank God was not fried egg but roast meat, exuding gravy into the bread.

"Here," Moody said, gesturing with his elbow, "take this book away, willyuh, before I drop something on it."

"Roast pork," LeBeau said. "If you had come along, you would have gotten mashed potatoes and red cabbage too. I won't mention dessert or it would bring tears to your eyes."

Moody had noticed that married men always cared more about

food than single guys: it had in fact been true of himself when he
was married, even though his second wife could hardly boil water
and in fact rarely visited the kitchen except to get cans of soft drinks
and packaged junk snacks.

" 'Glenn-Air' looks like it might be his place of business," Moody
said, trying to hold the sandwich through the plastic bag. "I called
it but didn't get an answer."

LeBeau frowned. "But you just got the address book."

"You don't miss anything, do you? Daisy called me from the
house."

LeBeau was looking through the book. "Most of them are first
names only."

Moody had already eaten half the sandwich. Carrying the other
half, he went to the water cooler. At the moment, only he and LeBeau
were on the floor, but other homicide detectives were at work elsewhere in the city, especially the team handling the case of the high-
school girl whose raped, mutilated, and murdered body had been
found three days earlier in a public park. Moody wished he had reminded Dennis that the coffee machine was out of order: he had to
wash the sandwich down with water.

When he returned to his desk, he and LeBeau divided up the
phone numbers, Dennis taking A through L. It was Moody therefore
who got the painful job of calling the number listed for "Mom." The
most he could hope for was that the number was that of Lawrence
Howland's mother. But it was one of the established truths of homicide work that the kinder alternative was rarely the operative one.

Had the number been local, he would have gone to the residence
personally. That was departmental policy, but he liked to think he
would have done so even when not under orders. He knew the public
erroneously supposed that those whose work concerned appalling
crimes therefore were soon made callous by them, whereas precisely
the reverse was true: the hundredth sight of fresh blood might be
less shocking to the nerves than the first, but it was much harder on

the soul, representing as it did not novelty but rather the inevitable, reminding you once again that you could do nothing to keep it from happening.

He was granted a temporary reprieve now: the number failed to answer after a dozen rings.

He gave the area code to LeBeau and asked, "Where's that? Downstate someplace?"

"Dunno." LeBeau was taking down some of the numbers from the address book, before handing it back over to Moody. He looked up. "Why don't we just Xerox this? Wouldn't that be simpler?"

"Why did it take us so long to come up with that idea?" asked Moody, striking his forehead with a flattened hand. "Not an example of our usual laserlike approach."

"No, it's a perfect example," LeBeau said, rising. They often disparaged themselves as a team, but would not suffer others to do so. He went to the corner where the copying machine stood. The bulb in the nearest overhead light had burned out two days earlier but had not yet been replaced. He shouted back, "I can't see a thing!"

Before surrendering the book, Moody had penciled several numbers on his notepad. There was one for "Marty," another for "Muriel," and a third for "Mr. and Mrs. C. K. Mitchell," with a street address in the state capital. Like all other entries throughout, these were written in the same rounded, precise hand as the stubs in the register that accompanied the book of checks imprinted with the names of Lawrence and Donna Howland. Similar writing appeared on a grocery list that had been held to the refrigerator door with a magnet. It was likely to be Donna's.

Moody dialed the number listed for "Marty." A man answered on the first ring. Moody identified himself. "I'm calling from an address book found at the Howland residence at eleven forty-three Laurel. Do you have some connection with Donna or Lawrence Howland or both?"

"Howland . . . Laurel . . . Yeah, I installed a washstand and commode in the new lavatory they put in, about a year ago. And they called me once, I think, for a repair to an existing fixture—kitchen sink, I believe. What's this in reference to, Detective? Am I being accused of something wrong?"

"No," Moody said. "There's been a problem, but not about the plumbing. When was the last time you were to the house?"

"Gee, I'd have to look at my books."

"Sure. Listen, you think you'll have a minute maybe to talk a little to us tomorrow if we need to?"

"Any time at all," the plumber said. "I ain't got a problem co-operating with the police."

"That's nice to hear, Marty. It *is* Marty, isn't it? Marty what?"

"Marty Conway." He spelled it out.

"Can I call you Marty? Or do you want 'Mr. Conway'?"

"Please, Marty's fine. 'Mr. Conway' is my old man."

"Swell, Marty. Uh, you can't say more or less when you were to the Howland place the last time? Put me in the ballpark?"

"Lucky for me, I been busy as hell the last few years, putting in ten hours, maybe, six days a week. I'd need to look at my books."

"You don't have them at hand? This is your business number?"

"Yeah, but I'm on the extension in the house. I work outa my converted garage, out back. My books are out there. You want me to go out there?"

"Naw," Moody said almost scoffingly. "We'll be talking to you again: you'll know by then."

"Absolutely. I can give *you* a call."

"Don't worry about it," said Moody. "Listen, Marty, are you what you would call social friends with Donna and Larry?"

Marty hesitated briefly, then asked, "The Howlands? No, I just did that work for them, is all."

"You remember Mrs. Donna Howland? I guess she was there when you did your work."

Marty answered after a long moment. "Not much."

"A nice-looking woman."

"A lot of them around these days," Marty said. "But looking at 'em too much can get a plumber in trouble." His laugh was hollow. "If you know what I mean. I'm a married man, Detective."

"Well, okay, Marty, we thank you for your help."

"Got a wife and two boys, eleven and nine. . . . Uh, would you mind telling me what this is about?"

"We'll talk again, Marty," Moody told him. "Could you just give me your address?"

LeBeau had returned from the Xerox.

"That was swift," said Moody, taking his share of the proferred sheets.

"There weren't that many pages to copy. There's not a lot of numbers here."

"I was talking to this plumber, Marty," said Moody. "He did a couple jobs for the Howlands, but he claims he doesn't know them socially. Is that the usual thing? Write down just somebody's first name when he's just your plumber, not a personal friend?"

LeBeau, now seated opposite him, lifted brow and shoulders simultaneously, as if dubious, but said confidently, "Sure. We got this kinda handyman, jack-of-all, you know, named Hal. We don't know him like a friend, exactly, but he does stuff for us once in a while, paints the porch and so on. Crystal will just say, 'I'll give Hal a ring,' and everybody knows who she's talking about. But me, I don't even know what his last name is. I doubt she remembers."

"You sold me," Moody said. "Say, that sandwich was fantastic. It was even salted just right."

"She knows your ways as well as she knows mine."

"Only way I can keep a wife," said Moody, "is if she's someone else's." He added hastily, "You know how I mean that."

The addendum was needless. Your partner was closer than your brother—closer certainly than Moody's, with whom he had fought bitterly when they were boys, and whom he simply did not see nowadays—and was not likely to misinterpret anything you said.

LeBeau returned the address book to the plastic bag in which it had been delivered. "Do we talk to the plumber again?"

"I don't know," said Moody. "But he bothers me a little. He claims he never noticed what Donna looked like, though he was there more than once. He put in the fixtures in the lavatory."

"Well . . ."

"She was beautiful," Moody said. "What man wouldn't even notice that? I know, *you* wouldn't admit it, but I also know you're normal. He claims to be, with a wife and kids. Does that mean anything?"

"I don't know," LeBeau answered. "Maybe. That's pretty iffy, unless there's something more. We can remember him if Howland turns up clean."

From the parking area behind the building, a siren started up, but diminished quickly as the car from which it came sped away. The precinct downstairs had gotten an emergency call.

Moody, now with A through L, decided to start from the back, mainly because the entry for "Lloyd" was accompanied by more phone numbers than any other in the whole book. There were also three different addresses, all of them crossed out with pencil strokes so light that no information was obscured. This was true as well of all the numbers. He dialed the last, which began with a downstate area code.

"Don't know nobody of that name," said a fatherly voice when asked to identify a "Lloyd." "But I'm only the night watchman. I guess you should call daytimes."

"Just what sort of business we talking about?"

"Lumberyard, see."

"What community?"

"This here is Little Falls, though it's the Rosedale postal district."

"I'll try tomorrow," Moody told him. "Thank you kindly." Hanging up, he asked LeBeau, who had himself just completed a call, "Can you gimme that state map of yours? Ever hear of Little Falls or Rosedale?"

His partner rooted through a desk drawer while saying, "I got a waiter in some restaurant over in Oakwood. Says he thinks he remembers a guy named Lloyd worked there last year, mopping floors, cleaning grease traps, and all. Thinks he just stopped showing up. Says he'll have the manager call tomorrow: guy's out with the flu at the moment." He found the tightly folded map and tossed it across to Moody.

Little Falls was too small to be listed in the index of towns on the reverse, but Rosedale was there. Moody pinched his fingers and made a rough estimate, based on the printed scale, of the miles from here to there. "I make it two, maybe slightly more."

"You're talking hundreds."

"Yeah. Like west-southwest. Looks like a mostly rural area except for Rosedale. What's that? Apples, cabbages, tin cans? What do they make or raise out there?" Moody smirked and shrugged.

LeBeau's phone rang. "Yeah, I'll accept. . . . Go ahead. . . . Uh-huh, uh-huh. . . . Yeah. . . . Look, sir, next time it'd be best if you waited till you were pretty certain. We're on a limited budget over here, and I don't know how many collect calls we can pay for, unless they really deliver something we can use. Know what I mean? Thanks. You take care." He replaced the handpiece and sighed at Moody. "One of *those* guys."

"There'll be more."

"He's the waiter I talked to earlier. Been calling up fellow workers, but every one of them had a different theory. Lloyd's a last name, one said. Another claimed the name was not Lloyd but Roy. Meanwhile the manager still has the same flu he had half an hour ago."

Then Moody's phone rang.

"Officer," said a voice that sounded out of breath, "I happened to put on the news just now, and that murder or rather those murders were on it, and I noticed the name. So I called that special number they gave, and told the officer who answered there what I had to say, and when I was done he gave me your number."

Nobody had bothered to coordinate this procedure with Moody. The number given on TV in such cases was monitored by one person, sometimes even a civilian employee of the department. Always there were people who complained they tried all night to get through but finally gave up after hours of the busy signal. Meanwhile those passed along by the call screener would tie up Moody's line with mostly useless information.

"Yes, sir, and just what is your name, sir?"

The voice became petulant. "My name doesn't matter. I'm talking about the *victim*'s name: Howland, am I right?"

"I have to take your name, sir."

"You most definitely do not," cried the voice. "Just let me say what I'm going to, will you? This name Howland, if I've got it right, well, I discharged an employee today of that same name, and he became violent, threatened me with a box-cutting knife."

It was standard to try to force an informant out of anonymity, for disembodied statements were often without merit. But not always. People sometimes really had good reasons for hiding their identities while telling the truth, but finding the perpetrator and assembling the evidence that would convict him was what the taxpayers had hired Moody to do, and this effort could be hindered by not knowing whom you were dealing with. However, you had to be careful not to drive away what might be the unique source of information that would break the case.

"Yes, sir, and what kind of work do you do?"

"Produce manager in a supermarket. It belongs to a well-known chain."

"You can't tell me where?"

"In town," said the man. "I don't want to lose my job. I know it's not the store's fault if this person is a criminal, but it sure won't please the front office to get this kind of publicity."

"Oh, I don't know," Moody said. "Business picked up after that holdup last year at the big Greenleaf over on Three-oh-one. You remember, I'm sure, being in the same trade. Guy came in with an Uzi?"

"I didn't realize that."

"Tell me more about *your* Howland," Moody asked. "Like his first name and where he lives, if you got that at hand."

"After the knife attack, I took the trouble to go upstairs to Personnel and take a look at his records. I was seriously considering preferring charges. I committed his address to memory. I didn't have to write it down. Would you believe he didn't have a phone of his own? Since our regulations insist on it, he gave one where a message could be left for him."

"Okay, give it to me."

"Got your pen or pencil?" the produce manager asked pedantically. He gave the street address. "Now, *that* I'm sure of. I'll give you what I *think* is the phone for messages. I could be off on one of the digits, but the address is absolutely correct. I've got pretty nearly a photographic memory unless something distracts me, and that—"

"Got a first name for him?" Moody demanded.

"Lloyd. Lloyd Howland."

"Look, sir. If it turns out something comes of your information both you and your store's name are sure to be known—and you won't regret it, neither you nor the store, because you'll get a lot of credit for your help—so why not give your name to me right now."

"I've reconsidered," said the produce manager. "I'm Jack Duncan, and my store's the Valmarket on Seventeen East."

Moody got Duncan's private and store numbers, asked him some questions about Lloyd Howland, thanked him, and hung up.

LeBeau was back on his own telephone, but had finished when Moody returned from the water cooler. "No return call from Howland as yet," Dennis said.

"We got something maybe better. This Lloyd: his last name's

Howland, and he's in his early twenties." Moody told his partner the rest of what he had learned from Duncan. "What's he to Lawrence? Brother? Cousin? He's too old to be a son. He's got a permanent attitude, according to his boss. But he was extra mad today about the firing, and he drew a knife on the man." He paused to elevate his right shoulder in a personal gesture of triumph. "Here's the big one: the phone he gave the store as his was Donna's: three-oh-three eight-seven-six-eight. Said he didn't have his own but messages could be left for him there."

Lloyd had not gone to his brother's house since the argument with Donna (if it could be called that) in February. He could not face her again until he had made something of himself or at least held the same job for a whole season and bought a usable car or rented a respectable apartment—anything, really, that he could show as an accomplishment. Yet here he was, three months later, in the familiar situation, or probably worse, if he was now considering stealing some woman's purse from a shopping cart. He had never before fallen that low.

All he wanted now was a drink to blunt the edge of a bad day. It wasn't much to ask, yet he could not afford it. He kept telling himself that, so as by means of inflated indignation to acquire the nerve, or the lack of shame, to enter the big PriceRite and do the deed. The most available victim would be the young mother with a toddler in tow and thus too distracted to watch her purse, someone very like Donna.

Next door to the supermarket was an overstocked liquor store, in which, as could be seen through the big front windows, several artificial aisles, made up of stacked cardboard cases of bottles, narrowed or even obstructed those between the permanent racks of horizontally displayed wines. He looked for and identified the big mirrors mounted just below the ceiling at various points around the room and angled so that they could be monitored from the checkout counter. Whether there might still be a blind spot or two that eluded their ken could not be determined without going in, and if he once crossed the threshold he would perforce be treated as a suspicious character until he made a cash purchase: he was young, unshaven, and he had a naturally sullen expression unless he faked a smile. He maintained no illusions about his appearance. So why did he not do something about it, as Donna might ask? Well, he had tried to shave on getting up that morning, and look what happened. He had ruined his razor, which led to losing his job, which led to his needing a drink, which led him here, about to commit his first serious crime. Everything was linked in an unbroken progress he was powerless to alter.

. . . But he had not yet fallen so far he would steal from a woman. He would take his chances on the liquor store, where, since he had been watching, no one had appeared behind the cash register or in fact anywhere else, and the entire place was visible through the floor-to-ceiling panes of plate glass that made up the front wall. It was possible that all who worked there were temporarily in the rear storage area, directing or helping with an ongoing delivery from a truck at the back door, the kind of job he had done at the Valmarket. If so, he might have time to step inside, seize the nearest bottle, and get out with nobody the wiser, unless of course there was a chime or buzzer that automatically announced the opening of the door. Even so, many clerks were lackadaisical in their response to such a signal. Some would only poke out or lift a head, then return to a preoccupation; some did less than that. In any case, he was very fast on his feet.

Thus far it was all projection. He would reserve the right to make a decision on the moment.

He pushed the glass door open and stepped quickly inside, listening for the alarm, hearing none. But there were those that signaled silently, with a storeroom light, for example. Big green jugs of weak table wine were nearest the door. He must go beyond the checkout, against the left wall, to reach the hard stuff.

He seized the first half-gallon container he could reach—amber-colored whiskey of some brand—and in the next second was passing the unattended cash register on his way out. It was at his mercy. But had he become sufficiently criminal for *that*?

The question was made meaningless by what he saw when he looked at the till. Its drawer was extended. Pausing for an instant at the counter, he saw that as much of the compartmented drawer as was visible at his angle appeared empty of money. He leaned farther across the cool smooth off-white Masonite counter—and saw a quarter of blood-streaked bald head and one shoulder tip of blue broadcloth.

The store had been robbed and the only evident employee badly wounded or worse. Lloyd's first impulse was to leave as quickly as he could. It was purely by chance that he had happened upon the scene. The laws of fate, which he respected, would not be defied by his fleeing the premises. He had not so much as seen any part of the crime as it was taking place, had not even noticed another person near enough to have been the perpetrator. Yet the robbery had occurred not long before: the pool of blood around the victim's head was obviously fresh.

There was nothing Lloyd could do for the man on the floor. He had a memory of CPR from school demonstrations, and also of that maneuver you apply to someone choking on a mouthful of food, but neither was appropriate to a head wound. If the clerk was not already dead, he was well on his way, and if Lloyd stayed much longer, a customer would come in and assume he had done it. You could count on that, and though there was no evidence against him—what had he done with the money?—he would be arrested, tried, and convicted just because he was who he was, the guy people hated on sight. He just wished he could explain that to Donna.

He left the store, remembering to walk steadily, purposefully, head lowered as if in thought. What he forgot, until he had gone thirty feet into the parking area, was that he continued to carry the half-gallon of whiskey, unwrapped. It was an advertisement of shoplifting. He should have taken a brown bag from the stack within reach on the counter. He scanned the nearby blacktop for discarded paper products. They blew all over the vast parking lot in front of the Valmarket from which he had just been fired, but either this strip mall employed better cleanup workers or it was another example of bad chance: at the moment he could not see a fragment.

He noticed a telephone cubicle on the other side of the rank of clustered shopping carts under the covered walkway in front of the supermarket. He went there and, retaining the large bottle on the little phone-side ledge with his elbow, dialed 911. He told the operator all he knew about the apparent holdup of the liquor store, but naturally withheld his own name. Maybe he was thereby saving the clerk's life, if any was left to save. He was not quite the total bastard people thought he was.

Immediately on hanging up the telephone he saw a crumpled brown grocery bag in the bottom of an empty shopping cart that stood free of the long, clustered files of its fellows. He went to it and seized the bag, which turned out to be torn but would serve to mask his stolen bottle with superficial legitimacy.

He had trekked only halfway through the parking lot when he heard the *whoop* of the oncoming police car, followed soon by the siren's wail of an ambulance. Both vehicles hurtled in through another entrance to the parking area than the one to which he was heading. He glanced back at the crowds coming out of the PriceRite and the satellite shops, because it would have been suspicious-looking not to.

Then he hiked back to the room he called home in lieu of anything better, leaned against the tiny sink in the kitchen niche, and opened the half gallon. He had not noticed the label before pouring himself a coffee mug full of liquid and taking a hefty gulp. He choked briefly and almost spewed it out: it was scotch, which he put in the category of cleaning fluids, fit to swab out toilets, open drains, but not for human use. . . . But the same properties that made it so filthy at first encounter served quickly enough to stun the very sense of taste by which it was obnoxious, and in no time at all, his palate anesthetized, he had not only drained the mug but refilled it. He was anxious to get to that level of consciousness at which he could contemplate his next move. Liquor worked best for this purpose. He had never tried a drug that did not dull his faculties whatever its reputation as stimulant.

4

As soon as they had obtained it, the detectives ran "Howland, Lloyd" through the computer but found no criminal record listed for a man of that name. They stayed up all night, part of which they spent revisiting the scene of the crime at 1143 Laurel.

Next morning Moody was an observer at Dr. Pollack's autopsy of Donna and Amanda Howland. Little in police work was more unpleasant. Though having attended many such events in his years in Homicide, Moody never became habituated to the sight of a human body laid open with a scalpel and was more squeamish than LeBeau, on whom he might have tried to foist the job had his partner not been the father of a daughter near the age of the smaller victim.

You could close your eyes, of course, but that was no defense against the odors that permeated the mask over your nose and mouth, and if you pinched your nose shut, you still tasted it or thought you could. The process took hours. He did not get back to his desk until early afternoon. He had eaten no lunch but would not have an appetite before dinnertime, if then.

He filled LeBeau in. "Donna was killed by a blow to the back of the head. Pollack wants to study the wound more before coming to any final conclusions about the weapon, but it must have been heavy to do what it did. The knife wounds were made with an edge as thin and sharp as one of his surgical scalpels."

"And the little girl?"

"The cut across her throat," Moody said curtly. "She wasn't otherwise hurt." He consulted his notebook, though he needed to read nothing there. "Neither one had been touched sexually."

At least LeBeau had meanwhile notified the woman whose number had been listed next to "Mom," who turned out in fact to be the mother of Donna Howland, a Mrs. Elizabeth O'Neill, in Elkhart, Indiana. But she was not at home. The next-door neighbor who watered her plants directed him to call the hospital, where Mrs. O'Neill was currently a patient with a serious heart condition. According to the neighbor, Donna was an only child, and she knew of no other relatives. Mrs. O'Neill was a widow. So Dennis saw no way out of the unhappy duty of informing a very sick woman that her only child had been violently murdered.

Moody visited the water cooler, where he swallowed two mint-flavored digestion pills.

When he got back to his desk, LeBeau was just hanging up the phone.

"Larry Howland came home."

The partners went down to their car, and Moody drove to 1143 Laurel. Across the street from the crime scene was a crowd of onlookers and also a scattering of media people. LeBeau and Moody ignored the shouted questions of the latter, ducked under the yellow tape, and walked to the house.

The officer on duty had detained Howland in the living room. The detectives took over.

Howland was a tall man going a little soft around the middle. He had curly dark hair cut neat and short. He was closely shaven but had the kind of beard that always casts a shadow. He wore a suit of medium gray, a shirt with a thin blue stripe, and a blue tie with a small red figure. His only visible jewelry was a gold wristwatch and a wedding band. He looked a few years older than the thirty-two they had established from Motor Vehicles records. The blue Escort parked up the street, just beyond where the yellow tape turned the corner at the driveway of 1143, was his, according to the number on the plate.

Howland's face was colored with indignation. He shouted at the detectives. He claimed not to know what had happened here.

Moody asked him, "You are Lawrence Howland, and this is your home? Your wife is Donna Howland, and your daughter's named Amanda?"

The answer was given at high volume. "How much longer do I have to put up with this? Where are they? What's happened to them?" He seemed more angry than worried. But the visible evidence of emotion could be highly deceptive.

"This won't take a minute," Moody said. "Would you mind just telling us where it was you really went yesterday? Because you weren't on any of the airlines that fly in and out of Los Angeles—at least not under the name Lawrence or Larry Howland. Also your employer, Glenn-Air, states they never sent you to any kind of conference or convention or whatever, in L.A. or anyplace else."

Howland was suddenly no longer angry. "God Almighty," he pleaded, "show me a little decency. What's happened to my family?"

LeBeau spoke, with a harder voice than Moody's. "We've got some serious business here, and therefore I'm going to give you your rights at this point. You have the right to remain silent . . ." He went through the litany, pretending to read from the card he took from the leather folder that also contained his ID and shield.

But before he had finished, Howland cried, "Do I have to get my lawyer to force you to answer a simple question?"

Moody decided it was time to hit him with it. "Mr. Howland, your wife and your daughter are deceased."

Howland nodded his head for a moment, looking at nothing. At length he lowered his fleshy chin and closed his eyes. The two detectives stood flanking him, in front of the couch he refused to take a seat on when they asked him to. There were all sorts of possible reactions to such news as he had now received—if in fact it *was* news to him—and in Moody's experience none was likely to be indicative of either guilt or innocence, though you might pretend otherwise. The most ruthless of murderers was quite capable of a display of shock and grief that was at face value much more credible than the sometimes mild reaction of the clean-souled.

"Now maybe you want to sit down," Moody told him, gesturing. "Mr. Howland?" The man seemed in a stupor.

"Excuse me," Howland said finally, turning as if in appeal to LeBeau, who previously had been the less friendly; but it was not LeBeau who had brought the worst news. "I want to get this straight." His eyes seemed to have shrunk in diameter as his chin receded and his nose grew more pointed, but his color stayed the same.

Moody repeated the curt statement, this time replacing "deceased" with "dead." When the substance of what you said was of this character, there was no means of not being brutal, at least so he believed. But he still might try when addressing someone who could not possibly be a perpetrator, such as Donna's mother. Which is why he was relieved that Dennis had taken that job off his hands.

Howland nodded as he had earlier.

"Sit down," LeBeau said sternly. He touched Howland's shoulder.

Howland flinched. He cried defiantly, "This is my house. Don't tell me what to do! You're on my premises here."

"Mr. Howland, you listen to me," said Moody. "Something happened here that changes a lot of things. You don't want to work against us. You want to help us find out what happened to your wife and little girl. At least I'm hoping you do."

Howland all at once screamed, taking the officers by surprise, and thus was able to dash as far as the hallway before LeBeau, with his quicker reflexes, could pursue him and halt his progress, being careful, however, to avoid strong-arming the man. Luckily nothing of the sort was needed, despite his apparent burst of hysteria. Howland came to a rigid stop at the touch of his elbow.

"Mr. Howland," Moody said. "Listen to me. I'm sorry there's been a misunderstanding. We're going to tell you everything we know. The reason why we want you to sit down is you're going to hear some nasty stuff."

Howland violently shook his head, without, however, disarranging his hair. He did not focus his eyes anywhere. He came slowly back into the living room, touching the woodwork and the pieces of furniture he passed, as though seeking orientation. He still would not sit down.

Moody told him about the murders. Howland covered his face, and his shoulders heaved, though he made no sound and no tears emerged from beneath his fingers. After a while LeBeau returned to the questioning, for one of the best times to get straight answers was when a subject was genuinely overwrought and grief drained the supply of energy needed for misrepresentation. But it was also true that one of the worst times was when the emotion was being faked. It would take a while before they could decide about Howland.

Howland took his hands off his dry face. Between shattering sobs, he proceeded to admit he had invented the story of going to L.A. for business or in fact for any other purpose. He had not been out of his home county since leaving 1143 the morning before. But the lie had been fabricated to delude his now dead wife, certainly not the police. The truth was that he and a lady friend had been at the Starry Night, one of those motels specializing in facilities for romantic trysts, the rooms of which featured hot tubs, water beds, erotic videos on closed-circuit TV, and bottles of pink champagne. Moody and LeBeau remembered the place as where, some years earlier, a transvestite was beaten to death by a man who picked him up at a bar. When the victim's body was found next day, a faint growth of beard had pushed through the heavy makeup on his cheeks: whiskers take a while to learn the game is finished forever. The killer, a manual-arts teacher at the public high school, turned himself in by late afternoon. He said what enraged him was being taken by surprise, that he had nothing in general against the type.

"I believe that," Moody said. "Otherwise you wouldn't have sodomized the body after killing the individual, would you?"

"What I figured," the husky teacher said, "was I was out an awful lot of money, adding up the drinks, the expensive room, and what I gave this, uh, person, and I still hadn't gotten what I went there for, so I had something coming."

Howland finally began actually to weep tears. He sat down or rather fell onto the sofa, where he continued to sob. "The cop wouldn't tell me what happened. I kept asking to talk to Donna, but he wouldn't put her on. I thought, well, maybe it's a burglary or something."

"You weren't that worried," LeBeau said coldly.

"I'll tell you what worried me," cried Howland. "You don't know Donna. If she knew I was with somebody else—look, maybe she'd rather be dead." His eyes became wild. "You think I'm kidding?"

"Is that why you killed her?"

Howland's expression immediately turned bland. It was a remarkably rapid transition, but Moody had seen its like on people who proved guiltless. Howland proceeded to loosen the knot of his necktie. Then he ripped his shirt at the top button—the cloth tore, the button remained. The shirt was probably ruined, as Moody did not fail to notice and, considering his own meager wardrobe, to deplore.

"I know how it might sound at a time like this," Howland said.

"What's that supposed to mean?" It was LeBeau.

"See, if this hadn't happened, it would have been just sex. It looks so bad now because while I was—well, you know, in bed and so on with someone else. . . . But look"—his eyes flared wildly again—"I wouldn't have been home in any case. I would have been calling on customers or doing paperwork in the office. I'm never home before past six."

"Who could have done a thing like this?" asked Moody.

"Nobody!" Howland shouted. "Everybody loved Donna." He sank to the couch. *"And my little girl."*

Moody leaned toward Howland and said, "Take your best guess, Larry."

Howland was moaning softly into the hands over his face. After a moment his thick fingers parted to make a fence through the interstices of which he peeped at the carpet. "I could never get her to keep the door locked. Maybe the front door, okay, but never the back. It was just too much trouble when you were running in and out, she said. I should have insisted more, but I could never argue with Donna." He lowered his hands and frowned. "She was real straitlaced, you know. But I won't go into that."

"What does that mean?" asked LeBeau.

"Well, nudity and so on." Howland wet his lips. "You know . . ."

"No, I don't," Moody said. "Tell me." He drew up an upholstered chair and sat down facing Howland. "I could use some help here, Larry." He moved his chair closer, so that their knees were almost touching.

"I'm in no position to hold back on myself," Howland said, red-eyed, wet-cheeked, sneering bitterly at the ceiling. "Man, what this must look like!" He appealed to Moody. "It was just sex, believe me. This woman, she's married, and she didn't want a divorce any more than I did."

Moody was holding his open notebook. "I really have to get the name. Things have gone too far, Larry. We'll find out anyway."

Howland stared at him. "Where are my wife and daughter now? They have got to be given a decent burial." He found a bright white handkerchief in an inside breast pocket and without undoing its crisp folds he blotted his wet eyes.

"It won't be much longer. I'll give the ME a call and find out when. Now let's have your friend's name."

Howland sighed. "Do you know what would have happened if

Donna found out? She didn't understand the first thing about any kind of sex, but—I mean, she knew it existed, but out in the world somehow, with people who had something wrong with them, and so on."

Moody gestured with the notebook. "The lady's name is . . . ?"

"Gina Bissonette. She lives over on Lowell Drive. She's my boss's wife. She's got nothing to do with this and doesn't deserve to get in trouble for it. If you could check with her when he isn't around, it would be the right thing."

"You let us decide what's right, Larry," LeBeau told him, coming across the room, staring him in the eye.

Howland did not look away. "I want to get my wife and child," said he. "I don't care about myself, but I'm going to phone my lawyer now. You're not going to keep me away from my family."

"What you could have done," LeBeau said, "was call from just around the corner. You lied about calling from L.A. Maybe you're not telling the truth now about calling from the motel." An instant later he added disingenuously, "Oh, I forgot: the call would show up on your bill, wouldn't it?"

"No," said Howland. "I made it from the pay phone outside the office, there near the parking lot."

Moody said, "Larry, we're going to ask you to come down to the bureau with us. I know you want to cooperate in every way you can. If I promise you that the bodies of your loved ones will be released as soon as possible—you have my solemn word on that—can you see your way clear to going along just a little while longer?"

He did not wait for an answer. He went to the front window and peeped out through the draperies that had been pulled shut so as to discourage TV cameramen, who were denied access to the lawn but might have been able to get a shadowy picture from the street, using the zoom.

Moody returned to Howland and used the situation to advantage. "We're not going to embarrass you in front of that pack out there.

We'll have the officer lower the ribbon so we can pull right back into the driveway, and you can exit through the rear door. You'll be in the car before they get focused. You can put a raincoat over your head."

Howland seemed grateful for Moody's kindness, having lost all energy. His nod was feeble.

Moody kept his promise, taking Howland out the kitchen door while LeBeau brought the car back, but the Kellers, the old retired couple whose property was just across the blacktop driveway on the west, had, for the excitement of it or perhaps even a fee, admitted some members of the electronic press to their side yard, and there was nothing the detectives could do about the cameras that were trained on them and their charge from close range. To the shouted questions, though, they could and did remain silent, and Moody advised Howland, his face swathed in the coat, not to be provoked by the raucous cries, "Didja kill your wife and child?"

Lloyd was awakened by the urgent need to urinate. In the aftermath of his monumental drinking spree of the day before—at least he assumed it was only one day earlier—he carried on his shoulders a head that felt as though encased in one of those old-fashioned diving helmets, the kind with a window behind a cage, offering only remote and fragmented visibility. He felt so dizzy that he had to take another few minutes of sleep, and it was during this period that he pissed the bed. After the briefest instant of wet warmth, he understood what was happening but went ahead anyway and emptied his bladder. Any attempt at self-discipline would have been useless at this point. It was not the first time, nor the tenth, that the malodorous, stained old mattress had been urinated on by someone, though *he* had never done so before. He would not anyway be sleeping on it again.

Lloyd's intent, when he could finally extricate himself from the slough of standing urine (which for some reason was not being absorbed), was to clean himself up soon as possible, leave town, and keep on going. It had been a mistake to come here in the first place. He had put himself under too much pressure while at the same time having no clear aim. How could anything good come of that combination?

Once he got to his feet he was not quite as weak of leg as he had anticipated, but his head throbbed with an aggressive pain, and his tongue was so sour that his teeth tingled from contact with it. At the corroded tap of the stained sink he made a drinking fountain of his hand, childhood-fashion, and swallowed water, which no matter how long it ran remained at the same tepid temperature as that from the hot-water faucet.

Had he single-handedly drunk the entire half gallon of scotch? But where was the empty bottle? And where had he emptied it? Instead of a memory of places and events, he retained only impressions, shadows, fragments of sound, textures, sensations, some unpleasant but not all.

Having gulped his fill of the water, rinsing with and spitting out the last mouthful, he raised his head to the mirror and saw the scabbed wound that extended on a long diagonal from the cheekbone to the edge of his upper lip. He had no immediate memory of its origin, but examining the nearby skin by eye and then by touch and, detecting only a faint shadow of beard, he supposed that at some time since the ruining of his electric shaver the morning before, he had found an edged razor somewhere and, using it, cut himself.

The matter sent him on a search of the medicine cabinet, some of the items in which had been left behind by former tenants. And there the implement lay, between an empty bottle that had once held rubbing alcohol and a plastic jar a quarter full of Vaseline. It was one of those disposable razors. Had he found it and used it before going to work, the day might have turned out differently.

If the water in the washstand was always warm, that which emerged from the showerhead, in the curtainless rusty-metal stall, was habitually unheated. Today it was as cold as ever, but in his current condition, with a body temperature that felt feverish, he derived some strength from the icy gush. In turning to clean his back, he encountered underfoot a soaked grayish cloth which when eventually retrieved and examined proved to be a T-shirt, presumably his own. The water had smudged but not washed away the streaks of red in its weave. He had apparently bled more from the facial cut than he would have thought.

Obviously the garment would not dry before he hit the road, so he took it to the kitchenette and stuffed it into the plastic bag he kept under the sink for refuse. There was no other garbage on hand because he had bought no food recently, except for the box of chocolate-covered doughnuts that was still in the half-refrigerator under the counter. It had probably been a long time since he had last eaten, but his sour stomach ruled out any thought of breakfast. He would leave the doughnuts behind for the obese super, who was the kind that pilfered from tenants anyway.

He stuffed his sparse supply of extra underwear into the old backpack he had found the year before among the junk Larry and Donna had gathered to contribute to a Goodwill bin.

"Don't tell me you're taking up the great outdoors," Larry said in the joshing tone that was standard with his brother.

"And why not?" asked Donna, in gentle challenge. She was playing her habitual role of defender of each against the other. As happened so often, this served to make her Larry's target.

"Listen to who's talking," he cried. "When did you ever haul your fat butt along a woodland trail?" He reared back, hands on hips. "I don't mean now. I mean way back when you were young, if you can remember that far back."

Lloyd could have punched him, but Donna did not seem to mind. "Hey," she said, laughing in the throaty manner, chin thrown up, which was at odds with her normal ladylike ways but never less than attractive. "If *you* remember, my backside wasn't fat in those days."

Nor was it now, but it was not Lloyd's place to make such an

immodest observation. He turned his head away, so she would not
be further humiliated. He addressed his brother. "The pack might
come in handy. I move around a lot."

Larry rolled his eyes. "And you're not expecting to gather much
moss, if that's supposed to hold it. That's for hikes, not real camping.
Used to use it on picnics, in college days: couple bottles of wine
cooler, going out. Coming back, it would be carrying another pair
of panties for my extensive collection!"

Now Donna's reaction *was* negative. "Oh, Larry. What a way to
talk in front of your brother."

Larry laughed with a flash of extra-bright front teeth. "He's a
grown-up, isn't he?" He grinned at Lloyd. "She makes you sound
like some kinda sissy."

"No she doesn't," Lloyd said levelly, turning away before he
would be tempted to go further and attract her disapproval from
Larry to himself. "I can use the pack. Can I have it?"

The three of them stood at the open door of the garage. Larry
toed the ex-liquor carton on the blacktop apron behind the car.
"Anything else you want? I keep telling her if you call the Salvation
Army to come pick up stuff, they give you a blank estimate form you
fill out yourself for the IRS. But you don't get a deduction at the
Goodwill bin: you're anonymous."

"Look at this collection," Donna said, gesturing with a flowerlike
hand. "I wouldn't have the nerve to ask for a write-off."

"That's because you don't have to pay the bills." Larry tossed his
big head to emphasize his exasperation. He sought support from his
brother. "She never made any money even when she worked!" He
winked. "She never made the most of the assets she has. I tell her
it's still not too late, but it's not going to last forever."

Lloyd certainly did not cooperate in this ugliness. He hung the
pack on a shoulder and looked away.

Donna shrugged good-naturedly. She wore a loose gray sweatshirt
over baggy white dungarees of the housepainter type. This was her

trash cleanup outfit, and both garments were shapeless. She looked like a dream to Lloyd. He preferred her this way, without makeup, and not all fancied up, her natural coloring being what it was, and he preferred not to see much of her body, either in the form of bare shoulders and legs or snug-fitting apparel from the waist down. Larry on the other hand, in what had to be perverse in a husband, was always urging her to show more flesh, buy a strap bikini, wear miniskirts, and was capable, after a few drinks, of getting downright disgusting, at least in front of Lloyd, on the subject of underwear. "Black garter belt and mesh stockings! Put a little zing in your dull life!" He would shake his head at his brother. "But *no*, not Little Miss Muffet there, in her pantaloons." Donna of course would have turned maroon by now. But on the few occasions when Lloyd protested against this treatment, it was she whom he offended, not Larry, who never took him seriously in any event, yet always urged him to drop around to the house.

It was while filling the backpack now that Lloyd consciously remembered the scene at the liquor store, and immediately thrust it back into the labyrinth of mind in which he stored such material. He had not committed the robbery nor done the mayhem, nor did he know either perpetrator or victim. He *had* shoplifted the whisky, but also he had reported the greater crime to 911. He had done the right thing when it was required. Maybe this was an odd pretext by which to feel a sense of accomplishment, and one perhaps too complex to explain to anyone else, but at least it was not another failure.

Afterward he must have gone home and drunk scotch until he passed out. Or so it seemed. What was hard to understand was why he could not find the big bottle this morning. Could he have thrown it out the window at some point? Perhaps in the direction of the barking dog that could be heard every early morning from somewhere beyond the trash-filled areaway on which his only window looked down. And at one point he had cut himself shaving. But why had he shaved in the midst of an orgy with the bottle?

The whole thing had begun when he realized he needed a drink before going to see Donna. It was absurd when you thought about it: he had required solace after a bad morning that began with the accident with the electric shaver, which in effect got him fired, and then with no money he could not buy liquor, so he stole the bottle, narrowly missing being either shot by the robber who had gunned down the clerk or arrested by the police, and when he finally got home after that ordeal he drank so much of the whisky as to lose consciousness, but revived, at least dimly, to shave and cut himself with the throwaway razor, only to collapse again and piss the bed before waking.

The longer he had been up, the more ill he felt. It was the kind of empty-stomach sickness that could not be relieved by puking. Something to eat and a cup of coffee would no doubt be the best medicine, but he was no less broke today than he had been yesterday. All the fight had gone out of him. He now regretted having gone to the supermarket to alienate his boss further. If he had apologized to the man, he might at least have been able to collect the wages due him. Maybe, if he had been pitiful enough, he would not even have been discharged, though that approach had never been known to work with a male superior. With women bosses, of whom he had had a couple thus far in life, counting an after-school job, it was effective if they were old enough to feel maternal. If one was near his own age, forget it: she was even worse than a man.

Should he swallow his pride and go see Donna in his current condition, get a free meal and a sympathetic ear? At least he had never asked her or Larry for money, and he would not do so now. Nor had he ever gone to their house without a little gift for Amanda. He could not break that tradition, which was all he had left.

5

Patrolmen Jack Marevitch and Art McCall were en route to the variety store where the shoplifter was being detained.

Marevitch asked his partner, "Are you old enough to remember the real five-and-dimes?"

"It wasn't that long ago, was it?"

Marevitch was driving the unit. "The one down at Mulhavill and Sixth even had a pet department, at least for birds and goldfish. I loved that place when I was a kid."

McCall chuckled. "Now, the pets were before my time."

Marevitch swung the car into the parking lot for the strip mall, which was two miles northwest, same road, of where the liquor-store killing had occurred the day before.

"That's it," said McCall. "There in the middle: Just Nickels. That's a chain, you know. Guy who founded it was really named Nichols. Bet you can't buy much there any more for five cents."

Marevitch stopped in the zebra-striped no-parking zone directly in front of the store. The Just Nickels show windows were all videocassettes on one side, assorted novelties on the other.

A fiftyish man with very dark hair on top but gray sideburns, the latter looking more synthetic than his scalp, awaited them impatiently just inside the door. He wore a plastic name tag on which was printed MR. SAWYER, MANAGER.

"Back here." The store was empty of customers. He led the officers, past some gawking female salespeople, behind a partition in the rear and on to a large storage area, only about a third of which was stacked with cartons. Under a hanging light bulb, the only illumination in the windowless place, stood a husky black man in a security guard's uniform. He was unarmed, so far as could be seen, but he was conspicuously powerful-looking, tall and wide, with biceps that made blue sausages of his shirtsleeves. A young man much smaller than he in every dimension stood next to him, presumably detained only by the implied threat of what the guard could do to him, for he was under no physical restraint. Stores had to be careful in such matters. They were vulnerable to lawsuits, and not only on the part of those unjustly accused. It was the fashion for professional criminals to sue those who legitimately nabbed them in the act, and not at all unusual for today's juries to award them hefty damages as victims of brutality.

Marevitch was prepared to stare narrowly at the security officer: it was not unprecedented to recognize such an individual as a felon you had collared within recent memory, and then you had to decide whether he had really turned his life around or was planning to rob the place from inside. But he knew who this man was.

"Hi, Winston." He put his hand out. "Jack Marevitch. I saw every game you played in."

The big man shook hands with a very gentle grip. "Thanks a lot." His voice was a high tenor, incongruous given his size.

"Meet my partner, Jack McCall. This is Winston Merryweather. He was—"

"You don't have to tell me about Winston Merryweather!" McCall cried with enthusiasm. "It's an honor, Winston. You're still the best linebacker ever played for the Bulldogs."

Merryweather had been a high-school football star a decade or so earlier. He went to State on an athletic scholarship but got badly hurt in his first practice scrimmage and never played again.

"What you got here, Winston?" Marevitch asked, looking at the smaller man.

Mr. Sawyer broke in. "*I* stopped him at the door. Here." He showed the officers what the accused had been about to leave the premises with, sans payment: a little rubber duck, yellow of body, red-beaked and blue-eyed.

"What have you got to say about this?" Marevitch asked the youth. "Did you steal this toy?"

The young man had a long scratch on the right side of his face, but it was not fresh enough to have been received in the current encounter. His eyes were slightly bloodshot but very defiant. "I didn't leave the premises. That's not shoplifting."

"It's been a long time now that a shoplifter doesn't have to actually leave the store. If he picks up something and heads for the door without showing any intention of paying, then the presumption is theft. You ought to know that. What's your name?"

The suspect hesitated. "Uh, Bob. Bob Masters."

The first name might have been the real one, but the last was obviously false.

Marevitch drew the manager aside and murmured, "Is that toy worth the trouble? You'll have to come down and testify. How about if he pays for the merchandise, and we promise if we see him again, it's an instant bust?"

Sawyer made a scowling pout. "I'm getting sick of this stuff, Officer. It's happened once too often, for my money."

"With this same individual?"

"I don't know. I don't catch everybody. I got missing inventory you wouldn't believe. I want to get the word out that if you shoplift here, you go to jail."

"Well," said Marevitch, "see, that's up to the judge, Mr. Sawyer, and take my word, this kid won't do time unless he's got a sheet already, and I just doubt he has if a rubber duck is all he grabbed, when you got those calculators and radios and all."

Marevitch went back to the suspect, who was flanked by the security guard and McCall, who were talking sports. McCall was six feet and weighed one-ninety; Merryweather was as much larger than he as Art was larger than the so-called Masters.

Marevitch shook the toy animal at the youth. "You might offer to pay for it, and then we'll see what happens."

The young man shook his head. "I can't," he said. "I don't have the money."

"Well, now, that puts a different complexion on it," Marevitch said gravely. "Turn your face that way again. How'd you get that scratch?"

"Shaving." The youth was getting more sullen by the moment.

"Nobody touched him here!" Sawyer cried. "He can't get away with that."

McCall grinned at the big security guard. "He wouldn't of just been scratched if he took Winston on. He would of got his head handed to him."

The ex-linebacker shrugged but retained his heavy-eyelidded, impassive expression. He had habitually worn it on the field, and some people even called it sleepy—admiringly, for he could strike with the speed of a panther when need be.

"You got some ID, *Mister Masters*?" After all these years, Marevitch still could not stomach calling lawbreakers Mister, but that had now for years been regulation, and included junkies rolling in their own wastes, those who raped children, and someone who had just shot a cop in cold blood: they were all to be addressed, at least in public, as gentlemen.

The suspect shook his head silently. McCall read him his rights and, having taken him to the nearest wall, had him lean forward, two hands against it, while he searched him. He found something immediately and asked, "What's this?"

The youth turned his head to the side to look at what the officer held over his shoulder. "A box cutter. I use it at my job."

"Which is what and where?"

"The Valmarket."

"The one on Seventeen East?"

"Yeah."

McCall had finished the search without finding anything else but a few squares of toilet paper folded into a pad, probably a makeshift handkerchief. He turned "Masters" around. "What's this for?"

"Wiping my nose."

"Got a problem there? Been putting something up it?"

The youth shook his head.

"You're right about having no money. Why's that?" He returned the toilet paper to its owner but held on to the knife.

"I got fired."

"Which explains why you're here, stealing this man's merchandise, instead of being at work. Is that right?"

Masters maintained a sullen silence.

"Where you living?"

The young man's chin came up. He gave an address in a seedy part of town, but said he was hitting the road to look for work elsewhere.

"What's the duck for?"

"To give to a girl I know," Masters said. "As a joke."

"You don't go around looking for little kids to pick up, do you?"

"Oh, for God's sake," the youth said in disgust. "Look, it's a little rubber toy. I didn't get out the door with it, and I didn't run or resist when I was asked to stop. I could have, and nobody here could have caught me, because the big guy was in back. But I faced the music. Can't I work it off? Do something here in this storeroom? That's what I've been doing lately, stacking or opening cartons and so on at the Valmarket. I'm no criminal."

Still crowding him, McCall asked about the knife. "It's not just a box cutter, though, is it? You loosen the screw and extend the blade, and you got quite a weapon, wouldn't you say? It's a utility knife, really, isn't it? You don't use that in fights or anything, do you, Mr. Masters? Or maybe to hold up stores not guarded by big fellows like that?"

"I told you what it's for. If I wanted to use it in a fight, I'd have to carry a screwdriver too, to open the blade."

"Or a dime," said McCall, grinning. "Just a dime."

"Or just a penny," said Marevitch, who had come up to them. "But you don't have one, do you?" He smirked at the youth and went back to where Sawyer and Merryweather remained standing. "Mr. Sawyer," he said in an undertone, "of course if you want us to arrest this kid, we'll do it, but in my opinion he won't come back here again if you let him go this once. It's gonna take a lot of your time if you prefer charges, and in view of the value of the merchandise, he'll certainly walk. They haven't got cell room for all the real bad guys."

Winston Merryweather suddenly said, in his tenor, "He'll be welcome to come to my church program for kids like him."

Sawyer said, smiling benevolently, "Winston's a preacher. He just moonlights here." Thinking of this apparently put the manager into a more conciliatory mood. "All right, Officer. I guess you know what you're doing."

"See," said Marevitch, "it would be different if a lot of big-ticket items had been boosted."

Mr. Sawyer had another, bleaker thought. "What's the latest on the liquor-store killing?"

Marevitch nodded soberly. "They'll get 'em, you'll see."

"Does it look like the same gang who's been doing it to all those others?"

"I tell you, that's not my department, but I know the detectives will nail it down soon. They always do." He did not mention that he and his partner had been first on the scene of the Howland murders, for he did not want to discuss the case with Sawyer. As to the liquor-store robbery-killings, they had all taken place in other precincts than theirs.

"It's just been the liquor stores so far," Sawyer pointed out, "but you worry they might change to other retail businesses one of these days. They come in shooting, don't they? Winston's unarmed. You know they won't let security guards carry guns."

"City ordinance," Marevitch said. "I tell you, the kind of people on the city council, you're lucky the *police* can carry weapons. But don't quote me on that, Mr. Sawyer. Now let's take this villain off your hands." He smiled at the big black man. "Great to meet you, Winston. Or is it Reverend Merryweather?"

"Either," Merryweather said. "But just remember I got that youth program. We like to get the youngsters into sports and away from crime. We got hoops, we got boxing equipment, all equipment donated by local merchants like Mr. Sawyer here."

"But most importantly of all, they got you, Winston. I'm still a fan."

"Open to all colors," the ex-football player said.

Marevitch joined his partner and the young punk who called himself Bob Masters. He took the utility knife from McCall and tapped its end lightly against the back of his left hand. "I'm not even going to measure this blade to see if it violates the concealed-weapon ordinance. You lucked out this time. It's too much trouble for all concerned to run you in. My advice is not be seen around these parts again, or your ass is ours."

The young man stared. "You're letting me go?"

"Don't boast about it," McCall told him.

They escorted him to the doorway. "Now," said Marevitch, "you walk straight down that aisle there and right out the door and don't look left or right. If you stop for a second, we'll change our minds."

Customers had reappeared, either new ones or those who assumed the threat was over. A place of business was usually quickly cleared out by anything that suggested crime. This had changed, in Marevitch's memory, from the old days when for many curiosity took precedence over fright. Nowadays, for good reason, everybody was scared. Winston Merryweather's escorting the shoplifter to the back room had probably been enough to empty the store, even though in this case the burly, menacing-looking black man represented virtue.

Before the officers left, Sawyer thanked them and said, "Policemen and their family members are always entitled to ten percent off here. I know there's some regulations against gifts, but I'm talking about a discount when you're off duty and out of uniform, with wives and kids. You just say hi to me when you come in, and it'll be taken care of."

McCall grinned and said, "Be seeing you, Mr. Sawyer."

Back in the car, he took the wheel. "He's got clothes there. He's got jeans and sneakers and all, over across from the toys."

Marevitch removed his cap and wiped the cracked leather sweatband with a handkerchief. The balder he got, the more his head perspired: you might suppose it would be the other way around. "I'm just thinking about Winston Merryweather. What a tough break. I maintain he would have made All-American and probably gone on to become a rich man as a pro. Had it all, power, speed, and the killer spirit, though you wouldn't know it to look at him." He opened the glove compartment and tossed in the utility knife.

McCall was nodding with reference to Merryweather's gridiron days. He had himself attended the rival school and had football ambitions but was too small even by the sophomore year to go out for the team. With the irony that so often obtains in human affairs, he began to grow to his current size only after forgetting about his own participation in the game. He reminisced about this to Marevitch, who had heard it many times but listened politely now. McCall finally cut it short to say, "I wonder if we should have gotten that kid's real name and run it. What do you think?"

"You know my policy of keeping down clutter," Marevitch replied. "With the computers it hasn't gotten better, but worse. Have you noticed any less paperwork?" He chewed his lip. "A kid steals a rubber duck ain't going on to rob a bank any day soon. . . . Listen, Artie, you better wait awhile before taking even any discounts anyplace. I told you, Internal Affairs is going on the warpath right now. I know that for a fact." As a veteran of the force, Marevitch had a few friends in the department, people in jobs where they could do some modest spying for him. There had been a time, way back, when he never paid for a restaurant or takeout meal, in or out of uniform, and when he got all his wife's home appliances, as well as the clothes for her and all three kids, at prices no higher than the respective store owner's costs. But in those days it was also true that he was pulling down less than fifteen a year, not to mention that he kept himself clean when offered big money by the same drug dealers who were more successful with other cops, leading to the big scandal of twenty years back when a dozen officers were thrown off the force and two went to prison.

It did not occur to Lloyd to feel he had been lucky to avoid arrest. Instead he believed he had added another misfortune to the series of such that had begun the morning before. It would have been morally preferable to be caught while stealing an object of value. He had been humiliated in a way that permitted no restitution of pride. Should he have taken on the gigantic guard over a rubber toy?

He absolutely could not visit Laurel Avenue without bringing a present for Amanda, who always came running to him with that in mind as soon as he set foot in the door. It had probably been a mistake to start the practice in the first place, which was all his doing and could not be blamed on a niece who, in the early days of her awareness of other persons than her parents, had shrunk from him and, when he persisted, screamed in aversion, embarrassing Donna, though, as was to be expected, brother Larry thought it hilarious. "You got quite a way with women, kid." On subsequent visits Lloyd eventually proceeded to bribe Amanda to tolerate him, bringing toys

that squeaked or rattled and distracted the child from whatever it
had been about him that scared her.

Then he lost his local hardware-store job, which had only been
temporary from the first, but for a change he got along with his
employers and colleagues and had hoped to be kept on when the
regular guy came back after recuperation from major surgery. However, the budget could not take it in a poor season for retailing. Nor
could he find work anywhere else in town at that time. Extending
his search, he ended up out in the western part of the state, picking
fruit, and when the harvest was over, he stuck around in the region.
They were big on high-school sports out there, with a college-style
stadium and a fast-food franchise to service it. Lloyd roamed the
stands with a hot-dog carrier slung from his neck. This had been a
student job when he was himself in school, but it was part of a bigger
business here, not confined to Friday-night games. The stand was
also kept open every afternoon at practice sessions, for the considerable crowd who gathered to watch those phases they were permitted to see, and then for the players themselves, for whom, as active
young athletes, few calories were excessive. Once practice had concluded for the day, they were allowed to grab snacks before going
home to gorge on massive suppers. Husky young giants who fre-
quented the gymnasium weight room whenever they were not on the
football field, they were the kind who might have bullied Lloyd, he
was sure, had he been their contemporary, or, worse, might have
been polite to him in a condescending way, but he at least had
learned how to pull rank by means of age: he had a few more years
than they in which to see more of life than truck farms and orchards
and high-school locker rooms.

When he next came back to Donna's house, Amanda was no
longer a baby but rather a self-propelled little person who could even
talk, and she liked him immediately, so much so that she climbed
into his lap without invitation. He had saved his money, and he
brought Mandy a big doll that could speak a dozen sentences. Don-

na's gift was a thick-walled perfume bottle of green glass within which sparkled little stars of gold. Larry received a bottle of scotch.

"Gosh, Lloyd," Donna said. "I know what those things cost. You're too extravagant." So he knew she was impressed. Donna addressed her daughter. "Did you thank Uncle Lloyd?" The child's version of thanks really was special: she said she loved him.

The trouble (which, as he had painfully learned throughout the years beginning with adolescence, proved to be the trouble with so much in life) was that the consequences could not be foreseen at the outset. He naively failed to anticipate that there would be times when he could not afford to buy any gift, let alone one that would startle Donna with his generosity. His brother did not really figure in any of this. Sometimes Larry was not there when Lloyd visited, even when by special invitation to a dining-table meal. Or Larry would arrive halfway through Sunday dinner, or come for the roast but leave before dessert. Once he did both, came late and left early, and there were occasions when he did not appear at all.

Lloyd took the unhappy experience at Just Nickels as final and sufficient warning that it was time for him to leave town promptly, lest the next reverse prove to be one of permanent damage. He returned to the discount drugstore, down at the west end of the strip, where he had left his backpack, having for once used a regulation for his own advantage: a poster mounted at the entrance warned against bringing into the interior of the store any parcels, packages, or articles of luggage, and offered a free parcel-checking service.

He reclaimed the pack from a pudgy young clerk who was officially sullen, probably because he made no concomitant purchase. She should have understood, as *he* always did when working at a job in which the real profits were made by others, that it was no skin off her personal butt.

*   *   *

Moody and LeBeau took Lawrence Howland to the less well equipped of the two interrogation rooms. The better one had the two-way mirror and an efficient system for making a fairly understandable audio recording, as well as video when the camera was in operating condition, but it was in use at the moment. Their colleagues Detectives Arnold Lutz and Warren Payton, Arnie & Warnie, were interrogating a white teenaged male who probably knew more than he had yet said about the body of the fourteen-year-old female found in the park near where certain elements from Central High gathered to drink and dope up on weekend evenings. Arnie & Warnie didn't think he'd done it, but they were sure he knew who had.

"What's this?" Howland asked as LeBeau ushered him into the little room filled with a large table and four chairs. He stared at the blank walls, gesturing. "You said you'd take me to my wife and child!"

"Please." Howland had stopped just inside the doorway, blocking the detectives' entrance. Moody spoke to his back. "We said we'd do that soon as we could, and we will. Now just please go in, Mr. Howland."

Howland turned and stridently said, "Okay, I want my lawyer."

LeBeau began. "Can't we just—?"

"You know my rights," Howland said. "You're trying to trick me. I want my lawyer!" He looked more petulant than sincerely angry, but of course they had to let him make the phone call. There went such edge as they might have had. His attorney would successfully stifle or obstruct any effort they made to discover the truth, even if Howland himself wanted to cooperate.

When the lawyer showed up, he turned out to be a sallow-skinned man even taller than his client but thinner. His name was Harold Loftus. He was not recognized by either of the detectives, and thus was likely to be not a criminal defense lawyer but rather an attorney used by Howland for civil matters, real estate and the like. For a moment Moody and LeBeau, seeing Loftus' unfamiliarity with felony procedures, thought better of the situation and still hoped Howland might be permitted to help them, but as soon as the counselor was brought into the presence of his client, he reverted to type and said, "Larry, my advice is that you say nothing further unless you are formally charged."

Howland clutched at Loftus' hand. "I just want to see my wife and child! I didn't *do* it, for God sake."

"Just one question, please, Mr. Howland," asked LeBeau, less hostile to the suspect now. "Is Lloyd Howland any relation of yours?"

Loftus turned, scowling. "I might just stop by and ask your captain if your hearing has been checked lately, Detective."

"This is a proper question in a criminal investigation, Counselor," LeBeau said, but when Loftus continued to stare at him, he sighed, and he and Moody moved away to allow the two men to leave.

"Dammit," LeBeau said across to Moody, when they were back at their facing desks. "We should have asked Larry about Lloyd before we left the house."

"Loftus doesn't know anything about criminal law, that's for sure," said Moody, leaning back in his chair, which meant he had to raise his voice to be heard by his partner, for the place was noisy today with phones ringing and people coming and going. "I better call the DA's office." An assistant district attorney was usually assigned to a murder case at the outset, so that the state would be fully prepared when it had a defendant to try. The cops hastily passed all legal problems on to this guy or, sometimes, woman.

Warren Payton, of the white-and-black Arnie-Warnie pair, walked jauntily to his nearby desk and scooped up a file folder.

"Are you looking good?" Moody asked him.

"He didn't kill her," Payton said, "but he was one of them, four or five, who got in on the rape."

"The little South Park girl?" asked LeBeau.

Payton's mahogany forehead glistened in the reflected light from the ceiling fixture high above him. "He said he knew it was wrong but could never get any sex on his own, and she was unconscious, so it would hardly matter to her. Besides, all the others were doing it."

Arnie and Warnie were good detectives, but they were also notorious publicity hounds and darlings of the TV newspeople. They regularly violated departmental policy but were allowed if not encouraged to get away with it by the brass, on the theory that the police could use favorable attention in an era when law enforcement often got bum-rapped in the media.

Before Moody called the DA's office, an assistant district attorney named Sydney Logan phoned him and asked what was happening with Howland, by which he meant the case, not any of the individuals of the name.

Moody filled him in. "We are short on a motive," he continued. "This morning Dennis checked with all the major insurance companies and couldn't find any policies on the wife or child. Howland's got one on himself through his company's benefits package, but there's nothing on the wife except the little one with the automobile club, which applies only to car accidents."

"What about the bedroom?"

"He's putting it to his boss's wife, so he says. He claims he was in a motel with her at the time of the murders, but he claims it's just sex, not love. We're going over to interview her soon as I get off the phone. Dennis called the motel clerk, who confirms someone matching Howland's description checked in yesterday about noon, but doesn't know when he left. Also didn't see a woman with him, but that's normal, and Howland did pay for a double. We're going to see the clerk soon as we can. We haven't got any sleep since night before last."

"You fellas do a good job," Logan said diplomatically. "That a local motel?"

"The Starry Night out on Three-oh-one. If the man provisionally identified by the clerk is Howland, he's been there a time or two before. He signs as 'Phil Owens,' and he pays cash, in advance—but they all do that. The clerk didn't see him after he checked in: most of the rooms are entered from around back, and you can leave the rear parking lot by the side road. . . . We better get going and find this woman of his, and see if she's just tail, as he claims, or somebody he'd kill his wife and child for. Oh, somebody else we're looking for is another man, apparently a younger guy, named Howland, first name Lloyd. He was in the wife's book. Maybe a brother. Got a bad reputation, at least with coworkers at some of his many jobs: threatening and so on, at least once with a knife. Seems like a drifter. Having a hard time getting a firm location on him."

"Sounds like you fellas have a good handle on it," Logan said. "We got too much on our plate over here, as usual. If you would just give me a holler when you've—"

"Sure thing, Syd," said Moody, who was always pleased not to have someone riding herd on him, and by now he was long inured to the district attorney's practice of grabbing as much credit as he could when the city detectives had brought in the perpetrator of a major crime.

LeBeau was on the phone too. "We're looking for him, Miz Jones. Where could we find him, do you think? . . . Yeah. If you could. Think real hard. Try and remember everythi—Yeah. No, we came up empty there. Sure. . . ."

Having hung up with Logan, Moody waved at his partner and punched the lighted button on his own telephone, putting him on LeBeau's line. "Miz Jones, this is Detective Nick Moody. Miz Jones, I know we asked you this before, but could you please try real hard to remember again if you saw or even heard any sound at all from next door at eleven forty-three during early afternoon? You think somebody could have pulled into the driveway but not far enough back for you to see their car? You could only see it from your place if it was all the way back in front of the garage, am I right? Otherwise the Howland house would block your view?"

"I told you no," said Mary Jane in her girlish voice, "and it's still no. What I'm calling about, what I told the other man—"

"Detective LeBeau, ma'am," said the same, "and I'm still on the line."

She went on as if Dennis had not spoken. "You're committing a miscarriage of justice, you should know that. It's just an outrage! Larry Howland didn't kill Donna and the baby. He adored them. You must be criminals yourselves if you arrest a fine man like that. Who's paying you off? That's what I want to know."

"Lawrence Howland hasn't been arrested," Moody said when he could get a word in. "Please just listen to me, Miz Jones: he is not in custody. He's walking around free. Now what you could really help us out with is this—"

"No, *you* listen," cried Mary Jane, her usually high voice deepening when she turned up the volume. "You're lying in my teeth, and meanwhile I'm watching it all on Channel Three Headlines-on-the-Hour. You went next door a while ago and arrested him. I didn't even know he came home or I would have stopped him from going in that house. Why is that yellow ribbon still wound around everything?"

Moody nodded at his partner and poked at the phone. Dennis took over. "Ma'am, you don't want to believe everything on TV. Lawrence Howland has not been arrested, I give you my word. He was just helping us with our investigation. We brought him down here the way we did so he wouldn't be pestered by the reporters. We were doing him a favor."

"Well, I don't know . . ." But Mary Jane gradually allowed herself to be placated by LeBeau, whose charm for the ladies was still effective.

"Yes, ma'am, it's a fact," he said. "Trust me. . . . Miz Jones? Do you know or know of a man named Lloyd Howland?"

"I sure do."

"Tell me about him."

"He's Larry's kid brother, is who he is. Well, really, half brother: same father, different mothers. He's not much, nothing at all like Larry. Floats around. Dropped out of school as soon as he could, works now and then and here and there. I think he's been away for a while now. When he does come to town, he mooches meals from Larry and Donna and sometimes sleeps in the guest room. They're real good to him. I never liked the way he hangs around Donna, *looking* at her. She's his sister-in-law, after all—hey, wait a minute, you don't—"

Moody came back on the line. "We want to talk to him, but we can't find a working address or phone. How do you suppose we might locate him, missus?" She was silent for a moment, and he added, "Moody again, ma'am."

"*I* know you," Mary Jane said waspishly. "You're the shorter, old one. I was just trying to think, but I guess I never have had any idea where he lives unless he was staying on next door. I never cared. I never thought anything of him."

"How old's he supposed to be?"

"Early twenties, I imagine. He's somewhat younger than Donna, but a lot younger than Larry."

"What's he look like?"

"He's a little runt. He's shorter than *you*," she said with a hint of insult. "Kinda muddy-looking hair, brown I guess. You know how blond kids will sometimes, in fact usually, grow up to turn brown. My own youngest is like that, but he's a fine-looking six-footer. Eyes, I guess you want eyes, but I'm not so good at that. I'm partially color-blind, I think. Call 'em gray. But then I see lots of things as gray."

"Give us a ring if you think of anything else about him we should know."

"I will if I feel like it," Mary Jane said snippishly. Moody rubbed her the wrong way.

LeBeau chimed in. "We'd really appreciate it, ma'am. You helped us a whole lot, but we can always use more."

"How long's that yellow ribbon gonna stay up? It's attracting too many rubbernecks."

6

Larry Howland's boss and alleged girlfriend, Paul and Gina Bissonette, lived in a generally expensive district not far from the Holly Hills private golf course, but their one-story house was one of the less imposing on the street, in fact not more than a mark or two higher than one currently owned by Dennis LeBeau, which Moody pointed out as they pulled up at the curb.

"It's the neighborhood that always makes the difference," said LeBeau. As they went up the walk past a lawn that was deeper than it had first looked, he noted, "Nice grass. It's got a good start. Mine hasn't recovered from that dry winter."

There were two front doors, an inner one of wood and an outer, which probably could be called a storm door, but what took Moody's eye was the ornamental ironwork in front of the glass: it would not have stopped a bullet aimed through an interstice, but was a good defense against a nonprojectile weapon. He pressed the bellpush.

He was taken by surprise when Gina Bissonette, a flagrant adulteress with a gaudy name besides, turned out to be a slightly built, elegant, and petite woman who spoke quietly and had gracious movements.

It was his partner who displayed the shield and introduced himself and Moody. "Miz Gina Bissonette?"

"I expected you before now," said she, opening the ironwork door. "I was almost ready to call *you*."

"Why?"

"As you obviously know, I was with Larry at the time the TV reports say the murder was committed—the murders, that is."

She had a lot of self-possession. Moody knew he had no taste (having heard it said often enough by women), but he was sure he could identify someone who did, and this person was definitely of superior quality. She wore a pearl-gray blouse of some silken material that might well actually have been pure silk, and on it a necklace of pearls that just about matched the blouse. She looked close to the same age as Howland, as opposed to his late, much younger wife. Her hair was what Moody would have called dark blond or, again, light brown with golden highlights. She was small and slender but had all the body she needed. The obvious question was what she could see in Larry Howland, but Moody was aware the same could be asked with regard to the male intimates of any attractive woman since the dawn of humankind, and after all, his own second wife had been considered by many, including himself, to have been a knockout in a bathing suit.

Mrs. Bissonette led the detectives to a living room that was much larger than you would have guessed from the exterior of the house. It did not take long to realize that it had nothing in common with Dennis' home.

The furniture seemed several inches lower than the standard. She offered them the sofa, but they could never accept being manipulated by those they questioned, even when on the latter's property without a warrant, so Moody seated her in one of the low-slung leather chairs, while LeBeau perched on a wicker-and-wire rig nearby. Moody stayed on his feet, which kept him twice as high as anything in the room except for the pictures on the walls, which were either stark black-and-white or, if in color, distorted when the image was at all recognizable.

"Let me just check the spellings." Dennis read her name aloud, letter by letter, from his pocket notebook.

"That's correct," she said, her blue-gray eyes seeking out Moody. "If 'Bissonette' gives you trouble, the easy way to remember is that every second consonant is doubled." She raised her eyebrows to see if he got it, which after a moment he believed he did. He knew what a consonant was, but he had never heard the spoken word for it his life long except maybe in school so very long ago. She had the better of him thus far, notwithstanding that he remained on his feet.

LeBeau put on the grave expression in which his eyes grew larger. He said, as if apologetically, "I'll make this easy on you as I can, but I've got to ask you some questions."

"Don't mind about me," said Mrs. Bissonette. "*I'm* okay. I'm just concerned about Larry. I haven't been able to get hold of him by phone. How is he taking it?"

"We can't comment on things like that," LeBeau said. "Now, you do know Lawrence Howland?"

"Of course," she said, with a soft laugh that sounded to Moody like the sifting of sand. "I never go to bed with strangers."

Dennis looked down. It was possible that he was actually embarrassed, but more likely that he was pretending. There was a kind of woman who enjoyed being outspoken with cops, because she knew that they themselves could never be when speaking to her. Some of the most ladylike in appearance had the foulest mouths.

"You are presently married to"—LeBeau checked his notebook—"Paul Bissonette, and living with him on these premises?"

"Let me help you get through this quickly," said Mrs. Bissonette, crossing her slender legs under the dark drape of long skirt. "I am happily married to Paul. One of the things that make us happy, maybe even one of the minor things, is that we each go our own way in sexual matters."

Moody finally sat down with a haunch on the edge of the sofa, but he still just listened for a while.

"Yes, ma'am," LeBeau said impassively. "You are involved with Lawrence Howland?"

Her smile took on a very sweet character, perhaps near the edge of the cloying. "Okay. I guess you could say that."

"Would *you* say it?"

"I'd say I go to bed with him from time to time."

"Always at the Starry Night Motel?"

She looked at the silent Moody. "Once we tried another place along the road there, but it wasn't nearly so vulgar, and I hated it."

Dennis frowned. He probably was genuinely puzzled here. "Vulgar? You like vulgar?"

Mrs. Bissonette raised her fine eyebrows. "I mean the appointments of the room: the pink bathroom fixtures, the heart-shaped headboard, et cetera. The videos!"

"You like those things?" It was a flat question of the kind that expects no answer, and insofar as it was, it was unprofessional in Moody's opinion: LeBeau was at a disadvantage with a woman of this sort.

"I love 'em," said she, smiling graciously.

Moody spoke at last. It was only respectful to ask a series of questions as to the time she and Howland reached the motel and when he subsequently left it.

She said they arrived independently, she not till about 1:30 P.M. Howland was already there, in room 122, their usual. He handled all such arrangements, though she insisted on paying her half of the charges.

"Did Howland leave the room at any time?"

"He went to the outside pay phone to call his wife sometime in the late afternoon, maybe four, four-thirty."

"How long was he gone from the room?"

"Three-four minutes."

"He came back immediately? Did he say anything about the call?"

"No. It wouldn't have had anything to do with me anyway."

"Nothing to do with you?" asked LeBeau, one eyebrow rising.

"I've been trying to suggest, without being nasty about it, that our only connection was sex. I have no interest in anything else about Larry Howland. I mean, I don't dislike him. I simply don't find him very interesting."

It was hard for Moody to hear that Howland would be considered erotically desirable by any woman, let alone this one, but no doubt that was another example of how little he understood the opposite sex. He asked, "How long has this connection been going on?"

"With Larry?" Mrs. Bissonette counted on her delicate, ringless fingers, the nails of which were either painted in the most subtle of polishes or with nothing at all, but they gleamed. "Two months, give or take. And while I'm at it, you'll probably want to know where and how we first met: the office parking lot, when I went there to deliver some presumably important papers one morning when my husband left home without them. Larry was just coming out the door. He—"

LeBeau interrupted. She was taking too much of the initiative. And unlike his partner, he was not impressed by the woman: that was obvious to Moody, who could not help feeling superior to Dennis, for once, in the emotional realm. "Tell me this: did Howland ever do or say anything that had to do with his wife, or make any phone calls when in your company that might have had to do with her?"

The elegant woman stared sharply at him and then turned to do the same with Moody. "Oh, no, you can't be!" she wailed. "You can't really think that Larry had anything to do with—and his poor little girl! For God's sake."

Moody's question was put mostly for the pleasure of witnessing her response. "You yourself had nothing to do with these matters, Mrs. Bissonette? You didn't want to get rid of Howland's wife so you two could get married?"

"You just *had* to ask that, didn't you? Is it some kind of regulation?"

He smirked. "You see, Mrs. Bissonette, we take a while in dealing with exceptions. Even in this day and age, the free-and-easy way you are willing to talk about your connection with Larry Howland is still out of the ordinary. For that matter, the connection itself: you two seem like really different people, from two different walks of life. You yourself are an exception to the people we ordinarily deal with, whereas Howland is really not, and I don't mean just money: it's state of mind or whatever." He knew he was not what she would think of as the soul of articulateness. He smiled at her. "But here's the thing from our point of view: you and Howland are the only people who can vouch for either one of you. The motel clerk says he didn't even see *you*, and unless somebody else did and says so, we have only your word and Howland's that you were there at all, let alone when you say you were."

"You're not serious about this crap?"

So she had a coarser side. "The clerk can confirm that Howland checked in, but he wouldn't know if he left, since the parking is all around back and out of sight of the office."

"Who was that comedian who made the comment coming through customs about the contraband he was bringing into the country?" asked Mrs. Bissonette, baffling Moody. "And famous as he was, the customs officials took him inside and humorlessly strip-searched him? I forget the name. Anyway, I guess your sense of humor wouldn't be any better, so I *won't* say we sneaked out the back, committed the murders, and returned to the motel to pretend we hadn't ever got out of bed. I'll just say this: your idea is asinine."

"It isn't an *idea* of ours," Moody said genially. "We're just exploring possibilities." He enjoyed using the high-sounding phrase, though he knew LeBeau was probably suppressing a snicker. "Let me ask you something, Mrs. Bissonette. Is your husband aware of your intimate friendship with Lawrence Howland?"

She lowered her feathery eyelashes. "That takes some explaining. I doubt he knows of Larry. That I go to bed with other men than he, Paul is well aware. I admit I have felt a little guilty in Larry's case, because he works for Paul. Not that Larry and I have ever talked about that. Well, he probably would have if I let him, but I haven't. It wouldn't be right. It's just by chance."

"What is?" asked LeBeau.

"That Larry happens to work for Paul!" She smiled distantly. "It was purely by chance that I met him. He didn't even know who I was at the time."

LeBeau continued, "You've never told your husband, because he wouldn't like you being intimate with an employee of his? But what about if Howland *didn't* work for him? Would it be okay then?"

She nodded solemnly. "I don't see why not."

Moody clasped his hands. "Your husband doesn't mind you going to bed with other men?"

Mrs. Bissonette gazed at him for a while. "This will remain confidential?"

"We can't promise anything like that. But if it's something that doesn't affect the case—but we'll have to be the judge of that."

She included LeBeau. "I'm going to trust you. Paul is a homosexual. He would never have been taken on by Glenn-Air in the first place if they had known the truth, and even nowadays he couldn't have gone as far in the company as he has without a wife. So that's my job, and it's as good as any other so far as I'm concerned, and I am not apologizing for either of us. I do have needs, and I do what I must to satisfy them. I purposely avoid men I might find attractive enough to threaten my marriage. A deal's a deal."

Moody's feelings were in something of a turmoil. Had he not been a veteran professional at his trade, he would certainly have asked whether she and her husband had ever desired the same man—and if so, had ever both had him. But what he really said was, "We'll want to talk to your husband. We won't dwell on his sexual preferences unless we have to. But you understand, if you're sleeping with another man while that other man's wife is being murdered . . . I can't make any promises. And we'll probably want to talk to you again, so if you don't mind letting us know if you have any travel plans."

"I'll be right here," said Gina Bissonette, with the languid kind of smile that could mean anything.

The detectives pressed her for every detail of her activities on the day of the murder and then widened the area of inquiry to include the history of her affair with Howland and her acquaintanceship, if any, with his wife, child, and brother. She stated she had never seen any of them, and never even heard of the last-named.

On leaving, Moody gave her his card, which she accepted with the fine tips of two long slender fingers and brought slowly before her limpid eyes for an inspection which, for all that, looked indifferent.

LeBeau drove the car. He waited until he had turned the corner before glancing at his partner. "How about that?"

"Classy woman."

Dennis snorted priggishly. "Not exactly the words I'd choose."

"You think she's cheap?"

"What I'd say is cold and calculating."

Moody shook his head, which caused it to throb slightly owing to his usual hangover. "That would be true only if she was sneaky. But she's not. She came right out and said it."

LeBeau was driving carefully, obeying the stop sign posted at every corner, unlike Moody's practice. "But what kind of woman would make a deal like that? That's what I'm talking about. What about love? She's some kind of pervert."

"You're looking at everything through your own eyes."

"Whose else have I got?"

"I mean, it takes all kinds. What do I know? You actually like *liver*, for God's sake." Moody turned it into a joke because he was taken with Gina Bissonette, the kind of woman he had no hope of ever getting.

*   *   *

For half an hour Lloyd thumbed cars and got no takers, then despite the NO RIDERS sign at the corner of its windshield, he tried a big tractor-trailer, and with much aspiration of brakes it pulled to a ponderous stop.

He made the considerable ascent to the cab. The driver was a not fat but rather thickset young woman who looked about his own age. Her round pink face gleamed beneath a smudged red baseball cap. She put the big rig in motion again with much shoving of the gearshift levers and kicking of pedals with her heavy work shoes, meanwhile introducing herself as Molly Sparks.

After giving his own real name, Lloyd nodded toward the sign in the windshield and said he almost did not put up his thumb.

"Yeah," said Molly. "I keep it there so I can pick my company. A girl on her own, you know." She glanced at him. "Not that I always been right by any means. Couple months ago, out in Illinois, this kid, college kid, he gets too friendly right while I'm at the wheel, for God's sake. I don't know what was wrong with him. I gave him a good shove"—she demonstrated, with a thick straight-arm—"and I says, 'I don't know what ails you but you'll have to get out if you don't behave.' Turned out he wasn't the worst kid you ever saw, but he had a goofy theory about interstate truck drivers: he thought a girl behind the wheel would be the same as a guy. Guy would pick up a girl hitcher for one reason, therefore so would a girl driver. I says, 'You din't learn much in that college, I'll tell you that, if you din't learn girls and guys are totally different. Something's wrong with anybody doesn't know that." She glanced again in Lloyd's direction, her smile showing a hint of tip-of-tongue. "So he ups and apologizes. Nice kid. He learnt something, I guess. I hope." She chuckled now. Hefty though she looked, she did not have a double chin. The plaid work shirt was stressed at the button line down the center of her bosom. "How far you going?"

"I don't know yet," Lloyd said. "I ran out of opportunities here. I think I'll try someplace else."

"What kind of work you do?"

He surprised himself with his candor. "Anything that doesn't call for much in the way of ability."

Molly kept her eyes on the road. "You're pretty good at knocking yourself to somebody just met you. That's one talent you got, anyhow."

He thought for a moment about what she said, something he rarely did with anybody but Donna. "Sorry. I guess I never considered it that way. I say stuff like that about myself, but usually *to* myself. If anybody beats me to it, I get mad." He was in a weakened state after the big drunk, not so much in physical condition—he had steadily recovered from the hangover symptoms since the initial shock of waking up that morning in a pool of urine—as in a sense of identity. It was not like him to have been so passive with the policemen at the variety store. He had lost his spirit.

"You got that scratch on your face," Molly said. "Look under the seat. There's a first-aid box there, with some antiseptic spray. It won't hurt. They put something in it that numbs you, you know."

"I think it'll be all right. I got it shaving. I took care of it." The subject made him uneasy, and he sought to distract her. "Do you talk much on that CB?"

"Not really, except to get road conditions. I'm not all that sociable when I can't see who I'm talking to. What my dad hates is if I pick up somebody off the road, like with you. See, he owns this rig and would still be driving it if he hadn't gotten hurt. He says, 'I could care less about you, Moll, but where'd I get another rig if some hitcher took that one off you?'" She produced a peal of laughter. "You got to know my dad. He's comical. He's not kidding about it, though, in one way: insurance rates are so damn high for these things, he takes a lot of deductibles to keep down the cost, but then if something happens he's got to eat the losses." Meanwhile she had brought the truck cacophonously up through the gears to speed and what felt like well beyond. Suddenly there was no nearby traffic except that going the other way on the opposite side of the four-lane highway.

"You get to see a lot of the country, I bet," Lloyd observed, peering down at the road from a higher elevation than he had ever experienced in a vehicle. The truck was mountainous. To control it was no small thing. No wonder the men who drove them exuded a certain arrogance, but a girl was something else. Yet for all her bulk, Molly seemed completely feminine, even attractive.

"I could see more if my dad let me. We could get lots of loads for California if he'd take them. He used to drive as far as Oregon in the old days, before he got hurt, but he don't want me that far from home, so I don't argue when it comes to that. If it was just him worrying about me being in danger, though, I wouldn't go along with it."

Lloyd unaccountably found himself representing her father's case. "I guess he's right about how dangerous it is. There are real bad people roaming around who probably can't be handled like you did that college kid."

"Don't I know it," said Molly, flashing a white grin his way. "For those guys I got me a three-fifty-seven mag."

Lloyd felt the slightest hint of fear, as he always did when guns were mentioned. His mother had hated them so much that he was not even allowed to own toy versions as a child, which lack embarrassed him greatly with such playmates as he had. He asked, "Got a license for it?"

Molly set her jaw. "It's for self-protection."

Lloyd felt he had lost face by the question. As if he had a personal interest in public regulation. "You're right. . . . I know you got into driving through your father, but how would somebody do it from scratch?"

"You see those schools advertise on TV? I guess they might work. But the only real way is learning the road, mile after mile. I started out when I was pretty young, riding shotgun with my dad. My mom passed away when I was twelve. When my dad was driving, which was most of the time, I had to live with my aunt and uncle. Because of school I could only go on short runs until summers came. But I missed a lot of school too, which is why I'm so ignorant. I'm not proud of that, but what are you gonna do?"

She had turned the subject back on herself, but Lloyd did not mind. She was doing him a favor. "What do you mean, 'ignorant'? You can operate this big thing."

"I'm not dumb. I just don't know a lot of things. Half the time I don't have any idea what they're talking about on the TV news. I couldn't find a lot of countries on a map of the world, I'll admit that."

"I barely got through high school myself," Lloyd told her, exaggerating a little.

Molly was amazed. "You sure don't talk like it."

"My mother believed in correct English."

"I guess they felt sorry for me, letting me graduate. It's a small town, where everybody knows you. Still, school was wasted on me, I guess." She tossed her head. "But somebody smart like you doesn't even try."

"Why am I smart?" asked Lloyd. "Just because I don't say 'ain't'?"

"It's just a feeling I get."

They were overtaking some traffic on their own side, most of which stayed to the right, but a little red sedan was immediately ahead on the left and going much more slowly than Molly. She made two melodious but strident blasts of the multiple horns, and the red car found a space in which to insert itself into the right lane.

"I guess you always know where the cops are," Lloyd said when the road was their own again.

"You drive a lot, you store up information, like where they put the radar. For example, it won't go through a hill from the other side. Some place it might be is in a supposedly disabled car, pulled off onto the shoulder. There are areas where they use helicopters.

You get to know those and the times of day they are up. And there's usually some kind of markings along particular stretches of road, so they can time you from the air, where they don't use radar. And so on. Now there's laser, too, but you get on to the tricks of the trade. You compare notes with other drivers at truck stops. It's like any other job, probably. As you go along you keep learning and you get better at it."

"I rarely have stuck at anything long enough to reach that stage," said Lloyd.

"You have to find something that appeals to you. It's no mystery."

"You sound like somebody else I know."

"Your mother." She smiled benignly at the windshield.

"Someone else. My mother's been dead for a while."

"I'd be lost without my dad, I know that. I've always missed my mom, but I never wanted any substitutes. I hated any woman I thought he might be interested in. I know that might be unfair, but what isn't? Of course now, with me on the road, he's got to have some help around the house, with him in the wheelchair, but *I'm* the one who hires them." She grinned at him. "I been on the road since five A.M. It's almost eleven now. Time for my lunch. There's a truck stop in a couple miles. You can come along if you want or you can wait, but not in the cab, which I got to lock up, no offense. I just wanted to get that out of the way first. And another thing: the food here's not very good, and it costs too much. It's not true you get a good cheap meal where truckers eat. My dad told me there was something in it thirty, forty years back, but too many people found out about it. But drivers still go to such places because you get to know the folks who work there and then you see your friends in the same line." She sniffed. "Then for the men, there's the hookers who hang around. I don't mind 'em, because they keep some of them jerks offa me. Be surprised how many of those guys are horny early in the day. Damned if I get it, but then I'm not a man—nor want to be, it might surprise you to hear."

"Why do you say that?"

"Because of the way I dress and how I earn my living!" she cried. "That's what some fool will say if I turn him down: I'm a bull dyke, and so on." Her facial expression became briefly sullen. "And I can't punch him, because that would only prove the sonbitch's point!" Having said which, she paused a moment for effect, burlesquing a bitterness she was incapable of maintaining for long, then laughed heartily.

As it happened, Lloyd thought she was nice-looking, all in all, but he would not have known how to tell her as much at this point without seeming like a phony, a preoccupation of his, so he said only that he had eaten a late breakfast and would wait outside the truck.

But when she had pulled into the vast parking lot behind the restaurant and among the scores of vehicles found a slot into which to fit her rig, Molly turned off the engine and said, "C'mon, I'm buying. I know you might of ate an enormous breakfast but you're so skinny you make me uncomfortable."

He really was not hungry, but knew he would be lonely, and he saw no serious defense of pride in refusing.

They deboarded from their respective sides, but did not meet on the ground for a while, Lloyd going around the front, past the towering radiator, while Molly apparently had gone in the other direction. He found her making a check of the back doors of the trailer, after which she continued on to complete an inspection tour around the entire vehicle. She was taller than she had seemed when seated and much less hefty when her upper clothing was no longer bunched up. The wide leather belt was cinched around a waist that looked positively slender. She had left the baseball cap behind. Her short blond hair was tousled, and the sunshine brought out a saddle of pale freckles across her nose. Her eyes were almost on the same level as Lloyd's, who was five-five.

They entered the gymnasium-sized eatery, which already was crowded and clamorous, mostly with men, though here and there was a woman, usually looking middle-aged, with a lined and grainy face. Near the entrance, at the long counter, sat two state troopers. Molly led the way to a couple of free stools down near the other end, where the counter made its turn toward the wall. Men at tables en route ogled her, and a few shouted. She waved to some of these, whom presumably she knew.

When they were seated side by side, she leaned to though not against Lloyd and said, in an undertone he could hardly hear, what with the general din, "I never brought a guy in here before. They'll be talking now." Louder: "Take a menu if you want. There's also that stuff up there, specials for the day." She indicated the notice boards posted on the wall above the grills. "I always take something that can stand being cooked hours ago and kept warm, like stew, you know, or soup. The green vegetables are hopeless, and their salad will just make you cry if you let it, lettuce all wilted and tomato that's just red and wet."

They were sitting closer than in the spacious cab of the truck. He was surprised to catch a faint bouquet of perfume when she leaned toward him. "Stew sounds fine to me."

"I don't know," Molly said, carefully perusing the notice board just above them. "I might be in the mood for chili. One thing they do nice here: they put cheese on top and run it under the broiler. Chili's kind of spicy, though, and they don't serve beer." She waved her hand airily. "Be in trouble if they did. 'Course, you can have your own, in the rig, and you can smoke and sniff or whatever too, but you don't want to get caught at it. That's no problem for me, but some of these characters claim they can't drive the long hours unless they got some kinda buzz on. Well, maybe sometimes I need a sugar high, but that's all." She jerked her head. "See those cops up front? That's why you don't see no girls. The ones not already working inside the rigs are hiding out in the ladies'. Which reminds me, I got to go. Hope there's room in there to get in the door. When Dee comes, order me a beef stew and a cup of coffee, and get whatever you want for yourself—well, I draw the line at steak, which doubles the price, but you'd only be sorry anyway if you got one here; you'd need a hacksaw to eat it, and I'm not talking about the bone."

Molly had not gone long when the fortyish waitress arrived. She had bright yellow hair and wore glasses with some kind of decoration at the hinges and a name tag on which was printed DEE. "What's yours, hon?"

"Two beef stews, two coffees."

"For yourself or you got a partner who's making a visit?"

At his answer she scribbled rapidly on her pad and put out two sets of clean but use-dulled stainless-steel utensils and two squat glasses filled with ice cubes. There was a pitcher of water within reach and a dispenser of paper napkins.

By the time Molly was back, the waitress showed up with the plates of stew and said, "Oh, it's you, Molly."

Molly grinned up and said, "How's tricks, Dee?"

"Don't I just wish, Molly! But when you're old, you got to sling hash for a living." After putting down their plates, she produced, from under the counter, smaller ones holding slices of bread and a wrapped square of margarine each.

"Don't give me that," Molly laughingly cried, "when you own the place."

Dee leaned over the counter and winked in close-up. "I used to make a lot more with less work." She went away.

Molly leaned in to Lloyd and said in a confidential tone, "Dee used to be one of the hookers, you know, until she married the old guy who owns the joint. She does work like hell, I'll say that. They're open twenty-four hours, and it's rare to come in here any time day or night and not see her. That's her own idea. She says she spent enough time on her back."

"The cops are leaving," said Lloyd.

"Know what's in their paper bags? Steak sandwiches. Not the

lousy kind you get if you order one, either, and it's on the house. All they pay for is the coffee. I don't blame Dee at all. You wanna keep on the good side of cops these days, or nobody will show up when there's a holdup or hijacking."

"You bring your gun with you?"

"In my belt in back," Molly said. "Had to remember that in the ladies', so it didn't fall in the can." The plaid shirt that when bunched up had made her look so heavy was capacious enough in back to give no hint of the weapon. "Billy McCoy, I said hi to him on the way in? Redheaded guy? He was jumped a couple months ago, right near his rig. It was parked in the back rank, because it's quietest back there, and he wanted to catch an hour or so sleep. He had been on the road for twenty-four straight. They got his money, but another driver spotted 'em and pulled his twelve-gauge out, and they had a car back there and jumped in it and run off."

Lloyd had little appetite for the meat, though it was tender enough, but he forced himself to eat something, because if he did not, Molly would undoubtedly take note and badger him. He found the coffee easier to handle, because it was so weak to begin with and then he diluted it further with milk.

"Ever had to use your gun?"

Molly, eating, shook her head. "I let some guy know I carry it, though. He had a few too many. There's a kind of drunk who won't take no for an answer."

Lloyd grimaced. "I never even had an air rifle as a kid. My mother was scared of guns. She had lots of horror stories about them, people getting killed cleaning them, and so on."

"Well," Molly said comfortably, forking in food, "you should re-spect your mom's memory. I sure do. People would act better in this world if they all did. But the main reason I carry a pistol is the people nowadays who don't respect anything or anybody." Despite her having talked almost continuously since sitting down, she was already finishing the last of the food on her once-loaded plate. Yet she had eaten gracefully, unlike the heavy-shouldered man on the far side of Lloyd who made loud animal noises.

At least half of Lloyd's stew remained, though he had made a manful attempt on it. He patted his stomach in extenuation. "It's good, but I had a rough night. I should probably fast all day."

Molly buttered both her slices of bread, which until now had gone untouched, rolled them together into one thick but easily compressed cylinder, and with it mopped her plate so forcefully that the china showed a high gloss. But even this was done with deftness and delicacy.

She asked, "You want some dessert? Know what's good here? The pie. It's not really homemade, but it's that kind that's *like* homemade."

She had the kind of small-featured face that probably had not changed that much since childhood. There was something babyish about her, as well as something motherly.

"No, thanks," Lloyd said. "I'm really not hungry. You go ahead and have some pie."

"Not today. I'm trying to watch my weight." She peered impatiently up and down the counter. "Now where's that Dee?" Referring to the other waitresses on view, she added, "She won't let anybody else give out the checks, even to their own customers." She leaned against Lloyd and said into his ear, "That's the whore in her: she don't trust anybody."

He took a chance on her not being offended and asked, "How would *you* know?"

She thought about it for an instant and then laughed even more heartily than usual. "You got me there. If I said I did, what would that make me?"

Lloyd on the other hand considered himself something of an authority on the subject, if at second hand. The only women with whom he was not impotent were prostitutes.

7

Molly was back behind the wheel of the tractor-trailer, reinvigorated by the stew. "Food's what keeps me going on a run this long. I don't sleep at all if by not sleeping I can deliver within twenty-four hours. You're supposed to, so you just don't admit it if you talk to the troopers, and naturally you fix the log. You got to work fast or you'll lose the business. People don't realize that who don't drive a big rig. We got schedules to keep, and I tell you they get tighter and tighter when the competition is what it is."

Lloyd politely simulated an interest in her comments, though within a few miles he had lost his immediate impulse on meeting her to consider trucking as a profession he might try. The road was not that fascinating to him, and he would not have wanted to be responsible for a piece of equipment so big and expensive. He liked Molly, however, and apparently she liked him. Previously, truck drivers had rubbed him the wrong way, but they had all been male.

"So." She grinned over affectionately at him. "Were you kidding about not having any destination at all? Not going to see a girl someplace, are you?"

The question surprised him. "No, I don't have a girl. I'm just trying to get a new start. I was in a dead end back there." He looked anxiously at her. "You're probably wondering how it is I don't have any money."

Molly laughed deep in her throat. "What I figure is, if you're some kinda crook, you'd *have* money, right? You wouldn't have to hitch."

He joined her with a bogus chuckle, but it was a very naïve thing to believe, if indeed she did believe it. "I've got some problems," he said. "Let's put it that way. I admit I'm running away from them right now. But I swear I'll take care of them soon as I can."

She stared solemnly through the windshield. "You got a wife and kids."

His incredulous chuckle was genuine. "Oh, no!"

"They have 'em at a younger age than you," said Molly. "Look, it's none of my business."

"I'm not married."

"Me neither," Molly cried with energy. "I don't want to be tied down quite yet. Then there's my dad to take care of. I don't need kids on top of it. If I had a husband, he'd want to get me out of this rig, I bet. Even my dad don't really like me driving. It's only because he got hurt I got the chance. Which reminds me I have to give him a call soon. We're out of range now from the CB home base. We want to get a cell phone one of these days, but the service costs an awful lot."

Molly continued to talk in this vein—a rig this size cost as much as some houses, and her dad could hardly keep up with the payments, and so on—and Lloyd felt so protected by the very banality of her concerns and way of life that he fell into the first untroubled sleep he had known in a long time and did not awake until the sudden change in that continuum of motion, monotonous sound, and sustained vibration was registered by his startled unconscious.

They had stopped at the farthest island of pumps at an enormous gas station. Molly had left the cab. The sky was almost dark, but the vast terrain of concrete, under massed floodlights, glared as if in a noontime sun, the difference being that this illumination was so blue-cold as to cause Lloyd momentarily to shiver.

But then there was Molly, smiling warmly up from the concrete below his window. "You want to use the john, you better," said she. "This is the last stop till touchdown."

When he returned to the truck, Molly fired up the massive engine with a twist of the key and a thrust of her foot. After several strident changes of gear they were rolling along the highway again. Once off the glaring apron of the gas station, she had switched on the headlights, and now, with nothing on the road ahead at the moment, she hit the brights. The illumination inside the cab had changed by contrast. Her face was a kind of silhouette tinged at its edges, forehead, nose, chin, with reflected light from the dials on the dashboard. "I called my dad, and he's set up another job, a load for the return. But pickup's not till morning, day after tomorrow. That'll leave a day to kill."

"Good," Lloyd said, but realizing this was ambiguous, added, "It must cut down your profit considerably to go back empty." He wondered whether she expected him to comment on the free day at her disposal. He did not want to get trapped in anything.

Molly said she was looking forward to some rest first of all. "There's a bunk right there, behind the curtain." She gestured with her thumb at the vibrating partition of navy-blue cloth across the shelf behind their heads. "It's real comfortable. I just pull in to a truck stop and climb up there. Usually I'm so tired I drift right off. They got toilets and showers at the stops, and most of them now have ones just for ladies, so that's no problem."

"And you've got your gun," said Lloyd.

"That's for a last resort."

During the ensuing hours Lloyd napped sporadically while sitting up, as he had earlier. He was psychically exhausted and needed sleep but did not dare surrender more than temporarily to what even so was not real oblivion but rather a state posing as such and therefore extremely treacherous. More than once Molly suggested he mount to the sleeping shelf, but he insisted that he felt fine where he was.

Finally, after a longer nap than usual, for it had been black night when he had closed his eyes but was now gray morning, he was awakened by the lack of motion to find the truck at a loading dock of a factory building of some sort. He was alone in the cab. Men were coming and going on the ground outside. Looking down through the closed window, he exchanged indifferent glances with a few of them, but most were too preoccupied to look up.

Molly climbed in to get a clipboard full of papers that had been hanging on one of the knobs on the dashboard. "Hey," she said, "you're awake. They're almost finished with the unloading. In a minute we'll go somewhere for a real snooze. I could use one." Yet she looked as lively as ever. Her red baseball cap had been swapped for a clean one in royal blue.

"I guess I wasn't much of a companion the last few hours."

"I just liked having you there," said she, swinging out the door and seemingly jumping to the ground.

She was vigorously back before long, returning the clipboard and settling in behind the outsized steering wheel. She waved to someone on the ground on her side, whom Lloyd could not see, and said, "He claims he can get me a deal on a living-room set." She turned to smile at Lloyd. "Ever notice how much furniture costs?"

"I've never bought any."

"Even without the markup, it's plenty." She sighed and started up the engine. "This place makes furniture, I don't know how good. My load was foam rubber. The best stuff's upholstered, I think. Anyway, you can make real good time with a light load like that. Going back, it's auto-body parts. But there's this twenty-four-hour layover. Don't get me wrong. It's a whole lot better than going back empty. But it's no way to get rich." She put the truck in motion. "He asked me who you were, and I said my brother. Do you mind?"

"Not at all."

"I never tell people more than they should know," Molly said. "It's just a principle of mine."

"I know what you mean."

"I got my reputation to think of."

"It's fine, really," said Lloyd. He sensed she wanted something more from him, but he was unable to provide it.

"Did you see him?"

"Who?"

"The guy, the foreman. He's as old as my dad, almost. He never saw me before. Why'd he offer to get me a living-room set whole-sale? Think he's putting the moves on me?"

Lloyd struggled to get his brain working. "Not necessarily. In that case wouldn't he offer to give it to you free? Whereas he wants money. I'd say he's either talking about seconds that couldn't be sold retail, or it's furniture he pilfered from the plant. A man in his po-sition could probably do that and stash it away there near the dock, where it could be sold on the side to truck drivers who come in, and loaded like legitimate shipments. The guys who work under him wouldn't necessarily even have to know, or he might pay them off."

"Wow," Molly said admiringly. "I'd never have thought of something like that. You got the mind of a cop."

"Or a criminal," Lloyd said.

"Should I be scared?" She was laughing.

"Not with the gun you're packing."

Eyes dancing, she said, "Hey, that's right. I keep forgetting I'm not helpless."

"You wouldn't be helpless without the gun," Lloyd said solemnly and added, almost without thinking, "I envy you."

Unless he was working, Moody went to Walsh's most nights rather than go home early enough so that he could be bothered by his fellow tenants, whom the super, disregarding his request, had told he was a cop, which meant neighbors knocked on his door every evening, bringing problems from trivial—noisy kids in the hallway—

to grim: a young woman had been raped and beaten half to death
on the tenth floor a month before he moved in, and people were still
reporting sightings of evil-looking strangers. But that was a Sex
Crimes case and not one for Homicide. When he explained as much,
however, people were annoyed to hear that policemen pretended the
arbitrary distinctions among themselves were meaningful and not just
TV jargon.

When you ordered either bourbon or rye by its generic name at
Walsh's, not specifying a brand, you got bar stock of indifferent quality, but, paying only from half to two thirds of what the known labels
would run you, you could not say you weren't getting your money's
worth. The cheapest draft beer, a local product named Steinbräu
(pronounced *Stinebrow*), was of a somewhat higher order and in fact
superior to the other brews on tap, all nationally distributed dish-
waters called Lite. Moody sometimes drank a Steiner to refresh his
palate between shots of rotgut, but tonight he had only had one of
the former to an uncounted number of the latter.

Walsh's was owned by two retired detectives, neither named
Walsh. "I don't know if there *ever* was a Walsh," Sal Borelli was
telling Moody. "Me and Howie bought it off this German guy, a big
krauthead name of Gruber."

"I remember him," Moody said. "John Gruber. My old man used
to be a friend of his."

"It was already called Walsh's at the time."

"Let me tell you this," Moody said to Borelli, who was tending
bar tonight, "if it was Irish, your corned beef would stink. And listen
to me, I know whereof I speak: my old lady was Irish. I loved my
mother but she couldn't cook worth a damn, and it was worst of all
when it was supposed to be Irish."

"Jews make the best corned beef," Borelli said, sipping charged
water over chipped ice. "Howie buys all ours from some kosher outfit." He put the tumbler down with a decisive thrust of hairy forearm.
"I wasn't looking for you tonight, Nicholas my boy. Ain't you and

Dennis on the Howland?" Though retired for some years, Borelli kept current with all ongoing investigations.

Moody answered as if indignant. "We got to sleep sometime."

"This is sleeping?"

"You know me, Sal. I can't get to sleep any more without some help, and I'd rather give you the money than spend it on pills." He jerked his chin at his full shot glass. "Hit me again." He hurled his head back and emptied the whiskey into his open mouth, afterward lowering the little glass delicately between thumb and forefinger until it came to rest between the rings of moisture on the gleaming bar. He believed that no amount of alcohol had yet proved sufficient to affect his coordination. He was convinced he never staggered or slurred his speech, but he was aware that at a certain stage of drinking he gradually began to shed things that were the products of deliberate thought and give precedence to feeling. If he had not been drunk, for example, he would never have bum-rapped his mother's cooking. It hurt him to do so, because she had not intentionally prepared corned beef that was dry and tasteless; in fact, she herself thought it perfect and was wont to boast about it while disparaging the version sold at Golden's Deli, which it was doubtful she ever tasted and which happened to be great.

"Golden's," he said when Borelli delivered the refill.

"Huh?"

"Golden's Deli, over on South Main. They had terrific corned beef."

"Nobody's got better than us, Nick," Borelli insisted. "You should try some right now. You're not sleeping, and I bet you forgot to eat. Let me order for you. Sandwich or the New England boiled dinner? Why not the dinner? Vegetables and all. And you don't need no more hard stuff. Stick with a Steiner."

A large man leaned over the bar near Moody and after muttering something to Borelli turned his head and said, "Hiya, Nicky."

It was Walsh's co-owner, Howie Hersh, who in his day, a decade earlier, had been the city's most decorated cop.

"You remember Golden's cornbeef."

Hersh patted Moody's shoulder with a heavy paw. "They're my wife's cousins own it now. The old folks passed on some time back. We get our meat here from the same supplier. Chicago."

"There you are," Borelli said proudly. "If you're on your way back to the kitchen, Howie, ask Denise or whoever to run a platter out for Nick."

Moody's hands were raised, as if a gun were pointed at him. "I can't go to bed on a full stomach. Be up all night. Just let me have another shot, and I'll be on my way."

"Whadduh we gonna do with this guy?" Borelli asked.

To show them he was not drunk, Moody made joking references to how heavy they were, Hersh being probably thirty or forty pounds over what he had been as a detective, but he had a massive frame. On the shorter Borelli the potgut was more conspicuous. The restaurateurs enjoyed being ribbed by another of their own breed, who could be counted on, drunk or sober, not to say anything really to offend them, and they would return the favor and never bring up the subject of women in Moody's presence, at least nowadays.

Hersh lumbered away, and Borelli poured the new drink. After downing it, Moody stepped off the stool to go to the men's room. He needed all his resolve to walk steadily. The place was crowded with patrons, not all of whom were cops, whose numbers, counting even those who were retired, would not have been sufficient to keep a business in operation if it enjoyed only their trade. Some of the civilian customers, especially the females, were fans of the police and liked to be near them in a social situation, but there were always others who were ignorant of the basic character of the place and presumably found it only by chance.

One thing you could say about the men's room at Walsh's: there were no phone numbers scribbled on the walls above the urinals and no filthy graffiti. Walsh's was not exactly a family place, for liquor was served in quantity, but neither was it a dive. Hookers were not suffered on the premises, even though many detectives were on good terms with call girls and some were discreetly intimate, exchanging protection for free tail. Female police buffs, so long as they did not charge a fee for their beds, were more than welcome.

When Moody emerged from the toilet he saw a neat blond head above a cute round behind just leaving the adjacent ladies' rest room. She headed the other way, toward the eating area, but then halted suddenly and turned back. It was Daisy O'Connor.

Fond as he was of her, Moody hated to see her when he was in this condition. It did not help to notice her briefly flinch and then cover it up by asking briskly, "Hey, Nick, how you doin'?"

"How's your mom these days? I've been meaning to check in on her but haven't been able to lately with all—"

"She's fine," Daisy said, gesturing impatiently with her short un-colored fingernails. Moody could remember her from the days when she used to bite them and would pout if kidded about it. He always thought it strange that in the case of the O'Connors it was the daughter who had followed her dad into the department and none of the boys, but Bill was a career Marine. Terry had something to do with computers and was married to an Italian girl, who in fact was a niece to Walsh's co-owner Sal Borelli. Patrick worked for a Catholic charity and had a manner that had always seemed swishy to Moody, who however, in deference to his old partner, the late father of this family, would not speculate further.

Daisy gestured again, and he saw the coin between her fingers. "I got to make a call."

He realized he was blocking her way to the wall-hung phone but was careful not to apologize too profusely, drunk-style. He stepped aside. "Great job you did finding that address book." He was aware of her aim to be a detective like her dad. Ordinarily this would happen only after some years as a uniformed patrolman, but practices were changing now when it came to women. Daisy had been sent fresh from the Academy to a special FBI course in forensic identification procedures. She might well be able one day in the not too distant future to step from Ident to one of the detective bureaus without an interlude in a car, dealing mostly with that formerly standard duty of the female officer, the family dispute.

Daisy gave him a severe but not unkind stare. "You haven't had any sleep in two days, have you? Go home and go to bed, Nick."

"Remember how you used to hate to go to bed as a kid, Daze?" As the only girl in the family, she had a room of her own, while the three boys were quartered in the dormitory into which the former attic had been remodeled. The only O'Connor who slept by herself, Daisy had been lonely at bedtime. Moody hoped this was not still the case and that she was not looking for some bum at Walsh's to take her back to his place. She still lived with her mother in the family house.

"I got some sense when I grew up," she said now, passing him. "I just wish *you* did." She had gone by but stopped abruptly and turned. "I didn't mean it the way it sounded, Nick. What I meant was, you really ought to take better care of yourself. We all want that, you know." She turned away just as quickly and began to use the telephone.

Moody was touched by her words, sufficiently so that all at once he got himself together and plodded toward the door, past the bar, where he said good night to an obviously relieved Borelli, and then onto the sidewalk outside in the fresh air and, when he got beyond the canopy, under a sky full of stars that seemed at once smaller than usual but much brighter. His car was parked nearby in a forbidden loading zone marked with a sign and glaring yellow stripes, but no vehicle in Walsh's vicinity was ever ticketed unless it obviously belonged to some civilian interloper.

He was trying to insert the key in the door when he heard a sound behind him. His faculties were instantly in working order and focused. As he was turning, hand on the revolver clipped to his belt, he had a millisecond in which to think: now the muggers are going too far.

But it was Daisy O'Connor. If she noticed his unarmed hand falling to his side, she ignored it. "Nick," she said, "let me drive you home."

"Aw, I don't need that."

"Don't take it that way. You're tired. You've been working two days straight." She reached toward him, fingers twitching. "Let me do something for you for a change. Gimme the keys."

"You do plenty, in your job," Moody said. "Your dad would be proud."

Her eyes sparkled in the reflected light from Walsh's windows. "Don't make me hurt you. I was real good at hand-to-hand at the Academy."

"I bet you were. I wouldn't want to tangle with you."

"Dammit, Nick!"

"Thanks anyway, kid. Go back in to whatever you were doing. If it's a date, I'm sure your taste in men is a lot better than mine in women, so I won't try and give you advice."

Daisy's expression went quickly from affectionate concern to an apparent lack of emotion made even more pallid by her fair coloring. "I'm not on a date. I'm with the bunch from Ident, eating dinner."

"The corned beef is real good," Moody said, mendaciously implying he had had some. "Get back before your food gets cold."

She tried once more. "Nick . . ."

He opened the car with authority and slid in. He felt almost sober now that he had talked with Daisy, who was the kind of child he would have had if he could have. Maybe he would not have run around so much if he had had a daughter to love and respect him, at least until she was old enough to have boyfriends.

8

Molly was finishing up the piece of steak that Lloyd had no room for, about a third of the sizable portion served him, so he had eaten twice as much as he left, a heroic accomplishment, hunks of red meat never having been his favorite form of nourishment. Molly was also generous with sauces, inundating the sirloin with an oleaginous brown liquid from a bottle specially requested from the waitress, floating the French fries in ketchup, and drenching her iceberg lettuce in a bright orange dressing.

The café attached to this truck stop was only about half as large as Dee's, though the parking area was probably larger. The motel was adjacent on the west and was perhaps under the same management, though Molly could not say for sure, never having stayed there and in fact not knowing anybody in authority at this establishment, which for her was largely unknown territory.

About halfway through the meal she said, "If you want to hit the road after eating, go ahead. You don't have to be polite." She chewed a moment and then revised her previous utterance. "What I mean is, you want to go on, wherever you're heading, just do it. You don't have to provide me with company."

The food he found most palatable was the roll, eaten in dry fragments. The idea of butter was nauseating, for some reason. "I'm glad to be here," he said. "Really. I'm just not crazy about sponging off you. What makes me mad is I had some money coming from where I worked, but I couldn't get it."

Molly gestured at him with a sauce-smeared steak knife and squinted affectionately. "You wouldn't be some kind of hothead, would you? It's not healthy to keep it to yourself till you explode."

"Not much I can do about it."

"Well, there, in my opinion, you're wrong." She leaned back and ate a French fry with her fingers, but rather daintily, holding it by the quarter inch not covered with ketchup. "You can always do something about anything, though maybe you can't do everything about any one thing"—she swallowed—"or however it goes. What I mean is, you can try. Do I have ketchup on my face?"

"No," said Lloyd. "None at all."

"You could try saying something right away." She rolled her eyes. " 'Voicing an objection.' I saw some lady say that in an old movie. I wish I could talk like that, but I couldn't get away with it, the kind of people I'm around. Present company excepted." She smirked. "Anyway, if somebody blows cigar smoke in your face you can say, 'Hey, don't do that!' You don't have to kill him." She managed to add, "Wait till he does it a second time!" before breaking up in laughter. After a moment she solemnly peered at the unsmiling Lloyd and observed, "But I can see it's no joke to you."

"It's not that," said he. "I was just thinking. I wouldn't get mad if the smoke was blown my way by accident. But what about when it's done on purpose?"

"Uh-huh."

"They're always taking me on," Lloyd said. "Seeing how much they can get away with."

"Who?"

He threw his chin up. "People. Guys, usually. Like I have to keep fighting to keep from getting walked all over."

She reached across to put her hand on the back of his. "You don't have to put up with that."

"I don't! But that's how I get in trouble."

Molly nodded. "Maybe being as nice as you are brings out the worst in people with weak characters, because of the contrast, see?" She continued to press the back of his hand. "I know this: very few guys can take being thought of as not basically in the right. Sometimes one of the other drivers will say something to me so vulgar, so filthy dirty, that I can't let it pass. So I stop and ask, 'What would you think if somebody said that to your mother? You're no kinda man at all.' 'Keep my mother outa this.' 'How can I, when she made you what you are?' You'd be surprised at the guys who can't stand up to that. They'll say, 'Listen, I'm not a bad person.' " Molly took her hand off his and moved herself against the back of the booth. "To make it worse, nine times outa ten a jerk like that is wearing a wedding band. Bet he lets his wife push him around, too!" She had been grinning all the while. She now added, "And if that doesn't straighten them out, I always got my three-fifty-seven. Like my dad says, 'You try good sense before you blow 'em away.' " She sipped some coffee after puffing it cool and asked, "So if you're going to stay around, what do you wanna do all day?"

Lloyd was weary. The fitful sleep on the truck seat during the night had only exhausted him further. "I'm really tired out."

Molly dug out her roll of bills from a pocket of her jeans. "You won't get rested till you can stretch out." She peeled off some money. "If you catch the girl's eye . . ."

He was facing the right way, and he beckoned to the waitress.

"Couple hours in the bunk is what you need," Molly went on. "It's real comfortable back there."

"I thought you weren't supposed to leave me alone in the truck."

"You're pretty self-centered, you know, Lloyd." But she was winking. "I done all the driving, but you're the one's worn out. What about some sleep for me, too?"

When they got out to the rig Molly drew aside the curtain that was stretched across the bunk and gestured for Lloyd to precede her.

He felt an access of panic with the recognition he would be the farther in, imprisoned between her and the back of the compartment.

"Do you mind?" he asked. "I've got to be on the outside. I have this claustrophobia. I'm sorry. That's just the way I am."

"That's okay," Molly said quickly, but he believed she had lost a very slight part of her inveterate good humor, if only by a hair, though perhaps it was his imagination. "But I might have to crawl over you if I have to get out to attend to the rig before you wake up."

"Sure."

She boosted herself up, crawled in, and stretched out, her thick shoes splayed. The mattressed space seemed almost as wide as a standard double bed. Molly found a rumpled blanket and, in her supine position, folded it into a neat packet. "Here's your pillow. The regular one is pretty grungy. Sometimes I remember to bring a case for it." She displayed the object in question, covered with dirty striped ticking. Before inserting it under her head, she sneered at it in the light of the compartment, into which the bright morning sun came via the windshield.

Lloyd climbed in. He was unfamiliar with the experience of sharing a bed with anyone, having had no live-at-home brothers and no childhood friends with whom he spent the night. It seemed to him not out of the question that with space at a premium there might be some conflict while both parties were asleep. He had not suffered a nightmare for some time, but Molly was armed.

She asked, "Would you mind?" She was struggling with her shoes, while trying to keep from kicking him. "Just drop these down on the seat?"

Was the gun still in her belt? But he would not ask, lest so many references to the weapon make him seem cowardly. He would just have to keep his distance. He removed his own shoes.

Molly spoke behind him as he was reared up on his side, dropping the footgear. "Better pull the curtain closed, unless you can sleep in that light. I can't." When he had done as requested it was quite dark in the compartment. Molly added, "It's also good for privacy." When he made no response she said, "Don't worry about fresh air. There are these vents up here."

Closeted in this way, he could again smell her flowery scent that he had first detected in the restaurant. He murmured drowsily, hoping the sound would suffice.

But Molly was not ready to let him sleep. "You should give me a shove if I try to hog the bunk. I'm not accustomed to sharing it, you know, and I might forget once I'm asleep."

She really was considerate to think of the very problem he had anticipated, but he decided if necessary to drop down to the seat, where, with it all to himself, there would be plenty of room. He mumbled again and stayed on his side, facing the curtain. His claustrophobic apprehensions were concerned not with enclosed places, but rather with people who crowded him. He kept his eye on the slit between the end of the continuous curtain and where, had it been tightly drawn, it would have touched the metal wall.

"The doors are locked," Molly said close behind him. "It's real snug, don't you think?"

He stoically rolled onto his back. "Yeah," he said. "It's really nice."

"Lloyd . . . sure you're not married or something?"

He answered in as dull a voice as he could produce. "No, I'm not married."

"Not that it's any of my business."

"That's all ri—" While thinking he would not be so rude as to fall asleep while speaking, and resenting the obligation being so imposed upon him, he did indeed drift away.

Moody had no special hangover next morning and felt no worse than usual, maybe because he always felt lousy, with a sour stomach, congested head, and nervous tension that often caused his hands to tremble. He arrived at work before LeBeau, who as a married man and father had more to take care of than someone in Moody's position. Dennis quite rightly was a much better father than Moody himself had been twenty-odd years earlier. Moody could admit as much, but it might have been a different story had his wife from the first not turned the boy against him, so by the time the kid was old enough to do male things—go to ballgames, hunt pheasant, etc.— Franklin did not want to. He was not sickly but he preferred to stay inside and read books rather than hang out with his dad. It was abnormal, and Moody predicted to Ruthann that the boy would grow into a full-fledged you-know-what one day, but in fact that had not happened, so far as his father could gather, twice a year, on the long-distance telephone, despite that sissy form of the name that Franklin, like his mother, continued to favor. Since the divorce, years earlier, Moody had called him Frank.

When LeBeau showed up, Moody passed across a sheaf of papers. "Lab reports." But Dennis took so long to take off his suit jacket, after first searching unsuccessfully for something in his pockets, probably the glasses he wore only when reading, that Moody retrieved the papers and said, "There was semen on the sheets."

"Wife's bed?" LeBeau had sat down and was rooting through his desk drawers.

"Only. But I guess semen's not a rare find on the sheets of a married couple. O blood type."

"What's Larry's?"

Moody smiled. "The medical-insurance people who handle Glenn-Air employees furnished it. It's O."

"Uh-huh." LeBeau had completed his search of the desk and started again on his jacket. "Donna's body didn't show any sign of recent sexual activity, right?"

"Yeah," said Moody, "so far as they could tell, but she was cut through the pubic area, so it would be difficult to say for sure." He had had no sexual urge whatsoever since observing the autopsy. "Remember the guy, couple years ago, who beat that girl to death, then whacked off alongside her on the bed? His come was on top of her blood. That's not the case here. This guy shoots his load, *then* cuts her? But there's a possibility it's old semen: maybe the stain was already there for a while. It's hard to say how fresh it was, because the blood would have dampened it."

LeBeau speculatively cleaned his front teeth with the tip of his tongue. "He might have used a rubber and pulled it off there, and most of the stuff ran out."

"They took both the toilets apart and probed the drains," Moody said, though of course his partner knew all of this. "You know, it sometimes takes more than one flush to send something like a condom all the way out to the sewer."

"Marty the plumber would be well aware of that. Is that what you're thinking?"

Moody put his head at an angle suggesting briefly intensified thought. "Not to mention that with all that blood the killer must have got some on him. You'd think he would have to wash, at least in one of the washstands or the sink, maybe a complete shower. But they took all the traps apart and didn't find a trace of diluted blood or semen." He picked up a pencil and shook it. "It's what else they didn't find that's interesting, too. The drain caps in the washbasins: they were real clean; there wasn't even a single hair wound around that part that goes down, you know?"

LeBeau certainly knew. He was a homeowner who did his own repairs if possible. "Maybe Donna was a good housekeeper."

Moody shrugged. "Well, it's a thought." The DNA tests, sent out to a private lab, would not come back for weeks. If they needed to wait that long for an arrest, they would be in trouble.

LeBeau resumed his search and finally, going again to the wide middle drawer that he had already ransacked, resorted to a pair of narrow-lensed generic spectacles kept for such emergencies. These were much stronger than Dennis' prescription eyeglasses, and he blinked when he first looked through them.

He read through the report and asked, looking up over his miniature specs, "Who can we put in the house?" He peered at Moody in a personal way. "Did you get any sleep at all?" He stood up.

"Sure I did."

"You went to Walsh's?"

"Had a nightcap and went right home. Little Daisy turned up there, Daisy O'Connor, eating dinner with a bunch. We had a nice talk." As he rose from his chair he felt whether his weapon was clipped at the left side of his belt. He often removed it and stowed it in the bottom desk drawer when he was doing sit-down work, because however he adjusted its position on his belt it proved uncomfortable. Such a practice defied a regulation that was instituted in the early 1970s, a few years before Moody's career began, to the effect that all police officers must be armed at all times, a militant-radical group composed of black male criminals and white girls from wealthy families having invaded a precinct station on the South Side and wounded two desk cops with a spray of automatic-weapon fire. But that had happened so long ago that the regulation was nowadays ignored by many. LeBeau usually wore a shoulder holster with an elaborate harness, of which, however, nothing was visible unless he took off his suit jacket, which seldom happened except on the very hottest days, when the window air conditioners failed.

Dennis had strode ahead, and Moody had just begun to follow him when the phone rang.

"Are you the detective wanted to speak to me? I'm Paul Bissonette."

"Hold on," said Moody, then covered the mouthpiece with his hand while he shouted at LeBeau's back. But Dennis did not hear him and kept going. Moody moved his hand. "I believe Detective LeBeau talked to you yesterday morning, Mr. Bissonette. I was surprised when you left town later on."

"Wasn't I supposed to?"

"Let me ask you something, sir: where are you calling from?"

"I'm in Miami."

"Miami, Florida?"

"For a regional meeting."

"That's your firm? Lawrence Howland, was he supposed to go to this meeting?"

"No," said Bissonette. "Not Larry. This is on the managerial level." He had the kind of matter-of-fact voice that Moody once would have believed unlikely for a homosexual to produce, but it had got so in recent years that you were sure only that a man who spoke effeminately was almost certain to be straight.

"Would you call Larry Howland a friend of yours?"

"He works for me. I don't see him socially."

"You don't have him out to your house?"

"Not for dinner or anything. He may have brought me some papers when I was sick. But I don't remember even that. I think that was Reynolds."

"Excuse me?"

"Bob Reynolds, somebody else on my staff." Bissonette was silent for a moment. "No . . ."

"Did you ever meet his wife?"

"Aw, God," Bissonette moaned. "What a terrible thing! And the little girl, too. . . . I can't remember ever meeting his wife. I don't fraternize much with my people, and we don't have office picnics or whatnot. The national office discourages that sort of thing. We feel we make up for it with nice bonuses for anybody who produces."

"How is Howland at his work? It's sales, right?"

"About average. Maybe a little under."

"He wouldn't know *your* family?"

"I've just got a wife," Bissonette said. "Unless you mean my parents, who are both alive, and I've got an older brother, and a sister—"

"I meant your wife," said Moody, who saw Daisy O'Connor enter the room and waved at her.

"Now, there again I'd say not likely. She rarely comes to the office."

"Uh-huh. Listen, Mr. Bissonette, we'll want to take a look at Howland's files, his business papers, if they're at your office. Would you mind letting your people know, giving them a call?"

Bissonette's voice acquired a stubborn note. "It's not my decision to make, Detective. It's head-office policy to keep all files confidential."

"This is a criminal investigation, Mr. Bissonette. We can get a court order for anything we need."

"I'd lose my job if I handed over the files just like that."

"Worse can happen if you defy the law," said Moody.

"I didn't say I would disobey the *law*. What I said was I could not grant your *request*. Of course I'll obey a search warrant."

Moody was annoyed with this man. He asked harshly, "When you coming back here?"

"Day after tomorrow."

"Give me your number."

Bissonette did so and named a hotel Moody had never heard of, but neither had he ever been to Florida, which deficiency he knew he should do something to correct, because sometimes he talked of retiring there, far from the winters he could hardly bear nowadays.

Daisy O'Connor had stopped to read the notices and orders on the bulletin board outside the captain's office. She came to Moody now that he had hung up.

She was one of the few officers, male or female, who looked like the attractive figures on the recruiting poster the department had circulated through the public-school system in recent years, which had in fact been the work of an ad agency, using professional models: two whites, male and female, and a black man and a black woman.

"Listen, Nick," Daisy said and paused while Phil Meader, another detective, passed nearby, leering at her. "I just stopped by to say I was out of line last night. I apologize."

"Did I run into you someplace last night? I thought I went straight home from work?"

"Sure," Daisy said, reaching out as if to pat his shoulder but instead hesitantly plucked at her own regulation gold tie clasp that held the uniform navy-blue tie against the shirt of the same hue. "Well, anyway, Mom wants to have you over for dinner, sometime soon. She'll be in touch. Okay?"

Moody was moved. "That will be nice, real nice."

"Okay," Daisy said, with a radiant smile. "Okay, Nick." She turned and walked out in the spit-and-polish way the uniform brought with it for the right person, her navy-blue cap foursquare atop the short blond hair.

"You took your own sweet time," LeBeau chided when Moody finally reached the car and climbed in on the right.

"You found them? What'd you do, leave them here?" He meant Dennis' proper, full-sized, gold-rimmed glasses, which his partner was wearing while consulting his notebook.

"Oh, yeah."

"Daisy O'Connor showed up. Didn't you pass her?" He then told LeBeau about Bissonette's phone call.

When they reached the eleven hundred block on Laurel, Dennis was careful to park the car in a place where old Mary Jane Jones would not see it unless she came out to the curb and scanned the length of the street, but the effort would be futile if she looked out the window while the two of them were striding along the pavement. Moody wondered whether the extra walk was worth it.

Everybody living on both sides of the street all the way to the corners had already been questioned by either of them or, in the case of the more remote neighbors, by some of the several additional detectives assigned by the captain for this purpose. The Kellers, the old couple who lived to the immediate west of the Howland residence, had in interviews with the detectives denied seeing or hearing anything untoward next door during the probable time of the murders, but could not resist the blandishments of the media since letting the latter onto their property when Lawrence Howland was taken downtown.

"Crys says they were saying all kinds of stuff to Binnie Baines."

"Channel Five?"

"That tall one with the hair and big lips. I slept through it. I was out when I hit the pillow."

"What kinda stuff?"

"Crys says they claimed they heard funny sounds and looked out and saw a car leaving."

Moody groaned. "This is the crap I won't miss when I retire. So we'll ask them about it now, and it won't turn out to be anything at all: you can make book on it."

He looked over at the Howland place as they went up the walk to the Kellers'. The patrolman on duty inside was probably sitting before the TV set.

LeBeau's finger was steering toward the doorbell button when the door opened as if by itself and the large blob of Mr. Keller appeared behind the screen.

"I'm way ahead of you," he said heartily. "Knew it was only a matter of time you'd be back." He swung the screen door open. "Your name begins with a B. I recall that, and you"—he meant Moody—"you're Detective, uh, uh . . ."

"Mr. Keller," Moody asked, "have you still got that card I gave you first time we talked?"

By way of answer, Keller lumbered to the mantelpiece over a hearth on which stood a tall vase filled with multicolored paper flowers. He brought back the little white rectangle.

"That looks like it," said Moody.

"This *is* it, sir," Keller said smugly.

"Then how come you never called me when you remembered some new information, like I asked?"

Keller was staring at the card as if its legend were written in a foreign language. He had a thick head of coarse gray hair for a man in his early sixties. He said, "Your name's Moody."

"Yes, sir. Why didn't you give me a call?"

Keller included LeBeau as, looking from one to the other, he said, "I swear I told you every single thing I know, if you mean what happened next door."

LeBeau was flipping through his notebook. He looked up. "Why didn't you tell us what you told Binnie Baines on Channel Five last night?"

"What did I say to her?"

"Now, Mr. Keller," Moody said, not unkindly, "don't ask me to put words in your mouth."

Keller lowered his heavy head in deliberation. "I'm trying to recall. You know, they put that on tape yesterday morning. It wasn't anywhere near the time of the broadcast. And in fact, I never talked to Binnie herself. I don't know if you noticed, we're never shown in the same picture. The questions were asked by some little guy. But when they put it on the air, they show Binnie asking, and then me or my wife doing the answering. I guess they can do that on TV."

All three men were still standing just inside the door, which here meant at the edge of the living room. The Keller house was a gabled two-story, older than the Howlands'.

"Okay," LeBeau said impatiently. "It doesn't have to be word for word, but didn't you tell her you noticed something about three P.M. the day of the murders?"

Keller shook his head, while displaying a long-lipped moue.

"Something about a vehicle?"

Keller nodded but answered in the negative form. "No, nothing except what I told you fellows."

"You told us you didn't see or hear anything," Moody said sharply.

"Well, I mentioned that, uh, truck, didn't I?"

"Truck?" Moody raised his voice. "There was a truck there?"

Keller groped for the word. "Not a truck, but a—you know, one of those closed things, kinda high and so on."

"Van?" asked LeBeau. "A van?"

Keller threw out an index finger. "I guess."

"Where was the van?" Moody asked. "Parked there?"

"In the street." Keller was not being cute. He was simply one of the many people from whom it took a strenuous effort to elicit any information at all, and when you got it, it was usually inconsequential.

"Driving by? Did you see the driver?"

"See," Keller said, "my trouble's I don't really know what you mean by a van. It wasn't a car. It was what I would call a panel truck, I guess."

"Was it special in any way? Anything about it you can recall? Sign or anything?"

"I didn't think you would care about the traffic that went by."

"Why'd you mention the panel truck?" asked LeBeau.

Keller sighed as if in relief. "Because it was backing out of the driveway next door."

Concealing his exasperation, Moody asked, "The driveway of eleven forty-three? The Howlands' driveway?"

"That's correct." Keller frowned. "It could have been just turning around, though, you know?"

"Did you recognize the driver?"

"I didn't see much of him. When I looked was just when he was almost finished swinging around to drive that way." Keller thrust a pointed hand eastward.

"How'd you happen to be looking out at that moment?" LeBeau asked. "You heard something next door?"

Keller grinned sheepishly. "This little TV guy—not Binnie—kept after us about didn't we hear anything and finally I said, well, maybe, and he said, better make it definite one way or the other, so I—"

"You didn't hear anything suspicious, did you, Mr. Keller?" asked Moody.

"No. I was just looking out because I do that now and again for no reason. I'm not nosy: I just like to see what's going on if any. You know, I worked five days a week for forty years. It's not easy to fill the time nowadays, so I'll look out on occasion and see what's going on outside."

A stocky little white-haired, eyeglassed woman entered the room from the archway centrally located in the west wall and minced to her husband's side. She vaguely resembled a relative of Moody's when he was a boy, except Aunt Patsy would not have been caught dead in pea-green pants.

"I am Mrs. Keller."

"Yes, Miz Keller. We talked the other day, if you recall."

But she did not seem to, and she said, "How do you do?"

"Miz Keller, did you see this panel truck Mr. Keller is telling us about? The one that maybe was backing out of the Howlands' driveway?"

She smiled sweetly. "Not really."

Moody said, "Well—"

Mrs. Keller was not finished. "I only saw it when it was heading away, toward the village."

"Village?" asked LeBeau.

Keller smiled down benignly on his wife. "She uses the old word. When her mom and dad first moved here, West View was an independent village. She means where the shops are."

"The few that are left," the woman said.

Moody asked if she had seen enough of the truck to describe it. He had a hunch the woman would display more precision of mind than her husband, and he was right.

"It was a van, not a panel truck. It was dark blue."

"Black," Keller corrected, shifting from one foot to the other like a kid who has to pee.

"He's color-blind," scoffed his little wife. "It was navy blue."

"What lettering was on it, if any?" asked LeBeau.

"If there'd been any," said Mrs. Keller in a saucy way, "I'd have told you without you asking." Dennis was not having his usual success with a female. Moody was more on Mrs. K's wavelength. Perhaps age came into play.

"If you saw the van from the back," Moody said, "you couldn't have seen the driver."

The little woman nodded briskly. "That's true. But *he* did."

Moody turned to Keller. "I thought you said you didn't see much of him."

"That's right. Not much."

"But *some*?" Moody asked him to describe what he saw of the person driving the van.

Keller winced in apparent despair, slowly shaking his head. "See," he said at length, "I . . ."

"Just take your time, Mr. Keller. You'll remember a lot more than you might think if you're patient and let the scene return to your mind's eye, like they say."

Keller raised his eyebrows. "That's not my problem," he said brightly. "I don't know what name to call them. You're both writing this down, and it might come out sometime in court or in the media that I used the wrong name, and we might be picketed or worse."

LeBeau was annoyed. "Just what do you mean?"

"Oh, come on, Gordie," Mrs. Keller said to her husband. "Cut it out." She addressed Moody. "What he means is the changing of the name, you know, from 'colored' to 'Negro' to 'black' to 'African-American.' "

Moody squinted at her husband. "This van was driven by a black guy?"

"You got it."

LeBeau asked, "Real black or lighter-skinned?"

"I don't know about that."

"You can't say what kind of color?"

"The window was up, and there was reflections on it." The man suddenly glowered at Dennis. "I'm just lucky I seen anything at all."

"What time we talking about?" asked LeBeau.

"Three or so, take or leave."

"Could have been three-thirty?"

"Maybe."

"Two-thirty?"

The question was near disdain, but Keller deliberated, head down, giving them a look at his scalp. "Couldn't have been two-thirty. Definitely after three."

"Three forty-five?"

"I doubt it," said Keller.

"What time would you say, ma'am?" Moody asked.

Mrs. Keller's lips were marked with those vertical lines some women get with age. She wore eye makeup and shadow, Moody recognized. She was late to arrive probably because she was getting fixed up. He found that touching. She might or might not have been pretty in her youth. She said, "Oh, Gordie's probably right about the time. He's better than me at that."

"Definitely nothing written on the van?" LeBeau asked, and then added, "That you could see?"

"I coulda seen the writing if any," Keller replied.

LeBeau drew the man to the trio of close-set front windows. "Help me out here, sir." He chose the middle one. There was clear glass between the flouncy curtains. "Was this where you looked out?" He stood at the angle required to see the end of the Howland driveway and its junction with the street, now still banded with yellow police tape. No media vehicles were in evidence at the moment, which meant that the detectives' pedestrian approach had probably not been observed by any neighbors. Moody stood at the window on the right. When he stepped away, LeBeau took his place and Keller drew nearer to the middle window, bending slightly to bring his head below the place where the flounces flared away from each other.

Back with Mrs. Keller, Moody asked, "Did *you* hear any sounds from next door?"

She nodded decisively, but then said, "I couldn't really tell exactly where they were from, though."

"Is that why you never mentioned them when we talked the first time?"

"That's exactly why," said Mrs. Keller, smiling triumphantly behind her glasses. "I think you have to know what you're saying when you talk to the police, wouldn't you agree?"

"You can use a little leeway, though," Moody told her. "We're trained to evaluate information. You shouldn't make up anything, but you really ought to tell every single detail you can remember." At this, she acquired a spark in her eye, and Moody asked, "Is something coming back?"

"No," Mrs. Keller said soberly. She left the room on the same route by which she had arrived.

Keller waited till she had gone, and then he said, in a lowered tone and a confidential manner, "She's got a little Alzheimer's, see. I didn't see a Negro driving the van. She just made that up. I couldn't see the driver at all. The truck window was tinted. She got out of the house couple weeks ago while I was in the bathroom. They found her down on Clare Street. She didn't have any idea where she was."

"You've helped us," Moody said. "Anything else comes to mind, you've got the number."

LeBeau had continued to look out the window. He shouted now at Moody. "Look who it is!"

Moody lost no time in bursting out the front door and onto the steps. A dark-blue van was moving slowly, crawling, along Laurel Avenue. It stopped briefly, red lights igniting, in front of the Howland residence, then continued in the easterly direction, going toward what Mrs. Keller called the village. It was already too far away for Moody, at his perspective, to read the legend printed on its side in bold white letters, but he could easily identify what was printed on the back: CONWAY on the left-hand door; PLUMBING on the right.

Dennis had now joined him. "Let's catch the bastard." They dashed for their car, which was pointed the wrong way and had to be turned in the nearest driveway.

9

"Lloyd? . . . Okay, stay asleep," said the female voice. "I'm gonna go get cleaned up."

He kept his eyes closed but had begun to remember where he was, and once that happened the wonderful feeling of well-being began quickly to be conditioned by other memories, not necessarily bad ones but very different in texture from the matter of sleep.

"All right."

"You're awake? I wouldn't of bothered you, but it's been more than eight hours."

He opened his eyes at last and saw that the curtain had been drawn back, to do which Molly had had to reach across him. He turned his head politely toward her, but she was not in the sleeping compartment. He had it all to himself, in fact was pressed against the rear wall. He squirmed to the forward edge and looked down.

Molly sat behind the wheel.

"Been there long?"

"I'm a lighter sleeper than yourself. It's been real noisy around here today. But I got a few hours . . . I was just thinking," she said. "Maybe we could go see the movie over there tonight."

"If you like."

"All right, then. I'm going over the showers. Could you just hand me down that duffel bag? I'll put on a change of shirt and pants."

He fetched the bag from where it was stowed, beyond his feet, and handed it down to her.

She pointed through the windshield. "Looks like the men's place is around that side. I never been here before. You never know what a bathroom's like till you try it."

Lloyd swung his legs around and descended to the seat. "I'd better hit the road."

Molly stared bleakly at the big steering wheel before her. "Why don't you hang around till tomorrow? What are you going to do now, anyway? It's almost six. Start out early tomorrow morning if you want. More likely to get rides then, aren't you?" She looked at him, her eyes large in reproach. "I thought you were staying."

Lloyd was embarrassed by her appeal. "I just think it might be better."

"Was it something I did or said?"

"It's nothing personal."

"That's what's wrong with it," Molly said quickly and began to step out the open door.

"Hey, don't be mad," he said. "I mean, I really have to get started making something of myself."

She shoved herself back onto the seat. "If you want to try trucking, finish this run with me, and we'll talk to my dad. We don't have enough work at this time to hire another driver, but maybe business will pick up soon and be too much for me to handle by myself. My dad will have some ideas. He knows lots of the other independents. But you might even want to get some training and then start out with one of the big lines as an apprentice, though you wouldn't want to stay with them long, I guarantee. You get some experience on the road, maybe you can drive for us later on. I'm not going to keep doing this when I have little kids."

"Kids," Lloyd repeated. "Yeah. I'll bet you'll be a good mother, too."

"Thank you." She was still staring at him. "How about it?"

He nodded. "I'll certainly consider it. It's just I was thinking of going on west, maybe all the way to the Pacific Ocean."

"When did you get that idea? While you were sleeping?" Her right eyebrow was arched. She shook her short hair. The red baseball cap was hanging on one of the gearshift levers. "You're just talking miles. There's other ways to get a fresh start that don't call for traveling, you know. Anyhow, wherever you go you'll be taking yourself along, right?"

Her grin made him wonder whether she was making fun of him, something he could not have tolerated had it been done by a man. But maybe she was simply being nice again. If so, he was touched. "All right," he said levelly. "I'll stick around awhile, at least until you head back, and I will think about what you said. But only on the condition that whatever happens I'm making a list of what I owe you, and I'm going to pay it back as soon as I can."

"That's your problem. Now, come on, if you're going to the showers. Because if you are, I'll lock up here. Go on ahead, if you want. I first got to go to a phone and call my dad."

"You must be the best daughter in the world," Lloyd said.

She inspected his face, as if to determine whether he was speaking in derision. "It's no strain on me. I guess he really wanted a boy, and I'm just trying to make it up to him."

"How'd you know he wanted a boy?" Lloyd asked indignantly. "Did he tell you?"

"No!" Molly said. "He'd never do anything to hurt my feelings. I just figured it out. All the stuff he likes to do most, or liked to do before the accident—fishing and hunting and all, and going to football games—wouldn't it have been more fun to do them with a boy?"

"Maybe it's even more fun with a girl who cares so much about you she will do things to please you that she wouldn't otherwise consider. You might look at it that way." He did not know where this wisdom, if it could be called such, came from. He was not accustomed to deliberating on the problems of others, because you could be reminded that way of how inconsequential your existence was to the rest of the world.

But Molly seemed to value it. "What a nice thing to say! You know, Lloyd, I really have a hard time trying to figure you out. You can say such nice things, but then you were just going to take off."

He was more puzzled than she, however. "I don't see that the two matters have any connection."

"See?" she asked, chuckling. "You're weird." And then she quickly leaned across and kissed him on the cheek, so quickly she was out her door before he could react.

Moody and LeBeau had caught up with Marty Conway's van at the intersection of Laurel with Warren Avenue and, after identifying themselves, asked him to follow their car to Homicide, but only if he did not mind. Moody also asked for permission to ride as passenger in the van.

"What's the emergency?" Conway asked. "I was just on my way to see you, in fact."

"Lucky we ran across one another, then," Moody said. He took the little rights-card from the case that held his shield and picture ID. "Just let me read this. You have the right—"

"Hey!" Conway complained. "What is this? Are you charging me with something? *What?*"

"Just to be on the safe side, Marty," Moody said. "We want to ask you some questions, and we're just protecting all parties. You ought to thank us."

The plumber made a cynical sound as Moody resumed the reading, but he said nothing more until the ritual was finished, then asked again, "What *is* this?" Conway seemed to be of average height, though as yet Moody had not seen him out of the driver's seat. His build was wiry, as was his sand-colored hair. He was one of those scrawny people who wear skin-tight knitted shirts with very short

sleeves that show as much of their muscleless arms as possible. He
was also a cigarette smoker, judging from the lingering odor in the
van, though no pack was in evidence and the ashtray was closed.

"It's a murder investigation," Moody answered. "So we got to be
sure we don't do anything to jeopardize any information we collect.
That's how we have to spend a lot of our time nowadays, Marty.
First I better ask what your preference is, Marty or Mr. Conway?"

"Marty's fine."

"You can speed it up a little," Moody told him. Conway had been
driving at about five mph through streets of sparse traffic.

"Hey, sure," Marty cried. "You can fix a ticket!" But he acceler-
ated only slightly.

"I'm not going to distract you by asking anything much till we
get to the bureau," Moody said. "So you got time to get your story
straight."

"Come on, man," Conway said with spirit. "I ain't got a *story*.
You're making me nervous, with all the pressure you're putting on
for no reason. So I was in the neighborhood on a job, so I drove
through Laurel. I admit I was rubbernecking the house. After all, I
done work here in the past. It'd be natural for me to want to look
at it now."

"You watch TV?" Moody asked. "The house is all over the news."

"So? Come *on*," Marty wailed. "If you don't want people driving
through the street, why don't you block it off, then? Is there a law
against looking?"

He continued to maintain the same note when they reached the
interrogation room, or more or less the same, but the detectives
made the most of minor inconsistencies. Had he repeated himself
word for word they would of course have accused him of having
memorized a prefabricated story.

"What you told me in the van was you just found yourself in the
neighborhood, so you swung through the eleven hundred block,"
Moody pointed out after Conway now specified he was coming back

from a service call in the district called Ashwood, a mile or so to the
northwest of the Howland address. "So let's have the name and
phone where you say you had this call."

Marty was not taken aback by the request. He said, "I didn't mem-
orize it, but it's down in the van." He smirked with only one side of
his mouth. "But it'll be in the book: L. T. Upchurch."

LeBeau got up. "I'll check it out," he said, and left.

Marty looked smug, from which Moody assumed he was telling
the truth about this part of the matter. "Ordinarily I'd take Disney
Road all the way to Linton, then come right back on Linton into
Grove Street. Instead I hung a left at Bronson, and—"

"We're not the Auto Club," Moody said. "I just want to know
what you were doing cruising the house."

"*Cruising?*" Marty asked. "What's that mean? Looking for sex?"

"You mention sex. *I* didn't. Why would that idea come to your
mind in connection with the Howland place?"

"It was just that word of yours," said Marty, sniffing.

"Uh-huh." Moody was silent for a while.

"Don't they use it for what those, uh, guys do through that alley
off Acorn?"

"What are you talking about?"

"That meat rack down there, where the young boys hang out and
the old queens cruise, you know."

"You go down there, Marty?"

"You oughta know better than that." To dramatize his exasperation Marty scanned the blank walls while breathing heavily. "Didn't
I tell you I had a wife and kids?"

"I think you know that's not an answer," Moody said.

"No, for Chrissake, no, I'm not queer!" Marty looked worried.
"Can you still say that?"

"What?"

" 'Queer'? You're supposed to say 'gay'?"

LeBeau briskly returned. "It checks out. He—"

He was interrupted by Marty's triumphant outburst. "What did I tellya?"

Dennis resumed. "Upchurch woman said he put in a new kitchen sink."

"Porcelain was cracked. Somebody dropped a heavy object in—"

"All right," said Moody. "But I happen to know those streets well, and you have to go way out of your way to come anywhere close to Laurel, and it's 'Brownson,' not 'Bronson,' and it's one-way *west*, so you couldn't make a left turn into it from Disney."

Marty stared briefly at each of them in turn, and he sighed as if the jig were up for him, but what he said was of another character. "So I got lost. I drove all over the place. I never had a call from Ashwood before. She got me out of the book, I guess, but I don't know why. Maybe the closer plumbers were busy. Maybe her checks bounce and they all now refuse to come. Maybe I been suckered."

"So it was completely by accident you found yourself on Laurel?" LeBeau asked, while reclaiming his chair, which faced Conway.

Marty groaned. "Do I have to go all over that again? What does it matter how I got there? I didn't do nothing but look, and I explained why."

Moody crossed his forearms on the table and put the weight of his upper body on them. Marty sat at a right angle to him. "I bet if we asked you nice, Marty, you would let us take a little sample of your blood."

"What for?" Marty looked solemnly at each detective, then threw back his head and laughed at the ceiling, momentarily calling attention to his gnarled adam's apple. When his face came down he said, "Now I get it. You're trying to cross me up. Well, it's a waste of both our times, gentlemen."

"You mean you're too smart for us," Moody said.

"No," Marty answered. "I'm actually dumb to sit here, going along with you guys as if you've really got something on me, whereas you don't."

"How would you know what evidence we got, Marty?" It was Dennis' question.

"There can't be any, because I didn't do anything—unless somebody is trying to frame me."

"Do you have enemies who might do that, Marty? Or is that something you saw on TV? Be accused of a crime and claim you're framed?"

Moody did not wait for an answer: the question was not that kind. Instead he asked another. "Why did you say you were on your way to see us? Don't tell me you can't remember that either."

Conway was wearing an almost garish smile. "Don't give me that *either*," said he. "There isn't anything yet I couldn't remember, and you know it. Sure I said I was coming over to seeya. I guess you're the one forgot when you called the other night I told you I'd have to look it up when I did the work for the Howlands. Okay, I did. I got the worksheets down in the van. I would of brought them up if you hadn't taken my mind off 'em with this crap."

LeBeau for a while had been crouched as if to spring across the table at Conway, but he now leaned back in his chair. "The worksheets for what you were doing, time of the murders?"

"I don't know exactly what the time of the murders *was*, though."

"They've told it often enough in the media."

"You're the detectives," Marty said. "I'm a plumber. I got the workbook for the whole month. Let me go down and get it."

"Whyn't you go by memory first?" LeBeau asked in a menacing drawl.

Marty whined. "What *is* this? I got the records, and now you don't want 'em?"

LeBeau put his hand out. "Gimme the keys."

"The van? It's my property. I say I got the workbook, and I'm going to go get it, voluntarily." He glared at LeBeau. "If you ask me, I'm doin' you a favor, not calling in a lawyer, and you know it. But I'm not gonna get shoved around. I don't work that way."

Moody rubbed his hands together. "Looks like we got off on the wrong foot, Marty. Dennis and I just want to save you some trouble. Now, whyn't you just give him the keys and he'll go down and get the book while you and me will get a chance to have a little talk that will probably settle the whole thing before he's back."

Marty shrugged and meekly surrendered the van keys to LeBeau. But then he said to Moody, with resentment, "Settle the whole thing? What's there to be settled?"

"You're getting supersensitive," Moody told him as Dennis left. "It was just a thing to say."

"All I did was drive through the block."

"Here's something I always wondered about, Marty. You know there's all kinds of jokes, but does it really happen with plumbers?"

"What?"

"Do they get a lot of tail from female customers?"

"I'm a happily married man. I told you that more than once."

"Getting a little on the side don't mean you're not happily married," Moody said with a smile. "I mean, hell, it's offered, so you take it. Who's to know?" His smile became lofty. "I don't mean this personally. I'm just getting your professional opinion. Here we've got this real good-looking babe, and her husband's away. What do you think? You've been there alone in the house with her, yes? How'd she act? She come on to you in any way?"

Marty curled his lip. "That's a lousy thing to say about her. She was a nice person, way I remember it, just polite and that's all."

"Give you a cuppa coffee, piece of pie?"

"I bring my own thermos, and I buy my lunch."

Moody got up and walked to the chair vacated by LeBeau. He leaned against its back, hands on the top crossmember. "Why don't plumbers ever show up with all the tools they need?"

Marty pushed his chair away from the table. "I don't have to take this crap. I'm on my way here voluntarily and you haul me in and harass me. I'm going to file a complaint."

"Now, settle down. Here's my partner, back already."

LeBeau showed Marty a sheaf of papers inside a hinged cover made of scratched and dented metal, held shut by a thick rubber band. "Is this what you meant?"

Marty reached for it, but the detective kept it just beyond his grasp. "That's my property," the plumber said. "You can't keep it from me. I'm not under arrest."

Ignoring him, LeBeau took Moody's old seat and opened the tin cover of the workbook. He brought his glasses from their case and began to examine the top sheet.

Moody said, "Okay, let's take a look at what the book says Marty did on the seventeenth."

Dennis leafed through the worksheets. "Here we are. . . . What's this name? Wilton?"

"That's right," Marty said eagerly. "Wilton, on Melrose."

"I can't find the time of day, though."

"About eight-twenty," Marty said. "Takes twenty minutes to get there from my place. I start at eight."

LeBeau read some more to himself. "You write like a doctor, Marty. What's this say?"

The plumber reached for the book. "If you'd give it to me, I could tell you."

"Just tell me from memory if you can."

"I put in the toilet seal. Then I think I went over on Addison, party name of Bigelow, water on the basement floor. Turned out to be a busted hot-water heater. It had to be replaced. You can't repair something like that, but people don't understand, so some of them give you an argument because it's a fairly big-ticket item and they think it should last forever."

"See?" Moody said soothingly. "That's all we wanted to know. How long's a job like that take?"

LeBeau examined the workbook and whistled. "You charged them for *five* hours, Marty?"

"I got to go to the supply house and get the tank, don't I? I was working by myself. You find anybody who can do it in better time."

Moody held out his hands, and LeBeau gave him the book. "So," he said, reading one page quickly and then turning to the next, "you charged them two hours for the toilet seal: means you finished up on Melrose ten-thirty or so. Address on Addison is maybe fifteen minutes away. By time you got the van parked and go in and look at the water on the cellar floor, it's near eleven." He peered at Marty. "Who gets charged for lunchtime?"

"I don't take time out to eat."

"You just said—"

"That I buy my lunch, yeah. I stopped off for a takeout coffee and burger, coming back with the tank. I ate 'em at the wheel."

"Five hours, starting at eleven," said LeBeau. "That leaves you free right in time for the murders." He smiled as if he assumed Marty would be eager to agree. "Two-two-three Addison's about a half mile from the eleven hundred block of Laurel."

Marty took no visible offense. "Oh, sure," he said, making his eyelids heavy, "I do heavy labor from eight in the morning on, don't knock off even for lunch, and then finish up the day by killing somebody I hardly remember."

"Did you go right home after finishing the Addison job?"

Marty poked the air in the direction of the workbook. "What does it say?"

"Oh, you mean this." Moody put his face nearer the paper.

"It's right there," Marty said, still pointing. "I did an estimate."

"How'd you originally get the Howlands for customers?"

The plumber scowled impersonally at the wall. "Now, there you've got me," he said at last. "I keep records of the work done, but how I first acquired a customer, now, that never come up before, and there's no reason to keep that information. If I had to say something, though, I'd say they found me in the yellow pages."

Moody nodded and continued to leaf through the book. "By the way, I don't find any work here you did for the Howlands."

"No," Marty said, "that was a couple years ago. It's in the book for that period." He looked at LeBeau with scorn. "You didn't get it? It was right there."

"I brought the only one I saw."

"It's in the black binder, for God's sake. I use the tin cover only for the current jobs." He turned to Moody. "You guys don't have any idea what you're doin'. You're just wastin' my time."

LeBeau went down to the van to fetch the binder.

Moody decided to ingratiate himself with the plumber. "Thanks a lot, Marty. How about a cup of coffee while we wait?"

Marty's mood had changed. He looked suddenly as if he were about to cringe. "I think I should tell you something just to get it out of the way." He pressed his dirty thumbs together. "You might find out about it on your own, and it wouldn't look good, so I'm telling you. Some woman back three, four years ago didn't want to pay her bill, and said she was going to file a complaint against me for exposing myself to her daughter. This kid was fourteen years old. She wasn't even home when I did the work! But what could I do? Who would of believed me if she got together with the kid?"

"So you made a deal," said Moody.

Marty nodded. "And this woman had a lot of money, big house out on Worthington! I offered twenty percent off, and she bought it." He punched the air. "She was the kind who would of taken a deal even if I did what she said."

"Did you, Marty?"

"I'm telling you I didn't, ain't I? You wouldn't know about it otherwise."

"Yeah, that's what puzzles me," Moody said. "Why *are* you mentioning it now? She took the deal."

"I'm just covering my ass in case she welshed. People can be rotten. You don't know what they might do. What if it gets around that you're talking to me now?"

"You mean she hears about it and decides to tell us about the incident you referred to? Three, four years later?"

Marty grinned bitterly. "I got her back, see. I screwed up the dishwasher before I left. That's why I was there, to repair it, see. I ran it through a speeded-up cycle while I wrote up the adjusted bill. I had time to do a dirty little job on it."

Moody was silent for a moment and then without warning he said, "Marty, you oughta know that we've got eyewitnesses who place you at the Howland home around three P.M. on Tuesday."

Marty's mouth twitched soundlessly for an instant. "That's what this is all about? You finally tell me?"

"I thought we'd take a while to get to know one another first," Moody said. "So whadduh you got to say?"

"It's a dirty lie is what I say. Those people are lying or they're nuts. What was I supposed to be doing there?"

"Pulling out of the driveway in your van."

"Which my name's written all over. That makes sense, don't it?"

"Yeah, if you acted on impulse, if you did the killing and panicked and had to get away fast."

The plumber was violently shaking his head, perhaps not so much in negation as to clear it. "I don't know, you just work all the time to make a living, and you get into something like this, somebody can say anything they want, and you're hauled off to jail . . ."

"You're not in jail, Marty," Moody said almost genially. "You're just giving us a hand here, like the good citizen you are. Now, you really haven't answered the question. Were you or were you not at the Howland residence or property on the seventeenth?"

The plumber made his back rigid. "I was not there. I never murdered anybody."

"Another little thing, Marty," Moody said. "Give me the name of that woman you just told me about."

10

Lloyd had the uncomfortable feeling that Molly had designs on him of a personal nature, that friendship would not be enough for her. She began to touch him at dinner, reaching for his hand to make a point, nudging him with her knee under the table. There was no graceful way to avoid her without possibly hurting her feelings, and he had a horror of doing that even to strangers, let alone a benefactor.

Afterward, walking to the movie theater, she bumped him occasionally, and then she leaned lightly against him as he examined the posted film titles.

"I don't know about you," she said. "But there are five pictures, and not one I would really like to see. But I'll go along with your choice. What do you think, the vampire one?"

Lloyd groaned.

Molly squeezed his arm. "A killer sent from outer space to do a hit in present-day California?" She cocked her shining face at him. "Ever watch those old black-and-white movies from years ago, on TV? With ladies and gentlemen, all dressed up, hats and all? Course, *I* should talk. But then I don't want to see myself after being me all day. I want to see somebody with class." She touched shoulders with Lloyd.

"I'll tell you something you maybe won't understand," said he. "I still laugh out loud at those old cartoons. I mean the really silly ones, where the cat gets blown up with dynamite over and over again by the mouse, and houses fall on people. Well, not humans but cartoon animals, and a little canary can lift an iron safe and drop it on its enemies, but nobody ever gets hurt in a permanent way. In the next scene they're back to normal."

"You can only find that in a cartoon."

"Yeah," Lloyd said ruefully. "I probably ought to get over it."

"Watching a cartoon isn't going to hurt anybody." Molly pulled him with one arm while pointing down the highway with the other. "See that motel sign? It says they got cable. Why don't we go over there? I don't know about you, but I wouldn't mind sleeping in a real bed tonight, with a private bathroom." She raised her eyebrows. "There'll probably be cartoons on TV."

"All right." It was not as if he could have suggested an alternative.

After they had checked in and inspected the room, which was luxurious by contrast with his recent accommodations, with a huge television set and what would seem to be twin double beds pushed together into one enormous soft surface, they fetched their overnight gear from the rig.

As soon as Lloyd closed the door, Molly presented him with the TV remote. "I know I had that shower, but I'm going to take myself a bubble bath now." Apparently she had already inspected the bathroom. "They give you a little complimentary bottle of it, along with a basketful of other stuff, shoe-shining cloths and sewing kits. When I pay these prices, I try to get my money's worth." She had dropped her duffel bag on the right-hand segment of the bed. She delved inside it now and found a toothbrush in a plastic container. "I didn't expect to be spending the night under these conditions. All I got to sleep in is this extra shirt." She displayed a rumpled workshirt of blue chambray.

"That's fine," said he, sitting down at the foot of the left-hand bed, brandishing the remote.

"Okay then. So I'll be in the tub for a while: there's no sense in doing it unless you get a good long soak. If you want to get a Coke or anything from the machine down the hall, the change is right here." As Molly spoke she was transferring a handful of clattering coins from her jeans pocket to the top of the low, blond-finished piece of furniture that followed the wall for almost the length of the room. "If you do go for soda, just remember to take the key: door's the kind that always locks when it shuts."

He smiled at her. "Enjoy your bubble bath. I'll be fine." He slipped off his shoes and propelled himself to the top of the bed with his stockinged heels. He pummeled the bolstered pillows into a cushion to support his neck against the headboard. He pointed the remote at the now distant television screen and began to manipulate the buttons at random, running through a series of pictures and alternating between sound and silence, in an exercise that provided satisfaction in the degree to which it was pointlessly compulsive, like thumb-twiddling or a child's kicking the back of a theater seat.

He was suddenly hallucinating. He could see nothing but Donna's face. In desperation he closed his eyes. When he opened them the image was gone, but sweat continued to well from his forehead. He rolled onto a hip and groped for the handkerchief in his back pocket. It should have been reassuring to hear water running behind the bathroom door, but instead he was terrified that Molly would come back for some forgotten item and find him in this condition, which was made worse by his inability to identify it. Was he simply insane?

He sponged his forehead with the balled handkerchief and looked again at the television screen, on which a hand-held microphone was being thrust toward the face of an elderly man. There was no sound whatever. With his indiscriminate button-pushing, he had apparently pressed the mute.

In the next moment the camera pulled back from a close focus on the man's grave countenance to pan across a front yard and the driveway between it and the house at 1143 Laurel Avenue.

*   *   *

The two bodies had been released by the medical examiner, and a
funeral was held as soon as possible thereafter, with no preceding
wake. Moody and LeBeau observed the comings and goings of the
mourners from a car parked across the street from the nondenomi-
national chapel of the undertaking establishment, Dennis sipping de-
caf from a container garishly logoed by the fast-food place where
they had lunched. Moody's was filled with real coffee, but, dyspeptic,
he drank little.

Surveillance of those in attendance at the obsequies of a murder
victim was standard operating procedure. Only a few persons came
to the funeral of Donna and Amanda Howland, most of them neighbors from Laurel Avenue, for Donna was survived only by her ailing
mother in the Indiana hospital, and apparently no one came from
Larry's side of the family, and nobody from his company, though
several persons from the Glenn-Air firm, most with female names,
had joined together in sending a floral piece, as did Mr. & Mrs. Paul
Bissonette with a separate basket (the largest of all), though neither
of the two appeared.

It was Moody who checked the flowers at the mortuary, LeBeau
having had an uncharacteristic problem with his automobile, which
unlike Moody's was always well maintained and furthermore had
been purchased only two years before as the car named by a con-
sumer poll as being the most reliable of the domestic models.

When a child was murdered it was the unofficial policy of the men
and women of the Homicide Bureau, even those not principally involved in the investigation, anonymously to drop contributions into
a cardboard box thumbtacked to the bottom of the bulletin board
near the captain's office, and this money was used to send a floral
piece to the funeral. In recent years the box had seen much traffic,
what with children regularly slaughtered in the crossfire between
gangs and those beaten to death by the boyfriends of their unwed

mothers. Moody had shaken his head over the meager bouquet you got nowadays for forty dollars.

"I didn't expect many of the neighbors would show up," he said now to his partner.

"That's something it took me a while to get used to," said LeBeau. "How somebody loses a loved one in a violent crime and then is shunned by a lot of their friends and even relatives."

"Maybe some of the neighborhood thinks Larry did it. . . . They're coming out now. . . . No, those guys work for the undertaker. . . . Here they come. . . . Who's that?"

LeBeau had his notebook out and turned to an earlier page. "I think that's Manelli, Mr. and Mrs. T. J. They're down at eleven twenty-five Laurel." He looked up. "They told Brill they hardly knew the Howlands. I did the second interview. Mrs. Manelli said she wouldn't even have recognized them if she had run into them away from the block."

"That's the kind come to funerals, though," said Moody. "The Kellers, right next door, stayed home."

"They had to give more media interviews, I guess."

"Now what's the holdup?" No one else had yet emerged from the building. A modest-sized crowd was being kept back by uniformed officers. The television trucks were parked half a block away. Several shoulder-mounted cameras could be seen behind the police line.

"Who's that coming out now?" asked LeBeau.

Moody squinted. The bronze-and-glass door had opened and a tall man strode out, but after only another step he turned and lingered. He looked in his early forties. He wore a snugly fitted double-breasted suit in navy blue and a very white shirt with a black tie. "I think that's Mary Jane's oldest son," Moody said. "Yeah, and . . . there comes the old babe herself. Looks nice, doesn't she?" He winked at his partner. "Your girlfriend." Mary Jane was wearing a black hat and a black dress that made her seem taller than ever. She poked her arm under her son's.

"I guess that's over now," Dennis said. "She sure got mad when we brought Larry in for questioning."

"He's a tall guy, but he's not that much bigger than his mom," Moody observed. The undertaker's employees were serving as valet parking attendants, shuttling to and from a side lot. One of them now brought a long, low, sleek silver-gray car to the curb in front of Mrs. Jones and her son. "Look at that chariot, will you? What's that? A Jaguar?"

"It's rented." They knew that from the number on the plate.

"Regal Rentals has got even higher-priced iron," Moody said irreverently. "What do you suppose a Rolls costs for a day? But you wouldn't want to drive a Rolls yourself: you'd want a chauffeur."

"Who *is* this guy?" LeBeau asked rhetorically, though they knew it was Mary Jane's elder son, Alfred, a commodities trader in Chicago, who had been at the exchange in that city while the murders were being committed next door to his mother's house: the detectives had by now checked out such matters with multitudinous phone calls. Her younger son, Duncan, a dermatologist, had been on vacation for a week in Hawaii, with his wife and six-year-old son. "Who's *that*?"

Moody identified the skinny bald man in the baggy brown suit. "He lives down at the corner of Locust. Harry McClintock." McClintock was the owner of a deli over on Hillside, where he'd stayed all day on Tuesday, from five-thirty A.M. to nine in the evening. He was a widower.

"There you've got another one hardly knew the Howlands, right?"

"Donna traded with him a little, but you know deli prices are sky-high."

"How'd our flowers look?"

"Cheap-ass," Moody said. "We'd do better, now the weather's warming up, to cut some real flowers from somebody's garden. . . . Hey, who's that little guy going in?"

"Probably somebody works for the undertaker or making a delivery?"

It took another second for Moody to notice an irregularity in the outline of the newcomer's clothing. By that time the young man, moving briskly, had stepped through the doorway of the building.

Shouting, "*He's carrying a piece*," Moody was out of the car before he reached the last word. LeBeau's sprint proved faster. They converged on the entrance, Moody slightly behind, breathing heavily from the run. Each checked the position of his own pistol but neither drew it. They entered the mortuary in tandem.

"May I help you, please?" An unctuous-faced man stepped from a doorway in the softly lighted hallway, dry-washing his plump hands. He was wearing a white carnation.

"A kid, a young man just came in here," Moody said. "Where'd he go?"

"I didn't see him," said the undertaker's man. "I was just in the bathr—"

The detectives ran to look in the viewing rooms, one off the hallway on the right, another to the left. Both were empty of humanity dead or alive, but the floral pieces remained in the right-hand room. Moody recognized the pitiful little basket sent by the homicide squad.

They trotted to the end of the hall. Moody turned and shouted at the carnation man, who had followed tentatively behind them.

"How do you get out this way?"

The man gestured fussily and came to join them. LeBeau flashed the gold shield at him.

"Oh, gosh," the functionary gasped. "Right through there."

The detectives went down a flight of stairs, opened another door, and were outside, at the edge of the asphalt parking lot. The hearse was drawn up at a big door farther along, and into it men were sliding the smaller casket.

"Where in hell *is* he?" Moody cried. "Did we miss him inside someplace? They bring the coffins down by elevator, I think."

He went to look in the hearse while LeBeau questioned the undertaker's people. When they were back together, Moody said, "I can't find Larry, either. Come on!"

They returned to the building at the run. Acting on instinct, Moody now at last drew his weapon. They began a systematic search of the rooms on the main floor. The second door they tried was that of a tiny lavatory, a facility apparently used by the public, as opposed to the one from which the carnation man had come.

Larry Howland was there, backed against the wall in the space between the washbowl and the toilet stall, by the young man they had seen at the entrance of the building a minute or two earlier. The latter was pressing a large revolver against the midsection of Larry's dark suit.

Moody put the muzzle of his own short-barreled .38 an inch from the back of the man's skull and identified it for him as a gun. "We're police officers. Now, very carefully, you put your weapon into the washbasin. Don't drop it. Just reach over and put it down real careful, so it won't discharge."

The young man failed to comply. It was as though he had not heard the order. He was short and slender, scarcely more than a boy. He could easily have been lifted off his feet from behind, or knocked off balance, but if his finger was on the trigger (Moody could not, at the close-quarter angle, see), such moves would be too dangerous to attempt.

Four men were crowded into a space that would have been uncomfortable for two, unless one remained in the stall. There was no urinal here. Was it a ladies' room?

"Come on, son," Moody said. His heart was racing, but he simulated calm in his exterior self. "Give it up. You're not getting anywhere."

Cowering against the wall, Larry was trying to speak. He finally succeeded in producing a sound between a whisper and a scream. "*He's crazy.*"

The young man with the gun stayed silent. LeBeau was half behind Moody, half to his side. Moody could feel the tension in his partner. "Look, son," he said in his avuncular tone to the fair-haired crown just beyond and below his chin. "Put the gun in the washbasin. Nobody's gotten shot yet. Let's keep it that way."

LeBeau was suddenly struck in the shoulder by the outer door, which opened as far as it could, the smooth face of the man with the carnation peeping in through the aperture. "Will you be much longer?" he asked. "They're ready to start for the crematory."

"Go away," Moody told him. It was easier for him to reach around Dennis to slam the door than for the latter, at his angle, to bring up a hand.

"Crematory?" asked the lad with the gun. "You're cremating them?" He uttered a howl of anguish. He dropped the weapon on the tile floor, hung his head, and sobbed. While this sequence was in progress LeBeau reached around and seized him, flung him against the closed door, brought his wrists into the small of his back, and cuffed him. The boy offered no resistance whatever.

Moody picked up the heavy pistol. It was a blued-steel .357 magnum. All the cylinders were empty. He asked LeBeau to look for ammo in searching the young man's pockets.

He addressed Larry Howland, who had remained against the wall for the reason that there was noplace else to go at the moment. "Did he take anything from you?"

"He's my half brother," Larry said.

"Let's get out where we can breathe." Moody helped LeBeau open the door and move the prisoner into the hallway. The carnation man was lurking nearby. "Tell 'em to turn off the motor," Moody said. "Nobody's going anywhere at the moment. This is a criminal investigation. You don't want to obstruct it."

"I certainly do not, Officer. You're absolutely right."

"Is that the men's or ladies' room?"

"It's for anybody. It's the only public one." The man hustled away.

"What did you do with the bullets?" LeBeau asked the prisoner, completing the body search.

The young man spoke for the second time. His face was wet. "I threw them away."

"What's your name?"

"Lloyd Howland."

"Where's your ID?" asked Moody.

"There's nothing on him," LeBeau said.

"We've been wanting to talk to you for a couple days, Lloyd," said Moody. "Where've you been?"

Lloyd's head fell. "I would have been here if I only knew. I would never have gone away."

"Let me tell you something, Lloyd. When we ask questions, you have to answer them," Moody told him. "It's a serious crime to menace somebody with a gun even if it's empty, and I'd be surprised if you had a license for it in the first place. So we got plenty to book you on."

Lloyd raised his pale eyes, from which tears were suddenly flowing again. "He did it."

"Who's he?"

"I should have killed him. I should have kept the bullets and killed him. But he's my brother."

Moody asked LeBeau to read Lloyd his rights. Larry was staying in the bathroom. Moody returned there now and found him throwing cold water on his face and, inevitably, wetting his tie and shirt front.

"Do you want to tell us anything before we take him down to be booked?"

Howland turned his streaming face to Moody. "Do you have to arrest him?"

"He was menacing you with a deadly weapon."

"It was unloaded. You said so yourself."

"What were you doing, listening at the door? Then you must have heard him also say he wishes he had killed you."

Larry winced. "He overreacts a lot. He's overemotional. He was real close to Donna."

"What do you mean?"

The tall, soft man shook his head. "No, not that. He . . . well, he might be gay for all I know. I don't really think so, but at least he doesn't seem interested in sex. Anyhow, Donna wasn't either. I can testify to that." Larry tore several paper towels from the dispenser, made a pad of them, and patted his now mottled cheeks. "I'm not saying he didn't throw a scare into me with that gun in my gut, but it's different if it wasn't loaded."

"What about his regret he didn't kill you?"

"I don't believe it," Larry said into the mirror. "Lloyd's a little screwed up, but he's no criminal. He was crazy about Donna and Mandy."

"He thinks *you* murdered them."

Larry turned to face him. "You shouldn't be talking like that!"

"What did he say to you?"

Howland resumed patting his forehead with the pad of paper towels, though moisture could no longer be seen there. "He was babbling. I didn't understand what he was saying. He grabbed me. I was on my way out to follow the hearse. I didn't know what he wanted! He didn't say a coherent word. I was in shock, I guess. I mean, not only was he waving that gun, but I never had a slight difference of opinion with him, ever. This isn't like him."

"I thought you said he overreacts a lot."

"Oh." Larry dropped the padded towels into a tall white waste can with a squeaky swinging top. "He's had run-ins with people everywhere he's ever worked, at least according to what he told Donna, and he changes jobs all the time. If you ask why, he mentions the boss or his coworkers having it in for him."

"Think he ever got violent?"

"No," Larry answered quickly. "I mean, I never talked to any of the people worked with him, but I wouldn't say from the way I've known him he was a violent person. I think he might do a lot of mouthing off." He stared defiantly at Moody. "I refuse to press charges against him."

"It's not your say-so. Two police officers were eyeball witnesses."

"The gun was unloaded!"

"That might mean less than you think."

Larry pushed past Moody without touching him, a feat in the constricted space. He turned at the door to say, "You let Lloyd go. He's harmless! And when can I get back to my house, for a change of clothes and some other personal items?"

"I think a supervised visit can be arranged," Moody told him. "It might help if you're a little more cooperative in giving us simple information."

"You've got my word on it."

The detectives booked Lloyd Howland on as many charges as they could associate with the incident in the washroom of the mortuary, among them menacing, illegal possession of a deadly weapon, resisting police officers, battery, threatening bodily harm, and others, the purpose of the excess being so that some of it could be thrown out in the inevitable deal made between the state, the defense, and the judge. As cops they were only too aware that any lawyer could render most of these counts ineffectual, with an unloaded gun and a supposed victim who refused to testify against the alleged assailant, but their principal interest in Lloyd concerned the murders of his sister-in-law and niece and the arrest provided an excuse to keep him for a while at their disposal. Even so, a lawyer could have sprung him on low bail within a few hours.

But as it happened, Lloyd refused to seek legal counsel, which refusal, if immediately convenient, might well be troublesome in the longer run, for though it would be easier to interrogate him without the obstruction of an attorney, if he decided to get one at any time in the future the first thing the counselor would arrange was a repudiation of everything his new client had said without legal representation. The fact was, the entire system was run so as to keep cops at a disadvantage, or so it was seen by all law-enforcement personnel.

Moody assumed his paternal manner in the interrogation room. "Like something to eat or drink, son? Did you have lunch? How about a burger?"

The wan young man silently shook his hanging head.

"How'd you get that scratch on your face?" LeBeau asked. "Look at me. That cut or scratch, where'd you get it?"

Lloyd stared dully at him. "Shaving."

Leaning back, as if relaxed and confident, Moody asked, "Where'd the three-fifty-seven come from?"

"What?"

"The gun."

"I stole it."

"Who from?"

"From a gun store."

"It's not new," said LeBeau.

"Don't they ever sell used guns?" The lad was not an experienced criminal, whatever else he might be. This sounded like a genuine question.

Moody asked, "Have you used this weapon to commit other crimes?"

"No, of course not."

"Why did you want to kill your brother?"

Lloyd closed his eyes. "It's personal."

"There you're wrong," said Moody. "It's illegal to threaten to kill somebody. You want to fight with your brother, it's nobody's business only if you don't break the law."

Lloyd's face suddenly looked as if threatened with disintegration, and he clutched at it. His shoulders were heaving. For an instant, until the tears came through the fingers and coursed down the backs of the young man's hands, Moody thought it might be a seizure of the epileptic kind.

LeBeau wore a faint sneer. He was always distrustful of suspects who interrupted the rhythm of an interrogation. He now coldly repeated Moody's earlier question. "Why'd you want to kill your brother?" But Lloyd, lost in his weeping, made no answer. Dennis became more contemptuous. "What are you really crying about? Because you got arrested?"

Moody carried a little packet of Kleenexes, which often came in handy throughout the day and cut down on his laundry, and he now produced it and peeled off a couple of sheets and gave them to Lloyd, who politely thanked him.

"It would make a better impression if you answered the questions," LeBeau said ominously. "It really would." He angrily rose from his chair and stalked out of the room, slamming the door behind him, in a display of fake emotion.

Moody settled back again and spoke paternally. "We wanted to talk to you for a couple days but had a hard time finding you. Mind telling me why you gave your brother's phone number to the Valmarket personnel people?"

"I didn't have a phone of my own."

"And I hear from"—Moody flipped his notebook back to the appropriate page—"Jack Duncan, produce manager, that you didn't do much of a job. In fact he fired you—and you drew a knife on him?"

"That's a dirty lie!" Indignation superseded grief, to be replaced by bitterness. "But I doubt you want to hear the truth."

"You seem intelligent," Moody said. "Use your head. Why wouldn't I want to know the truth? Because this Duncan is paying me off in fresh cabbages? I'm trying to get your side of it. Give me some help."

"I had a utility knife to cut cartons with. It was the store's property. When he fired me I was just trying to return it."

Moody chewed on his stubbly upper lip. "You can see how that might have looked if you were arguing with the man. But there's these other jobs where you didn't get along with people. Like this restaurant in a place called"—more flipping—"Oakwood. You want to explain that?"

"Are they accusing me of something?"

"Should they be?"

"I ought to be the one to do that! There were lockers for your street clothes. They gave me one where the lock was broken, and somebody kept stealing stuff I left in my pockets. Nothing really valuable. I didn't have anything worth much. But you know, a comb and so on. Small change."

"Other employees would steal these items?"

"I tried to figure out why," Lloyd said. "They all made more than me. I was at the bottom. I was supposed to share in the busboys' cut of the tips, which is some small percentage of the waiters', or so I heard only after I got fired. I actually never collected a cent of it. I didn't even know I had it coming. The others never said a word about it, so it wasn't *that* that caused the trouble. I just got fed up having my locker pilfered. So this big bastard is the one who takes me on."

"How?"

"I complained, and this guy says, 'You got a big mouth. That's the way to get a sore ass.' "

"How far did it go?"

Lloyd shrugged. "If you let them do that to you, you'll never hear the end of it, but I don't like to get the hell beaten out of me, believe it or not. But I just can't let certain things go. This guy was a head taller and had forty-fifty pounds on me. What am I supposed to do?"

Moody was shaking his head. "All that matters is what you *did*."

"What Duncan says is a complete lie, but this time I really was standing next to a big chef's knife on the butcher block where they had been cutting chickens up. I told him, 'You better worry about your guts and not my ass.' I just glanced at the knife. I never even touched it. But he goes and gets me fired. The manager says, 'You're just lucky we don't press charges.' "

"Knives again," Moody said, as if wearily. "Now you've switched to guns, is that it?" He rose slowly from the chair and strolled about the limited space available to him on that side of the table. "You see how it looks, Lloyd? I'm trying to understand, but it always seems to come down to you threatening somebody—or anyway *they* think so, whatever your intentions were according to yourself." He stopped and stared. "It never goes beyond that? You don't ever use any of these weapons? It's always just you saying something and somebody else getting the wrong impression? It's always just talk?"

11

Patrolmen Jack Marevitch and Art McCall were talking to a florid-faced man wearing an undershirt that was stained with what looked like blood, sweat, and other substances not so easily identified but which may have included ketchup, car oil, cooking grease, and excrement. The man had let them into the second-story apartment through its back entrance, up a flight of outside stairs from an asphalt driveway and through a screen door with a cracked frame and torn mesh, into a kitchen. He held a beer can in one fist and a lighted cigarette in the other. He was unshaven and stank of beer and a mixture of foul personal odors.

"Sir," Marevitch said, "I'm going to ask you again to put down the can."

"Yeah," McCall added, squinting as the smoke came his way, "and drop the butt in it."

The man crumpled the can in his right hand and hurled it into a porcelain sink mounted on the farthest wall, but he retained the cigarette.

McCall was tall and fit but nowhere near the size of the smoker. Holding his horizontaled baton at either end, belt-high, he stuck his face up at the man's big nose and asked threateningly, "You got a hearing problem?" It was of course legal to smoke and drink inside your own home, but the officers found it useful to start off by bullying a mutt of his type, and all the more so given his size.

The cigarette was launched to join the accordioned beer can. "I want you to throw the book at her," the man said through lips that had difficulty in forming the words.

"How much did you have to drink?" Marevitch asked.

"She was the one assaulted *me*. I wanna swear out a complaint."

"What's your name?"

"McCracken. Mac McCracken."

"Is Mac your real first name or your nickname?"

"It's Avery." The kitchen was typical of those on domestic-disturbance calls: all flat surfaces were crowded with empty take-out food containers, sticky ex-liquid receptacles, slimy plastic plates, and forks with solid matter clogging their tines. The general odor was sweetish-rotten. "You going to arrest her?" McCracken glared down at the officers.

"Let me tell you something, sir," Marevitch responded aggressively. He was a head shorter than this man. "*You're* the one going to find yourself in jail if you say any more with that tone in your voice."

The man produced a combination of whine and howl. "Me? Arrest *me*? I'm the one *called* you, for Christ Almighty."

"Then calm down, sir. Here we are. Now, who's 'her'? Wife? Girlfriend? Sister, mom, or who?"

McCracken lifted his chins and closed and opened his bleary eyes. "Fiancée."

"Is she here at this time?"

The big man seemed to take offense. "All right, don't believe me, goddammit. I'll just go get her."

"You stay right here," McCall told him, pointing. "Take the crap off that chair and sit down in it. I'll go find your fiancée. What's her name?"

McCracken closed his eyes again and for an instant swayed as though he might fall. The officers stepped aside, having no intention of catching him and getting befouled. But he remained on his feet and finally said, "Della."

"Della what?"

"I forgot."

"You forgot your fiancée's last name?" asked McCall.

The big man patted the protuberant belly of the stained T-shirt and suppressed a belch. "You know how it is," he said.

Calling out "Miz Della?" McCall went through the inner doorway. He could be heard repeating the name for a while. Then, after a moment of murmuring, he came running back. "She's okay," he told Marevitch and kept going toward the door.

Marevitch too had got the call on his own epaulet radio. It was a 10-31, crime in progress, at a liquor store on Central Avenue. "We got to go, Mr. McCracken," he shouted at the big man, who now seemed to have gone into a trance. "You try to dry out for a while, and I bet it'll all work out with your lady."

The officers trotted down the desiccated wooden steps of the outside staircase and, skirting the rusty pickup truck parked off the asphalt in the muddy yard, reached their unit.

Marevitch took the wheel. "Did you find her?"

"Yeah. She's okay. She's a little bitty woman. She admitted beating up on *him*."

They got a laugh out of that. Marevitch turned on the flashing light and the alarm that he still called a siren though it actually made a whooping sound, but only a few of the private automobiles and commercial vehicles made voluntary way for the police car.

"Look at that guy." He bared his teeth. "And they get away with it. The only time you could catch them is when you don't have time to do it." He cut the wheel sharply and darted through a suddenly opened space to pass the offending four-wheeler, at the driver of which McCall shot a finger. "If I could get away with it, I'd put the flasher on sometime when it wasn't a hurry-up call, and bust everybody who wouldn't clear the way."

The liquor store was for once not in a mall but on a street of middle- to small-sized shops, heavily traveled, the metered parking places always filled. It was probably because of the difficulty of access by motorist customers that the store advertised sizable markdowns in its placard-covered windows. In a quick eyeballing of the facade, Marevitch managed to register that his prosperous brother's brand of sour-mash bourbon was discounted here by almost 15 percent.

He double-parked the unit, the first to arrive, and he and McCall approached the liquor store, Marevitch with the old-fashioned, familiar .38 revolver, an empty shell in the chamber under the hammer, making it only a five-shot, and his partner with the twelve-gauge pump gun.

"Goddamn those signs," McCall complained. "You can't see inside." One that advertised jug wine covered even the glass of the front door. He took his billed cap off, put it under his left arm, and, bending, went along the glass looking for a hole in the paper or an open joint between two panels.

A poodle-haired white-blond woman stepped out of the beauty salon next door, and Marevitch waved her back inside with his free hand, though all she could look at was the gun in the other.

He told her not to let anyone else come out until they were told. He spoke into the radio at his epaulet, asking the ETA for backup units. But it was still a long moment before he heard the sirens. Meanwhile, McCall had come back to the obscured front door in his reconnoitering tour.

"Here they are," Marevitch said, with reference to their distantly audible support. "Wait up, willya?" He could never understand, looking back, why his partner did not do so. McCall had never been a hotdog or showboat, eager for commendations or promotion. Not to mention that his wife was seven months pregnant.

Yet Art chose this moment to be foolish for the first time in his career. He returned the cap to his head, extended the barrel of the shotgun before him, and with its muzzle pried a narrow gap between the edge of the glass door and the metal frame of the doorway.

At his own angle Marevitch could not see into the gap. He was reluctant to shout another warning, lest someone inside be alerted to his partner's presence. Therefore he was watching silently when McCall's cap was blown off by a burst of heavy-caliber automatic fire that also pulverized the glass of the door. McCall's body was twisted and hurled aside by the impact.

Seeing the spray of blood and brain matter, Marevitch for an instant believed Art had lost the entire back of his head, but finally recognized he was looking at where his partner's face had been.

Artie still had a faint heartbeat when they put him into the ambulance, Marevitch accompanying, but it was gone by the time they reached the hospital.

Lloyd slept well in jail, despite the noise and the lights, which were not extinguished or even dimmed as day became night and vice versa, as he had to assume continued to happen, though there was no window by which to confirm it. If he had had a watch it would surely have been taken from him, as was everything else removable except his underwear and socks, in return for which he received a shirt and a pair of pants dyed navy blue and slip-on shoes with pale canvas uppers and black rubber soles. CITY JAIL was stenciled in white across the back and on the breast of the shirt and, in smaller letters, down the seam of both trouser legs. His cell was furnished with a combination washstand and toilet, with the basin where the water tank of a normal toilet would be, an ingenious fixture new to him, efficient and space-saving. The cot, with a continuous metal frame, was fixed to floor and wall and covered with a gray blanket over a firm pad that was no less comfortable than some of the surfaces he had slept on when free.

Here in jail he slept better than he had for quite some time on the outside, except when watched over by Molly (guilty memories of

whom he tried to suppress now), and he ate breakfast from the compartmented plastic tray with better appetite than he had known for
days.

He was aware that the detectives used certain techniques of ma-
nipulation that really had nothing to do with him as an individual
except in the role as specimen. He returned the favor, having no
personal interest in them or in fact anyone else alive. They were
doing what they had to do. He had refused a lawyer despite the
judge's stern advice at the arraignment. He said he had listened to
and understood the charges against him, which was not true, and
pleaded guilty, which did represent something closer to the truth, if
not to the letter thereof, but then what was? The truth was that he
had first unloaded the pistol and then gone to shoot Larry with it,
and that was an impossibility, but no more of one than that Donna
and Amanda had been violently murdered, of course not literally by
Larry, who could have had no motive. What Larry *was* guilty of was
consorting with other women while his wife and daughter were alive:
for this he deserved to be shot, but Lloyd could not have done that,
for they were brothers, hence the unloaded gun. He could never have
explained this to the police without compromising Donna's memory.

Not long after he had cleaned up the breakfast tray Lloyd was
manacled at the wrists and shackled at the ankles and taken by elevator to a room on the floor below.

The older detective was waiting for him there. "Hi, Lloyd."

"Your name is Moody."

"Thanks for remembering." Moody asked the guard to remove
the prisoner's restraints. "How they treating you here?"

"Okay," said Lloyd. "All right." The guard pushed him down
onto the chair so the leg irons could be removed.

"Getting fed?"

"The food is good."

The guard smirked as he unlocked the handcuffs. "You must like
the taste of spit."

"Knock that off," Moody said, scowling. The guard left with the clinking hardware.

There was a window in this room, but behind thick bars the glass was covered on the interior with dense mesh and was barely translucent, masked on both sides with a veneer of filth. The only effective light came from the embedded ceiling fixture inside its protective cage.

Moody sat some distance back of the table between them, maybe so he could cross his legs. But he uncrossed them now and brought up an attaché case from the floor. "Do I have your permission to tape-record our conversation? I'll ask you the same question when the tape gets rolling. This is what we have to do nowadays. . . . And I'm going to level with you, Lloyd. It will probably have to be done all over again if you get a lawyer."

"What could a lawyer do for me?" Lloyd asked. "I'm guilty."

Moody stopped fiddling with his little machine. "Are you willing to repeat that on the tape?"

"How could I deny I had the gun when you and the other detective took it away from me? And my brother was there too."

"You're just talking about the gun," Moody said, as if disappointed. He apparently had started the recorder, because he spoke some ritualistic language at it, identifying himself and Lloyd, along with the time and place.

"Now, you admit you are guilty of the gun charges."

"That's right."

"I was wondering"—Moody writhed in his chair and grimaced slightly—"I was wondering if there's anything else you would like to admit to doing. Right now, you know? Like they say, get free of the burden."

Lloyd frowned. "I can't think of anything."

Moody smiled at him. He was old enough to be Lloyd's father. Lloyd often failed to get along with other men, but the conflict was never started by him. He usually felt neutral toward them until they began to criticize him. He had nothing against Moody, who had thus far been fair.

"What we're really interested in is not so much the gun charges, Lloyd—though they're serious—but there's something else you might give us some help with. Matter of fact, that's why we've been looking for you."

Lloyd lifted his chin. "I didn't know that. I wasn't running away." Which was true only in the sense that he had not been intentionally evading the police.

"What did you mean at the funeral parlor?" Moody asked. "You were accusing Larry of something. His wife and little girl were murdered, had their throats cut, the bedside rug like a sponge, the little girl's mattress was soaked through to the spring, you wouldn't think a three-year-old child had so much in her. What kind of person would do a thing like that? Your *brother*?"

Lloyd had covered his eyes with his hands. He felt a boiling in his depths, and his fingers were icy against his eyelids. His answer was a sobbing no.

"No? Then what did you mean?"

Eventually he lowered his hands. "I don't know. I didn't realize what I was saying."

"Lloyd," Moody said in an avuncular tone, chin lowered, "I'm going to have to ask you a question that might upset you, particularly the second part, but I hope you will answer it truthfully. Did *liking* Donna go a little bit further? Did you ever have any intimate relations with her?"

Lloyd shook violently. "Oh, my God—"

But Moody, though still friendly, was implacable. "I want an answer."

"For God's sake, no," Lloyd said softly, addressing the tabletop.

"Now, here's another question I've got to ask. How about little Amanda? Did you ever do anything with her you shouldn't have?"

Lloyd was less disturbed by a question that was essentially worse, perhaps because it was so absurd. "Of course not. They were my sister-in-law and my niece. I'm no pervert."

Moody leaned away, placing his hands on the edge of the table, and asked, almost idly, as if it were not important, "Do you like women?"

"Yes, of course." Lloyd paused, and then said, "I'm not a homo-sexual, if that's what you mean."

"You're not. Uh-huh." Moody nodded. "You mean you don't go to bed with men. But that's not what I asked. I asked if you *like* women. I didn't mean for sex."

"Certainly."

Moody pushed himself back in the chair and stood up. "I've known a lot of gay guys in my time—we've even got one or two on the police force nowadays: that's the law, you know—and I'll tell you, I have never known any of them to *not* like women. On the other hand, you take the men who kill females, nobody but females, your Ted Bundys for example: they're not gay. They're *only* inter-ested in women! You might say they're fascinated by women, else why kill so many? But you can't say they *like* women, now can you?" He sat down again, pulling his chair so close that the table made a crease across him, just below the chest.

"I like women as friends," Lloyd said, "if that's what you mean. In fact"—perhaps rashly, he suddenly trusted the detective—"I'll go so far as to say I prefer them as friends."

"Meaning—?"

"Not for sex. No, I'm not gay. I like sex, but not with girls I like."

"Wait a minute, Lloyd," Moody protested. "You're getting out of my depth. I'm a cop, not a psychologist. Go over that one again."

"Then love is something else," Lloyd said. "There's liking, there's sex, and then there's love, so-called. At least that's the way I see it."

"Where would murder fit into the pattern, would you say? Take

Bundy—you know who he was: a guy who killed lots of girls out West, then went to Florida and killed some more—would he have had these different compartments?"

Lloyd shrugged. He did not recognize the name; he had no interest in crime. "You'll have to ask him."

"I'd have to go to hell to do that," said Moody. "They burned him in the Florida chair, couple years back."

"For killing women?" Lloyd asked.

"If they'd done it earlier, some of those girls would have been saved, but he escaped from a courtroom while being tried the first time. What do you think about capital punishment, Lloyd?"

"In this case it certainly made sense." He briefly felt more rage than sorrow. "Whoever did that to Donna and Mandy should be put to death."

"Even if it was your brother?"

"Larry didn't do it."

"Did *you*?"

The question had come without warning, though no doubt he should have expected it. He felt as if slapped in the face. "You shouldn't ask me something like that!"

"But that's why we're here, Lloyd." Moody's tone, however, was soothing. "We've got to find who did this awful thing and take him off the street, don't you agree?"

"How could it be me?" Lloyd cried. "I loved them."

"I thought you just said you *liked* them as family, and then you said there were differences between liking and loving and sex was a third category. So what do you mean now by loving them? If you mean like sisters, which you said they were to you, then that's a fourth category, isn't it?"

Lloyd sat in silence.

Moody reached for the little black machine. "Let me run it back for you."

"No!"

The detective smiled. "Can listening to yourself be that bad? . . . Or is that what you meant by love in the first place? Love for your mother, your family members, maybe some close friends, but not ever for what goes on between men and women, which is either just liking or just sex?"

Lloyd felt nothing but resentment. "I don't even want to think about it. Out of nowhere you accuse me of this awful—"

"I haven't accused you of anything," Moody said levelly. "Except the gun charges that you admit to. . . ." He leaned to check the little top window of the recording machine, where Lloyd could see the reels turning. "But let's get away from the theorizing and into what actually happened. Let's set up a chronology."

Lloyd had not yet recovered his composure, but as this was an essentially neutral exercise, he complied, tracing the events of his morning, staying literal except for the episode at the liquor store, the relating of which would only have complicated matters and perhaps even got him accused of the robbery and the shooting down of the clerk. But in remembering the matter now, so as to evade it, he realized that he had put it utterly out of his mind until this moment. He had never before come so close to the consequences of violence. He must have missed the crime itself by only minutes. Could the loss of memory have been caused by shock? In any event, he had to admit to himself that the lapse was shocking, in another way than the crime.

But Moody was sharp. "This liquor you had—scotch, was it?— how'd you get it without money? You told me the beef with your boss was about getting the pay they owed you, right away. Or did you have enough for a bottle?"

"It was one of those half-gallon jugs," Lloyd explained. "I had it around for a while. It was almost full. I'm not much of a drinker, ordinarily."

"You're not much of a drinker—and you're not the kind of big heavy guy who might be able to hold a lot—yet you emptied a half gallon of scotch and lived to tell the tale?"

"Well, that's just what I don't know," Lloyd said. "I couldn't find the bottle next day."

"But you stayed home the whole afternoon and night? If you never left the place, where'd the empty bottle go?"

"Maybe I didn't look thoroughly enough," said Lloyd. "Though the place is so small . . ."

"Let's get this out of the way, Lloyd," Moody said earnestly. "Mind giving us permission to take a look around your apartment? If a bottle's there, we'll find it."

"I don't think you need my permission. I paid rent by the week, and the week was up. That's one of the reasons why I left when I did. I couldn't have paid."

"I understand," Moody said. "But the legalities are so complicated nowadays that we have to be extra careful. Just give me the address if you will." He wrote in a black-covered notebook, and while it was still open, he looked up and asked, "Oh, can we get a blood sample from you without going through a lot of hassle? All you have to do is sign a couple permission forms for all of this. Keep it simple. That's my motto. Don't you agree? You're a reasonable guy."

Lloyd's resentment had dwindled away by now. He willingly assented to all that was asked of him. Not to have done so would be to suggest that he was a criminal rather than somebody whose situation was as yet too complex even for him to understand.

12

Even though Lloyd was well aware that Moody could hardly be a friend of his in the true sense of the word, he had not been able to keep from trusting and even liking him a little: that naturally happened when you were treated decently. And the reverse was as true. LeBeau was only doing his job, but it was impossible not to react adversely to him when he started right off on an obscene note.

"This sister-in-law of yours," the detective said. "She was a good-looking woman, and I never even saw her alive." He leaned into the table, as if to receive a confidence. "How was she in bed?"

Lloyd kept himself under control: this was only to provoke him. "I never touched her." This was literally true. Though Donna sometimes put her hand briefly over his, when seated near enough, or steered him into a room, her fingers on his arm, and sometimes kissed him hello or good-bye on the cheek, he never touched or kissed back.

"What did you use, a rubber?" LeBeau asked. "A condom? And then you pulled it off, spilling some gunk on the sheet? Or did you get so excited cutting her that you had to jerk off?" His grin displayed the lines of cruelty from nose to the corners of the mouth.

"You're disgusting," Lloyd said.

"Then what did you do to little Amanda? I mean, other than using the knife. What did you make her do first?"

"You can talk that way all you want, but I won't have any answer except the same one I've been giving. I know what you're trying to do."

"Your brother says you always wanted to get in Donna's pants."

Lloyd could not help inwardly cringing at this coarseness, but he said firmly, "No, he didn't."

"How do you know what he says behind your back?"

"Because Larry hasn't ever hidden his low opinion of me face-to-face," Lloyd said. "I've got to hand him that."

"You hate each other?"

"I don't hate him. He's my brother."

"Half brother." LeBeau squirmed in his chair. "You just mentioned his low opinion of you."

"You can think little of somebody," Lloyd pointed out, "without hating him. You can also hate somebody while having a high opinion of them, in the sense of them being good at what they do."

LeBeau smirked. He was a younger, better-looking, and much fitter man than his partner. "But all this philosophizing is missing the point, though, isn't it, Lloyd? You don't want to think about Donna, laying there in all that blood, or little Amanda with her throat cut from ear to ear. It's easier to bullcrap about who thinks what of somebody."

"But it was you just asked me," Lloyd said. "I was only answering what you—"

"You know, Lloyd," the detective said, "we're doing you a big favor. You got this special private cell all by yourself only because we arranged it. This jail is full up. On the top level they're three to a cell. If we didn't ask, they'd put you in with two big black guys, and they'd be putting it to you night and day, at both ends. You complain and they put a shank in your belly." He showed his dirty grin again. "Of course, maybe you'd enjoy it, for all I know. You like sex with guys, Lloyd? Is that it?"

This was now getting more ridiculous than offensive. But even though Lloyd was aware that no tape recorder was running now, he knew he would do well to avoid making ironic or sarcastic remarks. "No, certainly not."

"Larry's got quite a taste for tail, hasn't he? He's quite the cock-meister, I hear."

"I don't know about that."

"Why's he got this low opinion of you, according to you?"

"I don't stick at jobs, for one thing," said Lloyd. "I guess that's a good part of it."

"Why?"

"I wish I knew."

The detective massaged an earlobe. "It wouldn't be because you threaten your bosses with knives, would it?"

"That's a lie. I've already gone over that incident, and the other one, with Moody."

"What became of the weapon you showed to the produce manager at the Valmarket?"

"It wasn't a weapon!"

"Where is it now, Lloyd?"

"I lost it."

"Exactly how?"

"How do you know how you lost something?"

LeBeau stood up and walked to the dingy, barred window and remained there for a while, his broad tweed back to the table, the kind of thing he certainly would not have done if closeted with a dangerous criminal. . . . But then Lloyd realized that, dirty and obscured as it was, the glass nevertheless provided a usable mirror image of the room: the detective was being neither negligent nor contemptuous of him.

Addressing the window, LeBeau asked, "The regular box cutters used at the Valmarket, they don't cut very deep, do they? Be real hard to kill somebody with one. But you take a utility knife now, with the blade run all the way out and locked, you could sure go deep across a throat, severing the jugular and windpipe and all." He turned. "Would you confirm that, Lloyd? You're the expert."

"I used it to open boxes," Lloyd said flatly. "Because it worked better than the regular ones, which were all dull. I didn't threaten Duncan. He was always looking for an excuse to blame me for something."

"Like your brother?"

Lloyd tried to explain, though it was probably a waste of breath. "Larry never *blames* me for anything. When you don't think somebody can do something, you're not blaming them. You like to see them, because it makes you feel superior by contrast. Larry was always asking me to come around for dinner, also to stay overnight. I could have lived there rent-free, eating off them: that's the impression I got."

"Now there's brotherly love for you," said LeBeau. "Why would Larry encourage you to be even more of a leech than you already were?"

"I don't know."

"But the thought must have occurred to you? Or didn't it? Maybe you're so pleased with yourself you didn't even notice."

"Hardly."

LeBeau returned to his chair. "You and Larry didn't grow up together."

"We didn't even know each other till a couple years ago. . . . It was a big surprise to me. I grew up never even knowing I had a half brother. My mother finally mentioned it; I was eighteen or nineteen by then. I guess she hadn't before because he was not her son. But then she rarely mentioned my father, whom she hated."

"Why?"

"He ran away with some other woman."

"You were how old?"

"Three. I don't remember him at all."

"How'd you finally connect up with Larry?"

"I just looked him up in the phone book. I just took a chance. I didn't even know his first name. There were only two Howlands with male names in the city book. I got the right one first time. I asked if he was the son of Willard Howland, and he was."

"Would you say with Larry, it's like father like son?" LeBeau asked archly, wrinkling his brow. When Lloyd failed to respond, the detective said, "But not you, huh? You're the mama's boy. Though your mom must not have been too straitlaced. Didn't she take your old man away from Larry's mother?"

"I wasn't alive at the time," Lloyd said icily. "I can't say."

"See," LeBeau said, "what's interesting is everybody else you're related to has had a kind of spicy love life. But not you."

"I talked to Moody about that," Lloyd told him. "It should be on the tape. I'm not going to keep repeating it. It doesn't have anything to do with why I'm here."

"That's not a decision you can make." LeBeau pointed a finger at him. "Don't kid yourself, Lloyd. I think you do that a lot, and you get in trouble as a result. I didn't bring a machine along, and this room isn't bugged. That's so you can talk to me straight. You don't have to perform for the grandstand. It's just man to man. And I'll tell you this, I'm tough but I'm fair. You give me the truth and I'll respect you. But you lie, I'll be all over you." The detective cleared his throat and suddenly turned, if not positively friendly, as Moody had seemed at times, then at least receptive. "I'm trying to look at this situation from your point of view. Moody and me, in an investigation we see eye to eye. I'm a little younger, for whatever that means. Sometimes you'll find a guy who likes to talk to somebody closer to his own age, is all. . . ." He put his earnest face forward. "Tell me about Donna. And speaking of age, I believe she was a lot closer to your own than Larry. Did the two of you have a lot in common?"

Lloyd frowned. The change had only been a simulation. "If you're getting back to sex, no."

"That's a funny answer. I didn't say a word about sex, yet you had to bring it in." LeBeau drew back. "I meant the way you two looked at the world."

"Current affairs?"

LeBeau shook his head in annoyance. "Come on, Lloyd. You're not helping. What does a guy talk about with a woman his own age, or pretty close?"

"I don't know about anybody else," Lloyd answered. "But me, what I talked about to Donna was always myself. Looking back now, I can see how selfish I was."

The detective seemed amused, his square jaw moving. "That's what women usually accuse men of. You're saying it about yourself?"

Lloyd wanted to deal with this matter whether his questioner believed him or even listened to him. "It bothers me now. But I still don't know what I could have done about it even if she *had* told me her troubles."

"What troubles did she have?"

"I don't know. That's what I'm telling you. I didn't want to go into the matter, because I didn't have the power to change anything. But maybe I should have tried anyway instead of just dodging the issue. Maybe she'd be alive today."

LeBeau snorted. "She's dead because somebody used an edged weapon on her," he said flatly. "That's why she's not alive today: no other reason. How could talking have changed that?" He paused for a moment. "Unless it was *you* with the weapon. Is that what you're working up the nerve to tell me? Because otherwise you're not making much sense."

Was this serious or a part of the technique? "All right," said Lloyd, "suppose she was in some kind of, uh, situation—"

"That is a very interesting choice of words, but I don't have any idea of what you mean by it. *What* kind of *situation*? Financial? Domestic? Bad health?"

"I don't know, is what I'm saying," Lloyd insisted. "I really didn't want to know, because if I did, I would feel I should do something about it, and what could I do about anything but probably make it worse?"

"Why should you feel the need to do something?" asked LeBeau. "She was just your sister-in-law."

"Because I was in love with her," Lloyd said. The admission was for himself. He could never have made it as long as she was alive.

Marevitch was cleaning out Art McCall's locker when a burly patrolman named Carl Pingatelli stopped by to tell him to see Captain Novak before leaving.

"I'm in charge of the collection for Rosie," Pingatelli said. "I went to school with Artie, starting the sophomore year, when I transferred over from Macon."

"You guys were on the same team, year you were all-city champs." This was common knowledge of the kind that would have been unbearably boring to hear repeated again had McCall not been killed. Had his partner still been alive, Marevitch would have done anything to avoid Pingatelli, but now he was warmed by the encounter.

The commander's door was open when Marevitch got there, but he lingered on the threshold until the baldheaded captain looked up from some papers and noticed him.

"Jack. Come in. . . . Take a chair." Novak walked briskly to close the door. Despite his desk job he had never developed a potgut, unlike Marevitch, who had always been on the street. Back behind his desk, the captain scowled across it. "I don't want to hear you saying Artie's death was your fault in any way. You just let the investigators draw their own conclusions, see." He gestured with a fist. "Art made a mistake and he paid for it with his life. He went in there without waiting for backup. He never had SWAT training, goddammit." Novak pounded the desk, the papers bouncing.

"He was a brave man."

"He was an idiot," the captain shouted. "What did he accomplish? He got himself killed for nothing. They'll use him at the Academy as an example of an officer's judgment at its worst." Novak struck the desk again. "Is that what we're here for, to bury our own?"

"Captain, I'm turning in my shield."

"Like hell you are. You're gonna see the psychologist. You're gonna take a couple days off. And then you're gonna come back and get in the car. You got police work to do, and I can't spare you."

Marevitch tried to be angry. "Don't tell me what I'm going to do."

Captain Novak said quietly, "Look, Jack, you're not all alone in this. I know what it is to lose a partner. Maybe you don't remember: it happened to me when we were rookies? Joe Malone."

Marevitch looked at the floor. "Sure, I remember."

"You're one of the few old guys left," Novak said. "I can't run this precinct without you. Besides, you're the only other Polack."

Marevitch was in no mood for levity. "What I should of done was order him back," he said desperately. "I'm the ranking officer, if it comes down to that. But give your partner an *order*? Whoever heard of that?"

Novak stood up. He was a good six-three. "You tell that to the doctor, Jack. That's where you take it, not to me, because I know it's crap. She won't."

"*She?* I got to go see some *woman* doctor?" He began to unfasten the silver shield on his left breast pocket.

"Jack, if you give that to me I'm going to stick it up your ass," Novak said. He smiled expansively. "Hell, wouldn't you rather have a woman than some little know-it-all pansy with a beard and long hair?"

"You mean what you said about making an example of Artie? That's not right, Captain."

"I'm putting him in for a citation, Jack."

Marevitch lowered his head again. "Thanks, Captain. . . . All right, I'll go to this woman doctor."

"She might have some good ideas, Jack," Novak said. "Anyway, it's out of my hands. It's department policy, like everything now, like putting in a bigger locker room for the three female officers than we ever had for all the men. Jack, you remember way back when we joined the force, when all a cop had to do was collar the villains?"

13

Lloyd Howland and Molly Sparks were sitting on a bench in the spring-green park across from the big gray cube of the municipal jail with its barred windows. He said resentfully, "Did I ask you to bail me out?"

"All right." Molly spoke wearily but without apparent offense. "But I notice you didn't refuse to leave when you had the chance."

"I didn't know what was happening," said Lloyd. "They don't tell you anything in there."

"Look at *him*," she said with delight, pointing at the squirrel that sat within a foot of Lloyd's right shoe, staring up at him with huge eyes seemingly all pupil.

"I'm sorry," Lloyd told the animal, which rapidly flicked the bushy tail erected behind its head, "but I don't have anything to give you." He scanned the nearby reaches of the park. "See that old lady over there? She's got stuff."

"She just ran him off with her cane," said Molly. "She's feeding the birds. We could go over to that deli and buy peanuts for him, unless you just want to sit here all day and gripe."

"Not *we*. *We* wouldn't be buying them. *You* would be." He turned his head away in chagrin. The movement scared the squirrel into a quick retreat up a tree with bark that was as thickly textured as tread on a tire. "You're always doing me favors I don't want. How do you think I feel about you taking your savings for the bail?"

"I just had to put down the ten percent for the bondsman," Molly explained. "*He* pays the rest. I won't owe any more unless you take off."

"I ought to," Lloyd said, turning back. "Teach you a lesson. I bet that percentage amounted to your whole savings. Admit it!" He spoke so loudly that he briefly caught the attention of the bird-feeding woman across the way.

"Not quite." She avoided his eyes.

"I don't know how you even found me."

"The arrest was on the news when I got back."

"Oh, my God."

She shook her head at him. "You didn't expect it to be? The murders of your sister-in-law and niece, and you show up at the funeral with a gun? Why wouldn't that make the news? Incidentally, the gun was mine."

"You don't think I committed the murders, do you?"

"Would I be here if I did? But it *was* you waving my gun around."

"That's all I was charged with."

"That's the only reason I could make the bail," Molly said.

He spoke more gently. "You're too nice a person to hang around with me. Not to mention the kind of trouble it will get you into with your father when he hears about it."

"He won't. It's none of his business. I did the run and brought the rig back, and I got to go out on another job tomorrow. You can't come even if you want to, because it's out of state and you got to stay here or your bail will be revoked and you'll be considered a fugitive."

"You've really got me tied down, haven't you?"

"Come on, you know that ain't, isn't, my idea!" She squirmed on the bench. "You're free to do what you want."

"Just take off, jump bail, and disappear."

Her brown eyes were fixed candidly on him. "Sure. If that's what you have to do, then do it."

He gazed across the park, past the bird woman, over a sweep of unpeopled greensward, to the thronged baseball field at the far side, occupied by scurrying players and bracketed with onlookers in multicolored clothing. The day was warm and sunny but did nothing for his sore heart. He saw no improvement over being in a windowless cell. "I'm not going to do that. I wouldn't know where to go."

Molly twisted again. "I'm never going to ask you about your problems," she said. "But I want you to know that if you ever *do* want to talk about them, I'll listen, and I won't offer any advice. But I have thought a lot about you, and I think I can tell a good guy from a bad."

"Please," Lloyd said uncomfortably. "There's not always a distinction. . . . Here's something you should know about me. It's only fair. I don't—" He looked away. "This is hard to say so it won't be misunderstood. It's nothing against you, but I'm not interested in a romantic attachment. . . . But 'interested' still isn't the right word." Neither was "impotent." Yet without using it he nevertheless, rejecting the claims of pride, employed a term that would probably be taken as synonymous. " 'Incapable' would be better."

"All right," she said without a change of expression. "We're not making a deal. I'm just trying to be a friend. You can look at it in any way you want, except as pity."

He was grimly amused. "What if pity's just what I want?"

"Oh." Molly frowned as if serious, then quickly proved she was not. "Then get yourself another sucker, buster. You've got all you can squeeze out of this monkey."

Lloyd assumed she was simulating the dialogue heard in an old movie from the days when there were ladies and gentlemen and both wore hats. "That's what you should have said a long time before now."

"I might have, except I wanted my gun back." She still seemed to be joking.

"I guess they'll have to give it back when this is all over," said

Lloyd. "No real crime was committed with it. I unloaded it and threw the bullets away—"

She groaned. "You know what bullets *cost?*"

"Anyway," he concluded, "I told them I stole it from a store. I kept you out of it."

"It's unregistered," Molly said. "They'll never give it back. I just hope my dad doesn't ask to see it one of these days."

"I'll add its cost to everything else I owe you," Lloyd promised. "I'll start looking for work right away. I don't exactly have good references, even without this thing hanging over me, so I'll have to find somebody who hires for day work, off the books." He felt some concern for her. "How long you think you can keep your father in the dark, if you insist on involving yourself in my affairs this way?"

"I'll get around to telling him eventually. I just have to make the effort, is all. It won't be like the usual fights."

"You fight with him?"

"All the time."

"I thought you two were really close."

Molly laughed with lips that were pinker than usual. He realized that she was wearing makeup. "That's why we fight! Because we're so close." She frowned. "Don't you understand that, Lloyd?"

"I don't doubt your word."

Molly elucidated. "I don't mean throwing punches. I mean arguing, and we both get real mad. Didn't you ever do that with somebody you loved?"

"No," said Lloyd. He was not at all reluctant to make the confession.

"Didn't you ever love anybody?" Immediately she lowered her head. When she came back up, she said, "I'm sorry. I was out of line."

Nothing she could do would hurt him, but he sensed that she would not like to hear that. What she wanted was an intimacy that he could not furnish. "I don't mind," he said. "I *think* I have loved certain. . . ."

But if it has to be according to someone else's definition. . . . Look, I tangle with plenty of people. If I love somebody I want it to be different from the situation with everybody else. I don't want to fight."

Molly made a disarming, girlish grimace. "We probably are talking about different aspects. The kind of thing I mean is you wonder how some person you think so much of can be so stupid in a particular instance. Yet if some outsider attacked this person for just the same thing, you'd defend your loved one, and you'd use his very argument! Funny how that works." She peered at Lloyd with bright eyes.

"I understand." He did not, but it was the least he could do under the circumstances. He changed the subject. "You're wearing a dress. It's very nice."

That was certainly the right thing to say to please her. "You really think so? I figured when you come to bail somebody out, you oughta be dressed respectable." The dress was of a blue-green figure, and her shoes were heeled. He actually preferred her in the trucker outfit, baseball cap and thick soles, which had not asked so much of him. It was as if she were attired for a date. He slapped his thighs and stood up. "I'd better make the most of my freedom and get going and find a job."

"Till your first payday, what are you going to do about eating, and where you going to spend the nights?"

"There are places where you can get food and lodging."

"Soup kitchens? Homeless shelters? God Almighty, Lloyd."

"How about jail?" he asked. "I wouldn't have the problem if I was still there."

Molly hopped up from the bench and pointed. "I just had a brilliant idea. My cousin Joe's a skilled carpenter, and he's also got a handyman business. He can't keep up with all the calls he gets. He's been looking for a helper but can't find the right guy. If they have any skills they want too much money. If they aren't good with their hands he can't use them." She peered into Lloyd's face. "How do I know you don't belong in the second category? I don't. But I think you could try, and it won't cost him to experiment, because I'm gonna tell him you'll take fifty cents under the minimum wage. That'll appeal to him. He's a big cheapskate."

"Oh, listen—"

"No, Lloyd, just shut up and play along for once. I know it'll work out."

Flat on his back, Marevitch was fighting for his life. He grasped at his holster but could not find it.

"Jack, Jack!"

Illumination appeared. When his eyes were half opened he saw it came from the pink lamp on the table at the far side of the bed. To see it he looked past his wife, between her plump nightgowned back and the crumpled pillow; she was sitting up.

"Jack," she cried again. "You're having a nightmare."

He made a sound that was incoherent to himself.

"Come on, Jack, will you wake up, for heaven's sake?"

"I'm awake."

"No, you're not! What day is it?"

"Oh."

"You're still asleep!"

He wanted to argue but could not.

His wife said, "It's three-thirty in the morning."

"I was dreaming, I guess."

"Sure you were."

"I was down, and I couldn't find my gun." He realized with shame that he was literally sniveling. He asked Stephanie for a Kleenex, and she turned and pulled a clump of several from the box on her bedside table. After he had wiped his face he said, "Artie wasn't there at all, and I couldn't find my weapon."

"You're okay," Stephanie said. "You're right here with me."

"I didn't know who they were. All I knew was they had me down and I was helpless."

"Well, it was a dream, Jack, and now it's over."

His pulse had not yet begun to decelerate. The ultimate shame would be to die of a heart attack in his bed, like a civilian.

"Novak is going to put Artie in for a decoration."

"Yeah," Stephanie said. "That's great."

"I told you that already?"

They had been married for eighteen years. She was a good twenty pounds heavier than in the old days, when she had never been exactly slender. But he had always gone for full-figured gals, as what's-her-name called them in those commercials. "Yeah, Jack, and more than once, and I was glad to hear it every time. They don't come any better than Artie."

"If Artie was there, I wouldn't be helpless, see?"

"It was just a dream, Jack. Nobody had you down, and you didn't need to find your gun."

He had continued to lie supine, but now he rolled onto his side to face his wife, who lowered her head to the pillow. He said, "I got to go see this doctor. She's a woman, for God's sake. What's she know about police work?"

"I guess she's qualified or they wouldn't of hired her."

"Are you kidding?" Marevitch asked. "Politics. Like everything the department does."

"I doubt it will do you permanent harm," said Stephanie. "You could just go see what she has to say."

"I've got no choice."

"There you are," said his wife. "That's the way to look at it. It's not your idea. You can't be blamed for it."

Marevitch felt his features contort, as if on their own. "If I had only—"

"No, Jack," his wife interrupted, so forcefully he could feel her breath from a foot away. "You go tell that to the lady doctor, but don't mention it to me again. I don't want to hear how you should of laid down your life for Artie, because what would become of us if you did? And you know I thought the world of Artie. You just go tell the lady."

Suddenly it made sense to Marevitch: he was not allowed to spill his guts to his intimates or colleagues, but a psychologist had to listen to anything you said. "You're right," he told Stephanie.

She raised her pale eyebrows. "You mean it?"

But he did not want to tell her of his new understanding. "Civilians think cops are the ones who give orders. That's wrong. Most of the times cops *take* orders."

"All right, Jack, I'll give you another one: go back to sleep. I'm right here. I won't let anything happen to you."

Moody and LeBeau were at the barren so-called studio apartment where Lloyd Howland had lived for the preceding weeks.

"Zee," said the super, a bulbous-bellied, thick-eyebrowed man named Denarius Glotty, who spoke with an accent neither detective could identify, "iss cleaned op for new guy."

Further questioning established that the place had already found a new tenant, a man who had paid an extra week's rent to Glotty to give the room a thorough cleaning of the kind it had obviously not enjoyed in recent memory if ever. The super also informed them that the new guy was bringing his own people in to install a reinforced door and unspecified security devices, from which the detectives suspected the newcomer was a drug dealer, and they would give the address to Narcotics.

Moody asked whether the previous occupant had left anything behind, anything at all, however insignificant. Glotty failed to recognize the name Lloyd Howland until LeBeau hand-printed it on the page of a notebook, peering at which the super scowled and pronounced a word that sounded like *Hoomar*.

"Racks," he said disdainfully. "Old racks."

"What did you do with those rags?" asked LeBeau.

Glotty had put them and other sweepings into a plastic garbage bag and the bag into one of the garbage cans the contents of which had been collected by a sanitation truck the morning two days earlier.

"How about a knife, a blade of any kind?" Glotty continued to look baffled, so Moody made a sawing motion with an index finger across the knuckles of his other hand. "Something that cuts?" They had already searched the kitchen alcove. "No cooking or eating knives?"

"Used to have farks and knives and alls," Glotty said, popping his thin lips in disgust, "but dey break ebryting or steal."

"So while Howland lived here you didn't provide any kitchen utensils?"

"Hail no."

"What can you tell us about Howland?" LeBeau asked. "What kind of tenant was he?"

"Shart," Glotty answered, holding his hand at a level that would have made Lloyd about three feet tall, though by Moody's assessment, Howland was probably a little taller than the super.

"Did you ever fight with him?" The question had to be repeated and rephrased several times. What Moody meant by it was not confined to physical violence, and that was difficult to communicate to Glotty. Eventually the detectives came to believe that the super had, in the time-honored fashion of such functionaries, avoided the tenants so assiduously that his description of any would not get beyond the generic.

"Place is supposed to be furnished, isn't it?" LeBeau asked. "So what did you do with the furniture?"

Glotty thrust his double chin at the doorway. "New guy donwannit, so took table and chair and frame of duh bett down cellar. But dat faking mattress full of piss!" He roared what were probably curses in whichever language. He wasn't going to carry it anyplace, said he, so he took the sash out of the window and dropped the mattress into the rear areaway.

The detectives immediately went to the window, which had been put back together but remained open and screenless, and they stuck heads out and looked down at a blackened mess.

Moody came back. "You burned it?"

"Naw. Dem kids, dat night."

"Neighborhood youths?"

"No loss," said Glotty. "But maybe landlord will nail my ass. I was gonna just let it dry, then bring back."

Moody and LeBeau went right down to examine what was left of the mattress, which had fallen atop a collection of other rubbish, surely also airmailed from above. Its top cover had burned away entirely, along with all but wisps of the filling and a few knots of the twine that had held the springs, but the sooty springs remained in place. LeBeau squatted and peered into them.

"Bottom cover's still there." He wrinkled his nose. "You can still smell piss even after all the burning."

"Somebody peed on it since the fire," Moody said, sniffing. "Maybe to put it out."

After poking through the other refuse with lengths of rusty metal found on the site and discovering nothing useful for their purpose, Moody stood guard while LeBeau went out to the car and put in a call for a team to come collect the remains of the mattress and test the table, chair, and bedframe from the cellar for the presence of dried blood or whatever else might be pertinent to the case.

Their next job was to get as much help as they could talk the captain into providing them, find the dump for this sanitation district, and look for the plastic garbage bag into which Glotty had placed the rubbish left behind by Lloyd Howland. That there might be nothing therein that could be identified as Lloyd's, let alone anything incriminating, was likely. That among the thousands of similar bags in the dump the one with the Howland-Glotty association could not be recognized even when opened could even be called probable.

14

To reach Molly's cousin Joe's place you went through an alley in the middle of a string of shops that had seen better days, crossed a service road, and were suddenly in an almost rural setting of trees and weeds, amid which sat a one-story structure that had apparently formerly been a cottage but had undergone sufficient degeneration by now, with flaking paint and curled roof shingles, to be called a shack. The underpinnings of the screened-in porch had collapsed at the far front end, slanting its floor in two planes, and the screening was torn in every panel but the one above the crushed support.

Molly stopped her father's car behind a gleaming black pickup truck equipped with an immaculately white cap that covered its bed.

"Look at the difference between his machinery and his house," said she. "That's Joe for you." When they were out of the car, she told Lloyd that the porch had been fallen in for years. "We have to use the back."

The garage at the end of the dirt driveway was also in better condition than the residence. Through its big open doorway could be seen the furnishings of a carpentry shop: floor-mounted power tools, walls hung with shelves or pegboarded hardware, wood in many forms—horizontally stacked lumber, barrels blooming with clustered dowels, giant plywood sheets on end—and unfinished pieces: a doorless cabinet, an inverted table with three legs in the air, the bottomless frame for a drawer.

As they approached the building a loud whine issued from deep within. Sporadically this became a groan or a scream or a howl, all noises made by the same lathe according to which tool was applied to the cylinder of wood revolving on its longitudinal axis or whichever section of the grain was under the blade. The tall skinny goggled man supplying human direction did not hear the arrival of Molly and Lloyd, nor did they exert any effort to gain his attention until he at last switched the machine off, killing the sound instantly. The last of the spray of sawdust ceased to descend a moment thereafter.

"Hey, Joey," Molly shouted at high volume as though over a power tool that had not been silenced.

The man turned, pushing his goggles up. Seen at closer range, he was more sinewy than skinny. He had a long jaw shaded with a faint growth of whiskers, and black hair brushed straight back from a high pale forehead. He seemed to be in his late twenties. He squinted in their direction. He wore jeans and a sawdusted shop apron.

"Hey, Moll!"

"I told you about Lloyd," Molly shouted. In a lower tone she informed the latter, "He can give you something to do and also a flop. I didn't spell it out earlier because I didn't want an argument. You got one now, we can call it off."

"You're really something," Lloyd observed. It would have been embarrassing for him to back out at this point, not to mention that he had no better offers.

Joe shook hands with a limp, diffident grasp. He addressed his remarks to his cousin. "I didn't reckonize you there for a minute. You're all dressed up." A fact that did not seem to please him greatly.

"I'm back behind the wheel again tomorrow A.M.," said Molly, as if in apology. "I got to be going now, to buy food for my dad and then get it all cooked. If I don't leave him enough to heat up, he'll feed himself, and you know what that will be—eggs fried in bacon grease."

Without warning, Joe spoke to Lloyd. "She's a good cook, too."

"I might take the hint and cook you guys something too if you ever clean up that kitchen." She began to step backward. "I really have to get going. You need me for anything, Lloyd, you get Joey to call, huh? Not for the next couple days, though: then I'll be on the road." She was heeling the threshold. "Thanks again, Joey, you're the greatest. Take care, you guys." She was gone before Lloyd remembered he should have said something to acknowledge what she had done for him.

The two men stood there awhile, continuing to watch Molly's departure after it was over. They could not see her car owing to the presence of the van in between. Lloyd believed it was probably his place to say something, since he had been, in effect, imposed upon the other, but nothing whatever came to mind, and finally it was Joe who spoke.

"I guess you're her boyfriend?"

"No," Lloyd hastened to say. "Just a friend." They both continued to look out the doorway of the garage and not at each other. "She's been helping me with some problems."

"That's old Moll," Joe said. "That's her all right. She's got a good heart. You're the first *person* she ever brought over, though; the rest have been animals: dogs, cats, all hurt or sick, and the baby squirrel was an orphan. 'Hey, Moll,' I used to say, 'what am I, a vet?' But the idea was, see, I got this place where there's extra space, and then it bothers her I'm by myself. I had a dog once, but he got out to the main street and was hit by a car. I can't go through that again." At last he turned to look toward if not precisely at Lloyd. "She brings birds that fly into the picture window over at her and Uncle Bob's place. They don't get killed usually, just knocked out. She brings 'em over here." He jerked his elbow. "Right now I got a sparrow she brought last week. It's on the front porch. It got well after a couple hours, but stayed around. All those holes in the screening? You'd think it would find one and fly away. I tried to catch it, to *take* it out, but if you know birds you know that didn't work. So there it stayed, and I give it bread crumbs to eat. Damn if I didn't go there yesterday and the bird flew and landed on my shoulder. How about that?"

"I've never done much carpentry," Lloyd told him, "though I have sold small power tools when I worked at a hardware store. But I can haul things and clean up and so on. I don't mind work. I'm not a charity case."

"All right," said Joe. "That's fine with me. Let me think after I finish turning this table leg. You can go in meanwhile and see where you're gonna stay. It's the front bedroom. It's not much, but there it is. Your sack is already in there." He elucidated. "Molly brought it this morning."

Lloyd had forgotten leaving his backpack behind at the motel. In jail he had been provided with the necessary toilet articles except for a razor. On arrival he had been quickly, coarsely shaved, with an electric razor, by a prisoner-barber, the guard impatiently waiting in attendance.

"Okay," he now told Joe. "Then I'll come back and make myself useful."

Joe had pulled the safety goggles down over his eyes. "You might want to take a look at that bird I was talking about."

Lloyd found the interior of the house, beginning with the kitchen, reasonably clean and in order, at least by his lights, whatever Molly's feeling. Perhaps the main reason for this was that the furnishings were almost as sparse as they had been in the one-room apartment he had lately vacated. A crudely made table, the top of which was but a sheet of unpainted plywood, sat in the center of a sizable kitchen and was accompanied by two folding chairs. Then up a bare hallway, past a room stacked with cardboard boxes, to the bedroom assigned to him, where nothing movable was to be found but an air mattress on the floor beneath the side window, and the blue cotton blanket heaped upon it. He opened the door to the closet and saw his backpack on its floor.

Another window looked onto the slanted front porch. He glanced out but could not see the sparrow. Either the bird was at the other end or had finally removed itself to the thickly foliaged grove of trees between Joe's hideaway and the busy commercial street that was only a hundred and fifty yards away but from which only muted sounds penetrated the greenery.

In his own company for the first time since leaving the cell, Lloyd was convinced he carried about his person the stench of the disinfectant of which the jail reeked, an odor so strong he wondered why Molly had failed to mention it. But then he considered the possibility that the smell might be the work of his imagination, which was perhaps rebelling against the constraints he had placed upon it since learning of the murders. He crossed the hall to the living room, another place barren of furniture. One wall was painted in pale blue, and newly so, with a drop cloth stretched along beneath it and cans of paint and turpentine nearby, alongside a tray filled with a cloudy liquid in which a roller was soaking. This was the source of the odor, which closer up was so different from that of disinfectant that he must have misidentified it for reasons other than a simple matter of smell.

He stepped out the door onto the porch. He still did not see the bird but immediately heard a faint whirr of wings and felt as if a fallen ball of cotton had lodged in the thick hair on his crown. When he gingerly reached up not to seize the creature but to verify its presence, the sparrow flew to the second-highest eminence on the porch, the tip of the handle of a push broom leaning against the flaked white paint of the siding. Its eyes were as bright as those of the squirrel in the park across from the jail, but, being smaller, seemed quicker and more sensitive. Aware that the slightest movement on his part, the crooking of a little finger, could send the bird elsewhere, he stood frozen and exchanged stares with it. Even so, in another moment the sparrow winged from the broom shaft to the collapsed end of the porch and landed on the angled floor, where it plodded about on large but frail-looking claws, beak down, poking between the desiccated boards.

Lloyd was accepted by being disregarded, if not trusted, by a creature so small it had reason to fear all who were larger. Next time he visited the porch he would bring along something the bird could eat: there was no other service he could provide it. For Joe, he could begin by painting the rest of the living room. He yearned to be useful, not simply to submerge himself in a task but to be able to look at an accomplishment when he was done and know it would endure for a while at least no matter what happened to him. He had never yet decided what to think about the dead, whether they could know of the subsequent histories of those they left stranded in life, but if it was possible for Donna to be aware of him, he would like finally to gain the respect she could not possibly have felt for him when alive.

Before the detectives could get far with a search for the garbage bag discarded by Denarius Glotty—LeBeau was still trying by phone to find a Sanitation Department official who could say for certain exactly which dump was used by the trucks that collected along the seven hundred block of Claussen—Larry Howland called Moody.

His voice was plaintive. "Can I get over to my house sometime today?"

"We're up to our necks—"

"Can I ask you something? Who bailed Lloyd out of jail, and where is he? He doesn't have any family but me, and I never knew he had any friends."

Being a professional, Moody concealed his surprise and asked, "How'd you find out about it?"

"I went to see him," said Larry. "Or tried to. I'm over here now, at a phone in the park across from the jail. Can't I find out where he is, at least? *They* won't tell me a thing."

Moody thumbed through his notebook and found Larry's new address. "Got your phone in yet?" Larry gave him the number. "Does he know you moved?"

"I don't know how he could. I haven't told anybody but you."

"And the hotel and phone company and the PO, I bet, and how about your place of business?"

"He's not going to hurt me," Larry said. "I'm not worried. If *you* really are, then you would have notified me he was out, right?"

Ignoring the jibe, Moody said, "Sit tight. We'll get back to you."

LeBeau had just hung up his own phone. He was glowering. "How about this? They haven't—"

"Lloyd's been bailed out."

"By who?"

"Not Larry. That was him on the line. He doesn't know, either."

"Does he want protection?"

"He didn't seem worried," said Moody. "Lloyd probably doesn't know his new address. But we better find where the little bastard is. If he's in the wind again—!"

LeBeau called the jail. After a short conversation he lowered the phone and told Moody, "Martha Sparks, two-oh-six West Etheredge, Clareville." This was an incorporated village north of the city.

"She met the bail? Where's Lloyd?"

"Care of a Joseph Littlejohn." LeBeau was reading from his note. The street was one neither detective had heard of, but the ZIP code indicated the middle of town.

Moody ran the names: neither Sparks nor Littlejohn had a sheet. Down in the car, he took the local street guide from the glove compartment. "Welling . . . K-*fifteen* . . . Welling, Welling . . ." LeBeau meanwhile had started the engine. Moody shook the folds from the map attached to the guide and was tracking a finger across it. "Here it is, Welling. . . . Looks like Lloyd suddenly picked up some friends someplace."

"He's still a creep," LeBeau said.

*   *   *

Marevitch's worst fears were not realized: the female psychologist was neither in her twenties nor was she especially pretty, at least according to his taste. He preferred fair hair, and furthermore Dr. Andrea Gilbertson looked undernourished to him, the kind who ran in the park in the early morning and ran the risk of being waylaid there and raped.

Dr. Gilbertson leaned across the desktop and shook Marevitch's hand in a firm but womanly grasp, not the macho kind, relieving him of another of his fears. She asked him to be seated. He was wearing civilian clothes, a brown serge suit and a shirt and tie chosen for him by his wife.

Dr. Gilbertson asked him to tell her about Artie's death.

"Yes, ma'am."

When he had finished the account, the doctor said, "Thanks. I know that wasn't easy."

"No, ma'am."

"You don't have to address me so formally, and you don't have to sit at attention. This isn't a disciplinary hearing, and I don't have any authority over you. Authority's something police officers worry about a lot, I know. And they should. That's their profession."

"Doctor, if I can just say this before we go further: I'm not in any danger of committing suicide or anything like that. I just regret not doing more to stop Officer McCall from endangering his life."

"What more could you have done?" Dr. Gilbertson asked. "You warned him to wait for the backup."

Marevitch winced. "It wasn't exactly a warning: I don't wanna take credit for that. It was more like a suggestion."

"But he heard you, didn't he?"

"I guess so."

"But he decided he knew better, didn't he?" Dr. Gilbertson said, her eyes bright. "He was a younger man, with less experience, but he knew better."

"I wouldn't put it that way," said Marevitch, staring into his lap.

"But it's true, isn't it?" the doctor asked implacably. "The fact that your partner was killed doesn't change the truth, does it? Officer McCall was taking a risk that shouldn't have been taken."

"Too much is being made of that, too goddam much." Marevitch suddenly seethed with emotion. "How could we have known what was going on inside there without looking? The windows, even the door, were all covered with signs advertising cut-rate prices. Somebody might have been dying inside: we wouldn't know. We don't have X-ray vision, for God's sake."

Dr. Gilbertson nodded briskly. "I think you're right. McCall was doing the only thing he could have done in view of the existing circumstances. He wasn't taking an unreasonable, unprofessional risk. In a situation like that, time counts, doesn't it? Waiting even a minute or two for the backups to arrive could be too long. The perps might be going out the back door or they might be hurting people, even killing them. Every second matters. He was doing his job. He was doing the right thing. Being a cop is always a risky business."

Marevitch's head had been lowered during her remarks. His face came up slowly now. "That's what the perps did anyway: they exited the alley door after they killed Artie. There were just two of us; we couldn't cover the back. The SWATs were only half a block away by then, with a vanload of men with automatic weapons, stun grenades, what-have-you. We didn't hear a sound from inside. They weren't shooting anybody at that point. They had already killed everybody in the store and were probably looting the place. Probably if we had just sat tight they would have been there when the SWATs arrived. They might not even have known we were there: we killed the siren before we hit the neighborhood."

"Well," Dr. Gilbertson said solemnly, respectfully, "then it was *not* the right thing to do."

"No." He was relieved by the admission.

"What you really feel, underneath it all, is resentment. Artie shouldn't have done it. He shouldn't have got himself killed, depriving you of the best partner you ever had."

So as to avoid the ultimate capitulation a while longer, Marevitch squinted at her and asked, "How did you know that?"

"Because a cop's current partner is always the best he's ever had. Am I right?"

"Because you've got to rely on him," Marevitch said in assent, but he was almost annoyed that she knew so much.

Dr. Gilbertson answered his unspoken question. "My dad was a police officer all his adult life, and so was my late husband, though for a shorter time."

Marevitch felt as though a burden had been lifted from him. He looked again at the nameplate on her desk: "Gilbertson." He could not remember anybody with that name. "Our force?"

"My dad was Anthony Accordino."

"Chief of detectives, what, twenty years back? He passed away some time ago, didn't he?"

"He did," said Dr. Gilbertson. "My late husband, Trooper James Gilbertson, was a rookie in the state police. He was shot through the head by a driver he had stopped for a broken taillight. He didn't have a partner."

"Yeah," Marevitch said. "I recall: wasn't that on a state road west of Summitsburg somewhere? About fifteen years ago?"

"Nineteen," said the doctor. "Anyhow, that's why I know more about police work than I learned at college."

"I think you do," Marevitch said with gratitude.

"But what really matters is if you yourself understand how you feel about what happened the other day at the liquor store. I'll tell you how *I* felt when Jim was killed: for a while I hated *him* for letting them do it to him, for leaving me stranded. And I felt so guilty about feeling that way that for a while I thought I might shoot myself with the gun that, goddamn him, he never drew to save his own life!"

The sight of her distress after all these years evoked Marevitch's paternal sympathies. "I'm sorry about that," he said. "I'm real sorry—a young man like that. Artie was young, too. His wife is just a kid, with her first baby on the way." He shook his head vigorously. "But you're right: I guess I feel deep down pretty much like you say. But that's while I'm awake. Sometimes when I'm sleeping it's a different thing." He told her about his bad dream.

Dr. Gilbertson wore a faint, sad smile. "Notice who the victim was in your nightmare."

"Yeah." He snorted sheepishly. "Me."

"That's healthy."

"It is?"

"You're alive, aren't you?"

"I see what you mean. I mean, I think I do."

"My job is a lot simpler than police work," Dr. Gilbertson told him, smiling widely for the first time. "It's just calling attention to the obvious. . . . You'll be okay. I can recommend something to help you sleep, if you want."

"No, thanks. I might get too fond of it." Marevitch moved his tongue across his lower teeth. "Uh, you're going to give me a clean report for the captain?"

"Count on it." She rose and put out her hand. "I'm real sorry about your partner. He sounds like a fine officer and a fine man. He won't be forgotten by those who served with him."

"Thanks, Doctor." He wanted to tell her she was doing her dad proud, but not knowing whether it was his place to make such a comment, he refrained. He could not wait to tell Steph how well it had turned out, but he had no intention of doing the same with Novak, lest the captain think he had had a real problem.

15

"All of a sudden," said the younger detective, the one named LeBeau, "you've got all kinds of friends to bail you out and give you a roof over your head and all."

"Yeah, well." Lloyd did not know what he should say: it was not really a question. He stood alongside the detectives' car. What with the din from Joe's machines out back, it was only by chance he had seen them getting out of the vehicle after a quiet arrival. He had gone to cut them off before they came in. He did not want Joe's generosity to him repaid by the intrusion of policemen.

"Who's Joseph Littlejohn?"

"A guy I know."

"Is that him making that noise back there? Running machinery?"

"He's got a carpentry shop."

Moody had not spoken except politely to say, "Hi, Lloyd." He had not offered to shake hands as he had always done at the jail. Now he suggested that they conduct the conversation in the car. Lloyd was directed to take the front passenger's seat, with LeBeau behind the wheel.

LeBeau asked, "Littlejohn an old friend of yours?"

"He's not exactly a friend. He's a guy I work for."

"What kind of job is it?"

"He needed somebody to be his helper. Clean up, carry tools, and so on."

"So you get out of jail only a few hours ago," LeBeau said dubiously, "over on the other side of town, and right away you've got a so-called job over here."

Moody leaned close to the back of the front seat. "Lloyd, who is Martha Sparks?"

Lloyd was half turned in the seat, but it was difficult to see much of Moody at the angle. The name honestly meant nothing to him, and he said so.

"You *don't know* the woman who went bail for you?" It was LeBeau's harsh question.

"Oh, I'm sorry," Lloyd said. "I guess I forgot her last name. I only heard it once. I never knew her formal first name. She calls herself Molly."

"Well, who is she?"

If they already knew her name, presumably by reason of the bail thing, he could not see how he could keep Molly entirely out of it, but maybe he could restrict their interest in her to the minimum. "She's a girl I met hitchhiking. She's not involved in anything you're accusing me of."

"That's not quite accurate," Moody said. "It's not against the law to put up somebody's bail, but naturally we're interested in the person who did it in your case, when we never heard of her before and you didn't seem to have any friends."

"And now," LeBeau chimed in, "you got two real good ones, it looks like, ready to bail you out on a felony charge, even hire you and give you a place to live."

Lloyd found nothing to reply to here.

Moody asked, "That gun of yours, the one that got you in trouble: you wouldn't have borrowed that from your friend Joe, would you?"

"I told you, I stole it from a store."

"Thing is, all handguns sold by legitimate gun shops have serial numbers which the shop owner keeps a record of," said Moody. "Yours wasn't reported stolen or purchased by any shop in the state."

"I didn't say it was this state."

"What state was it?" asked LeBeau.

"Hey, Lloyd!" The distant shout could only have come from inside the workshop.

"Do you mind?" Lloyd asked the detectives. "Can I just go see what he wants?"

Moody gestured with his left hand. "Why not?" LeBeau turned his head away in apparent disgust.

Joe was standing in the doorway when Lloyd reached him. "Is that a car back there?" His van was blocking most of it from view. "Somebody to see me?"

Lloyd had neglected to ask Molly what she had told Joe of his problems. "They're some guys I know," he said, which was strictly true.

"Oh, sure. Go on back. I didn't mean to interrupt you."

"That's okay. They'll wait. Did you want something else?"

"Your room okay?"

"It's fine."

"It's not much," said Joe. "The whole place needs work, I know that, but I just can't seem to find time for it."

"Maybe I can do something," Lloyd brightly offered. "Maybe I could finish painting the front room."

Joe's mouth was thin-lipped but broad. He used all of it now in a full smile. "Hey, that's an idea."

"I'll start in on it as soon as I get finished with these guys."

"Swell."

Lloyd returned to the car and appealed to Moody. "Since I'm ready to take my punishment for what I did, can't you just let it go at that, without involving anybody else?"

LeBeau asked eagerly, "You're admitting you killed your sister-in-law and niece?"

"Why don't you just stop asking that?" Lloyd said. "You know I'm talking about having the gun."

"Where'd you get it, Lloyd?" This was from Moody.

"I stole it."

"What became of the knife you threatened the produce manager with?" asked LeBeau.

"What's the use of talking to you?" Lloyd said. "You don't listen to anything."

"What *do* you suppose happened to that utility knife?" Moody asked.

"Some cops took it away from me."

"Cops?" LeBeau shouted. "What cops? What are you trying to pull?"

Moody's face was close to the front seat. "Now we're interested," he said. "Tell us what you mean, Lloyd."

Lloyd told them about the aborted shoplifting of the rubber duck.

Even Moody now seemed irritated. "Why didn't you tell us this before?"

"I didn't think of it! They didn't arrest me. They let me go. The manager didn't press charges, so I thought the whole thing was over. It didn't seem important enough to tell you about."

"Lloyd," said Moody, his face still there, "you let us decide what's important. Now try real hard to remember anything else that happened to you that you haven't told us about."

"Was the knife in your pocket when you went to see Donna?" LeBeau asked with a sneer.

Lloyd kept telling himself the detective was only doing a job, but it was hard to keep from disliking him. "You can keep that up as long as you want, but I already told you everything I know." He saw no point in revealing his theft of the bottle from the liquor store. Policemen desperate to make an arrest could not be trusted to make fine discriminations. "If I remember anything else, I'll be in touch."

Moody patted him on the shoulder, but it was not a friendly gesture. "Oh, we won't be far away, Lloyd. You want us any time, just turn your head and look." Both detectives had taken out their notebooks. Moody said, "Let's go over the shoplifting incident again."

*   *   *

In their tracking of the utility knife, which for them took precedence over all else at the moment—the search of the dump was postponed—the detectives soon determined that the patrolmen who had made the confiscation were Marevitch and the late Art McCall, but neither had turned the knife in at their precinct.

"Lot of coincidences," LeBeau said at the wheel as they went looking for the car, which was back on patrol with a new team. "Same two officers: first at the Howland crime scene, then this business with Lloyd, then McCall is killed."

"You get coincidences now and again," Moody said from his wealth of experience. "Guy was a contract killer for the mob. He did something they would never ordinarily do: took a diamond ring off a guy he whacked. You know those pinky rings they all wear? This hit man goes on to the track. He has enough sense not to wear the ring at a place like that, where he might run into somebody who knew the victim, who was another wiseguy, needless to say, so he takes it off and puts it in his pocket—where a pickpocket lifts it off him, takes it to a fence, a fence who's also used by the mob and knows a couple brothers, soldiers in the DeCorsia family, one of them wears a pinky ring and the other's been looking for a match to it, and you know the type: it wouldn't occur to them to go to a legit jeweler and have him copy the piece. So when the surviving brother sees the ring, he doesn't yet know his brother's got whacked, so he buys it off the fence and puts it on his pinky." Moody stopped, remembering way back. "Bill O'Connor was my partner at the time."

"So," Dennis asked, eyes on the road, accelerating. "What happened?"

Moody shrugged. "It's an example of coincidences."

"Well, don't leave it hanging," said LeBeau. "Did the mob guy go ballistic when he found out about his brother?"

"Yeah, he—Hey, there they are." He pointed at a black-and-white patrol car that was slowly turning a right-hand corner in the next block.

LeBeau caught up with the unit halfway down the residential street and beeped. The cars stopped in tandem. Moody got out and went to the passenger's side of the marked vehicle, flashing his shield.

He spoke to the officer riding shotgun, a heavyset sergeant wearing a sandy brush mustache. "Your precinct says this is the unit Marevitch and McCall used?"

The sergeant looked apprehensive. "Yeah, it was."

"We're looking for a blade those officers might have taken off a subject. One of those utility knives, you know? They didn't turn it in, because he wasn't charged, I guess. Could you take a look and see if they left it in the car someplace?"

"Can we just pull up there?" the sergeant asked. He gestured at an open length of curb, up the block.

Moody walked to where the unit came to rest. Both the uniformed officers got out, and he saw that the driver was a large black woman. She was huskier than he and taller than either he or the sergeant. As with all the female officers Moody had ever seen, her uniform had knife-edge creases and her cap was squared away; and her posture, at least when around male colleagues, was as if on parade. The sergeant, on the other hand, was nearing slobdom, with a slack necktie knot and a spongy gut that overhung his pistol belt. The former regulation against excess weight had been abandoned as a consequence of a suit brought against the department by a fat patrolman at the prompting of the usual civil-liberties activists who did what they could to frustrate law enforcement.

"Sir," the black officer asked Moody, "did you want me to do the search or did you want to do it yourself?"

"You'll do a good job," he told her. "A movable-blade utility knife."

"I know what one is," said she. She inserted her large upper body into the car, her substantial navy-blue rear sticking into the street.

The sergeant did not offer to join the search. He planted himself heavily in place on the sidewalk and said, "Checking her out in the unit for a couple days. She's fresh from the Academy."

"Looks like she could handle the perps," Moody said, watching the husky woman in her careful search of her side of the interior of the car, which involved moving the driver's seat forward from the position in which she had put it to accommodate her length of leg.

"Did you know Art McCall?"

"No," Moody told him. "But I've known Jack Marevitch for years."

The sergeant smiled. He pushed his epauletted shoulder, with its attached radio, toward the curb. "She's his new partner."

"She is?"

"He's on leave for a few days."

The big officer left her side of the car and came around to open the door that the sergeant had closed on climbing out. She glanced at Moody as he stepped aside, and he nodded genially at her.

"You know Warren Payton?" asked the sergeant, whose name-plate, above the left pocket, read STOCKMEYER. "Worked with him last year on that torso homicide. One of my men found the canister."

"Yeah. He's in the squad."

The towering rookie pushed herself from the car and triumphantly held an object in the air. It was a utility knife.

After a glance at her nameplate, Moody said, "Good job, Ravens-wood. I hear you're going to be Marevitch's partner. He's a good man. Look after him."

"Yes, sir."

Moody had both Sergeant Stockmeyer and Officer Ravenswood sign a receipt for the knife. The latter's first name was Felicia. He returned to his car, waving his acquisition at LeBeau. When he was inside, he found a plastic bag in the glove compartment and put the knife therein.

The detectives decided to show the tool/weapon to Larry How-

land, and Moody called him and said that if he wanted to get into
1143 Laurel the time was now.

They waited in the car for his arrival, parked in front of the Keller
house. The yellow tape still discouraged the use of the sidewalk before the Howland residence. Larry showed up within twenty minutes
of the phone call. When he started to climb out of his car, Moody
gestured him back inside and went to join him.

"Ever seen this before?" He displayed the sealed bag.

"What is that?"

Moody sniffed. "You don't recognize it?"

"Huh-uh."

"You've never seen one of these?"

"What is it?"

"It may have belonged to Lloyd. Did you ever see it in his possession?"

"I don't think so," Larry said, blinking.

"You never owned it yourself?"

Howland shook his big head. "I wouldn't know what to do with it."

"It's a knife," said Moody, tapping the plastic bag. "The blade's
inside right now. You release it by unscrewing the screw. When the
blade's out as far as you want—you got your choice as to the
length—you tighten the screw to lock it in place. Or am I just telling
you what you know already? No? You wouldn't know anybody who
had such a knife?"

"I wouldn't even know it *was* a knife unless the blade was showing.
I'm not handy with tools. It was Donna who'd fix things that broke,
or she'd try anyway. I never saw her with a knife like that."

Moody shrugged and inserted the plastic bag into a coat pocket.
He left the car, carefully treading across the grassy strip so as to
avoid two piles of dog droppings, one fresh, one old and crumbling.
Larry came around to join him. Moody lifted the yellow police tape
and ducked under, whereas Howland, with his long legs, found a
sagging portion and stepped over it.

LeBeau was waiting for them up the driveway. He now went to the back door and knocked to summon the uniformed officer guarding the premises.

"Carmody," said Moody, reading the name on the plate over the officer's pocket. When they were all inside, he told Howland, "Okay, get your stuff."

Larry led them to the door of the bedroom in which his wife had been murdered, but he halted suddenly on the very threshold and turned back so abruptly that he almost collided with LeBeau. "I can't do it. I can't go in there. I thought I could but I can't." Nothing in his expression revealed the emotion that his actions suggested he was feeling, but that was a valid reason to believe it genuine. He appealed to Moody. "Could you get me a few items?"

But Moody was cold to the request. "You wanted to do this, so do it." Moody could still smell the blood, though the mattress, the box spring, and the bedside rug had been taken away and the floor wiped. The pale dust of fingerprint powder remained on many surfaces, though it was not conspicuous on the off-white woodwork.

Howland took a deep breath and entered the room in a brisk manner that could have been a simulation of decisiveness. He pointed to the sliding doors of the clothes closet that extended across the entire south wall. "Can I go in there?"

LeBeau slid open one panel and made the be-my-guest gesture of spread hands. Howland began to move rustling garments on their hangers along the horizontal rod. "Donna's stuff is all mixed in with mine," he said in a tone more wondering than complaining. "I guess you looked in here."

Neither detective made a response. Moody was standing at the foot of the empty bedframe.

Larry brought out a gray suit. He held its hanger high, at arm's length, for his own appraisal, then moved as if he was about to lay it on the bed while he made more choices. It was apparently only now that he discovered that the bed had no horizontal surface. He gazed helplessly at Moody, who stepped aside. "This is what I should have worn at the funeral, but I didn't have it. . . ."

Moody had had enough of Howland, and he went out to the kitchen, where Carmody was seated at the table. He pointed east, asking, "Does the old lady come over and bother you a lot?"

"Not on my shift," said the patrolman, sagging his chin.

"She's the neighbor."

"I never saw her," said Carmody, unwrapping his thick fingers from the mug-top of the thermos he had brought along. "But the old guy on the other side"—pointing—"he seems to be looking out the window every time I get here, and also when I leave."

"Keller. He's got a lot of time on his hands. I guess he's figured out when the shift changes."

Howland emerged from the master bedroom, arms full of clothes, in a lumbering stride. LeBeau was just behind him.

"Got everything you want?" Moody asked him. "Because we can't keep doing this."

Howland now turned testy. "I'm going to seek legal means to get my house back for me. You've had it long enough. It's not fair." When the detectives escorted him outside, he bobbed his head at the empty driveway and asked peevishly, "When can I get my own car back? How long are you going to keep it? Renting costs a fortune. Why do I have to pay for all this? I'm the one who lost my family." In his sudden agitation of the armload of clothing he carried, a pair of balled socks, riding unrestrained on top of the pile, fell to earth and rolled to the edge of the asphalted driveway.

As they walked down the driveway, Moody looked up and saw Keller at the window. The old man first shied away, letting the curtains swing together, but immediately he parted them again, smiled broadly, and showed an affirmative thumb-up to Moody.

16

Moody was at Walsh's, alone at the bar, but tonight had only nursed a beer for a good fifteen minutes while conversing with Sal Borelli, and now was using the second mug to wash down the first real meal he had eaten in several days, a plateful of brisket with onion gravy, carrots, mashed potatoes, cole slaw on the side. It was not unprecedented for him to go off the hard stuff on occasion, but during the last year or so the intervals between the occasions had grown ever longer. What ruled him this evening was a determination that if Daisy O'Connor showed up again tonight he would not be in the weakened condition in which she had found him here last time.

"Now you're talkin'," Borelli said as the plate of food was hand-delivered by Howie Hersh.

Hersh rested one heavy hand on Moody's shoulder as he leaned in to deposit the dish in place. "I hope they're gonna get serious now an officer's been hit."

The liquor-store gang had begun as primarily the responsibility of the robbery squad, with Homicide assisting since the first clerk had been killed some months earlier, but Moody's allegiance embraced all cops on active duty, even when the criticism came from a former colleague.

"They've been on it," he told Hersh. "What they need is one good break. These bandits do their homework; they don't just pick any store. They pick those with good escape routes, and they pick times when there aren't many customers for that particular store. The times differ, depending on the area. There hasn't been one real description. They wear masks and gloves, so nobody even can be sure of their race. Nobody's lived who heard them talk, for Christ's sake. So far they've killed everybody in every store they've taken."

"How you and Dennis doin'?" Borelli asked, rattling within the ice-cube bin below the bartop.

"Tell you soon, maybe." Moody swirled his mug, foaming the two inches of beer.

"So book the husband and be done with it." Borelli was still doing something with both hands plunged into the ice: maybe looking for some object he dropped in.

"I only wish!" Moody told him. "He gets on my nerves. You remember how that goes."

"Tell you this, though, Nicky," Hersh said behind him, touching his shoulder again, "you want nerves, you run a bar. You tell him, Sal. The regulations, the insurance, the taxes: they drive you nuts."

"Now you're disillusioning me," Moody said, stepping down from the stool. He stayed to swallow the rest of the beer and smack his lips with greater satisfaction than he felt. "Good brewski. I should stick to it. . . . Going to make an early night of it. Funeral's in the morning. I don't want to show up all hung over." He paid his tab with Borelli, winked good-bye to Howie Hersh, went back to the wall-hung phone between the restrooms, and called Dennis' home number.

Crystal answered, in her optimist tone. "He went over the Jackson Mall, Nick. Hardware Is Us got a sale on power mowers. Denny doesn't like the sound of the motor in ours. Listen, he's due back any minute now, and I've been holding dinner. Whyn't you come over and get a good meal inside you for a change? Chicken-in-the-pot, hot gingerbread and, unless you're watching your weight like me, real whipped cream."

"Kid, you got the same figure you had when cheerleading," Moody said. "But *now* you tell me. I just ate."

"I only wish that was true. You live on junk food and your girls are always sluts. You're an awful man, Nicholas. Why do I care about you?"

"It's the wardrobe." She sounded a contralto chuckle, and they exchanged more chaff before he had to depress her by stating the reason for his call. "I forgot to check with Dennis if he's going to the patrolman's funeral Monday morning. Do you know?" Crystal did, and Dennis was. Moody then said he'd pick him up. "Crazy about you, kid," he told her, and she uttered a reciprocal sentiment, along with still another invitation. "Thanks for the great sandwich the other night," he remembered to add. "Next time I come for a meal, *I'm* bringing the steak. Your old man can grill it, but I'm buying." She wouldn't let him take them out for a meal, because little Bridget was a pain in the neck in a restaurant and Crys could not find a baby-sitter she would trust.

Moody drove home and parked his car in the basement garage. He left the elevator at the fourth floor and walked to the adjacent east wing, in which his door was first on the left. He found his key ring and opened both locks. The living room was dark, but light shone from the entrance to the bedroom, off the shallow hall. His weapon was in his hand as he stepped across the threshold. He never forgot to throw a switch when leaving. Anyway, the sun rose before he did in this season, and the bedroom window looked east. He had not needed electric light that morning.

He kept quietly to the carpet, avoiding the obstacles in the darkened living room. He had reached the top of the hallway before he heard a sound, and then it was a slight rasp of labored breathing. He lifted the .38 and quickly stepped into the open doorway.

On Moody's bed a naked man with a hairy behind was violently thrusting himself between the legs of a nude woman, whose face under the tousled short blond hair, eyes squeezed shut, nostrils flaring, pink mouth gasping like that of a beached fish, could, despite the distortion of feature and the incongruous venue, be recognized as Daisy O'Connor's. It took him another moment to identify the man servicing her as Dennis LeBeau, for though Moody had showered alongside his partner, he had never seen him from the rear at such an angle.

"Oh, Christ." It was Daisy, her bright blue eyes wide open now.

What immediately occurred to Moody, absurdly, was how her father, his first partner, would threaten to slap her face when as a child she used the Lord's name in vain. He holstered his gun and left the room.

He was in the kitchenette, rinsing out a dirty glass, when Dennis arrived, wearing the striped boxer shorts his wife bought when there was a sale at Jones & Jones, the expensive menswear shop on Main, and punching into a V-necked T-shirt, so white it seemed fluorescent.

The glass slipped from Moody's wet hand and fell into the sink and did not break, but he seized the rye bottle by the neck and drank straight from it.

LeBeau said nothing, just stood there in his underwear, frowning with exaggerated eyebrows.

Moody swallowed slowly so that his throat would not be overwhelmed.

At last Dennis said, "I should have checked at Walsh's. But I was so damn sure you'd be there all evening."

"Doesn't matter." Moody took another pull on the bottle. "That's why I gave you a key: so you could bring pussy here at your convenience."

"Come on! You're out of order." LeBeau's jaw was thrust forward, but Moody knew this was bluster.

"Come on yourself, *partner*."

"You got it wrong, Nick," LeBeau said. "I was going to tell you, I swear." He had already abandoned his show of pride, but Moody was not pleased by the surrender.

"Have a drink," he said falsely, waving the bottle at LeBeau but not offering it to him.

Dennis waved a hand, whatever that was supposed to mean.

"No?" Moody cried. "Then get dressed and get out. I want some privacy."

"I interrogated Lloyd Howland for a good hour," LeBeau said. "In case you think I came here instead." He gritted his teeth in an odd way. "In fact, we just arrived."

"Oh, forgive me," Moody moaned. "Then go back and finish. I'll be so quiet you'll never know I'm on the premises."

"Gimme a break, Nick."

Daisy came around the corner. She was fully dressed in civilian shirt and jeans, but her hair could have used more combing. She began, "Nick—"

"Good-bye," said Moody.

"Nick, don't be that way."

"Just leave." Moody turned a shoulder to her.

"Come on," said LeBeau, but Daisy pulled her forearm away before he could touch it.

"You're going to hear me out," she cried savagely to Moody. When Dennis asked her again to come along, she said angrily, "*You* go. I'll do better on my own."

LeBeau now displayed sheepishness toward both of them. Daisy was not looking at him, so he shook his head at her back. He trudged toward the bedroom, presumably to find the rest of his clothes.

"How about a drink?" Daisy asked irritably.

"Get a glass," Moody said, taking the bottle with him to the coffee table in the adjoining living room. He dropped himself into the worn armchair that had been one of the few items of furniture he could claim as his own in the last divorce. Its stained upholstery was concealed under an elasticized pink coverlet generically sized, slightly too large for the piece: the gift of one of the few women he had brought home more than once.

By the time Daisy had indeed found a glass and washed it thoroughly and then asked where the clean dish towels were and he said no place, and she went next door to the bathroom and came out, drying the tumbler with a ball of toilet paper, LeBeau was emerging from the bedroom, in his sports jacket and wearing a badly knotted necktie. With a feeble wave at Moody but without a word or gesture for Daisy, he left the apartment, closing the door as if it were a delicate object.

Moody did not offer the bottle to Daisy, so she helped herself. When she leaned over the coffee table just beyond his knees, he smelled her perfume and found it nauseating. But with her small gold earrings, the scent was her only specifically feminine touch. Otherwise it was jeans, the button-down oxford shirt, the white running shoes. She unscrewed the cap, wiped off the mouth of the bottle with the heel of her hand, and poured herself a good three fingers. So she was a boozer as well as a slut.

Moody glared at her. "Where's your weapon?" Even when off duty, all police officers were required by the department to carry a gun unless they were inside on their own premises.

Daisy dropped to the couch and pulled up the right leg of her jeans, having some trouble owing to its narrow taper. Then she rolled down the thick-knit top of the white athletic sock, revealing a small ankle holster that held a diminutive automatic pistol.

He sneered. "What's that, a twenty-five? And by the time you got to it . . ." He leaned across and brought back the bottle from where she left it, near her side of the table, though he was not yet ready for another drink now that she had joined him. He wanted to do nothing in common with her.

Daisy took no notice of his gesture. She sipped some whiskey while breathing deeply. She had her mother's blue eyes and the short, not quite pug nose of her father. She had been a cute little girl, with many freckles that by now had vanished. She was attractive in the way you would like a daughter to be. Any connection between her and sex was too repugnant for Moody to consider.

She began defiantly. "I could say it's none of your damn business, Nick. You're not my father, and anyway I'm well beyond the age of consent—let me finish! I know it's your apartment, but . . ." She put down the glass she had thus far only tasted and put her hands before her. "I know, I know, he's your partner and that makes it different and—"

"No, it doesn't," Moody said. "He's a married man with a family. He doesn't get enough time as it is to spend at home with his wife and kids, and—"

She wailed, "I know, I know!"

"You don't know anything at all," said Moody. "You *think* you know, but you don't."

She lowered her dropping hands and went back to resentment. "*You* should talk. What about your *wives* and *families*?"

"I lost them," he said. "I lost them just this way."

"Not *this* way," Daisy cried. "We're in love. I know you can't conceive of anything between two people but sex, but it's not like that with us."

He shook his head. "You dumb kid. You're saying that guy who just ran home, with his tail between his legs, to eat the dinner his wife's waiting to heat up in the microwave, you're saying that's a man crazy in love? You're saying that guy who'll check first to see if his kids are tucked in, that guy who'll later put on the outside lights to see how his lawn is coming along—"

"You ask him," Daisy cried. "You just ask him if he's in love. You'll see. You're talking about what he has to do to be a responsible person. I love that about him. I want him to be that way. I certainly wouldn't marry him if he wasn't."

"Marry him?" Moody disdainfully blew air from his mouth and looked ceilingward.

Her eyebrows were proudly lifted. "That's what I'm trying to tell you, if you'll only listen. This is not some dirty, sneaky business. It might look that way at this point. But it's not."

"Hell it's not," Moody shouted back. "You're too dumb to see it's the *love* that makes it dirty and sneaky. I'm not going to say so-called love, or what you think is love but isn't, is only infatuation or what-have-you. No, I accept it as love. Remember, I'm an authority on the subject. I won't say I fell in love with every woman I went to bed with, but I did with too many of them, and that was my problem. Sex in itself doesn't mean that much, at least not to a man. But since he's been my partner I've never seen Dennis much attracted in a sexual way to any woman we've run across, and you know most of the married guys on the squad get it on the side, if not from regular girlfriends or one-night stands, then freebies from hookers. Sex is easily available for cops: most of them think it's part of the remuneration, like discounts at stores and free meals." He would never use her dad, his first partner, as an example, but he could have; yet there had never been a better husband and father.

Daisy's lower lip was extended, reminding him more than ever of the little girl she had been. "Yeah, well, that's them, that's you. That's not Dennis: you admit it isn't. He doesn't fool around. He doesn't have to prove he's a man."

"Are you listening to anything I say?" Moody asked. "I just said he wasn't, didn't I? And what I'm saying is: I wish he was. He ought to be. It's normal. And what's wrong with *you* is you're *not* a whore, you're a stupid kid and you don't know what you're doing. You ruin that marriage of his and I'll never forgive you as long as I live." He was aware that it was not much of a threat: since the age of puberty she had shown no interest in having his approval in any regard, not even—and that hurt him—when she was in the Academy. But at least it was a statement from his heart.

She astonished him with quite another response than he expected. "Believe me, I feel awful about that. I lie awake nights. I wish I had the answer." She smiled sadly. "Fact is"—a habitual phrase of her father's, from whom Moody had picked it up years before—"fact is, I was trying to work up the courage to come ask *you* for advice."

He could not remember another occasion on which he was at once so appalled and yet so flattered. For a moment he lost his sense of outrage. But it returned soon enough. "If you're serious, then I'll *give* you my advice. It's simple enough. Just stop what you're doing. Knock it off with Dennis. Tell him to get lost, and go find yourself a single man. Don't try to break up his marriage. And look, I'm speaking just as much for your interests as I am for his wife and kids', because, between you and me, I don't think you *can* break it up, which means you'll be the one out in the cold. Either you'll get dumped eventually or, worse, you'll hang on with false hopes. You'll be the one spends Christmas alone. He'll keep on making more children." From her expression he saw he was hitting the mark. It was cruel but no more than the truth.

She finally took a real swallow of the whiskey. Over the glass, which she held just below her lips, she said, "I should have known better."

"Yeah," Moody made the mistake of saying, "you should have."

"Asking *you* for advice, I mean," Daisy cried, lowering the glass so forcefully that some of the liquid splashed onto the top of the coffee table. "I should have known what you'd say. The great authority on love! With the experience to prove it."

Moody became bitter again. "But my bedroom sure comes in handy."

Daisy had brought along the wad of toilet tissue she had used to dry the glass. She now used it to sponge up the spill of whiskey. Then she asked, in a resentful tone, "Why *does* he have a key?"

"He's my *partner*," Moody said soberly. "If I drink too much some night and fall down and hit my head on something, he's the only one would come looking for me. But it's also a place for him to catch up on his sleep when the baby's screaming all day and night at home, or have a quiet beer and watch a game if that leech of a brother-in-law comes visiting. He can't stand anybody in Crystal's family, for that matter. This is his hideout."

"That's all okay, but you object that he sees *me* here."

Moody looked at the dirty, curtainless window behind her head. "Does what you just said make any sense?" He lowered his eyes to her. "You're putting those things on the same plane? I offer my partner a place to catch a nap or whatever, to make himself at home—you're saying I should cheer him on when he goes to bed with *you?*" He sneered. "When you came around the bureau the other day: that wasn't to apologize to me, was it? You came to return his glasses. He left them behind last time he was with you. But you two would have left together if you had been here. So where'd he leave the glasses, in your *car?* Where you *parked* somewhere? Don't you have any decency at all? What in hell has happened to you?" Tears were welling from her eyes. Maybe he had gone too far.

She sprang to her feet. "I should have known better. You can always be counted on to let me down."

He too stood up. "What does that mean?"

"I wouldn't be caught dead here again," she said in a voice that though of moderate volume had the intensity of a scream. "And from now on, it's only professional between you and me."

"That's what it ought to be between you and Dennis. Your superiors will be all over you if they find out."

"You going to tell them?" Rage altered her features: he might not have recognized her on a photograph taken at this moment. "You son of a bitch."

"That's enough," Moody said quietly. "Get out of here."

"Gladly," Daisy said. "Soon as I get my linen."

"What?"

She had already started toward the bedroom. Without turning she shouted, "*Our* sheets. Think we'd use those filthy things of yours?"

*   *   *

Joe made a tasty supper, crumbling hamburger into a skillet and adding a block of frozen mixed vegetables and, once the latter had thawed and the meat lost its pinkness, a couple of shots from a chili-sauce bottle.

"This is really good," Lloyd told him at the kitchen table, where they were eating off plates of porcelainized metal spatter-colored in blue and white.

Joe chewed until he could swallow the food in his mouth. "I guess it's healthy," he said at length. "Though all the flavor comes from the chili sauce, I guess. . . . How about the plates? Molly give 'em to me. I generally ate right out of the pot or even the can. Her and my uncle Bob used them camping, I guess, and then came his accident and they don't go any more. Anyway, she brought 'em over here." He gave Lloyd a defensive glance. "She's always getting after me to clean up my act." He went for bread from an almost exhausted loaf, penetrating the deflated package up to mid-forearm. He withdrew and held up the piece. "You want this? There's only the heel left."

"No, thanks," Lloyd said. "I still have some."

"You're doing a good job in the living room. God knows when I would of got around to it."

"I'll get going on the second coat after supper."

"Well, it might feel dry," Joe said now, with the surer fix of eye he employed when speaking professionally, "but it's best to give it overnight at least, especially with this humidity." He picked up his empty plate, which he had polished to a high sheen with bread. "That reminds me, I got some lumber I wanna bring in the shop before it rains."

"It's going to rain?" The afternoon had been unconditionally sunny, so far as Lloyd had been able to see through the living-room windows.

Joe showed his extra-white front teeth in his version of a grin. "I always get old Molly with my weather predictions. I don't take 'em from the TV. I get 'em from the feel of the wood. She don't believe me that if you work with wood all the time like me, you can feel the moisture content. But you can." He took his gleaming plate to the sink and ran hot water across it. He turned, still grinning in the chipmunk manner. "But I'll admit I ain't always right. Just because there's a lot of moisture in the air don't necessarily mean it'll rain."

Lloyd carried over his own plate. "Let me clean up here and then I'll be out to give you a hand."

The dishwashing was soon completed, involving as it did only one skillet, two plates, two forks, a spoon, and one ceramic mug and another of plastic. There was a crumb or two on the table and a few on the floor. In a closet Lloyd found an old broom, its head slanted from use, and a cracked plastic dustpan. He was about to put them to work when a telephone rang.

By the time he located the instrument, on the wall beyond the refrigerator, the ringing had stopped. But a moment later he heard a shout outside and went to the door. Joe was waving from the entrance to the shop.

"Pick it up! She wants to talk to you."

Lloyd returned to the kitchen extension. Molly was on the line. "So how's it goin'?"

"Okay. Fine." He heard the sound as Joe hung up the workshop phone. "Your cousin's a nice guy."

"He feed you?"

Lloyd told her about the supper, and when she groaned in mock pain, he protested, "No, it was really good!"

"But then," Molly said gleefully, "what do you know? You never eat anything."

"I cleaned my plate! I was hungry for a change." He told her about painting the living room. "Of course, it was just a start. I got the second coat to do, and all the trim. . . . Listen, I saw the bird you brought over. He's recovered. He can fly all right, but he doesn't want to leave."

"Sounds like you're doin' all right," said Molly. "I'm glad to hear that. Now Joe's off the phone I can tell you he's not the easiest person to get along with. Hell, I don't care if he *is* listening. I've told him to his face: he's too bossy. That's why he never found a girl who would marry him."

"Funny," Lloyd said. "I thought he was easygoing."

"To another *guy*. If you were a girl you'd see. He'd be running everything you did. You see how he acted when I showed up in my good clothes? I guess I was supposed to ask *him* what to wear?"

"The position I'm in," Lloyd said, "I couldn't be critical no matter what."

"Oh, I'm not criticizing. I'm just making a point. Joe's my favorite relative. Trouble is, he knows it. Well, I got to get back to the rig. I'm at Dexter. Remember? Where we got the fill-up on the way out? I was wondering about how you were getting along, that's all."

"I'm fine," said Lloyd.

"I'll seeya day after tomorrow, if you want."

"I'll be here," Lloyd said. "Don't worry about that: I'm not going to lose your bail for you."

"Hey, come on! That's not what I mean." She snorted. "I hope you ain't gonna pick up any of old Joe's sarcasm."

Lloyd suddenly felt concern for her. "I hope you're going to be careful out there. Because of me, you don't have your gun any more."

"Oh, you had your reasons," said Molly. "I'm sure of that. And it's nice to have you thinkin' about me. But don't worry: I got me a double-barreled sawed-off my dad used to carry in the rig before he got the three-fifty-seven."

"Oh," said Lloyd. "Oh, good. Well, thanks a lot for calling, and get back safe, Molly."

"It's real nice of you to say that. I'll seeya, Lloyd."

Lloyd quickly swept the floor and then went out to join Joe, whom he found at a stack of boards behind the shop. The back door to the building was narrow, so care had to be taken to guide the planks through. Lloyd could have carried more than two at once, since they were light though long, but Joe told him two were the optimum number that could be easily negotiated through the clutter inside, en route to the place where there was room for restacking. Molly might have called this bossy, but it was a sensible instruction: it was Joe's shop and Joe's lumber.

Only when the task was completed—soon, with the two of them—did Joe ask about the phone call. "She ain't in some trouble, is she?"

"Oh, no," said Lloyd. "I'm sorry, I should have told you. She was just calling to say hi. Nothing's wrong."

Joe leaned against one of his machines. "She was probably worried how I was treating you. She don't have a high opinion of the way I operate."

"She thinks the world of you."

"She does?" Joe showed his broad smile. "Well, I do of her too, but we always fight a lot. I worry about her out on the road by herself, and she sees that as a lack of confidence."

"I guess you know she carries a gun."

"That three-fifty-seven mag is way too big for her," Joe said, his smile converting to a downturn of disapproval. "But you can't tell her nothing. She can't shoot it worth a damn, you know. Uncle Bob's got a lot of land back of his place up there, and her and me been out back with that gun, and she can't hit a can at fifteen feet. But she's got to be the tough guy. Somebody her size oughta carry a thirty-two at most."

"She's got a sawed-off shotgun on this trip."

"Oh, for Chrissakes," Joe cried. "That'll knock her on her butt!" He lowered his long head and shook it at the concrete floor. When his face came up his mood was changed. "Say, Lloyd, I don't want to be outa line here, but I been thinkin'. I know that you say her and you are just friends, and I ain't calling you a liar, but she never brought anybody else around here before. I don't think she even dated much. . . . Now my uncle Bob's laid up, she don't have anybody else to look after her, so I guess I been elected. So it's me who's got to ask you: just what are your intentions with regard to this young girl?"

"She's just been nice to me," said Lloyd. "I don't know why."

The statement did not sit well with Joe, who scowled and asked, "Just how nice you mean?"

Lloyd hastened to clarify. "Not in *that* way! She's just been kind, like bringing me over here." He was not ready to say more unless he was pressed further.

"You don't know why?" Joe asked. "She's got a big crush on you, that's why."

"I don't know about that," Lloyd said, looking away. "You said yourself how nice she is to everybody and everything."

"Well, you ought to see the difference. . . . She's awful young."

"We're the same age, so far as that goes," Lloyd said. He brought his eyes back to Joe's. "Look, I haven't touched her. I'm not interested in her that way."

"You got trouble with the law, right? Those guys that came today, they were cops."

Lloyd nodded and said nothing.

"You don't have to tell me why or how," Joe went on, showing the angle of his sharp jaw, "but I done some time myself as a juvenile offender, not hard time but in a correctional facility, see, but I still remember what cops look like. It's like swimming—you don't forget. I still don't feel good when I see 'em, and I've kept my nose clean for years. They were right to bust me. Armed robbery, at fifteen? Lucky for all concerned it was just a pellet gun. If I could of got a real piece, I was so cocky I might of killed somebody who called me. So the cops probably saved a life or two, including mine. That's what they're supposed to do, right? But I tell you, I think what they do is right, but I still can't stand the sight of them. I don't like to be reminded, I guess. That's my problem, not theirs."

"My problem," said Lloyd, "isn't the police." Nor was it as simple as self-pity, much as it might have seemed so to Donna. "You're right: they're only doing their job." He was suddenly and briefly enlightened. "I envy them." He quickly glanced around the shop. "Have you got anything more for me to do out here? How about sweeping up?"

Joe raised a narrow eyebrow. "I don't think Molly would like me using you for just flunky work."

"Don't worry about her," Lloyd said. "I can still speak for myself. When it comes to being a flunky, that's the only work I know how to do."

"She warned me you might say that."

"Because it's true."

"Yeah," said Joe, smiling wryly. "That's just the way I used to be. But at the same time, along with this no ability at anything, I had a real high idea of myself. I thought I was way better than everybody else—and not because of not having a chance to show what I could do or whatever. No, I thought I was superior because I was useless." He laughed with an open mouth, looking foolish as he expressed wisdom.

"You were awfully young then."

"Old enough to try to rob a discount beverage store." Joe rolled back his upper lip with a little finger. "Three in front are false. Guy came out from behind the counter, knocked the pellet gun out of my hand, and hit me so hard in the mouth that he knocked out three teeth. Lucky for me they have to destroy all juvenile crime sheets. Guy who knocked my teeth out, for some reason he took pity on me, probably due to my age, and he used to come see me at the correctional facility. He sure didn't bear a grudge. I stayed a little cocky till the time when I told him he wouldn't of jumped me if the gun was real, and he says, 'It *wasn't?*' Till then he didn't know it! I asked him why would he risk his life to save what was in the cash register, and he said, 'Because it was *mine*. You didn't have no right to the money I worked for. I didn't steal it. You're not gonna take it from me without a fight.'" Joe pushed himself away from the machine on which he had been leaning. "When I got out, he give me my first job, and I kept my nose clean because I was scared of him, not of getting beat up or anything: I was scared he'd think less of me if I screwed up. I couldn't stand having a man like that think of me as a punk."

The situation was familiar to Lloyd, but there were significant differences when the person whose esteem you sought was a woman and you were furthermore obstructed by taboo.

17

If LeBeau attended the funeral for Patrolman McCall, he was not among the contingent of detectives, in uniform for the occasion, at either church or cemetery. Daisy O'Connor would have been in another division than Moody's, amid the large turnout from the city force, and he might not have seen her anyway.

Aside from the front pews occupied by McCall's relatives, the white-haired mayor, and accompanying officials, the nave of St. James's was solid blue.

At Brookside Cemetery the local cops were joined by a variegation of visiting officers from other jurisdictions, county sheriffs in khaki, state troopers in seam-striped breeches and campaign hats, patrolmen from big cities and little villages, and there were certain shoulder patches from other states, not all of them contiguous.

After the firing squad and the bugler had done their respective duties and the casket was lowered into the earth, Moody decided now was not an opportune time to say a word of condolence to Jack Marevitch, whom he had known since way back, even if he could have located him within the massed uniforms, so he sidled through the rear elements of the crowd, found his car after a brisk walk, and managed to get away before the traffic could clog the exit route.

Today was when he and LeBeau, assisted by whichever helpers the captain would provide them, were to search for the plastic garbage bags in which the super had discarded the rubbish from Lloyd

Howland's studio apartment. The dump had at last been established as the Department of Sanitation's No. 3, out where Highland became Route 1-B. It was the newest and largest such facility. Thinking of its vast acreage could make the heart fall, though there was some small solace in the precise identification of the quadrant used exclusively by the trucks that collected from the neighborhood of the shabby building in question. This area was probably no more than a quarter mile in each direction. The DOS would lend them coveralls, rubber boots, and heavyweight protective gloves, but they would be on their own if they wanted respiratory masks.

Dennis was at the desk across from his by the time Moody arrived at the bureau after a stop home to shed the uncomfortable uniform, still painfully tight at the waist even after the latest alterations.

"I would have been late for the church service," LeBeau explained, with eyes that sought more than usual from his partner. "I could have gone to the cemetery, I guess, but I thought I'd get some work done here. Lab didn't find any traces of blood on the utility knife."

Moody made no acknowledgment either in voice or gesture, though he had met his partner's glance straightforwardly. He sat down now.

"What I was thinking about the dump," LeBeau went on, "is if we could get the garbage-truck guys to give us some idea of how big a typical day's haul is. If we just had an estimate of how much they haul per collection, per neighborhood, we might be able to figure out about where the stuff from last Tuesday would be dropped." He tapped a pencil. "Some specific idea, you know? I mean, we got the general area, but if there was some way to zero in . . ." He stared across at Moody. "You got a right to be steamed about the apartment. I grant you that."

"I don't give a shit about the apartment."

"Sure you do."

"Don't tell me what I care about, goddammit!" Moody shouted. "You don't know me that well."

"Have it your own way," LeBeau said stoically. "What you don't have a right to be is a judge of my private conduct. You're not Crys's father."

"I'd rip your guts out if I was."

"And you're not Daisy's father, either, though you might think you are."

"In other words, I'm not supposed to have any reaction at all?"

LeBeau looked away. "I didn't mean that."

"You're going to have to decide what it is you do mean," Moody informed him. "You're a mess, Dennis."

LeBeau reared back. "That's your theory, is it?"

"Well, look at yourself."

"Look who's talking."

"I don't set myself up as an example," said Moody. "Except as something to be avoided."

LeBeau grimaced. "You might just listen to my side of it. It's real, Nick. I'm not just playing around. I never did that. I'm in love with her. But that doesn't mean I don't also love Crys and the kids. I can't just walk out on them. You're right. It *is* a mess."

"Listen to me for a minute." Moody dropped the indignant tone. "This is an idea I came up with. Before you do anything you'll be sorry for, just think about maybe trying this. You and, uh, her"—he could not bring himself to utter Daisy's name and so acknowledge their illicit connection—"why don't you just try this: set a time limit on it, see. Like as of a certain date, if you still feel as you do now, then see what happens. Say like the end of the month. That should give you time enough to make an intelligent—"

"What are you talking about?" asked LeBeau. "Did you hear what I just said? I'm in love, Nick."

Moody shrugged. "Yeah, and this is my answer. Think about it. That's all I ask. Take a little time."

"Don't you think I've *been* thinking about it?"

"I just now told you."

"Not what you said," LeBeau cried. "I've been thinking about the situation. I can't sleep because of it. . . . How in hell can I tell Crystal?"

"Don't," said Moody. "Like I say, give it more time."

Dennis leaned forward. Moody had never before seen him in a beseeching role. After the momentary novelty, it was degrading. "Nick, you don't. . . . Look, it's okay if you disapprove. Hell, you can say what you want about me, I probably deserve it. But I was just wondering if *you* could say something to Crys. It might be easier for her that way. She thinks the world of you. You know, she was always on your side when it came to Dawn. She never could stand her."

He was referring to Moody's second wife. This was as good an example as any of how naive Dennis was in matters concerning the relations between the sexes. Moody didn't want to hear criticism of Dawn from anyone else: he had married her. He shook his head at his partner. "Man, you're hopeless. I'm supposed to explain what I don't understand myself?" After a pause he said, "I think it's wrong. I think it's stupid. I don't think it's love. I think it's crap. I'm not going to say anything to Crystal. I'm not going to say anything more to your girlfriend, and I'm never going to mention it to you again, you can count on that. From now on, our partnership is strictly professional."

LeBeau's face hardened. He leaned so he could get a hand in his pocket. "Here's your keys." He threw them clattering over onto Moody's desktop.

Moody dropped the keys into the waste can at his knee. He sneered across at LeBeau. "I already had the locks changed." He stood up, adjusting the gun clipped to his belt. "Come on, let's go to the dump."

Lloyd had a good night's sleep on the air mattress, though it was not as comfortable as the prison bunk. He got up when a shaft of bright sunlight reached his face: long after dawn, for the sun had to climb over the topmost trees in the tall grove at the front of the property.

Having assumed that his host would be an early riser, he was surprised to hear a snore issuing from beneath the heaped blankets on Joe's bed as he passed the open doorway en route to the bathroom.

Lloyd breakfasted on instant coffee and dry graham crackers from a half-depleted box found in a kitchen cabinet. He dunked the grahams in the coffee mug and usually succeeded in getting the wetted portion to his mouth before it fell off, an exercise he had not practiced since childhood. After washing and drying the mug and cleaning away such crumbs as had fallen, he went to the living room.

He had painted about half the longest wall before Joe finally appeared, in jeans and T-shirt, but barefoot, fists grinding into eyes, gaping, still not wide awake.

"Lloyd! I forgot you were here." He squinted. "You do all that already this morning? Takes me a while to get going." He yawned, crucifying his sinewy arms. He went closer to the area of new paint, peering. "You done a real nice job cutting in around the molding. Do that freehand? Not bad." He gave Lloyd the once-over. "I was gonna say you can borrow a pair of coveralls, but I don't see a drop of paint on you."

"When you're wearing the only clothes you got, you're careful," Lloyd said. "Look, I owe you some explanation—"

"No, you don't. Molly—"

"Picked me up hitchhiking. She's known me for all of two days. I'm under suspicion of murder. They're just looking for enough evidence to charge me."

Joe studied his face for a while. "Are they gonna find enough?"

"That's just it. *I don't know.*"

Joe's right eye became heavy-lidded. "Lemme get this straight. You don't know if they'll find it, or you—"

"I don't know whether or not I'm guilty." Lloyd had managed to say something that only a moment before he could not have imagined putting into words for another person. "I was drunk, drunker than I ever had been in all my life. I was all upset about losing still another job. I can't remember what I did for half a day and a whole night. All I know is I woke up next morning in a pool of piss and my face had this scratch." He touched his cheek. "It's healing up. It looked a lot worse originally."

"Nobody saw you during this time?"

"The last I knew, I was home. I was still there when I woke up, but what if I went somewhere meanwhile and forgot about it?"

Joe nodded. "Was this in town here? My TV's been broke for a while."

"Molly hasn't mentioned anything?"

"Naw." Joe chuckled, but as a courtesy, not in humor. "I guess she was worried I wouldn't let you in if I knew your story." He waved a hand toward his guest. "Sometimes I get to working on a job back there and don't see anybody for days in a row. Couple years ago there was a war that was over before I heard it started. I was doing some inlaying, every piece of it hand-cut, and if you don't keep your mind on it every second, you're in trouble, at least if you're me. I can't think of two things at once."

In a rush, lest he break down before he was finished, Lloyd told Joe as much as he knew about the murders, which he realized only now was not much. He had avoided learning the details: he saw that all he had really cared about was his own deprivation.

"I don't know," said Joe when Lloyd was done, taking a moment for conspicuous thought, with furrowed forehead. "Wouldn't you of gotten some blood on yourself?"

"It looked like my shower was used sometime during the period I can't remember." Lloyd chewed his lower lip. "There was a T-shirt on the shower floor that looked like it might have had some blood on it. It was pinkish and soaking wet, like some attempt had been made to wash it. Maybe the blood came from the cut I *maybe* got when shaving."

Joe stared at him. "Why would you of committed these murders, Lloyd?"

"Not for any sane reason."

"You mean you might be crazy?"

"It happens, doesn't it? People lose control and do something terrible for no reason?"

"I'm a carpenter," said Joe. "I guess if you really want to find out, you ought to go to somebody who specializes in that trade."

"A psychiatrist?"

Joe shrugged with his long arms. "Whoever it takes. . . . I mean, that is, if you really want to find out."

"I don't know if I've got the guts."

"Well, you can always just wait around for the cops to pin it on you," said Joe. "If they got the idea you're the one, they'll be glad to nail you. It's their profession, you know?"

"I've never had a profession," Lloyd said. "I've never got to where things begin to connect and make sense so that next week you can look back and see where you've been and how you got there and what you have accomplished. . . ." He bent to pick up the roller. It had absorbed too much paint. He ran it over the corrugations at the high end of the tray, to squeeze off the excess.

"Hell," said Joe, "there's no hurry about that."

"I'd like to get it done before I have to go back to jail." But suddenly he dropped the roller and straightened up. "Look, if you didn't know all of this about me, then I'm here under false pretenses. You thought I was just in some kind of minor trouble with the law?"

Joe spoke in mock horror. "Yeah, I'm not going to forgive that Molly, bringing around somebody like you, might cut my throat while I'm sleeping!" He grew sober. "You *could* be crazy and dangerous. Some people are, I'm told, and others around them don't

find out till it's too late. But maybe *I'm* nuts—I got a hunch about
you. You worry too much about what don't matter—no, that's not
right, either. It *does* matter, but not in the way you think. . . . I only
wish I could say what—" He frowned, then brightened. "It's what's
necessary. That's the only thing to worry about."

"How do you decide what's necessary?" Lloyd asked. "That's my
problem."

"I guess it's between what you can live with and what you can't
live without."

"I guess that's it." Lloyd reached down again for the roller and
brought it up to the wall.

Marevitch assumed that the funeral would be the worst experience
that remained for him to survive, but he was wrong. There really
was a useful purpose in such ceremonies, which transformed what
was personal and weak and limited into the institutional, with all its
resources and possibilities. Though a functional atheist, he could
nevertheless agree with Stephanie, who was not, that Artie somehow
was able to look down and see the display and be made proud.

Afterward a couple of dozen members of the department closest
to Art McCall, and their families, gathered at the Marevitch home,
where Stephie, assisted by their daughter and several other cops'
wives, put out a buffet of baked ham, fried chicken, meatballs, and
accompaniments. Jack directed people to the tub full of beer cans
and melting ice cubes, back on the kitchen counter. Big bottles of
soda were on hand for the kids, and Marevitch saw that the teenagers
stuck to the sanctioned beverage and did not grab a brew, though
he was under no illusions that any, including his seventeen-year-old
daughter, were teetotalers when not under surveillance—or virgins
either, for he had spent his own teen years getting drunk and looking
for tail, which did not mean he would tolerate the same in those who
were youths now he was an adult: that was the way standards were

maintained, as many elements of society had forgotten to their peril or, worse, had never learned.

His new partner, Patrolman Felicia Ravenswood by name (he had yet to meet her face to face), being one of the cops who had to stay on duty while the others were at the ceremonies, crime taking no holiday, therefore could not come to the house and give his wife a chance to look her over, as he knew Stephie was anxious to do despite her pretense of indifference. His own concern was much greater, but he could not yet admit as much even to himself. He was still capable of very little except to point the way to the beer. He had not yet even been able to deliver the carton of Artie's possessions, taken from the locker, to McCall's twenty-three-year-old widow, married a little more than two years and seven months pregnant with their first child.

There was a moment when he caught Stephanie's attention, and she worked her way through the throng to join him inside the kitchen, away from the trafficked doorway.

"I got to get Artie's stuff to Rosie."

His wife was a stately figure in her black dress, which trimmed her weight to almost what it had been a decade earlier. "Bring it along when you run her home."

"She don't have a ride?"

"She came over with the Monaghans, but I think you wanta give her a lift back to her mother's."

"Me?"

"Who else?"

"Well, if she's gonna stay at her mother's, I can't give her Artie's stuff," Marevitch said, wincing.

"I don't know about that," Stephie told him. "But it's time you said something to her, Jack. You simply got to."

A burly figure passed through the nearby doorway and stopped at Marevitch's shoulder to pat him and say to Stephanie, "Hiya, sweetheart." To Marevitch he said, "Jack, there was a lieutenant of detectives there all the way from Nebraska!" It was Sergeant Glen Heinz from the precinct. "He was in plainclothes. Hooper told me."

"Did you see Novak?" Marevitch asked him.

Heinz's big brushy mustache hid his long upper lip. He was proportionately no heavier than Marevitch but four or five inches taller. "The captain was called away, I believe."

"I was hoping maybe he could present the medal to Rosie at the ceremonies," Marevitch said. "Though I guess they do that at another time and not the funeral. But when I think she ain't got nothing to take home but that folded flag, you know . . . ?"

Heinz capped his shoulder with a large hand. "You got to hear this sooner or later, Jack. Captain Novak got turned down. He tried, but the chief won't buy it."

"That son of a bitch," Marevitch said. "*He* was there, right alongside the mayor and the commissioner, for the TV cameras."

"He says they reserve it for valor." Heinz rolled his eyes. "He says what Artie did was a mistake." He applied pressure to Marevitch's shoulder. "Can't blame the captain. He tried."

"Yeah," Marevitch said, balling his dangling fists. He turned to get Stephanie's support, but she had left. He urgently addressed Heinz. "Ain't there some way I can appeal? *I* was the one who saw the whole thing. Where's *he* getting his information from?"

The sergeant's jowly countenance showed alarm, his eyes growing smaller. "Now, you don't wanna question a decision at the top, Jack. That won't do you or Artie's memory any good at all. Pierce didn't get to be chief by changing his mind once it's made up."

"He got to be chief by sticking his nose up the commissioner's ass," Marevitch said. "We all know that." He strode away from Heinz, whose stripes were suddenly offensive, though they did not usually bother him much despite his four and a half years' seniority over the sergeant. He went through the dining room, looking for Rosie McCall. From bitterness he took sufficient courage to face her at last.

He found her in the living room, sitting quietly at the far end of a sofa otherwise occupied by two other women, who held filled plates in their laps. In Rosie's was the triangle of the folded American flag, taken from Artie's casket prior to the lowering of it into the grave. Above the flag swelled her belly. People came and went to her, yet she was utterly alone in the crowd. Despite her condition she looked smaller and younger than usual. Her fair skin, which tended to burn red in the summer sun, was paler than ever by contrast with the unrelieved black of her clothing.

She saw him, cried, "Jack!" rose with an effort, and came into his arms as far as her pregnancy would allow. She was not that much older than his daughter and slighter in every dimension.

"I can't hug you tight as I want," Marevitch said into her pink scalp. "Don't want to squeeze Artie Junior."

She pulled back an inch or two and said contritely, "Jack. Forgive me, Jack. I shoulda come to you before. I know that. I know what you meant to Artie." *She* was apologizing to *him*.

"Stephie told you, didn't she? I was real sick last night. I couldn't get to the wake. I was throwing up all—Listen, I got Artie's stuff. From the precinct, ya know. Extra shirt, civilian sweat outfit, sneakers and all." The workout clothes dated from when, two years before, Art had done a plainclothes job on temporary loan-out to Narcotics because the drug dealers wouldn't recognize him: he jogged around the park where the buys were made.

Rosie tried to smile. "I forgot about that. He hated exercise. You know that, Jack. He said he got enough climbing in and out of the unit."

"He always stayed in good shape," said Marevitch, wagging his head. "He was a natural athlete. He didn't need no extra jogging. I was sure glad to have him along when we had to chase some mutt through the alleys: Artie did all that. Me, I drove the unit around the block." He patted his gut. "I got almost as much here as you, Rosie. I took a lot of heat from your old man on that subject. 'Come on, Jack, not *another* doughnut, for pity sake!' " McCall had of course used stronger language, but Marevitch revised it for the occasion.

"You were his idol, Jack. Most people learn to be cops, but 'Jack,' he always said, 'you take Jack, he was born to it. With him it's an instinct. You can't ever learn it like him,' he said."

One of the other occupants of the couch got up and pressed past them. She told Rosie she would call her in a day or so to come over. Marevitch did not know which of his colleagues to associate with this woman and asked Rosie.

"Marsha Hagenson . . . Ron Hagenson, the Fourteenth," naming the precinct in which Artie had served before joining Marevitch's Sixth.

"You want I should run you home now, sweetie?"

"I'll be staying with my mom for a while. I might sell the house after the baby comes, Jack. I don't know if I can bear to look at it anymore." They had only had the place, a fixer-upper, for a little over a year. Artie had spent most of his off-duty time working on it. Once or twice Marevitch had helped him out, bringing in big panels of Sheetrock from the home center, in a pickup they borrowed from Charlie Haseltine, a fellow patrolman who moonlighted as a handyman. Rosie made a wry face. "There's also the mortgage payments. I don't know if the benefits will cover them."

"Not time to worry about that," said Marevitch. "We'll get you home now to your mom." He left her at the couch, where she picked up the folded flag again. He went to ask Stephie for the keys to the family car: easier than searching forever for his own set.

But when he found his wife near the rented coffee urn, replenishing the supply of Styrofoam cups, he gave vent to the indignation he had hitherto suppressed for Rosie McCall's sake. "They're not giving Artie the medal." He clenched his teeth at her. "I'm turning my shield in tomorrow morning first thing. Don't try to talk me out of it." Someone in blue came for coffee. Marevitch turned his back on the man without identifying him, turned back when he was gone. "I'm not gonna put up with it, Steph."

"It's your call, Jack. You do what you gotta do."

"You agree with me, don't you? I had Novak's word."

"Yeah, you told me."

"I mean," Marevitch said, moving his chin from side to side, "what else can I do? He gave me his word, Steph. What kinda man would welsh on that?"

"If he's the one doing the welshing."

"What's that supposed to mean? You know something about this matter?"

"No more than you."

"Heinz?"

"He knew you were mad," Stephanie said. "He didn't want you to blame *him*."

"I never blamed him," Marevitch said disgustedly. "Goddammit."

"It's a lousy thing, Jack."

Marevitch hung his head. "I'm not gonna lose my pension over it. Artie wouldn't want that. I did what I could." Tears blurred his vision. "That's the second time I let him down."

"Rosie don't think so," Stephanie said. "I mean, about the liquor store. She didn't know about the medal business, and for God's sake, don't tell her!" Stephie on occasion could get fierce.

Marevitch blinked. "All right, woman," he mock-growled. "Gimme them car keys before I whip your butt."

"That'll be the day." Ordinarily she would have chuckled, but they had just buried Artie, so she only pressed her hip against him before going to the sideboard for the keys.

18

Moody and LeBeau stopped at Lloyd Howland's former residence to pick up Denarius Glotty, who, it was their understanding, had agreed to accompany them on their search of the dump, for only he was equipped to identify the trash that he had put out for collection. But when the super finally answered their repeated knocks at his ground-floor rear door, he denied all knowledge of the deal.

"Tings to do here. Cannat go away from building, I don' care, caps or no caps." And when further pressed, he added, "I got me some rights too, damn me." He wore a gray shirt that might have been clean but looked dirty, a puff of dirty-gray chest hair showing at the open neck. He smelled strongly of some substance, though it was nothing Moody could readily identify.

It was practical, however, to assume the man was drunk. "You got the right to help the police," Moody said menacingly. "That's how it works in this country."

"So now I'm a gottdam foreigner?" Glotty showed a grimace that could have been either serious or farcical.

"What we're doing, Mr. Glotty," LeBeau told him, in a genial tone, "is asking for a favor from you as a law-abiding citizen. Like you promised the other day, remember?"

Glotty snorted with force, sending another wave of the odor their way. It smelled somewhat like turpentine, but if he had drunk that he would have been dying. "I don' got to answer to youze, you know. My bozz is duh lanlard."

This speech made Moody want to lean on him with more spirit than had yet been exerted, but LeBeau said, "We got your boss's okay. You call him if you want."

Glotty's ridged forehead became smooth for an instant. "Hang on, I get my hot."

"You didn't talk to the landlord, right?" Moody asked his partner when the super had gone.

"Right," confirmed LeBeau just as Glotty returned, wearing a broad-brimmed felt hat that looked old-fashioned but was in almost new condition.

No help awaited them at Sanitation's No. 3 dump. The detectives assumed that this state of affairs was probably due to the delay caused by the funeral, and they sat in the car, smelling Glotty's stench even with all windows open and listening to his grumbling, for a good hour, until it was reasonable to suppose nobody was coming.

They were parked on the shoulder of the road, just outside a chain-link fence that was already rusty, though this was supposed to be a relatively new facility. A squat shed of stained corrugated iron sat just beyond the gate. No moving object had yet been seen on the vast undulating trashscape beyond except the quivering seagulls, but suddenly the roar of a poorly muffled engine could be heard, and from a depression invisible at Moody's perspective, a dirty yellow bull-dozer hauled itself into view. When the vehicle came close enough, the noise was too loud to bear except with fingers in the ears—at least for the detectives. Glotty seemed to have gone placidly to sleep.

A man wearing an orange safety helmet emerged from the shed to hail the dozer, which stopped. At the idle, its noise was reduced to the almost bearable.

Moody brought his hands down. "I'm gonna use their phone. We can't sit here all day." He climbed out, heading for the gate, and had just reached it when the man in the helmet and stained coverall saw him and advanced.

"Hey you," shouted this guy, pointing to the sign that hung on one panel of the swung-back gate. "Off limits to the public. Can't you read?"

Moody identified himself and the business at hand.

But the helmeted personage became no friendlier. "Nobody told me nothing about that."

Moody pointed at the shack. "Can I use your phone?"

"Out of order." When Moody gave him a dubious look, he thrust out his jaw. "So try it and see."

Moody returned to the car. Decades of experiences with other city agencies, and even sometimes with other divisions of the Police Department, had made him stoical.

"Let's find a phone."

LeBeau was staring at the reaches of the dump. "Look at those gulls. What are they, a hundred miles from salt water?"

Moody would no longer engage in small talk with his partner, else he would have noted that there were probably even more rats.

They stopped at a phone booth outside a gas station, and LeBeau got out and made the call. "Captain can't spare the men," he said when he returned to the car. "Due to the time lost for the funeral, and there's a new homicide."

"He knew about that when he told us," Moody said.

"He claims he never promised."

"Well, it's too much for two men only." Moody turned to address Glotty, now awake and scowling. "You're in luck, Mr. Glotty. We can't do it today. Run you home now."

The super's expression changed to the positive, and his accent was lighter. "I gonna get paid, though?"

Moody did not want to discourage him with the truth and therefore answered by murmuring the word "tomorrow." He was pleased to see that it worked, Glotty moueing amiably. Moody directed LeBeau to take a right on Markham, up ahead. "It intersects with Mulberry in about a mile. That's right around the corner from Laurel. Let me off there while you run the citizen home."

"But didn't you want—"

"No," said Moody. "Let me off there."

His partner took the hint and said nothing more till they reached the appropriate place, a street away from the eleven hundred block of Laurel, and Moody pistoled a finger at where he wanted to deboard. "What're you gonna do?"

"Walk the territory," Moody said. "Maybe I'll learn something." He had no ideas at the moment, but he wanted to be alone.

He left the car and started along Mulberry, past a series of single-family houses of more or less the same size and age though with slight variations in design, unlike the Howland block, where newer structures were distributed among the older.

"Hey you, sir!" someone shouted behind him. He turned and, after a moment during which time the tall figure trotted nearer, recognized the Howland neighbor Gordon Keller, who wore a snappy outfit for a man of his age and place, a multicolored nylon jacket, a brilliant green baseball-style cap atop his gray hair. He was shod in sports shoes, blue and red lightning-bolt stripes over basic white. "Hi, Mooney," said he. "You still on the same case?" He thrust his hand out.

Moody shook with him and forced himself to be affable, though he did not want the man's company.

"I sure am, Mr. Keller. In fact, I was just on my way to see if you or the missus have been able to remember anything else from last Tuesday. You know, you're so close by, and things come back sometimes, after all the excitement settles down."

"Oh," Keller said ebulliently, "it sure hasn't settled down. It's getting bigger. We're on TV tonight again, our own segment on the *Ten O'Clock Five Star Report*."

"Bill Arbogast and Natalie Featherstone," Moody noted. "I thought you were Binnie Baines' people. You went over to the competition?"

"Don't you know it." They turned the corner at Mulberry, into Laurel. Keller was half a head taller than Moody and had a much longer step, but the latter refused to quicken his pace. This caused the older man to temporize impatiently now and again, dancing in the jazzy sneakers. "I just been down the village, buying some new clothes."

"They paying you?"

"I'm a retired man, Mooney," Keller said testily. "We're living on a pension, me and her." He blew his cheeks out after a gulp of air.

"Name's Moody, Mr. Keller. I don't care if you make a little money, unless you're selling something you ought to be giving us, good citizen like you."

"Beg pardon for getting the name wrong, sir," Keller said, staring ahead, "and I deserve to be called on it. But I got responsibility maybe you don't understand. Wife of mine, she don't have anybody else in the world."

"I got a responsibility to the people of this city, including yourself and your wife. We can't afford to have murderers running around free."

"You're right about that," said Keller, with artificial vehemence. "But I got to look out for that poor wife of mine, on account of nobody else will. She can't look out for herself."

As they turned the corner into Laurel, Moody frowned at him. "Somebody staying with her now? You've been away from the house for a while, and she's back there alone?"

"I don't have that kind of money," Keller said, performing another of his little dance steps so as to slow down for his companion. "Anyway, people talk. I don't want nobody going around saying she's a loony, and they do that, you know. You pay a nurse all that money, and then they talk about you with their other patients."

"So what do you do about her when you go out of the house?"

"I keep her safe," Keller said. "You can count on that."

"You say it's Alzheimer's?"

"Pretty much." Keller licked his lips.

"Go to a doctor?"

Keller shook his head. "Nothing they can do."

Having arrived at the ribbon of yellow crime-scene tape that still denied access to the length of pavement in front of 1143, they had to leave the sidewalk for the gutter.

"Mind if I come in with you and talk a little with yourself and your wife?"

Keller was surprised. "Now?"

"If you don't mind."

"We was going to get ready for *Five Star Report*."

"You got lots of time for that," Moody pointed out. "I won't take long." He wanted to find out just what information the Kellers were selling to the TV program: it was sure to be new. Arbogast and Featherstone, whose show specialized in the provocative, would not pay for a mere rehash of what Binnie Baines and the others had gotten for free.

Moody followed the older man up the steps onto the porch, where he expected Keller would pause to use a key, but such was not the case, the door yielding with the simple brisk turn of the knob. So much for locking the wife in. . . . But he was immediately enlightened by what he saw on entering the living room.

The house was equipped with old-fashioned high-standing radiators of cast iron. To the one adjacent to the far arm of the living-room sofa Mrs. Keller was attached by a heavy-link chain that encircled her ankle and was secured at either end by a padlock.

Spousal abuse was not among the infractions of the law handled by Homicide. Moody would call the precinct to send somebody, but since the woman suffered no visible pain, he could spare a few moments for a more important matter.

"Hi there, Mr. Moody," brightly cried Mrs. Keller, getting up from the couch, chain clinking. Whatever her condition, she had a better memory than her husband, at least for names, and proceeded to do even better. "Where's Detective LeBeau?"

"He'll be along shortly," Moody told her. "Are you okay, Mrs. Keller? Chain doesn't hurt?"

She sounded a pealing, girlish laugh. "Oh, no!"

Moody turned to Keller. "Unlock her."

The tall old man had removed his cap and jacket and hung them on a hall tree beside the front door. "Naw," he said coolly.

"You heard me: I said take that lock off her."

Mrs. Keller sat down on the couch, pulled off her right shoe, a beige loafer with a run-over heel, and stepped out of the chain. Today her slacks were purple.

Moody felt like a fool, but you could not be a policeman and admit anything of the sort, or apologize unless there was some legal reason to do so. Therefore he asked sternly, "What's the idea?"

Keller raised an eyebrow that was still darker than his hair. "Sir?"

"If it's not locked—?"

"It *is* locked," Keller explained. "On both ends." He smiled at his wife. "That means a lot to her. Feels secure, but it don't stop her from getting up if she needs to go to the toilet and so on, you know. It's an ideal solution, keeps her safe and snug, yet don't restrict her, see."

Having had enough of the matter, Moody went immediately to more pressing issues. "Last time I asked about the day of the murders next door. What I want you to do now, if you would, is think back to the time before that, back when Mrs. Howland and the little girl were alive. Normal times." He included Mrs. Keller in the question, glancing at her from time to time, but she was taking elaborate pains in returning the shoe to her foot. "Tell me," he said to Keller, "what you would see the Howlands doing. You're just across the driveway."

"Yeah," Keller said indignantly, "but last time you rushed out the door soon as I started to talk."

"You told us about seeing the van," said Moody. "Did you want to say anything else?" He smiled. "Can I sit down?" Without waiting for permission he perched on the thick arm of an overstuffed chair that was probably, judging from the almost new condition of its up-holstery, for guests; whereas the adjustable lounger under the floor lamp was likely to be Keller's own favorite.

Keller remained on his feet. "I'd like your word you're going to listen," he said, scowling down at Moody. "And not run away soon as I start to say something."

Though his memory of the last visit to these premises had no resemblance to the version he was now hearing, Moody would not argue with a willing witness. "Sorry about that. We had an emer-gency call, I guess. I can't guarantee I won't ever get another, but I'll sure give you all my attention right now."

Keller seated himself at the opposite end of the couch from his wife. He crossed his legs, which brought one enormous striped ath-letic shoe into Moody's line of sight. With his jacket off, Keller's paunch bulged in the knitted shirt of pale blue. Moody, whose bald spot was larger every time the barber gave him a hand mirror, envied the older man for his dense crown. Keller must have been a hand-some guy, years before, on the order of Dennis LeBeau, square-jawed, clear-eyed, thick-haired.

Mrs. Keller had at last succeeded in shoeing herself. She stood up. "I'll let you fellas do your man-talk. I got to primp for the TV."

Moody rose courteously. "I might want to talk with you a little later, if that's okay."

"Believe me," said the little old woman, whose head would have reached her husband's breastbone had he been standing, "I am at your disposal, schedule permitting." She walked purposefully, with many rapid short paces, to the stairway against the far-right wall, but slowed her pace when mounting the steps, making each an event.

"How long has she had her condition?" Moody asked when the small feet had finally disappeared from view.

"Beats me," Keller said impatiently. "I can't remember anymore, it's been so long."

Moody resumed his seat on the broad arm of the chair. "You've been keeping an eye on what we're doing next door. I've seen you at the window. You waved the other day. That's your dining-room window, right? It's straight across from the bedroom where the homicides took place."

"I get it," said Keller. "You wanna know if I could of seen anything over there from our window. But the blinds was closed all the time just like you fellas keep 'em."

"Venetian blinds?"

"I wouldn't own a set of the things," Keller said bitterly. "We lived in a rental years back had 'em. You can't keep 'em clean, I tell you. They sell gadgets to clean 'em, but they just brush off dust, and hell, what you get after every couple weeks you can't call just dust. It's grease, for God sake, and I don't care how far from the kitchen, all the way through the place the venetian blinds will collect a layer of it, you need to use solvent on every strip, an old toothbrush or whatever. Guy at work once told me you drop the whole blind in a bathtub and run hot water with dishwashing detergent, but we never had a dishwasher in the days I mean. Lucky we had indoor plumbing. . . . You a married man, Lieutenant?"

"I'm not a lieutenant, Mr. Keller."

"I been married all my life to the same woman," Keller said, leaning back against the sofa pillows and thrusting his long legs out so far that the big striped shoes ended up more than halfway across the space between him and Moody. "We had a couple kids. Girl's married to a man in Arizona. Boy got mad we wouldn't loan him any more money and don't speak to us. He went away, we don't know where."

"What are you going to tell them on *Five Star Report?*"

"Deal is, they get an exclusive." Keller arched his dark eyebrows. "You better watch the show."

"I've gone too easy on you so far, Mr. Keller," Moody said. "I'm going to tell you only once more: withholding information from the police is a criminal offense."

Keller held up his big hands and fluttered them. "All right, all right." He retracted his lower legs and leaned forward, white-fisting both kneecaps. "Could you just do me this favor. Don't tell the *Five Star* folks I told you, till they give me my money? That won't be long. They're coming to tape in an hour."

"Let's have it," Moody said.

Keller moved his hands in that tone-down-the-volume gesture sometimes used by persons in an official capacity to quiet a demonstrating crowd. "Let's get it over with, then," he said. "Fact is, you can't see in her window with the slats of the venetian tipped up that way, the way you fellas still leave 'em. That is, you can't see past 'em if you look out of the window of the dining room in this house, right across. But you can from the upstairs bathroom. You can look down and at that angle you can see quite a bit through the slats when they're not closed tight and if a light is on over there, as it usually is, 'cause it must be dark in there even during the day with the blinds closed like that. What you see is in slices, you know"—he made horizontal motions with an index finger—"segments, between the slats, but at that distance they come together in your eye, and—"

"What did you see?"

"She was taking her clothes off," said Keller, his right eye in a knowing droop.

"Mrs. Donna Howland?"

"She did that a lot, right there and not over to the side where you couldn't see no matter if the blinds been open all the way."

"You were in the habit of watching her, is that it?"

Keller was deaf to any voice but his own. "I always thought it was just by accident—not knowing how it is with venetian blinds. You can cock them up at an angle that way, and from inside it looks, to you, like you got perfect privacy along with at least some light from outside, but somebody from above—"

"You said that." It was not an interruption, for Keller continued to speak throughout.

"—can see more than you know." He smiled faintly with the angle of eye and warp of lip that suggested how keen he was. "Because they're not looking straight on but down through the gaps. At first I thought she never knew that. It took me a while to realize she knew it goddamn well." Now he did stop and take note of Moody, who defied him and stayed silent. "Well," Keller resumed after a long moment, "that's about the size of it."

"That's what *Five Star* is paying you for?" Moody asked at last, with simulated disdain. "You saw her naked? They're gonna want their money back."

Keller was wounded. "Oh, yeah? You think you know it all because they made you a detective. But you're way off. I mean, she knew what she was doing, see."

"Yeah, she was changing her clothes."

Keller put up a finger and moved it like a metronome. "That's where you're wrong."

"She was doing it because she knew you were watching?"

"Now you're on the money," Keller said, stamping his shoes on the carpet. "She wasn't all that fine a person. Oh, I know what they say on TV and all, you'd think she was a saint, but far from it."

"She was a loose woman, you're saying?" Moody was letting him run with it. "Who're we talking about, by the way?"

"You're making fun of me," Keller said. "This is a joke to you."

"I'll tell you what it is to me: I think it's interesting you can smear this dead lady but never speak of her by name."

"I never knew her well enough to use her name," said Keller. "It would be pretty phony if I started using it now."

Moody displayed a smirk. "I guess she was built nice?"

Keller raised his chin and spoke almost loftily. "It was an indecent display. I think there's a law against that."

Moody abandoned the brief attempt to talk man to man and asked harshly, "Undressing in her own bedroom, with the blinds closed?"

"I told you they weren't closed."

"Not if you went all over your house looking for an angle you could partially see through them."

"I never went 'all over the house,' " Keller complained, though he was somewhat chastened. "Come on, be fair."

"What makes you say she knew you were watching? She wave at you or look up and wink or something?"

"Body language."

"Excuse me?"

"It's all over TV: how to tell somebody's interested in making your acquaintance in a bar or tavern, et cetera, way they hold their head, play with their hair and all."

"You go much to pickup joints, Mr. Keller?"

"At my age? Come on."

"Her name was Donna Howland," Moody stated. "What kind of body language do you say she was using?"

Keller snorted, glancing at the nearest wall for effect. "She went right to the point. Showed her bare topless."

"What?"

"They call it that nowadays. Topless."

"Topless *means* bare," Moody said. "Showed you her bare breasts?"

"I was trying to not use that word. All right, she did that. And then she bent over and showed her backside, stuck it right up in the air."

"That was naked too?"

"Sure was."

Moody nodded judiciously. "If she first showed her breasts, then she was facing you. To show her bottom she had to turn and face the other way before bending over. Is that right?"

"Wrong!" Keller made it a little triumph. "Her side was pointed this way."

"You were at right angles?" Moody sighed. "She did this just once? Showed the top, then the bottom?"

"That was the worst of it," Keller said, leaning forward to cup his kneecaps again. "She did it over and over."

"She was touching her toes, Mr. Keller. Doing exercises. Haven't you seen that on TV?"

"No," said the older man. "They always wear those special suits for that. She was naked, I tell ya. And you ain't heard what she does next. She lays down, across the bed, pointing my way, and she spreads her legs. I swear! She spreads them wide as they could go." Eyes gleaming, he demonstrated with his outflung arms. "I shouldn't have to look at things like that."

"That's another exercise." Moody raised his voice. "Tightens the thigh muscles. Women worry about their thighs, especially as they get older, but this poor girl never even got to thirty. Donna Howland was exercising in the privacy of her bedroom, while her little girl was taking a nap in the next room."

Keller scowled. "I know what I saw! And not for the first time by any means. But those people were trash. I never thought well of them."

"You did this peeping every day?"

"I wouldn't call it peeping. I wouldn't put it like—"

"What would you do, play with yourself while you were watching?" Keller showed what he wanted to be taken as incredulous outrage, but Moody needled him further. "Man your age, how'd you get it up?"

"Listen, you," Keller began, but he stopped abruptly and changed his tone. "You got it all wrong. Nobody ever wants to hear what I . . ." His eyes wandered as if looking for a point on which to focus.

Moody decided to strike without further preparation. "I'll be glad to listen to you. Just tell me how you killed her."

Keller's gaze fixed on an arbitrary point on the carpeted floor between them. He was sadly reproachful. "I don't know where you get off talking to me like that. I thought we were friends. I been cooperating all along. You come into my house and talk to me like I'm dirt. It ain't fair."

"How much did you have to drink before you went over there?"

Keller's indignation now seemed real enough. "I haven't taken a drink in fifteen years." He swept a forearm at the surrounding room. "Go ahead, look for a bottle. You won't find none."

"I *know* you did it, Gordon. I just need the details."

Keller was slowly shaking his grizzled head and smiling vaguely into the distance. "You got quite an imagination."

"Then how about giving me some facts?"

"*She* was the one exposing herself. I was the innocent bystander."

"You tell your wife about this?"

The man snorted. "Hardly."

"Jealous woman?"

Keller glanced furtively toward the stairway. "There was this girl, years ago, did some baby-sitting. I come home early. I thought my wife wasn't due back yet, and I, well, why go into it? Anyway, she come in, and she ran her out with a butcher knife."

"What were you doing with the girl?" Moody asked.

"Oh, a little touching's all." He widened his eyes at Moody. "I swear."

"She blamed the girl, not you?"

Keller silently shrugged.

"Are you saying she spotted you peeping at Donna Howland and went over there and cut her throat?"

Keller stared dully at him. "I'm not saying anything."

Moody stood up. "Let's go up and ask your wife about it. I want to look at that bathroom window, too."

"No, wait a minute," Keller said. "I don't wanna give you the wrong impression." He added, in a weaker voice, "My wife's a little off, but she's not like that."

"Well, you've succeeded in putting the idea in my mind," said Moody.

"Wait a minute. She's on medication." Keller rubbed his jaw, from the neck forward. "I made that up. She never went after any girl with a knife."

"Was there really a girl?"

Keller was silent awhile. "Maybe not exactly like that."

"Maybe like some other girl who forgot to close her blinds all the way?"

"Just give me a minute," Keller mumbled, then in a wailing tone said again, "Nobody will *ever* listen."

"I'm listening."

"Who will take care of her?"

"People who might do a better job than you," said Moody. "Doctors."

Keller shook his big face. "She won't go for that. She don't think she's that bad."

"Maybe she's right. We won't know till she's examined, will we?"

Keller's exploratory finger now found the long furrow that ran from the right lobe of his nose to the corner of his mouth. "I just got fed up, see? I know I made a mistake, I realize that."

"Tell me about it." Moody was trying to hold the line between overeagerness and a show of indifference. He had been taken entirely by surprise. He might have been embarrassed, a detective with his experience, had it not been that the same experience made him professionally immune to such an emotion.

"I'm no pervert," Keller said. "You got to understand that."

"If you mean you don't have a record," said Moody, "I know."

"You already checked?" The thought seemed to startle the man.

"That's routine in a homicide case where the perpetrator isn't immediately identified. We run all the near neighbors, relatives, co-workers, et cetera, through the computer."

"I've had a few parking tickets."

"They don't show up." He added, "Peeping Toms don't get a sheet either unless somebody brings charges, and that's rare."

Keller became agitated and slapped his thighs. "I wasn't worried about that! It would of been my word against hers. I got a good reputation in this town long before those people showed up. I always been fair with everybody, paid my bills on time, give to every charity that asks. . . ." He hid his face in his hands for a moment, and when he next revealed his features they were blurred, his cheeks ashen, his mouth an open, seemingly toothless oval. He moaned, "Oh my God, I can't, I can't. . . ."

"Sure you can," said Moody, as if only stating a fact. "Go minute by minute, take your time. Just tell what happened. You don't have to analyze anything: that would only complicate matters at this point. You can go back and do that later."

Suddenly Keller was transformed, for no apparent reason. He said blandly, "I don't know what you're talking about."

"Sure you do, Gordon, and you really want to tell me and get a burden off your shoulders. I've seen you watching us next door, afraid what we'd find out. That's over now."

All at once Keller let the air out of himself with a long exhalation.

Moody brought out the leather folder that held his shield and, in the pocket under it, the Miranda card.

Keller seemed to receive a certain confidence from the reading of his rights and in a strong voice answered where asked. Yes, he understood; no, he didn't need a lawyer to "tell my side of it" at this time.

Moody did not like the restrictive phrase. "Just tell what happened," he said, knowing full well that nobody ever was capable of that.

19

Moody answered the knock at the front door.

It was LeBeau, looking somewhat miffed. "Old Mary Jane came out and told me you went in here. I was about ready to go back downtown."

Moody stepped out onto the porch. In an undertone he said, "Keller is confessing."

"Keller?"

"I ran into him by accident. One thing led to another, and it suddenly hit me that he did it. So I just asked him."

"Christ." But professional that he was, Dennis had already lost his look of surprise by the time he was inside the house.

"Hi, there," Keller said affably, rising from the couch, preparing to shake hands. But LeBeau stayed back and acknowledged the greeting only with a shift of the shoulders.

"Mrs. Keller is upstairs, getting ready for another TV show," Moody told his partner.

"Five Star Report," Keller specified. "Bill Arbogast and Natalie Featherstone."

"Okay," said Moody, taking his chair again as Keller sat down. LeBeau remained standing. "What we're going to do, Mr. Keller, is take down your story." He displayed his notebook again. "Just tell me everything the way you remember it. You'll get a chance to look at all this later on, make sure it's accurate as possible. But first we

255

just want to get an idea of what happened." Moody liked a suspect
to believe that what would finally go on record was only an edited
and polished version of a confession, whereas of course the Miranda
warning was literal: every utterance of a person under arrest belonged
to the state and would be used, if possible, always to his detriment,
even though he might be confessing voluntarily. Fine moral toler-
ances were of no value in law enforcement.

"That's only fair," Keller said. He crossed his long legs in the
other direction and conspicuously moistened his lips. He raised his
chin, tightening the loose skin there, and closed his eyes. Then he
uncrossed his legs, placing both big shoes flat on the floor. He stared
into the middle distance through slitted eyes.

"Start anywhere you want," said Moody. "You were at the upstairs
bathroom window?"

"That's correct."

"What time would that have been?"

Keller shrugged. "Whenever, you know." He frowned at Moody.
"You said the details could be left till later."

"We need an approximate time."

"You tell me," Keller said, with the rising inflection of indifference, but then he appealed to LeBeau with a half-smile.

Dennis rejected him. "This isn't a joke, Mr. Keller." He moved
closer to the man by one step. This was intended to be threatening,
now that Keller did not expect him to be potentially a friend. A
suspect's home was not usually the optimum venue for an interrogation, but Moody had to take the matter of Mrs. Keller into consideration. He believed her husband might at this stage refuse to
cooperate if taken downtown. Of course, he might do the same if
the TV people arrived before the detectives had heard even a preliminary account of his role in the homicides.

Moody leaned forward. "You get your act together, Gordon, or
we're gonna go right down and book you this minute, and I tell you
this: you won't get out on bail if we do that. Give me a time."

"We don't eat till whatever show she watches is off at twelve-thirty. Then she opens a can of soup and so on. I always help her with the dishes, and after that's done I generally—"

"How long's it take you to eat your soup? Fifteen minutes, quarter hour?"

"Oh," Keller said, "hour, hour 'n' a half."

"For soup?"

"Well, there's more than that! I got a partial dental plate, and I eat slow. I also drink a lot of coffee, and by time I've helped her with the dishes, I need to go upstairs and pee."

"Use the upstairs bathroom, do you?"

"Well, yes," Keller said. "I could use the downstairs toilet, but that's next to the kitchen and it seems nicer to go upstairs. So while I'm up there, while I was drying my hands I happened to see out the window and I look down and there she is, over there, doing what I said she was in the habit of doing. You say exercises, because you never saw her the way I did. Oh, she was the bold one inside her bedroom. She wasn't the kind who would take sunbaths in the yard, wearing skimpy little bikini bathing suits, not her! That was all to make the public think she wasn't that sort. Her husband was away a lot. If you ask me, he don't even like women. Seen that walk on him? If my boy still lived here, I wouldn't let him talk to him, I don't mind saying that. I wouldn't want him talking to *her*, for that matter."

"Mrs. Donna Howland was nude?" Moody asked for the benefit of his partner, who had not heard any of Keller's foregoing remarks.

"Naked without a stitch. She was laying across the bed, legs spread far as they would go."

Moody made some jottings with a ball pen that was only intermittently inking the words. "You're sure she was looking at you?"

"Hell yes."

The pen had warmed up by now and was writing legibly. He waved it. "Go on."

"I got fed up," said Keller. "I'm no prude, but there's a limit."

"Her blinds were open?" LeBeau asked.

Keller stubbornly shook his head. "I ain't gonna go through it all again. I explained it already to"—he hesitated for a moment, then found the name—"Mr. Moody here."

Moody blinked. "He claims the slats were turned so you could see down through them if looking from above." He directed Keller to proceed.

Keller began, "I'm a broad-minded individual, but—"

"What did you do next?"

"What I went over there to do was just talk to her, I swear. I didn't want to make too much of it. I was willing to keep it between me and she. Imagine if that old Jones woman had something like this on her? It'd be all over town next day. These people'd be run out of the neighborhood. I didn't want that. I'm a fine person, you ask anybody."

"Let me get this straight," asked LeBeau. "You say she was heating you up on purpose, knowing you were watching? You didn't go over there with the idea of getting some, did you?"

Keller appealed to Moody. "I thought you wanted to hear my side of it. How come he's interrupting with his dirty mouth?"

"The detective is trying to get to the truth," Moody said. "Like me, Gordon. *Did* you make sexual advances to her?"

Keller seemed to be grinding his teeth behind clenched lips. "You're all alike in thinking the worst, ain't you? A man like me, do I look like a sex maniac?"

"You walk over to eleven forty-three. What's your wife doing at this time?"

"Watching TV in the living room."

"You come right down the stairs over here?" LeBeau asked. "Tell her where you were going?"

"She gets into her soaps, she won't pay attention to nothing else."

Keller said this with a smile, which faded when Moody put him at the Howland threshold.

"Back door or front?"

"Back."

"You went through to the kitchen in this house and out your own back door. Across the yard to eleven forty-three?"

"Correct."

"Just walked in over there?"

LeBeau's question exasperated Keller. "I don't barge into other people's homes without knocking. You can't seem to understand you're not dealing with some lowlife. I might of made mistakes, but I'm not trash."

"So you knocked. Then what?"

Keller began to agitate his head. "She come to the door after a while."

"With clothes on?"

Keller smirked. "No."

"Stark naked?" LeBeau asked with obvious and menacing skepticism. "I don't believe it."

"All right!" Keller wailed, shrinking against the cushions. "She had some kinda bathrobe on, but it was real skimpy, thin material, and I could see everything she had."

"Must have looked pretty familiar to you, just at closer range," said Moody. He now had the man's number and did not worry about offending him into silence. Keller's self-professed need was to be heard: needling him would only make him more desperate to talk. "She look hotter close up, or worse?"

"She turned my stomach! If she don't get enough from that queer she's married to, it ain't my problem!" Keller lowered his voice. "I didn't say that. I was polite, but I just told her straight I couldn't put up with it any more. She pretends she don't know what I'm talking about. She acts like I'm going to put my hands on her."

"Where are you now? Porch or in the house?"

Keller stared at the floor. "Wait a minute," he said as if to himself. "I'm inside by now. I remember there was a screen door between us, but then it wasn't there any more."

"You opened it and came in."

"I never would of done that without being asked, I guarantee."

LeBeau sneered at him. "Why would she have invited you in?"

"Because I'm a neighbor," Keller loftily replied.

Moody stared at him a while in silence. "So?"

"Oh," Keller said. "Okay. . . ." His heavy eyebrows were twitching. "I'm trying to remember. . . ."

"How'd you get in the bedroom?"

Keller nodded once. "Oh, sure. Well, way it happened was . . ."

"She run in there to get away from you?" asked LeBeau.

Keller extended his hands, long wrists emerging from the sleeves. "She had the wrong idea from the first."

"What does that mean?" asked Moody.

Some blood colored Keller's cheeks. "Like it was *me* who done the wrong thing. I mean, here I am, the injured party."

"She was scared of you?"

Keller turned his head away, snorting, and came back to say, "Yeah, me, at my age. What am I gonna do to her?"

"What *did* you do?"

"Nothing!"

"You killed her with a blow to the head," LeBeau said, "then sliced her from groin to breastbone."

Keller was heavily reproachful. "I mean sex. You know that: it was in the paper she wasn't touched, for heaven's sake."

Moody asked, "How'd you come to hit her in the head, and with what?"

"Wish you could of seen it for yourselves." Keller looked from one to the other. "Even then you would of found it hard to believe." He silently requested affirmation from each detective, but getting none, he hardened his nose. "Woman can claim anything, all you got's your word, and who will take that these days?" His jaw was shivering above his turkey neck. "She was gonna call the police! Can you top that? I says I was the one who should call 'em. She runs in the bedroom. She heads for the phone on the little table there. Nobody's gonna listen to me. I knew that. I hit her with a thing from the dresser."

"What thing?"

"A bottle. Real thick glass."

"Like a perfume decanter?" asked LeBeau.

"You tell me," Keller said, appropriately this time. "I can show it to you."

"You kept it?"

"Under the sink." He pointed kitchenward, over his shoulder, then waggled the finger in front of him. "I just wanted to slow her down, for heaven's sake. She was out of control. I didn't know what else to do. She wouldn't listen to anything I said."

LeBeau had been pacing, but he halted now. "The cutting—why did you do that?"

"Yeah." Keller's eyes showed a pain that was probably real enough to him, because its object was wholly himself. "I should probably not of done that, though it didn't matter to her by then. When I saw she was dead—I couldn't see any breathing, anyway—I knew I'd get blamed if anybody found out I was over there. Like the nosy old Jones lady. But if nobody saw me, then who would ever suspect a man of my reputation? I turned Presbyterian for *her* when we got married"—he pointed up—"and was an elder down at the church on Greenwood for many years." He grunted. "I wanted you to think it was a sex maniac. I didn't realize how that might make me look if you ever traced it to me, but I didn't think you ever would, see? Now you might think I'm weird. The other was an accident, but—"

"The other?" Moody asked.

"The thing with the bottle."

"Murdering her, you mean," said LeBeau. "That's what killed her: getting hit with the so-called decanter."

"Yeah, that's what I'm saying."

"No, you're not. Can't you say it?"

"Say what?"

"You killed her with the decanter."

Keller shrugged. His eyes were cold again. "It was an accident, I tell you. I'm admitting the other business, the cutting, might of been a mistake. I know it doesn't look right."

"What kind of weapon did you use?" It was Moody.

Keller leaned to the left so that he could reach into his right-hand pants pocket. He brought out an object. "It's not a weapon. It's just this. I always carry it. Comes in handy. The blade slides out." He was about to demonstrate when LeBeau quickly moved in and relieved him of the knife, handing it to Moody, and then ordered the man to his feet and frisked him.

Moody examined the tool that had been used as a weapon: it was a utility knife, but unlike the one taken by the patrolmen from Lloyd Howland, it was made of plastic and its blade could be extended by a thrust of the thumb, not being locked in place by the setscrew of Lloyd's model. He found an evidence bag in the third pocket he explored, and put the knife into it.

LeBeau meanwhile had reseated Keller on the couch and moved a few steps away. "Tell us about killing the child."

Keller nodded briskly and patted his long thighs in the gray suit pants he wore above the big striped sport shoes. "She was sleeping. The blanket was pulled up to her nose. I just reached under and did it. She couldn't of felt a thing."

"Why?"

Keller elevated his chin. "Because her mama was gone, and what kind of father was that guy? I couldn't of lived with that on my conscience. She would of been an orphan. *We* couldn't take her in.

We're too old, and she"—again he pointed at the ceiling—"well, need I say more?"

Moody spoke quickly, so that Dennis would not dwell on the little girl's killing at this time. "You cut somebody like you did Mrs. Donna Howland, there's gonna be blood all over the place."

"Well, now, that's true." Keller spoke affably. "But I looked around and found one of them real big towels in the cupboard, the kind they sit on on the beach? I was going to use it to cover *me*, but then I saw it could go over her and I could work underneath. If my sleeves was rolled up, I wouldn't get the blood on me except the hands. I saw that on a TV show. When I was done, I rolled up the towel along with her robe and the bottle and brought 'em over here. I put the stuff in the washer, but I washed the bottle off and kept it, because it's real nice, might be worth something. That was dumb, I guess, but I was raised a poor kid and can't destroy something of value."

"Where's the towel and the robe?" Moody asked.

"Threw 'em out in the garbage that night."

"Can was picked up by Sanitation?"

"Next morning."

It occurred to Moody that this confession would send him and LeBeau back to the dump after all. He stood up. "Let's get that bottle."

"Sure," said Keller, rising from the couch with the aid of only one hand. Moody could not have done that.

"Stay there," he told Keller and drew LeBeau aside, asking him in an undertone to phone for some help with Mrs. K.: there was a protocol for such matters; social-service liaison personnel would come to look after the old lady. He turned back to the suspect. "Where's a phone?"

"Kitchen," Keller said. "Bottle's there too. C'mon." He led the way at a fast lope.

They went past the stairs and through a dining room that was made smaller by a large table covered with a lace cloth in the center of which was a big cut-glass bowl empty except for a single paper clip. Moody glanced across at the house next door and saw the closed venetian blinds on all the windows. When they reached the kitchen, he asked LeBeau also to call the Howland number and tell the patrolman on duty there to come over.

Keller pointed to a wall phone identical to that in the kitchen of 1143. "Help yourself."

LeBeau too noticed the similarity. "You saw Miz Donna Howland went into the bedroom to use the telephone. What about the one in the kitchen?"

Keller smiled. "That's simple," he said brightly. "I wouldn't let her." He opened the cabinet door underneath the sink and, squatting, fished around in a cardboard box filled with empty cans and bottles until he found and brought forth what proved to be, when it was surrendered to Moody, a globe of thick green glass in the walls of which were embedded golden stars fashioned apparently of another substance, glittering, perhaps metallic. It was empty and had no stopper. "How about that?" Keller said. "How do they get them in there?" Meaning, presumably, the stars. He stood up and gestured down at the box. "I'm religious about recycling."

"Oh, here you are." It was Mrs. Keller, entering the kitchen with her distinctive walk. Her gray hair was arranged otherwise than when Moody had last seen her, more formally, as it were, swept up no doubt in the interests of the large disklike earrings. The dress was black, with fancy puffed sleeves and a long skirt. Evening attire? She was dressed for the TV interview, which he had not forgotten but was thinking of in another way: namely, that he wanted to get Keller away before the television people showed up, and time was running out. "Gordie," she chided, "you haven't changed yet? Better get going. I'll take over with these gentlemen."

Moody, summoning up all the courtliness at his command, took her arm in his. "You look beautiful, ma'am," said he. "But there's been a change of plans. Let's go in the living room and talk things over."

She pulled around to stare at the perfume bottle in the flat of his far hand, her eyes sparkling like its embedded iridescent stars. "Is that a little present for me?"

"Not really." LeBeau had already finished with the phone, and Moody asked him to escort Keller. He would wait for the reinforcements before he arrested and cuffed the man, though that event was overdue.

"Oh, I'm sorry," said Mrs. Keller. "It's for your own lady."

"No, ma'am." He dropped her arm and found another plastic evidence bag in the same pocket that the other one had come from. "I need it for my work." The bottle was the size of a small grapefruit or large orange, and hung heavily first in the bag and then in his jacket pocket.

"Your work must be very interesting," Mrs. Keller said when he had deposited her on the living-room couch. "What is the nature of it?"

LeBeau had brought Keller along behind them, and now put him in the big chair.

"I'm in law enforcement," Moody told her, supporting the skirt of his jacket with a hand, compensating for the sag of the weighty bottle.

"Gordie was in wholesale office supplies," said she. "I did substitute teaching. We're both retired." With the black evening dress she was still wearing the worn loafers in beige. She continued to smile as her husband was asked to stand up, turn around, and put his hands in the small of his back.

Keller's wrists proved so thick that the cuffs had to be fastened at the second-to-last notch.

When the social-service people, a solemn man and a young woman with a matronly air, arrived to deal with his wife, the detectives took

Keller upstairs and had him show them the bathroom window from which he had looked down on Donna Howland's bedroom. Then they took him out to their car. They pulled out of the eleven hundred block just as Moody, on a cue from LeBeau, who was watching the rearview mirror, turned and saw the van from *Five Star Report* swinging into the other end of the street.

Keller continued to be agreeable when interrogated at the Homicide Bureau. The video camera was back in working order, and the partners used it to record the confession that the man willingly repeated. He seemed to be enjoying himself, perhaps considering this as at least moral compensation for missing the *Five Star Report* deal. After several hours of such, he was asked whether he'd like a bite to eat, and he gleefully gave his order: two cheeseburgers with the works, apple pie à la mode, strawberry shake. But the detectives, who had to pay out of their own pockets for the treats, explained what they had in mind was coffee and sinkers. LeBeau made the run, bringing back a six-pack of mixed plain and powdered. Keller ate four and a half doughnuts.

Keller signed the typewritten version of the confession and several other forms averring that everything he said was of his free will, without official duress, and giving permission for the videotaping. He was also reminded from time to time of his constitutional rights but continued to dismiss the idea of a lawyer.

When the interrogation was finished at long last, at least in this phase, and all three men stood up from the table, Keller, cuffless throughout the questioning, extended his large right hand, that which had, reinforced by the fancy perfume bottle, killed Donna Howland with a single blow.

"You fellas do one whale of a job," he told Moody before including Dennis with a twist of his chin. "I'm glad to give what help I could, even if I did have to postpone the *Five Star* interview."

"What were you gonna tell them?" Moody asked. "That you did it?"

"I got to take care they don't get the wrong impression. I'm not going to let them call me a criminal. I've got to defend my good name. Okay, I might not of gone about it in the right way, but this was something new for me: I'm not some street-corner trash. Call it an error in judgment, but don't blow it out of proportion. Mistakes were made on both sides. A lot of any situation hinges on how it looks." He smiled again and extended his hand to Moody for a shake.

Moody, however, deftly used it to revolve him, and seizing Keller's left hand as well, manacled both in the small of his back.

"Is this necessary?" Keller asked when facing the detectives again. "I've got to get over to the TV station. It might not yet be too late for tonight's show."

"You're going to jail," LeBeau said. "You're under arrest."

"But I been cooperating with you. I thought we had a deal!"

After elaborating on his complaint and getting nowhere, he now demanded a lawyer.

"Place never looked this good before," said Molly, admiring the paint job. Lloyd had finished the living room.

He opened the door to the screened-in porch. "Come and see your bird." The sparrow landed on his extended finger while he was still speaking, and after a brief explosive flutter of wings established a balance that was not affected when Lloyd moved the hand to Molly's shoulder, onto which the bird gravely stepped.

Molly turned her head to try to get eye-to-eye with the sparrow, but it prudently moved around to the base of her nape, plodding, on its big but delicate feet, back toward her shoulder when she looked forward again.

"It will be cautious for a while," said Lloyd. "It trusts me now because I feed it."

Molly winked. "I know how birds are."

"I didn't want you to think I was alienating its affections."

"I don't know what that means."

"Oh. Well—"

"I was just kidding you, Lloyd: I can figure it out. It was never *my* bird."

"You saved its life."

"You can't own something living, no matter what," Molly said. "Not even if you save its life."

"It can leave any time it wants. Look at all the holes in the screening."

Molly looked around, hands on hips. She had left her baseball cap behind and instead of a workshirt wore a thin sweater in bright blue. "He wouldn't lose much if he pulled this whole darn thing down."

"Don't say that. It's my next project."

Molly snickered. "Fixing up this porch? That's big-time skilled labor. Joe has to pay you decent money for that. He oughta put you on hourly. I hope he don't think you're gonna do all his dirty work for just room and board."

Lloyd could chide her now. "You got him wrong. All I want is to do a good job. That end of the floor has to be jacked up. Then we got to think about putting some support underneath: railroad tie, maybe, Joe says. All the screening should be replaced, and this floor painted with deck enamel. I just hope I have enough time to finish it before—"

Molly impatiently broke in with, "Summer?" He had not meant that, and she probably knew it. "Don't put yourself on a deadline. This porch has been completely neglected for years, along with the rest of the house."

The sparrow left her shoulder and flew toward Lloyd. When it disappeared from his line of sight, he assumed the bird had gone past him to another destination. But then he felt a slight pricking from its pointed toes as they took a purchase on his crown.

"Bet it's a female," said Molly. "Jealous of me. It's giving me a dirty look."

"Hey, how you doin', Moll?" Joe came onto the porch, his weight having an effect on the floor. He proceeded to stamp on the worn boards, aggravating the tremor and scaring the bird off Lloyd's head. It flew to perch on the folded-back edge of one of the openings to the outside, but stayed inside the screen.

Molly complained to her cousin, "Are you nuts? It's gonna fall in any minute."

Joe shrugged. "Only a two-foot drop. Just break a leg or something." He smirked at Lloyd. "Save us jacking it up. Have to build a new one, which would make more sense anyway."

"When they handed out the brains, you must of been on vacation. I hope you don't think Lloyd has to do all this work to earn the gourmet meals and luxury accommodations."

Lloyd was quick to say, "Come on, Molly."

"Listen," said she, throwing a punch that did not quite meet Joe's midsection. "I know this guy from away back."

"Who taught you how to box?" Joe cried, putting up his dukes and further agitating the porch floor with a heavy-toed prizefighter's shuffle-dance.

Molly addressed Lloyd. "He's telling the truth for once. And he never heard of the idea that you don't hit a lady. I saw stars more than a few times."

Joe too appealed to Lloyd. "She keeps begging me not to take it easy on her because she's a girl. 'Slug me,' she says. 'I can take it.' She keeps this up till finally I throw a slow-motion left hook that takes about five minutes to get there, and I also pull it so I barely touch her chin. Jesus, you should of heard the blubbering!"

"Damn you, Joe, I never cried once!" Molly said. "You big bully. I was eleven."

Joe stopped moving and lowered his arms. "You're having a good effect on her, Lloyd. See how she cleans up her English when you're around?" Suddenly he thrust his head down and forward. "Is that the phone? . . . Yeah." He dashed into the house.

Molly looked fondly in the direction in which her cousin had gone. "Isn't he the greatest guy? But I don't ever flatter him to his face: that would spoil him rotten. . . . Did *you* hear the phone?"

"Not really."

"I think he must of done something weird to the bell," said Molly. "Only he can hear it if you're outa the kitchen."

Joe returned in a moment. "It's for you, Lloyd."

Lloyd did not ask who it might be. Only the detectives had this number for him.

He went to the kitchen and lifted the handpiece that dangled from the wall phone. "Lloyd Howland."

"Detective Nick Moody. You might have heard the news. But then I figured the kind of person you are, you might not have, either."

"No, I haven't."

"We made an arrest. I thought you'd like to know."

Lloyd shouted desperately, "Not Larry!"

Moody said, "No. Take it easy. Listen to me, Lloyd. Before I tell you, I want your promise you're not going to do anything foolish."

"*Foolish?*" He was still desperate.

"Do I have to spell it out?" Moody asked laconically. "Way you acted at the funeral? . . . You'll be back in trouble if you do. We won't put up with it. . . . Lloyd? You there?"

"Yeah."

"You sound like you still have some doubts. Take my word for it, you're off the hook. We've got our man. It all checks out."

"What a time to get blind drunk," said Lloyd. "I could have saved them if I had gone there. It was where I was heading."

"No, you couldn't. It was too early. If you had gone there mid-morning you wouldn't still have been around when the homicides occurred. The little girl was taking her nap."

Lloyd groaned. "Donna would have thrown me out long before noon. She couldn't stand bitterness. Donna hated anything negative, especially in me. She thought it held me back. Donna was always full of hope." He kept talking so as not to sob. "But maybe she could have gotten me out of it. She was good at that. That was why I was heading there." He resisted learning who had committed the murders: he would have to cope with knowledge no human being not a policeman should be forced to accept.

"I want your word, Lloyd. I don't want you to do anything you'll regret. You can hear it on TV, but I wanted to talk to you myself."

His account was clear, measured, and in a language that employed police terms in certain passages.

Lloyd stayed silent so long after the account was concluded that the detective asked again whether he was still there. "Yeah. I'm all right. I mean, I'm not all right, but I'm not—you don't have to worry about me. I won't go after him. What would be the use? . . . Oh, God . . ." Now his defenses crumbled, and he wept.

"The little girl would not have felt a thing," Moody said after a moment. "And Donna was deceased as a result of the blow to the head. She wouldn't have known of the rest. She was gone."

"You've already told Larry."

"He was duly notified, that's correct."

"He's not still scared of me, you think?" Lloyd was trying to make his voice less tearful. His grief was his own.

"I wouldn't know about that," said Moody.

"I haven't tried to get in touch with him. I didn't think I was supposed to. But it would be okay now, wouldn't it?"

"I'm not stopping you, if that's what you mean." Moody paused. "Uh, listen, Lloyd. The DA's office is going to drop the gun charges. . . . Lloyd, you hear me?"

"Sorry. . . . Detective?"

"Yes?"

"Is there any way I can get the gun back?"

"You got to be kidding. . . . Am I wrong about you, Lloyd? Are you really hopeless?"

"I don't mean for myself. It never belonged to me. I stole it from a friend, not a gun shop."

"Joseph Littlejohn?"

"No, not him. Someone I don't want to get into trouble, somebody who didn't have anything to do with—"

"It's been confiscated, Lloyd," Moody said in the harsh version of his voice. "Lucky for your friend there's no record it was ever used in the commission of a crime—other than that stunt of yours. Best thing you can do for your friend is tell them not to play with firearms in the future, or at least apply for a license."

"Yeah."

"What are you going to do now?" Moody asked in a gentler tone. "Work there for Littlejohn, doing carpentry and so on?"

Lloyd breathed out. "I don't know. It's all so sudden, not to have this hanging over me. It'll take a while to get used to."

"You sound like you expected to be found guilty. Mind telling me why? You weren't the perpetrator."

"Okay," said Lloyd. "I owe you an answer. First, I wasn't really sure I didn't do it. I've never been that drunk before. I wet the bed during the night, something I haven't done since I was a little kid. I woke up with this cut on my face, and apparently it bled enough to get on my undershirt, which was on the shower floor. I don't know if I had tried to wash it out or just threw it in there. The whole night is still a blank. That's the only time in my life anything like that has occurred. If I could black out for seventeen, eighteen hours, maybe it was because of something terrible that I did during that time." He paused. There was still no point in going into where and how he had stolen the half gallon of scotch: he could provide no information as to the identity of whoever had shot the liquor-store clerk and emptied the cash drawer. "The other reason I thought I might be charged with murder is—you say you want to hear it—I thought so long as you didn't have anyone else, you might just go ahead and nail me."

"Without any evidence?" Moody was not so incredulous as reproachful.

"I'm sorry," said Lloyd. "But you wanted to know, and I'm just telling the truth. I guess I thought that's what the police might do, the police in general, not you necessarily. It wasn't personal."

"That's a relief," Moody said. "I've got a son only a year or so older than you. He's a graduate student in sociology, out West. He and his mother don't live with me. With him it *is* personal. . . . But I'm not saying it's all his fault."

Lloyd did not feel it was his place to respond to that. But at least he could say, "Well, now I know different. You were always fair with me, and I really appreciate you calling me now. I guess it's more than time I grow up."

"Listen, Lloyd," said Moody. "You want to talk about anything, get my opinion for what it's worth—I *have* been around for a while—give me a call. I'll be interested to hear what you're doing with yourself. You get too bitter, like you say happens sometimes, get in touch with me before you do anything, I mean, get into a fight or walk out on your job. Maybe I'll have something to offer. If I don't, I won't waste much of your time anyway."

Lloyd was touched by this unique and modest suggestion. Not even Donna had actually invited him to tell her his troubles. He had assumed she would be sympathetic to him, and imposed them on her. By nature a kind person, she was probably just being nice, the way she had unfailingly been to everybody. "Thanks," he told Moody. "Thanks a lot for everything."

When he rejoined his friends on the porch and gave them the news, Molly hugged and kissed him, in the first embrace they had ever had, and Joe pumped his hand.

"Calls for a big celebration, buddy! I'll go get the pizza and six-pack."

"There you have Joe's idea of high living," Molly said. "If he won the lottery he'd order a slice of pizza and a brewski." But her round face darkened then, and she gently grasped Lloyd's hand. "It's a terrific relief, but it's not—"

Lloyd said quickly, "That's okay. It's no disrespect. She would understand." He grinned at Joe. "Pizza's fine."

"All right, then," Molly cried, "but not beer, for God's sake. This ai—isn't the bowling tournament, Central Hardware versus Mel's Auto Parts. The champagne's my treat, don't worry." She addressed the last words to her cousin.

Joe spoke to Lloyd in mock outrage. "She thinks I'm too cheap to spend five bucks on a bottle of champagne."

"I think it's gone up since the last time you looked, Joe old boy." Molly winked at Lloyd. "It might even be five-fifty by now."

"Ouch," said Joe, wincing. "That's why I stick to beer." But a significant look of his own at Lloyd meant he too was joking.

20

Captain Novak finally caved, if only to shut him up, and permitted Marevitch to return to duty after only three off-days.

"Take care of that new kid Ravenswood," Novak told him. "She was fourth in her class at the Academy."

"Then she should take care of me," Marevitch said. "I was at the bare-ass bottom of mine, and you should know: you were first. She's also six foot tall, I hear."

"Yeah, Jack, but she's a lousy shot. She barely qualified. Take her to the range with you next time you go. You're overdue this season."

Marevitch was not bad with the good old regulation long-barreled .38, but could hardly hit the backstop with the new automatic the department was thinking of introducing and having the men test. But the main reason he was often late with the required target practice was that each officer had to pay for his own ammo. He grunted now and started to leave, but the captain called him back.

"I know you're steamed about the valor medal turndown. But listen, it's just political. I won't go into the complications, but take my word for it. What's political right now won't necessarily be next year, if you get my drift. Then I'll put in for it all over again. Don't think all is lost forever."

Marevitch found the courage to say, "If Heinz told you about that, then he also must of said I cursed you when I heard."

Novak laughed toward Marevitch and then at the ceiling. "I

thought that was the way my men always refer to me. Don't tell me otherwise, Jack, else I'll think I'm doing something wrong."

So on the seven-to-three watch next morning, Marevitch was back in a unit, but the car was different.

He asked Felicia Ravenswood, whose large figure was behind the wheel, "What did they do with nine-oh-five?"

"Pulled it for a brake job," said she. "I hope while they got it they do something about that transmission as well."

"What's wrong with the transmission?" Marevitch asked resentfully. "I been in that unit for two years and everything works fine."

Ravenswood moved diplomatically. "You know how cars are. They'll run fine for some time and then all at once everything will break down inside one day. Windshield wipers are out, too."

"That I knew," Marevitch assured her. "Artie and me never got around to reporting that, I guess because of the long spell of dry weather." She was driving too slowly. "You can speed it up some. If you go slow along here, you make 'em nervous." They were on a cross street off the main drag in the black district. She ought to have known how her people reacted to a crawling police vehicle.

"I thought that was the idea," Ravenswood observed. "We want the bad guys to be nervous, don't we?"

"They don't start the serious dealing here until later in the day. Now we'll just be upsetting the good people, who are trying to get their shopping done before it's wartime again."

She smiled at him. "You might wonder why you had to tell me that. I don't live here and never did. I was brought up in Cassdale, and since I've been married we've lived over on Egmont. My husband's on the job: Traffic. If you can call that police work. I used to kid him like that when I wanted to get him mad, but then somebody he pulled over for running a stop sign pointed a nine-millimeter at him and would have shot him if it hadn't misfired." She made a *harrumph* sound. "That ended the jokes. It's also what got me to enter the department."

"You mean you *wanted* the risk?"

"I guess that would take a crazy person," Ravenswood said. "No, I just figured I might do more good with a shield than I ever could as a schoolteacher, where I was always outnumbered."

He thought of asking, "Even at your size?" but did not, in case she was sensitive about it, as he knew some women were, because he had gone to high school with a pretty but very tall girl named Elyse Miller who was touchy on the subject. Later in life she married an ugly little guy five inches shorter than she, and there were those who figured he must have made up in equipment what he lacked in height.

All this while both officers were scanning the streets they drove through; you could talk about anything and still be alert on the job. He and Artie sometimes even got into heated arguments, always having to do with local sports, the only area in which they could have serious differences.

"Where'd you go to school if you grew up in Cassdale?"

"Valley."

Marevitch nodded vigorously. "I went to Central. We always played you. Of course that was before your time."

"Hey, look at that mutt!" Ravenswood slammed her foot against the brake pedal. Luckily they were not going faster. Even so, Marevitch had to catch himself with a hand to the dash. She was already out the door.

A boy ten, eleven had snatched the purse of a gray-haired woman, who was now hobbling after him, screaming and shaking a cane as he put distance between them, sprinting east on Middleton. Marevitch would have made pursuit in the unit, leaving any foot chases to Art McCall, and the kid would probably have vanished between the buildings, on turf that behind the facades was unknown to the white police.

Now he watched in astonishment as Ravenswood proceeded, despite her bulk, to run the boy down within a block. It was her long legs that did it: each stride covered three times the ground gained by one of the kid's. The accessories on her gun belt flapped violently, but her cap stayed on, squared away as always.

Marevitch took the wheel and drove down the block to where his partner was holding the boy's skinny dark-brown wrist in a huge hand of the same hue. The lad had short-cropped hair, a small shiny nose, and flawless skin and wore baggy pants, an oversized shirt, and black running shoes. His dark eyes were sullen by current expression and not by nature.

With her free hand, Felicia, panting, gave the purse to Marevitch. To him, for the boy's benefit, she said, gasping for air between each phrase, "What do we do with this prize? He sees our car, yet goes ahead and does the crime anyway."

The derision had no discernible effect on the boy. Ravenswood was showing her inexperience.

"What's your name?" asked Marevitch.

When the boy failed to answer, Felicia shook him gently by the wrist, but she was so powerful that his entire body trembled.

Marevitch repeated the question, but the lad replied only with an obscenity. He quickly patted the boy down and was surprised to find no weapons.

"Put him inside, loose. His hands are too little for the cuffs to hold: they'll slip right out." And then they could be used as a weapon; it had happened. Marevitch leaned over and spoke into the brown ear under the blue cap. "We got an audience."

Dark heads were in the windows above, and a collection of persons was forming on either side of the street. This was not a gathering mob, but it did provide reason to proceed with discretion. Perhaps a videocamera was already running.

They went to the unit, and Marevitch unlocked the rear door. Not even he dated back so far as to remember the time when a police vehicle, even one with the engine running, was considered forbidden territory to the bad guys. Nowadays the attempted carjacking of a unit from two armed officers was not out of the question. So as not to be inflammatory, he did not draw his weapon or even unbutton the strap that kept it holstered, but he was prepared mentally for any kind of assault.

Felicia put the boy in the backseat. She closed the door with the thrust of a big hip and asked Marevitch, "We're turning him over to Juvenile, right?"

"I don't know if it's worth it."

"You don't mean you'll let him go?"

"We recovered the property."

"See, that's what— Well, I don't want to be out of line. It's not my place as a rookie."

"Go ahead, Felicia. You got a right. You just made a nice collar."

"I wouldn't turn him loose. I don't approve of that."

"That's all very well, Felicia, but Juvenile ain't gonna hold him, I guarantee." He looked past her. "Here comes the lady."

Close up, the woman looked older than when seen from the unit, with cheeks like eroded brown earth. Now that the police held her purse, she was prepared to turn her anger on Marevitch. But he seized the initiative.

"I believe this is your property, missus." He gave her the purse.

She was somewhat mollified, but, probably so as not to lose her self-respect, opened the handbag and, plunging her fingers inside, prudently counted the money therein without bringing it into view. She announced her surprise to find it all there.

Felicia turned her glower on the old woman. "You gonna thank anyone for recovering it?"

The woman was not fazed. "Fuh doin' you *job?*" She jammed the purse under her arm and clenched its protruding end in her fist. She left at a pace that was measured by her cane.

Ravenswood glared at the closest person on the sidewalk, a young man with a shaved head and a gold ring in the right lobe of his nose, and asked what he was looking at.

"Nothing, Mama."

"Then take a hike." She waited, hulking, until he moved, which to Marevitch's surprise he finally did after only a short stare-down, and then said to her partner, "Mind if I get in back and talk to him?"

"The kid?" He didn't get it, but said it was okay by him. "But let me hold your weapon."

"Really think he could take it away from me?" She was amused.

He was not. "I just lost a partner. You'll take whatever precautions I think are necessary."

"I'm sorry." Felicia unbuttoned the holster strap and handed him her pistol, butt first. She climbed into the backseat with the boy, who shrank apprehensively into the far corner at her massive entrance, and Marevitch went around to the driver's seat. Without looking directly at the people on the sidewalks or in the windows, he was nevertheless aware of the intentions of each with regard to his partner, the unit, and himself, in the veteran policeman's way that was based mostly on experience but also included intuition, a sense of luck, and a certain stoicism. His bulletproof vest would not stop high-tech cop-killer slugs nor, as with Artie, a head shot, and all bets were off when it came to the deranged individual, but the odds were he would live to collect his pension.

He drove to the now disused part of the once busy but still extensive railway yard and stepped out of the car to let Felicia talk to the kid. People still fished along that shore, down below the tracks, and, if they were black, ate what they caught and probably did not suffer for it, though most whites assumed that despite the cleanup efforts of decades the water was still polluted. Marevitch himself ate no fish whatever its origin, and as few vegetables as he could get away with.

For some reason, very few dead human bodies ever surfaced in that part of the stream, maybe because the current was too swift-moving there. In his years of service Marevitch had encountered many dead men, women, and children, most of them deceased by reason of accident or natural causes, and not murder, but it had been he and Artie McCall who had found the Howland mother and daughter. When you've seen little children who were beaten to death by blood relatives in their own homes, some of them after months of preliminary mistreatment, you could actually be relieved that the little Howland girl's face was unmarked and looked serene: so he told Stephanie, to whom such assurances meant a great deal, her association with what he did being vicarious.

He wanted to give Ravenswood enough time to do whatever she had in mind, but he was also bored. He could have walked down to the water, but it was a hundred yards distant and he did not wish to leave her there alone and unarmed. Thinking she would be able to talk some sense into a kid like that was another example of her naïveté, but then she seemed to be a lace-curtain type, from a bedroom neighborhood on the border of the suburbs, who had little sense of the urban lower depths.

He kicked a rusty rail. Either scrap metal was no longer worth much or the locals were too lazy to pry it up and sell it, for tons were still in place over the ties, which in themselves could be put to various uses, but not firewood, owing to the creosote. It took a special effort for him to stop thinking like a cop, and he saw no reason to exert such energy, for he liked what he was and did. In fact, he loved it.

From time to time he eyeballed whichever rear window of the unit he was nearest in the circuit he was pacing, and he usually saw Ravenswood doing all the talking. She could continue that till she was, as the saying went, blue in the face, for all the good it would do. A boy like that would have no father, a mother who drank or drugged up all her welfare money, brothers who were thugs, and sisters who were whores. You were going to tell him to clean up his act? Come on. Or, as his daughter told him to say now, thinking he actually wanted to speak a teenager's lingo: get real. There were lots of such gets. Get a life. Get it on. Get down. . . .

It was time to get rolling. He was walking toward the front passenger's door when Felicia backed carefully out of the rear compartment.

She closed the door with her hip technique and said solemnly, "Let's step over here." Meaning, as she proceeded to demonstrate, about twenty feet behind the unit.

Marevitch plodded with her. "So," he said when they stopped, "did you save his soul?"

Ravenswood ignored the derisive question. She stood in her usual somewhat round-shouldered posture when speaking with him if he too was standing, probably to diminish their difference in height, and as always he was more offended than gratified. "I got this idea," she began. "I just thought I would try it on for size, since you were going to let him go anyway. I mean, it couldn't hurt."

"Oh, yeah?"

With a finger to the bill, she poked her cap up about an inch and, thrusting out her lower lip, blew air up her face. "Hot in there, and I didn't want to open the windows. . . . Anyway, I thought I'd see if maybe I could get him interested in being an informant on what was going down around the neighborhood."

Marevitch winced. "Jesus, I wish you'd asked me. Kids'll just get you in trouble. Leave 'em to Juvenile. They know the ropes." He sneered. "Of course, what that means is they just let 'em get away with everything. They got ten social workers to every cop there. But hell, you can't do anything about that situation except walk away from it. I could tell you . . ."

Though impatiently scraping her teeth across her lips, she waited for him to finish, but when it looked as though he wouldn't do so soon, she broke in. "I wasn't prepared for the reaction. Right away he asks what it would be worth to us if he fingered the gang that's been robbing the liquor stores and doing all the killing."

Marevitch stared at her. "Oh, no," he said angrily. "That's crap, can't you see that? This little punk would know who hit Artie? Forget about it, Felicia. We wasted enough time already." He wanted to turn and go back to the unit, but she grabbed the elbow of his blue shirt.

"Just hear this, Jack. It's his cousin and some other boys. They're a few years older, though still in their teens. He wanted to join them, but they wouldn't let him. Said he was too little. They gave him a real bad time when he pestered them too much."

"So he's gonna do this to get back at them? Get real." Felicia shrugged and looked away. But Marevitch did not want to hurt her feelings. "You learn these things after a while on the street," he said, taking the harsh edge off his voice. "Little mutts like this will say anything to a cop. Then you turn your back on 'em and they zap you, if they got a weapon. Sometimes they'll do it to your face. Think this one wouldn't have used a gun or knife on you if he had one? Last year an officer in the Nineteenth took a shot in the stomach when he asked a kid this age to turn down a boom box."

Ravenswood nodded vigorously, a light in her eyes. "But would you mind if I told the captain about this thing?"

Marevitch sighed. "You want to waste his time, go ahead. I won't stand in your way. Only grant me this, please. Just be sure Novak knows it's all *your* idea. Just leave me out of it." He stretched, elbows back, and smiled. "I hope it won't break your heart if you never see that kid again once we let him loose."

"At least we got some names we could check." She patted the back pants pocket where she carried her notebook.

Marevitch snorted. "Take my word for it, the names will be phony. Think he really believes you could do something for him?"

"I think he'd like to get the reward."

"There's a reward?"

"The liquor dealers' association," said Felicia. "After your partner was hit, they got together and offered it."

Marevitch was embarrassed. This had happened while he was distracted by self-pity. "Then you better run with it, Felicia. You might get yourself a commendation, first time out." He decided it made more sense for him to be affirmative, to be proud of her, than to admit envy into a partnership that lived on loyalty.

Moody was at Walsh's, and tonight nobody tried to cut down on his drinking. The proprietors in fact were setting them up. Sal Borelli, working the bar as usual, even joined him in the first one, hefting a little shot glass of beer for himself while Moody put away two ounces of what Sal poured him, gratis: not the usual bar stock but mellow stuff from a special bottle.

"To the man of the hour."

"I had some luck," Moody said. "You remember how that can happen."

"Yeah, but I always took full credit." Borelli had the kind of laugh that sounded almost like a cough. "The department's on a roll, huh? The liquor-store gang's been collared too, huh?" He poured Moody a refill.

"Information received," Moody said before swallowing. After savoring the aftereffect—he enjoyed the taste of good whiskey while he was still sober—he explained, "Couple of patrolmen brought it in. Precinct commander does it by the book, gives it to Robbery, who've been liaising with Homicide, where"—he took another sip—"since the officer was hit, the Wonder Boys got into the act."

"Payton and Lutz."

"Arnie and Warnie. So you probably saw who took credit for the collars."

"Yeah, Nicky, you got upstaged. But some of that's your own fault, you and Dennis, and you know it. The TV news treated the Howland case like some kinda, uh, afterthought. And that *Five Star Report*, that pencil-neck geek Bill Arbogast, he says you fellas bungled it from start to finish. Why's he got a hard-on for you?" Sal stuck his five-o'clock shadow up close. "You don't stand up for yourself enough, pal." He pulled away and grinned. "So how's Dennis these days?"

"Wife's pregnant again," Moody said more gloomily than he would have liked, because he did not want to get into the subject with Borelli, who might know more than he was letting on. It would not be Moody who told him that Dennis had asked Crystal for a divorce, but Sal's grapevine had never needed help from him in the past. At Walsh's they had known of his own domestic troubles almost as soon as he did, and he could never figure out quite how, unless the women provided the information, but in fact both his wives loathed the place.

Throughout the succeeding hours, other officers, current and ex-, stopped by Moody's stool to offer similar sentiments and stand him a round, and after a few hours of this, his first hollow leg was filled to capacity and he was working on the second. He had a lot to drink about.

On the advice of the lawyer whom he had finally asked for and been assigned, a counselor from Legal Aid but as aggressive as those who charged high fees, Gordon John Keller had repudiated all of the several phases of his confession including that on videotape, on the ground that the police had abused him in various ways, among them the conducting of an illegal search of his premises and denying him food and drink when he was taken into custody, and in fact detaining him improperly. But dealing with this was now primarily the responsibility of the district attorney's office.

Dennis LeBeau had gone home after the interrogation of Keller and chosen that moment to tell his wife that though he loved her and the children he was in love with Daisy O'Connor, someone whose name Crystal had never before heard, so that for a while she assumed it was a wacky joke of his, chuckled over it, and then changed the subject to say the doctor had confirmed what she had more or less known but thus far had not mentioned: namely, that once again she was "with child," using that term to maintain the tone of levity he had introduced.

"You can imagine how I felt then," LeBeau told Moody the next morning.

"No, I can't," Moody replied.

"Take my word for it."

"I don't want to take anything from you."

Dennis leaned across the desk as far as he could without leaving his chair. It was obvious he did not want the other detectives, coming and going, to hear this. Not that there was much danger of that, given the volume of noise, most of it coming from the area where Payton and Lutz held sway.

"Daisy wants me to tell you she apologizes for what she said the other night. She was under a lot of stress. It was embarrassing. You're like an uncle to her."

"See," Moody said, throwing back his head. "That's what— Hell, what's the use?"

"What's that supposed to mean?"

"She can't tell me to my face? I've known her since she was four years old. . . . I can assure you of one thing, Dennis. This will kill her mother if you go through with it. Marie's from the old school. She never missed a mass in her life. Only reason she talked to me after my first divorce was neither Ruthann nor me was Catholic, so she didn't take the marriage seriously anyway. If she knew what you are doing with her baby daughter . . ."

"That's where Daisy thought you might come in. Maybe you could talk to her mom. A word from you in my behalf might do a lot. You were her husband's partner. Now you and me have been partners for what?, six years in August. If you can't vouch for me, nobody can."

"But I *don't* know you, Dennis. That should be obvious."

"You're turning us down? I can't believe it, Nick."

"Believe it. After you gave her the news last night, and she finally believed it and threw you out of the house, Crystal called me and talked past midnight. She blames *me*, for Christ sake."

LeBeau shook his head, probably in self-pity. "I stayed out in the van." He must have gotten back in the house in the morning, for he was clean-shaven and wearing the usual sparkling shirt.

Moody had enough of the subject. He pointed, with the by him seldom-used gesture of a detective first grade ordering around his junior partner. "Set up a visit to the dump, and make sure there's help this time. Should be somebody free, now the caseload's down by two."

At Walsh's he was reluctant to leave his glass and the camaraderie even for a short visit to the men's room, but eventually he had to. In his opinion he walked without a stagger, if more slowly than usual, and he was careful not to show an expression associated with drunkenness, the fixed smirk, the judicious scowl, etc. But on approaching the urinals he acquired a doubt that he could function while standing without bepissing himself, so made his careful way to the farthest of toilet stalls, almost sat down before lowering his clothes, but remembered in time, and began to urinate in the female position.

The room had been empty when he entered. Now he heard the sound of the opening door and, soon after, two voices, neither of them familiar to him, but it appeared their owners knew who he was and referred to him as they peed.

"Old Moody's feeling no pain tonight."

"Glad he had one more good collar before he drinks himself to death," said the other voice. "He's a nice old guy—good for him."

"He's settled down a lot with age. Time was, you didn't dare introduce him to a woman unless she was a working girl, or he'd be all over her." They flushed simultaneously. Then the same man added, "It'll happen to you too, my boy. One day you won't be able to get it up any more."

"Speak for yourself," said the other. They ran the water at the washstands and subsequently used the paper-towel dispenser. They departed.

There was a side fire exit at Walsh's, and Moody used it after he left the men's room. He assumed that all the drinks he had had were gifts from someone else. If not, Sal and Howie would not hold an unpaid tab against him. He was not sober by any means, but hearing what he heard had raised him to a level of inebriation at which he could move efficiently enough while thinking with greater clarity than had ever been available to him.

When he got home, after driving as carefully as in a dream, he recognized, seriously as opposed to theoretically, what a mess the place was in. Bad enough before, it had degenerated further since the episode of Daisy and Dennis. He had not remade his bed, nor in fact had he used the bedroom. He had slept on the living-room couch, sans bed linen, just rolling up in a blanket and using as pillow one of those that had accompanied the sofa for decades and gave off a sour smell when the face was pressed against it.

In the kitchenette the sink had not been emptied of its soiled glasses and dishes, and the adjacent countertop was a cockroach race-track. The refuse in the pedal can was piled high enough to prop the lid in the open position. His entrance would have momentarily scattered the mice into hiding, but unmenaced experience there had made them bold, and they would return at any moment, or "forthwith" as would be said in the police jargon that had been his unique written idiom through adult life. Had he commanded any other language, he might have tried to write a letter to his son at this point, providing a counterargument to the one Frank had heard from his mother, or on the other hand, agreeing with her—who knew what he might say if he had been able to express himself? As it was, he must confine himself to certifying, on a page torn from his new notebook (the old one, containing his notes on the Howland case, had been turned over to the DA), that it was he and he alone who had discharged his service weapon, of his own volition and not under duress, with no involvement of a person or persons unknown, through the roof of the mouth at a forty-five-degree angle, the slug exiting through the cranium and entering the back of the couch, in the upholstery filler of which it would probably have come to rest in a deformed state. After completing the statement he signed it as Nicholas T. Moody, Detective First Grade, and was about to place it on the coffee table, weighted in place with a frosted can of beer that he had taken from the fridge but decided not to drink, when he remembered something else, and added a postscript to the effect that his personal papers, copy of his will, etc., could be found in a shoebox on the shelf of the bedroom closet.

He pushed aside the wadded blanket so that he could sit flat on the far left side of the couch. He took the snub-nosed .38 from the clip at his belt. He moved the cylinder so that a loaded chamber would be in alignment with the falling hammer rather than the one kept empty for safety purposes. He wiped the muzzle with the clean portion of handkerchief he had established after much inspection and refolding. He scrooched down until his sacroiliac area was at the leading edge of the cushion and his crown was below the top margin of the back of the couch, so that when he squeezed the trigger his brains would be blasted into the upholstery rather than out the dirty curtainless window behind, and also in order that the projectile would not continue on and possibly harm the person or property of citizens who lived on the other side of the air shaft.

After further consideration, he rose and fetched the metropolitan telephone book, a weighty tome, and sitting down again, arranged it so that its thickness formed a barrier between his skull and the couch, further ensuring the well-being of his neighbors.

He inserted the muzzle of the weapon between his lips, biting down gently against the cold metal just behind the front sight, in an effort to assist his hand, which suddenly was not as steady as he needed it to be while arriving at the proper angle to tilt the barrel. He should have checked this in a mirror, but if he got up now, the phone book, held in place by the pressure of his head, would fall to the seat, and he was too weary to mount it in place another time.

He was still adjusting the weapon. He was at least a second or two from closing his forefinger against the trigger, and therefore, as he afterward told himself (he would never trust another confidant with an account of this incident), the call did not literally save his life, but it did prove opportune.

He could have let it ring. But given the likelihood that he was being called on police business—nobody would say he had ever been derelict in his duty, not even in the last moment of his life—he withdrew the .38 from his mouth, stood up, letting the directory thud down behind him, and went to the kitchenette phone.

"Detective Moody? This is Lloyd Howland. You spoke to me earlier today, if you recall. I got your number from the phone book."

Moody reached over and placed the weapon on top of the refrigerator, too late feeling with his trailing fingers the dust-laden grease that glazed that surface. "Yeah." His mouth tasted of metal. "Yeah, Lloyd. What can I do for you?"

"Is it convenient? I hope it's not too late."

Since the subject was raised, Moody glanced at his digital drugstore watch and saw that the hour was only nine forty-five. He had been under the illusion that it was in the wee hours of the morning. The events of the night had slowed the passage of time. "It's still early."

"Good," said Lloyd. "Because this is something of an imposition anyway. You don't owe me anything."

"Go ahead," said Moody.

"I got an idea. I've never known what to do with myself. I've never held a job longer than a few months, if that long." He cleared his throat. "I've been thinking about how you do your job. You believe in it, that's pretty obvious. I doubt it's a way to get rich, and it certainly can't be too comfortable at times. But it's something that's needed, that's for sure. You can be proud of what you do. There will always be bad people, no doubt, but through your efforts a lot fewer of them will get away with it. And that should give you a great deal of satisfaction."

"Lloyd?" Moody asked, but more matter-of-factly than in sternness. "Have you had something to drink?"

"My friends here brought some champagne, and I had a glass or two. Do I sound drunk?"

"Not necessarily," said Moody. "In fact, I myself had a few drinks this evening. I'm just not used to hearing praise for what I do."

"Well, listen, you deserve it. I admit I've had my own low opinion of the police; based on nothing—well, not nothing but maybe the idea of constraint. That's annoying, especially if you're young. You want to do something that doesn't seem wrong, yet somebody wants to stop you. I know you're a detective and you don't give speeding tickets or enforce curfews."

"I started that way, though," Moody said, surprising himself with a chuckle. "And I busted up noisy college parties and I arrested bartenders who served beer to underage drinkers. Hell, Lloyd, I did all of that, and I don't apologize for it. I did it because the law was being broken, and the citizens were paying me to maintain respect for the law. If I waited table in a restaurant I would bring your steak when you ordered it. I wouldn't eat it myself or throw it in the garbage. If I pumped gas for a living, I wouldn't fill your tank with air or water. What I do is enforce the law. If you don't want that done, then don't hire me. But if you do hire me, that's what I'll do. If the citizens decide homicide is *not* against the law, then I won't arrest anybody for murder. Am I making any sense at all?" Instead of blowing out his brains he was running off at the mouth. Both were expressions of self-pity.

"It makes sense to me," Lloyd said.

"I don't mean I'd do what I'm told no matter what. But that's never happened. We don't have a police state here. Anything but. Most felons go right back on the street." Even in his current condition he would not be oblivious to Lloyd's feelings and note that Keller would probably cop a plea. He was not addressing Lloyd's half brother. It was LeBeau who had called Larry Howland to announce the arrest of the murderer of his wife and daughter. He said Larry's first reaction was to demand immediate possession of the house at 1143 Laurel.

"I wanted to ask your opinion," Lloyd said. "Do you think I could join the police force? If the gun charges are dropped, I don't have any record, I gather. I'm of age and in good health. The one thing I'm worried about is whether I'm tall enough."

"Mind hanging on, Lloyd? Just a minute." Moody let the handpiece dangle and fetched the can of beer from the coffee table. He averted his face and pulled the tab but was conscious of less spray than anticipated. He took a swallow of what proved to be the most delicious liquid he had ever tasted, though the label identified it as the same old Steinbräu. "Okay," he resumed, "where were we?" He actually remembered without help. "Oh yeah. I don't think they have a height requirement any more. Nowadays the department has to take anybody who applies, I think, or they get sued." Only a minor exaggeration. He took another draft of exquisite cold beer, which he would have missed had he killed himself. "Problem would probably not be in getting accepted," he told the lad, "but in sticking with it. The job makes a lot of demands on you, and usually comes before your personal life. The public never sees the worst of what you confront day after day as a police officer. Sickening stuff you never suspected was possible, at least not in this country. I puked three times the first week I was a rookie. You're not only supposed to handle it but rise above it and go on to something else that's worse, and then rise above *that* and still be human." He took more beer, and then he laughed. "But if you're a certain kind of individual, it's what you were cut out to do. Nobody's going to like you but other cops, but *they'll* lay down their life for you. That's not the worst deal. Where else can you find it? Maybe in some elite units of the military, but you have to wait for a war to see."

"If I get accepted," Lloyd said, "do you think I could talk to you once in a while? I don't mean be a pest. Just ask your advice on certain things."

"Sure," Moody answered without hesitation. "I'll be glad to talk with you, Lloyd. If I don't know something about that subject, then I've wasted my life, because it's all I know. . . . Listen, you want to have dinner with me tomorrow night?"

"Really?" Lloyd seemed to be delighted. But next his voice fell. "I'm sorry. I just remembered: I promised to do something with my girlfriend tomorrow night. She wants to introduce me to her dad. She's the Martha Sparks you asked about, who paid my bail."

"Sounds serious," said Moody. "She wouldn't be your fiancée, would she?"

"Maybe, in time. I've got to clean up my act first."

"Here's an even better idea." Moody finished his beer in one gulp. "Night after tomorrow, I'll take you both to dinner. Great place, where a lot of cops hang out. You'll both find it interesting, I guarantee. You'll meet people who are good guys to know if you enter the department."

"That would really be nice of you. I don't know what to say."

"Just show up seven sharp. Now, you never know in my job if you'll get tied up, so this has to be tentative. But I'll leave word if I'm delayed, and dinner's on me in any event." He gave him Walsh's address. "I look forward to meeting the lady. Hope to see you there, son."

The conversation and the beer had lifted Moody from the depths. He was still drunk, but now in a way that could be soporific. He burned the suicide note in a dirty coffee cup from the sink. He returned his weapon to its holster after turning the cylinder around to the empty shell. He stripped to his underwear and, having swathed himself in the old blanket, which toward the far end had a large moth hole in which he sometimes caught a toe, he lay down and assumed the fetal position on a couch that was too short for him to stretch out.

If tomorrow he must deal with his partner's domestic troubles, the destruction his surrogate daughter was wreaking on her once promising life, and whichever homicide he was next in line for—maybe it was in the process of being committed at this very moment—he needed all the sleep he could get.